NO HUT

TNH OA

If You Were Mine ...

A Novel

by

Cynthia Scott Hutchinson

Bloomington, IN Milton Keynes, UK

authorHOUSE®

AuthorHouse™
1663 Liberty Drive, Suite 200
Bloomington, IN 47403
www.authorhouse.com
Phone: 1-800-839-8640

AuthorHouse™ UK Ltd.
500 Avebury Boulevard
Central Milton Keynes, MK9 2BE
www.authorhouse.co.uk
Phone: 08001974150

First published by AuthorHouse 3/8/2007

ISBN: 1-4259-3777-2 (sc)

Library of Congress Control Number: 2006904421

Printed in the United States of America
Bloomington, Indiana

This book is printed on acid-free paper.

The lyrics to "If You Were Mine" appearing in Chapter Thirty-One are composed and written by Fernando Ortega from his compact disc, "This Bright Hour" (1997, Myrrh Records, Division of Word Entertainment), and are used by permission. Their use by the fictional characters in the context of this novel is solely a product of the novelist's imagination and does not reflect the original intent of the songwriter's creation.

The lyric excerpts from "The Master's Hand" appearing in Chapter Thirty-Five are composed and written by Anne Herring from her compact disc, "Waiting For My Ride to Come" (1991, The Sparrow Corporation), and are used by permission. Their use in the context of this novel is solely a product of the novelist's imagination.

Scripture other than King James Bible quotations are taken from the HOLY BIBLE, NEW INTERNATIONAL VERSION. Copyright 1973, 1978, 1984 International Bible Society. Used by permission of Zondervan Bible Publishers.

For You, Gracious, Loving Heavenly Father,
Maker, Master of the Universe,
Mender of our brokenness,

With all my heart

Prologue

This story is about my first-born daughter, Jennifer. My beautiful, sweet and gracious, intelligent, kind and good daughter. My Jennifer.

I remember so vividly the day she was born in Hixson Memorial Hospital in Mobile, Alabama, on June 4, 1955. The doctor and nurses, smiling broadly, placed her in my arms saying, "Mrs. Jacobs, she is truly one of the most beautiful baby girls we have ever seen! She is going to be a heartbreaker, for sure!"

But as I took one long, glorious look at her through my heavily drugged, twilight haze—as was the fashion in child birthing during the Eisenhower administration lest we fragile, delicate young women should experience any part of Eve's curse, "greatly multiplying our sorrow in bringing forth children,"—I somehow knew that she, herself, was the one destined for heartbreak.

It's odd. I just looked into her tiny pink face ... and I knew it.

I didn't know how it would happen, but I knew it, way down deep in my brand new mother's heart. My daughter was going to have her heart badly broken.

And I wept, both for the joy of the day's offering, the birth of my very own little baby girl, and for the grief and pain, remorse and regret that tirelessly accompany us along our difficult, wonderful journey through life—pain caused mostly by our own benighted behavior, and yet so often we tend to blame God.

I suppose all of us experience heartbreak and deep emotional wounding at some point, and perhaps it was not a divinely inspired revelation to me at all that June day in 1955. Perhaps all new mothers realize that their precious babies will one day experience great heartache and distress, despite our best efforts to shield them. Perhaps that was part of Eve's curse in her greatly multiplied child birthing sorrows.

Nevertheless, as my own sweet Jenny was finally able to open up her heart under repair and share with me her sad, tragic story, before I was able to shed even one of the million and one tears I have since cried for her, I was immediately taken back there in my memory—taken back to the day of her birth when I tried to tell my obstetrician that he was mistaken. That my beautiful daughter was not born to be heartbreaker. But that she was certain to have her heart broken

What I was able to mutter through my drug induced fog, however, sounded like garbled gibberish to his ears, I am sure, and he just nodded, smiled kindly at me, and patted my hand absently as he observed my tears. It was just another day at work for him, this opening of my womb to introduce a brand new life into this grand, wild world. But for me, a first time mother, it was a most holy, most profound moment ...

I did not write this story. I could not, you see. I bear too much guilt and pain still in my own heart these many years later to attempt to tell my lovely Jennifer's story—my very lovely Jennifer, who deserved so much better than her father and I were able to give her. Although she has forgiven me and God has forgiven me, I find it difficult to release myself from my responsibility in her tragedy.

So I cannot tell her story. I am much too close to it still.

But as the author relates to you the life of my sweet daughter, my prayer is that you will come to love her and care for her as I do. And that you will have hope for her and for the millions of others who have lived through their own versions of her heartache and despair. Hope for a future for all the deeply wounded ones.

And hope for us as mothers to guide and direct our daughters and sons into the paths of peace. And of life. Life to its fullest.

Chapter One

*T*here are days in our lives that seem almost perfect—too perfect to last in this fallen world. And yet they appear sometimes as a gracious gift right out of the blue, shine their lovely, warm rays into our souls, and then fall away to that distant, dreamy land from which they came, just as suddenly and unexpectedly as they arrived.

Such was that balmy, bright, early April morning in Coburn, Alabama in 1975. Spring always arrives early in the Deep South, probably because its sojourn there is received so warmly and graciously by Southerners famous for their hospitality to far less desirable guests. A brief, dull gray winter is merely endured with the patient forbearance of Alabamians, but spring is welcomed just any old time to stay as long as she desires.

The sky was a soft but vibrant blue with just a trace of high, wispy clouds. The birds in the trees overhead seemed to be rejoicing at something wonderful and yet mysteriously unknown to the mortals all around them. The azaleas and the dogwood and the last of the late blooming narcissus and daffodils were putting on quite a show, spilling their fresh, revitalizing fragrances onto the pleasant spring breezes of the grounds of the college campus where Jennifer Jacobs, an attractive sophomore with dark brown hair and even darker brown eyes, sat in the grass and shade of the hundred-year-old oak trees on the grounds of the Commons, along with two of her friends, just soaking in the promises that spring always brings into the hearts of nineteen- and twenty-year-old young women. Promises of romance to come, love that lasts a lifetime, careers that satisfy, and hope that "springs eternal in the human breast," as Jennifer had just learned in her English Lit class that a wise man named Alexander Pope had once said.

The campus groundsmen were mowing the lawn, and the wonderful aroma of the freshly cut grass along with the rumbling sounds of the mowers awakened in Jennifer the happiest emotions of safety and security that her memory could offer. She involuntarily was taken back to her early childhood. Memories of lying in her bed on Saturday mornings in the Alabama springs with her window open, being awakened by the sounds of her father's lawn mower and the indescribable scent of the brand new spring grasses, flooded into her mind without effort.

Especially the smell of the grass. That was Jennifer 's favorite fragrance. She could see the pink and white checked curtains in the window by her bed gently floating in the breeze through the half-opened eyes of the little girl she once was, bringing in that clean, refreshing smell that promised so many good things. Promised a lazy, purposeless Saturday in which she could just lie in bed as long as she liked, daydreaming of Cinderella while listening to the droning of the mowers and smelling the newness of spring to her heart's content. It was such a happy memory.

And it was the last time she could remember that she ever felt safe.

For despite having the outward appearance of a pretty, self-possessed, intelligent young coed, the inner workings of her heart were far removed from that place of safety she remembered so intensely at that moment. Her parents' divorce that occurred when Jennifer was ten-years-old stripped away from her heart all the positive emotions that come from having a loving family, a home life that offers a place of refuge, peace, stability, and security—with one stroke of a judge's pen—leaving in their places an ominous feeling that many unnamed but terrifying monsters were lurking just out of sight, right around the corner somewhere, so that there was no longer a place of lasting safety.

The months immediately following the divorce had found Jennifer waking up in the middle of the night screaming for her daddy, her pajamas wet with both perspiration and urine, arousing her mother from a drugged sleep, as she tried desperately to calm her hysterical child.

But as the weeks and months and years had passed by, Jennifer had coped with her demons by becoming that perfect, model child that teachers, church workers, and fellow students loved and admired, an over-achiever in every arena she could master with her God-given talents. An adolescent of above average intelligence and beauty, she studied, prayed, read her Bible, dieted, exercised, and made up her face and coiffed her hair until at last she had arrived at that place of acceptance by both the adults in her life and her peer group.

There was love out there in the world for such a flawless person, Jennifer knew from observation, and she was determined to obtain it for herself. For the life lesson she had unwittingly internalized from her parents' divorce was that love was not freely given—it was earned. In men, it was earned through works and could be taken away if the works proved inferior. In women, works also had to possess an attractive appearance. Yes, love was earned, she had learned, and if the wages used to pay for it were substandard or lost their luster, love packed up and moved out. She could trust no one to give love to her freely. No one but Jesus, that is, she knew very well from her many Sundays at the Hillside Baptist Church. Jesus loves unconditionally, she had been taught.

But Jesus was in Heaven, and she was in Coburn, Alabama, just one of fifteen thousand students, a face in the crowd. So she had to make it the best face possible.

And although Jennifer sometimes believed she had finally tamed her monsters of insecurity and self-doubt by becoming one of the smartest, most attractive, and best liked girls in each and every school she had attended, the fact remained that she still occasionally woke up screaming at night, usually before a big exam or just after a blind date that did not go so well. Screaming, though not loudly enough to wake up her very sound-sleeper of a roommate, she would wake herself up, but quickly forget whatever it was that frightened her and go back to sleep.

And sometimes, not often, but sometimes, she would make herself throw up after she felt she had consumed too many calories and not exercised enough. Overweight women are not loved, she knew quite well. Her mother had been twenty pounds overweight and her husband had left her. This would never happen to Jennifer.

The voice of her friend, Beth, interrupted her thoughts and brought her abruptly back to the present.

"What a gorgeous day! I think all classes should be called off on days like this one. Especially after that dreary, rainy, depressing March that we had. And I have to go to the Black Hole! There is absolutely no justice is this world," she moaned.

The Black Hole to which Beth referred was a physics building classroom situated in the interior of an eighty-year-old structure with no windows and an annoying, malfunctioning, buzzing, light fixture overhead that made her fair complexion appear bluish-purple. This last part was particularly troublesome to Beth as there was a certain young man, a pre-med major from Valdosta, Georgia, with whom she was hoping to develop some sort of liaison. Beth was supposedly studying to become a nurse, just to fall back on in case she had not "snagged myself a med student by graduation," as she was known to repeat.

"Why should you bother about official days off?" joined in another friend, Sarah. "Don't you create your own Day's Off Calendar by skipping classes whenever you feel the urge?"

Sarah Cunningham was a very serious student who would never miss a class unless she was lying comatose in the infirmary, and was an almost extinct species at this university with the nickname, "Party U." She was her father's favorite of five daughters and took pride in his pride in her. And he expected her to graduate *magna cum laude*.

"Yeah, you're right, Sarah. I think I may just take a personal day today and head back to the good old Gamma House and hit the sundeck. I'm beginning to lose my tan from Spring Break," rejoined Beth, taking no offense whatever in Sarah's remark.

Sarah would always be a play-it-by-the-book type of person, Beth knew, and would miss out on all the fun that spontaneity and irresponsibility create, the enjoyment of which Beth had elevated to an art form. Beth didn't mind Sarah's barbs. Beth was a drop-dead, gorgeous, bottle blonde who was working very intently on obtaining her M.R.S. degree. And her father was rich enough to support her through as many years of college as it took. The pre-med Valdosta boy could be flirted with some other day.

For in the 1970's in central Alabama, no decent, lovely, young Southern lady would be caught dead on that college campus in April without the beginnings of a real nice suntan, because white legs looked just awful hanging out from the bottoms of shorts. And Beth had such shapely legs! So hitting the sundeck and applying baby oil containing iodine as a tanning aid were top priorities for the young coeds, who paid no attention to their mothers' warnings that baking themselves in the sun with no protection would one day come back to haunt them. The young women on campus would only laugh at that advice, knowing very well that they would not care at all what they looked like at forty. Life would be all over with by then, anyway. Today was what mattered.

"Yeah, I'm heading back to the Gamma House. I can catch up on this class ... oh, sometime later. Or better yet, I can ask that cute Valdosta boy if I can borrow his notes." She stood up smirking at Sarah and stretched her arms and legs luxuriantly before adding, "Anyone want to go to the sundeck with me? What about you, Jenny? You're looking a little pale these days."

"Jennifer? Look *pale*?" Sarah both questioned Beth's eyesight and took a little jab at her at the same time. "Her skin never looks pale, Beth. We can't all be make-believe blondes with fair skin, you know."

Jennifer had smooth, olive skin, which complemented her dark hair and eyes, and never really appeared pale but tanned beautifully. And though she not averse to cutting an easy class occasionally, she declined the sundeck this time while smiling at both girls so not to offend either.

"No thanks, Beth. I'd better not today. Anyway, I don't have a nine o'clock class. Just thought I would wait out here for my next one at ten. It's such a perfect day."

"I think she's waiting to see if *Michael* is going to ask her to breakfast again," Sarah observed, her eyes twinkling mischievously, a teasing tone to her voice. And the subtle change in Jennifer's facial expression let her know her guess was right.

Michael Evans, a junior, had been dating Jennifer for several weeks now and was known to seek her out at the Commons and ask her to go have breakfast with him at the Student Union Building. On Tuesdays and Thursdays she would have to cut class to go with him, and though she did this gladly, she would often feel a little guilty later. For Jennifer was a good student, majoring in the safety of a subject in which she excelled so not to have to risk failure at something more challenging. To Jennifer, failure was not an option. People who fail do not earn love.

She and Michael had known each other for several years. Together they had attended Hillside Baptist Church in their hometown of Mobile, had been active participants in the Youth Programs there such as choir, drama, and summer camps, had gone on a couple of mission trips with the group, and generally had the same backgrounds and interests. But Michael had never dated Jennifer until recently, as she was a year behind him in school and therefore not in his inner circle. Besides that, just about every girl at Hillside had been madly in love with him at one time or another, and he had always had his pick of the litter.

With golden, wavy hair and clear blue, dreamy eyes attached to a six-foot-two-inch frame that was strong, broad, and lean, he was devilishly good-looking, very masculine, and wore self-confidence and assurance the way a super model wears the latest designer fashions, parading down the runway of life with ease. Not only that, he had been the starting forward on the basketball team in high school as well as an academic All-American, possessed a wonderful sense of humor, and could sing songs he composed himself in a beautiful tenor voice while accompanying himself on guitar. Yet amazingly, with all his gifts and popularity, he was not terribly conceited. Truthfully, he possessed just enough conceit to make him believe he could accomplish any goal he set in life and make any girl love him. And he was not far off base on either count.

The fact that sweet and lovely Jennifer Jacobs was indeed in love with him was not only apparent to him, but also to all who observed them together. For try as hard as she could to be mysterious and intriguing and not to wear her heart on her sleeve, Jennifer could never hide the soft glow in her eyes and creeping blush on her face whenever he showed interest in her. And the despairing air of melancholy that surrounded her on days he did not call was obvious to anyone who cared to notice.

She did not want to fall in love with him until she first knew his heart. That much she knew for certain. She had been injured in puppy love once before, and that had brought much pain, hurt feelings, and wounded pride into her still fragmented, fatherless, little girl spirit. She did not think she could relive that type of rejection again.

And she hated the fact that she was desperate for some type of masculine love in her life. She wanted to be secure, strong, independent, and self-driven, like the feminists in the culture told her she should be. She scorned Beth's man-hunting ways, though she could not help but like Beth for her open, guileless manner.

But Jennifer knew herself too well to believe that she could ever become a radical feminist, denying her tremendous need for the love of a good man. For she was at her core tenderhearted and extremely sensitive, the type of personality that tended to internalize all the circumstances that life threw into her pathway, so that her parents divorce did not "just happen," but it happened "to" and "inside" Jennifer herself. She felt to this day that if she had been good enough, pretty enough, and smart enough, perhaps her father would not have left home.

It was because of her true nature, the design the Creator had made of her personality, that Jennifer could not now hide her feelings for Michael any more than she could hide her great need to be loved from those who knew her family history. The broken, abandoned little girl she thought was long dead still showed herself to the adults in her life at church, who had taken the time to really know her and pray for her, as well as to some, but not all, of her peers.

Had she known this, she would have been truly humiliated and angry, because Jennifer thought she valued strength and courage almost more than the more tender qualities of love and trust. Strength and courage were what you had to have to make it in a cruel world. Love and trust could disappoint and disillusion you, making a painful hole in your soul that had no healing balm. She had dearly loved and trusted her daddy, and he had left her.

But over the years, Jennifer had learned to repress and ignore the bad feelings she had about her parents' split up. What good did it do to cry over it? Years and years of crying and praying had done nothing to rectify the situation. It was better to just accept it and get on with her own life. She could look after herself. And God was there, too. Most importantly, she would make certain that she did not fall in love with a man who would desert her.

Surely there was a man somewhere who would not desert his wife and children. Her friends had fathers who came home every night and showed up at graduations, ball games, and birthday parties. There were good, kind, loyal, godly men at her church. They had let Jennifer know that they cared for her and wanted her to know the love of God. She could be safe with such a Christian man. Michael's dad, Dr. Evans, was a good example.

And Michael was such a young man. He composed and performed some of the loveliest praise and worship songs to God that she had ever heard. The congregation at Hillside praised him to the hilt. He often sang solos on Sundays back at Hillside and would perform at the campus church they attended on other Sundays as well. Michael was majoring in music with a minor in business and hoped to get into the gospel music industry in Nashville after graduation next year. He had already established some contacts in that arena through his singing and composing. His future looked bright indeed.

And as bright as his future appeared on such a glorious April day, he appeared in Jennifer's eyes with a sort of glow around him as he walked up to her and the other two coeds who were sitting and standing under the oak tree on the Commons just after Sarah had mentioned his name.

"Hi ya', Toots," he smiled at Jennifer, and plopped down by her side, semi-reclining and propped up on one elbow, spilling his books onto the grass and kissing her lightly on the cheek. "How about some scrambled eggs and grits? I know they're your favorite."

Not many young men of his generation could get away with the term of endearment, "Toots," the way Michael could. But it was the playful nickname his beloved, eternally young and mischievous grandfather always used with his grandmother, and Michael had subconsciously adopted it. It fell from his lips naturally and unapologetically, and Jennifer loved it. It suited her just fine.

"Yuck, grits!" Jennifer wrinkled her nose at him, beaming as usual in his presence. "You know I hate grits."

"You don't say!" Michael played along, winking at her. "Then it must be Bethie, here, who likes grits. How about some scrambled eggs and grits, Bethie? Or don't you want to miss that great physics class you should be heading for about now? I hear that Professor Knowles is a great lecturer. You and that pre-med guy from Valdosta could share some memorable moments in cosmic history in ' the Black Hole,' you know."

"Jenny! Must you tell Michael *all* my secrets?" Beth, flirting as usual, whined through a half-smile, her perfectly straight teeth showing through full, sensuous lips as she swayed seductively back and forth.

Beth could not resist flirting with every good-looking male in her vicinity even though she was not interested in Michael romantically. His career choice in the uncertain music world was too chancy. She had bigger fish to fry.

"No, I don't like grits, either, Michael Evans," she continued. "And I have an appointment with the sundeck about now. Anyway, Jenny here would likely scratch my eyes out if I accompanied you two," she observed grinning, and winked back at him.

"No, don't be silly, Beth. You and Sarah are both welcome to come along with us," Jennifer rejoined. *Does my insecurity show through that badly?* she thought. *I will have to work on that.*

"Then I'll take that as a 'yes,' Jen, to my original breakfast proposition," Michael stated, his attention now focused back on the lovely brunette by his side and away from the beautiful blonde standing over him. And he smiled, took her hand in his, and brought it to his lips.

Jennifer smiled back into his own grinning blue eyes and wondered, involuntarily way back in the deep, hidden places of her soul, how in the world she would ever get along without him and his easy going kindness and attention toward her should he ever go away. *Why, oh, why must I always think these thoughts?* she fretted.

"Oh, don't the two of you look like the cutest little love birds," Sarah chimed in with a singsong voice. "I will bow out of the breakfast plans, too, not just because three's a crowd, but because I need to go to class right now. Besides, I already had my breakfast, and there were no grits on my plate either, Michael," she grimaced playfully.

With that, Sarah stood up, grabbed her books, and with a "See ya' later" left with Beth, who was walking in the same general direction.

"Don't do anything I wouldn't do!" Beth called back over her shoulder and smirked at the pair.

"Don't worry! I won't try to 'snag me a med student', Bethie," Michael shouted back to tease her. "And I'll make darn sure that Jenny won't, either!"

Beth grinned unashamedly while Sarah laughed out loud at his remarks, and the two of them disappeared into the crowd making their way to various classes.

"So how about it, Jenny? Ready to go consume the most important meal of the day?"

He sprang up from her side, still holding her hand, and pulled her to her feet. "You sure do look pretty today. Is that a new blouse? I like the color on you. Red goes real well with your dark hair and eyes."

And as he said that, he brushed her bangs gently to the side of her forehead and then caressed a curl that had fallen down the side of her face before lifting her book bag onto his shoulder. With his other hand still in hers, they walked slowly toward the Student Union Building's cafeteria.

He would have been surprised to learn that these small, tender, physical demonstrations toward the various girlfriends he had dated over the years were received by the girls as evidence of a growing passion and concern for them. He was totally unaware that they communicated anything to the young women he accompanied, for they were natural responses to him, not contrived or planned to capture the affection of anyone. This lack of knowledge on his part had left a string of broken hearts in its wake, mostly unknown to him.

But to Jennifer, whose heart had ached for so many years for the tender embrace of a masculine figure, these gentle, sweet, non-sexual physical contacts went straight to her heart and answered a deep abiding need to be loved, cherished, and protected. She still remembered sitting on her daddy's lap as a very small child while he read her a story. She remembered the earthy smell of him and how strong and steady his arms felt around her. She knew then that she was safe and cared for, that nothing could harm her, that the world was a good place as long as Daddy was there.

The couple looked good together, both tall and slender in blue jeans and collared shirts. He fair and she dark. He always joking and she with a tendency to be serious while still enjoying a good time. And as they laughed and smiled and traded information about their day's agenda, their moods both matched the indescribable beauty, peace, and hopeful optimism of that early spring day under the dogwood blossoms in Coburn, Alabama in 1975.

Life can only get better and better, thought he.

Maybe... just maybe... Michael is the one who will truly love me and never hurt me, thought she.

Chapter Two

"Str-r-i-ike Three! You're out!" yelled the crowd at the annual Faculty vs. Student Body spring baseball game at Coburn University held the last Saturday in May, just prior to the end of the school session.

It was the bottom of the eighth inning and Joe Smothers, friend of Michael and Jennifer, was on the mound pitching to the more daring, most fit, and least haughty of the CU professorial staff. The score was sadly: Student Body 15, Faculty 2. Joe had been the star pitcher on the baseball team of Central High School, Michael and Jennifer's old alma mater back in Mobile, and had attended Hillside Church, too.

"Way to go, Joe-Man, old buddy!" Michael stood up and screamed over the din of the boisterous group sitting on the bleachers in the warm, late May sunlight.

"Good job, Joey!" Katie McComb, a petite, shapely auburn-blonde, shouted down to her boyfriend. Katie was Jennifer's roommate and was seated next to Jennifer and Michael in the grandstand.

The crowd was dominated by Student Fans, though there were a few jocular Faculty Supporters, mostly wives and children laughing at their husbands' and fathers' faltering attempts to hang in there with youths less than half their ages. The air of the annual fundraising event was light and joyous. The game was followed not only by numerous fraternity dances and parties that helped many of the fledgling academicians overcome their guilt at not having studied for their latest exams, but also by several more staid but still lively faculty cookouts in the backyards of some of the professors' homes, where liniment, condolences, and humble pie were passed out freely along with good natured taunts and insults. It was the annual End of Spring rite for the college and was appreciated by students and faculty alike.

The Student Body Team was now at bat, but the few student fans in the crowd who were actually following the game closely had a tough time seeing the playing surface because of those standing up and obscuring their vision.

"Hey! Down in front!" yelled Michael to a group of more than slightly inebriated Sigma Chi brothers who were on their feet applauding a group of scantily clad coeds making their way slowly down the stadium steps toward the ladies room. "I'm trying to watch my buddy at bat knock that baseball into the new football stadium next door."

"Hey, man, what's wrong with you? You wanna watch a guy hit a baseball when you could see *that* instead?" the Sigma Chi's responded incredulously as they directed Michael's gaze toward the girls.

The group of about six young women wearing swimsuit tops and very short, cut-off blue jeans now commanded the attention of most of the young men in the stands. On their heads were crooked sun visors, and each girl held a new can of cold beer to replace the old ones, thus necessitating the many trips to the ladies room. With each new trip, the group of ladies became less steady on their feet, and a couple of them were quite frankly holding on to the more secure walkers for dear life. One rather well endowed young lady in the bosom department was in danger of revealing her most prized possessions to the entire ballpark when one of her more tipsy friends reached for her arm but accidentally caught her bracelet on the side of her bikini top, pulling it slightly askew. Whistles and catcalls followed that episode.

Michael, who possessed the typical male appreciation for the female form, allowed his eyes to linger on the wobbly procession of feminine flesh until the sound of Katie loudly clearing her throat and the painful pinch on his arm inflicted by Jennifer let him know that his response was the incorrect one.

He quickly recovered by shouting back, "Yeah, but those girls are walking *away* from ya'll, but look at what I've got sitting right here *beside* me!" He pointed down to the two attractive girls sitting next to him.

As if on cue, Jennifer and Katie, dressed in more modest but still appealing tee-shirts and longer but still becoming shorts, their tan, slender legs and gently flowing curves in no way inferior to those of the imbibing coeds, stood up, smiled, and waved at the drunken frat boys, who whistled and applauded appreciatively back at them.

When they all sat back down again, Michael observed as he sipped at his soft drink, "It's going to be a long night for those guys, and for the girls, too. They haven't saved themselves much drinking to do tonight at the dances."

"And wouldn't you just love to have the Alka-Seltzer, Pepto Bismol, and aspirin concession tomorrow!" Jennifer joined in. "We ought to go out this afternoon after the game and buy up all the analgesics in town and sell them for double the money tomorrow morning."

Jennifer never drank alcoholic beverages so she could afford to be smug. Besides the moral and religious aspects that governed her decision to abstain from the partaking of potent potables, her personality required her to be in control too much to risk inebriation.

As she laughed at her own joke and the others sitting around her joined in, she shook her head slightly, and her long, golden earrings bounced and sparkled against her olive skinned, handsomely featured face, her large dark eyes glowed beneath the bangs on her forehead, and her brown, wavy hair fell gently to her shoulders. Michael thought how pretty she looked. She was not the most beautiful girl he had ever dated, but she was indeed lovely and had a softness about her and a vulnerability that she tried in vain to hide from him. She would try to tell him, in the words of the day, "I am woman; hear me roar." But he knew her roar was little more than a squeak.

He picked up her hand in his, held it high for those around him to see, and said aloud, "That's my girl! Always thinking!" He then looked into her eyes, winked, and gave her a quick kiss on the temple, enjoying the lingering smell of her shampoo and the silky texture of her hair as his lips briefly brushed her head.

"All right, Joey! Way to go! Whee!" screamed out Katie suddenly as she jumped up and applauded enthusiastically, cheering her boyfriend. Joe had just hit another home run off a rather beleaguered, fifty-year-old chemistry professor, who was clever enough to hold several patents on mysterious chemical concoctions but unluckily possessed a very "iffy" curve ball.

"Hey, everybody! That's my man! Yea, Joey!" Katie continued shouting. "Did you see that, Mike and Jen? A grand slam homerun! I'd say this game is about over."

The scoreboard now read: Student Body 20, Faculty 2, and the natives were getting restless.

"I'd say this game has been over since the second inning," Jennifer observed and Michael agreed, adding,

"Are we all still going to the dance at the Student Union tonight after the youth fellowship, or are we planning to crash the *SAE* party? I can't remember what we decided."

Joe was a member of the *SAE* fraternity and had invited his friends to one of their many bashes, but Jennifer did not especially like frat parties. Neither she nor Michael had gone the Greek route, partly on the principle that they did not want to be labeled and partly because the idea of rejecting individuals from membership for purely arbitrary reasons seemed somehow un-Christian to them. And Michael had promised rather solemnly to his parents that he would never have more than two beers in an evening. He had lost his uncle to a drunk driver and had relatives on his mother's side who were recovering alcoholics. He knew that fraternities were not the place for those choosing the abstemious path.

And Jennifer, who for the eight years prior to college had fought and won countless battles to be accepted by the in-group, was weary of jumping through hoops to try to please people. She was battle fatigued and had felt she needed a rest from all the burdensome toil of trying to obtain membership in a so-called "good" sorority. When she had told her mother that she was not going out for Rush, Betty had been somewhat surprised but more than a little relieved. Finances were tight for Betty and her second husband, Bill Miller, who had to pay a large child support payment monthly to his three children by a previous marriage. She could have asked Jennifer's father for more money, but her pride prevented that option, resulting in the fact that the extra money needed for sorority silliness would have been difficult to come by.

"Oh, come on and go with Joe and me to the *SAE* party tonight," pleaded Katie. "You know the theme is going to be a Roman forum, and the decorations are really nice. I saw the beginnings of them when we stopped by the house for a minute before the game."

"What decorations?" queried Michael, smiling playfully. " I can't imagine Joe, or any of his buddies for that matter, hanging crepe paper streamers and entwining Roman columns with ivy. In fact, knowing those guys, I'd be very surprised to discover that they had even bothered to clean the vomit from the floor or take the panties off the ceiling fans after the last big party."

He had to cover his head with his hands after that observation as both girls swatted him in feigned, light-hearted annoyance while exclaiming, " Oh, Michael, don't be so gross!" and, " Anyone can be crude!"

Then Katie defended her argument. "No, really, the *SAE* house does look good. We girls from the Alpha Gam sorority are the co-sponsors of the party and *we* are the ones who are doing the decorating. Do you think for one minute that we could trust the *guys* to do the job right?" answered Katie. "So come on and go with us. It'll be fun."

Katie, too, had been a long time friend of both Michael and Jennifer. She had been in Jennifer's class at Central High but had attended a Methodist church. However, when she and Joe Smothers had begun to date, she would often forget the teachings of John Wesley's Methodism and attend Hillside Baptist with Joe.

"What time are you expected at the youth group hayride tonight?" Jennifer turned to Michael in response to Katie's plea. "Will you get back in time to meet us at the dance?"

Michael had been invited to sing and be part of the chaperone/leadership group at a local church's high school youth group function this evening. He seldom refused these invitations as he genuinely enjoyed the company of the school kids. And he wanted to be a good example to them. He liked the way they all looked up to him because he was older—a college guy, even.

"Hey, you're coming with me to this hay ride thing, aren't ya', Jenny? It starts at 5:30," Michael inquired, surprised. He thought it was understood that Jennifer was coming with him.

"Sure, if you want me to," Jennifer beamed at him. "You know I love to hear you sing and strum your guitar. I'll come, that is, if you promise to sing *to me and me alone* later," she added, smiling a playfully seductive, mischievous smile and taking his hand in hers.

She loved to hear Michael sing. She could listen to his soft, tenor voice all night long.

"Wow! All right, then! Can't pass up that offer!" he responded with enthusiasm, squeezing the hand she had given him and kissing her lightly.

How exciting to his senses and soothing to his ego to have a sweet girlfriend like Jennifer who was not afraid to let him know how much she cared for him. It was intoxicating to him. He had dated some girls before who would play games and act as though they did not like him, even though they would tell their friends a different story. They would play hard to get to try to intrigue him. But not so with Jennifer. Jennifer did not believe in playing games, or if she did, she was a poor actress. He very much liked that about her.

Jennifer's affection for him was obvious in the way she absolutely glowed in his presence, gazed so sweetly into his eyes, laughed at his jokes, and was always able to change her plans, whatever they were, to be with him. It was even more apparent in the way she held his hand, snuggled into his arms as they sat side by side in his car, and kissed him goodnight, responding to his physical affection with a passion and fervor that he found surprising in such a sweet, innocent girl.

For even though this was the era in which the Sexual Revolution was relentlessly and ruthlessly marching its way into the minds and hearts of the culture at large, its arrival had been hampered somewhat in the great State of Alabama, as in the rest of the Bible Belt, by good, sound, Biblical teaching such as Jennifer and Michael had been raised on.

The principle of sexual purity—that sex was wonderfully designed by God to be exercised within the bonds of marriage only—had been taught to these young people over and over again by the Sunday school teachers, pastors, and youth group leaders at Hillside Church. The harmful consequences of sex before marriage were carefully explained to the youth, and they had been invited to freely express their questions and their own thoughts regarding this important issue. Their questions and comments were always taken seriously by the adult leadership, who prayed for, loved, worried about, and provided safe alternate forms of fellowship and activities for the precious young people the Lord had entrusted into their care. The public school system, also, had taught an abstinence based sex education course, as was desired by the parents in the community.

As a result, both Michael and Jennifer were still virgins, both of them by choice and by means of the safe places the adults had provided them. Jennifer, herself, had never been placed in harm's way as far as temptations of the flesh were concerned. Her previous boyfriend had been the respectful gentleman he had been raised to be and had placed no sexual pressure on her.

Michael, on the other hand, had experienced several opportunities to "go all the way," but had so far found within himself the strength to resist. He truly wanted to be the man of God he was fortunate enough to see modeled in his own father, a sincerely good, wise man—a doctor, obstetrician by specialty—who was well respected in the community and was a deacon at Hillside.

His father would tell him how sad it was to have unwed pregnant teenage girls in his practice, abandoned by their lovers to deal with their situations alone or with the aid of an angry, disillusioned parent. The implication to Michael was that he had better not ever be such an irresponsible young man. The point was driven home, and Michael had no intention of falling into such a pit. He, himself, had two beautiful younger sisters for whom he felt very protective, and he had already intimidated several unworthies whom he had discovered slinking around them.

But while he was committed to the *idea* of sexual purity as he had been taught, Michael, at twenty-one, also knew the tremendous, volatile power of sexual passion and had experienced some struggles in this realm, especially recently with the attractive brunette by his side.

And the problem was this: he just plain liked the way she responded to his physical expressions of affection. Lately, they found themselves spending a very long time telling each other goodnight at the end of their many evenings together. In fact, the amount of time spent before their ultimate parting was increasing steadily. Michael knew that he should perhaps take the initiative in bringing their passionate kisses and embraces down to a safer level. But being with Jennifer was just too exciting for him. He had never felt this way about any girl before.

Sure, he had dated a couple of girls with bad reputations who had been more than willing to oblige him sexually, though he had resisted. But it was different with Jennifer—sweet, vulnerable, innocent Jenny. He was not certain it was "true love," whatever that was supposed to mean, but he knew he cared deeply for Jennifer and found her to be the most engaging and lovable of any of his past girlfriends. And the still controlled, latent sexual side of her nature that was implicit in her response to his touch appealed strongly to his own growing desires. And now, she was requesting more time alone with him later this evening. How could he refuse?

"So then, what are the two of you going to do after the hayride? Come to the *SAE* party with Joe and me?" Katie's voice brought him back to the question at hand as she persisted. "Don't go to that tacky Student Union dance. You'll have more fun with us."

"What time do you think the hayride will be over, Mikey? Will there be time to go to either one of the parties?" Jennifer inquired.

She liked to call him "Mikey" and he allowed it from her and her only, because even though he hated the sound of it from anyone else, he loved the way her eyes glowed and the corners of her mouth turned up when she addressed him by her own affectionate nickname for him.

"Oh, yeah. We should be done by about nine o'clock, I think. Then we can go directly to the frat party," he answered.

"That's great!" squealed Katie with delight. "Then you are coming with us! But you can't come directly from the hayride. You have to dress in togas and Roman-style costumes with laurels made from vines on your heads and all that stuff."

"What? You must be kidding! I am *not*, repeat *not*, going to wear a toga! No way! Not in this life," exclaimed Michael in disbelief.

"Oh, come on, Michael! Don't be a party pooper. Everyone there is going to be wearing one … even Joe," Katie pleaded.

Michael began to chuckle, and then progressed to a loud, riotous, belly laugh until tears came into his eyes as the picture of his buddy, Joe—all six foot four inches of him, big burly Joe, heavy muscled, thick chested, dark and swarthy Joe, a 'man's man' Joe—wearing a toga on his body and weeds in his hair, floated across his imagination. He could even now see the thick, dark hair of his legs, arms, and chest making such an incongruous statement in a costume of that style.

"Joe … wearing a dress ... with a vine wrapped around his head! Oh, Katie, stop it! … Oh,stop it! … I can't catch my breath!" He was doubled over now and his laughter was quite contagious, reproducing itself up and down the rows of people seated in his vicinity. Jennifer, too, was laughing uncontrollably as he continued, "Where did he buy it? At Togas R Us? I hope they have a Big and Tall department … Oh … oh, it's too much! ... It's just too funny!" He continued for several moments more.

Katie, herself, could not help but chuckle along with the others. She liked the Togas R Us joke but pressed on, presenting her side of the case as best as she could in the midst of all the hilarity.

"No, he didn't buy it at Togas R Us, Michael. I made it for him out of some old sheets in my closet. Stop it! Stop laughing! I really did make it! And he looks quite good in it actually. Kinda sexy, I think. Jenny could make one for you. Oh, stop it, Michael. And you, too, Jenny. Stop laughing at me!" But Katie was now laughing, too, as she could no longer keep from joining in with the others who were no closer to stopping the merriment than they had been moments before.

"Poor old Joe," Michael continued hysterically, holding his aching side and drying his watery eyes. "He must have it pretty bad for you, Kate, if he's reduced himself to wearing a dress ... made out of your old sheets. Oh, stop it! ... And where did he get the vine for the laurel? Out of your flower garden? ... Make sure it's not poison ivy!"

"Quit calling it a dress!" defended Katie. "It's a *toga, a toga, a toga,* Michael!" And she slapped him lightly on top of his head. "All the Roman men wore them. Oh, Jenny, help me explain this to your boyfriend. That is, if you can stop laughing long enough yourself, you old turncoat. I thought you were on my side," she finished playfully.

"Maybe all the Roman men wore them, Katie," responded Jennifer when she could catch her breath, "but I don't believe that you're ever going to get this American man sitting next to me to wear one, much less wrap a vine around his head."

"Oh, you two! You're both exactly alike! Party Poopers Deluxe!" cried Katie in feigned exasperation.

Finally, the mirth and merriment spent itself, and as the fans were all now leaving the stadium, Michael turned to Katie saying,

"Sorry about that, Katie, but it was such a funny mental image..." and he was beginning to shake some more as he envisioned Senator Joseph Smothers, who did not know Caligula from Casper the Friendly Ghost, leaving the Forum dressed in a toga after a long, hard-fought battle with one of the treacherous, nefarious Caesars. However, he was able to stop himself as he could tell that Katie had had about enough and concluded, " We will be happy to visit the Forum tonight, but I am sure that Joe and all the other Noble Romans will excuse me if I pass on the toga and wear jeans and a shirt instead. Jenny can dress up in costume if she wants to, of course."

Just then, Joe, all dusty and sweaty, ran up to the threesome, kissed Katie ceremoniously and exclaimed, "Well, I'd say we pretty much humiliated the faculty again this year. I do wish I hadn't beaned my history professor with that line drive down third base, though. Oh, well. There goes my straight 'A' average … Hey, ya'll are comin' to the Roman party with us tonight, aren't ya?"

"I don't know, Joe," responded Michael, a satirical gleam in his eye. "My favorite toga is still at the dry cleaners. Maybe I could borrow one of yours!" And he doubled over again, convulsively.

"Oh, Michael! Enough already about the togas!" Katie protested.

"Wha- -What's going on?" quizzed Joe, his forehead wrinkled. "Oh, I get it. I know it's stupid, Mike, but after a couple of beers, you kinda get used to it. It's kinda cool, actually. I mean as far as air circulation is concerned and all. Much more comfortable than pants. What is it, Mike, old man?" Joe was still in the dark.

"Just do us all one big favor, Joe. Make sure you have on a pair of clean shorts! Preferably ones with no holes in them!" gasped Michael, laughing still and wiping away tears.

"Oh, Michael!" cried both girls, simultaneously. But they were smiling, too, though slightly red-cheeked.

"Yeah, right, buddy. Don't worry. I'll have everything covered, if you know what I mean," Joe smiled back at his friends, the light finally on. Then to Katie, he said, "Gotta go hit the showers now, Babe. I'll pick you up at seven thirty, okay?" With one more kiss from his girlfriend, he trotted off to the locker room.

"Well, if we're going to be at the church parking lot by 5:30, we'd better be leaving, Jen. It's four fifteen now. I'll take you both back to the dorm and I'll pick you up in an hour, all right, Toots?" Michael asked.

The three young people left the stadium eagerly anticipating the evening's festivities. Michael, for one, could not wait to see how close his mental image of Joe in a toga and laurel compared to the real thing, and he chuckled again as they made their way to his car.

Chapter Three

"*O*h, Jennifer! You look so beautiful! Michael will not be able to resist you in that gown," exclaimed Katie, Sarah, and Polly as they finished their preparations on Jennifer's costume.

The three girls had of necessity hastily thrown together a last minute outfit for Jennifer to wear to the *SAE* party in just a few hours. Polly, a helpful girl from Huntsville whose room was one door down, had volunteered her long satiny white, sleeveless nightgown which featured sashes that crossed the v-neckline in front and tied in the back. It was a simple, classic design that had a certain Roman air to it, and with her undergarments and Sarah's long slip on underneath, it was not apparent it was actually a nightgown. The clingy, creamy white fabric contrasted very nicely with Jennifer's olive skin and dark features. On her head, they had fashioned a garland of ivy taken from the window box of one of the dorm's first story rooms. The total effect on the young coed was breathtaking. She looked like a goddess, like Venus, the Roman goddess of love and beauty, her long slender frame and pleasing curves giving substance and shape to the simple lines of the gown while the ivy crown emphasized her large dark eyes and shining hair.

"Well, Jenny, Michael is going to take one look at you in that gown and want to marry you … or something," stated Sarah emphatically, stepping back and surveying with critical eye the final product. And Sarah was not one to embellish the truth. She called it just the way she saw it. And she saw Jennifer looking as pretty and virginal as any bride in any bride's magazine.

"It's the 'or something' that worries me," joined in Polly, smirking in a playfully wicked way. "Make certain that you have the wedding *before* you go on the honeymoon, now Jenny, dear," she sang out mockingly, intoning from memory the wisdom of all the mothers of the four young ladies who were now giggling at their friend.

"Oh, ya'll. Stop it. Michael has not asked to marry me. Nor will this 'dress'—and don't any of you dare tell him it is really a nightgown—induce him to propose to me," Jennifer complained, somewhat embarrassed as she preened herself in front of the mirror, her gold hoop earrings shining from beneath her hair.

" 'Induce him to propose to me,' " mimicked Katie, smiling. "Your parents' hard-earned dollars have been well spent on your education, Jen. Sounds like something out of a Jane Austen novel. I don't know if Michael needs any 'inducement' to propose marriage to you, Jennifer, but by golly, you sure could 'seduce' him in that gown if you wanted to! You do look like a bride!" And she stepped behind Jennifer and lifted the back hem from the floor as if it were a bridal gown train while humming the wedding march before being slapped away by the quasi "bride."

Her comrades were all enjoying teasing their pal because they knew that Jennifer was still very innocent, as indeed all of them were. But they were beginning to find themselves in a smaller and smaller minority, so that joking and laughing about sexual temptation made them feel at least a little more experienced and less juvenile.

"Look, she's blushing! Blushing just like a bride coming down the aisle," taunted Polly playfully, enjoying herself thoroughly. "Quick! Somebody call up Jennifer's dad and tell him to get his shotgun and come down here and make Michael Evans marry his daughter before it's too late—before Michael takes the lid off the cookie jar and his little girl is ruined!"

The girls all pealed with more laughter and giggles.

"Really, now ladies, you must be terribly bored and hard up for something to do to sit here and tease me like this," Jennifer observed, still crimson. "Here, help me out of this gown so I don't get makeup on it. I only have a few minutes to change into my jeans for the hayride."

With their assistance, Jennifer hung the Roman dress on the hanger and changed for the youth function. How close their comments had come to the truth, she hoped they did not know, and she wished for the hundredth time that she could learn to control her blushes. For she knew that she had been playing with fire to a degree in her private moments with Michael during the past eight weeks. His initial tender kisses of two months ago had progressed into more passionate, heated ones, and lately she had run into trouble keeping his hands away from places they had no right to be.

But what was troubling her more than his attempts to fondle and caress her was that she, herself, was finding it more difficult to push him away. She loved being with him, feeling so close to him, feeling that special, tingling excitement when they were kissing and embracing. It made her feel as if she belonged to him. It made her feel beautiful, desirable, womanly, and sensual, like the heroines of some of the novels she had read.

And yet, with all these positive emotions, a little warning bell was ringing in her conscious thoughts, telling her to be more careful and cautious. Telling her to think long-term and not just for the moment. All of the good reasons to wait for marriage were stored there, in her memory bank, and they made perfect sense to her logic.

But her body and her emotions were beginning to battle her more rational and, indeed, spiritual nature. The little warning bell was becoming more and more muted as her time spent alone with Michael in his parked car was becoming longer. She loved him and she loved being with him. She could no more hide that fact from anyone. And she was beginning to believe that he loved her, too.

Surely he loved her, too. How could he be so impassioned and yet so kind if he did not love her? He had not yet spoken those three little words that she so longed to hear. Nor had she spoken them to him. She was determined *not* to be the first one to say them. But, of course, he knew it even though she had been silent on the subject. And though he had also been silent verbally in expressing his feelings for her, his actions surely could not be construed in any other way than to say, "I love you, Jenny. You are my girl."

"Bzzz." The speaker on her dorm room wall interrupted her thoughts, announcing a visitor in the lobby.

"That will be Michael. Thanks so much for helping me with my costume for the dance, ladies. I'll see you later," Jennifer addressed her three buddies as she gathered her purse and sweater.

"Have fun on the hayride, and we'll see you at the party," responded Katie.

"Make Michael take good care of you," called out Sarah, waving.

"Don't come back with hay in your pants," teased Polly salaciously. "I don't want to have to phone your father!"

With an "Oh, Polly!" and a half smile, Jennifer walked out the door and down the short hallway into the lobby of the dormitory.

"Hey, Jen. Let's go! I'm running a little late because I got halfway here and had to turn around. I remembered that I had left my guitar back at The Cave, and I knew you wouldn't go back there with me to get it," Michael stated hurriedly, giving her his hand and leading her quickly to his car.

"The Cave" was Michael's nickname for his very small, very dark and dingy, very old, musty apartment situated in the older part of the small college town. Jennifer would never go in there with him as she said that the place was too depressing. His former roommate in his previous, bright and clean apartment had come up with the brilliant idea of cleaning the place with a garden hose through the window one day last semester after he had consumed a six-pack of a secret microbrew by himself. This inspired maneuver had caused both young men to lose their lease, sending Michael on a last minute, frantic search for suitable accommodations. The Cave had *not* been suitable, but it had been the only thing available, so there he was until next semester. The good news was that he no longer had a roommate.

"You're right about my not wanting to see that place, Mikey. Yuck! I don't see why you don't have nightmares every night in that place. It gives me the creeps," agreed Jennifer, shivering at the thought.

"You're a spoiled, spoiled woman, Jennifer Jacobs," teased Michael as he gently patted her bluejeaned leg. "But I think I'll keep you." And he kissed her on her forehead and tussled her hair gently.

They pulled into the church parking lot at exactly 5:40 p.m. There was an old yellow church bus filled with high schoolers waiting impatiently for them. Pastor Bob, the youth leader, came up to the couple with a relieved expression on his face. He was about thirty-two-years-old with an open, honest look about him, and appeared to be the all-American guy who lived next door.

"Boy, I'm glad to see the two of you! I don't know how I could handle this rowdy bunch by myself. Two of my chaperones and my wife had to cancel at the last minute for different reasons," Bob explained as he shook both of their hands. "We'll all take the bus out to the Carey's farm about five miles out of town for the cookout and hayride. I told the parents to meet us back here at nine o'clock."

The ride out to the farm was a boisterous, noisy one, with kids piled upon kids all talking at once. The exuberant *joie de vivre* of the youngsters reminded Michael and Jennifer that they were not quite as young as they used to be. The girls were all making eyes at Michael and then at each other and giggling. Jennifer remembered how silly she had been at that age and chuckled silently to herself as she placed her arm through Michael's and held his hand, as if to say, "Settle down, girls. He's taken."

The Carey farm was buzzing with activity just a few moments after the bus stopped and the youth spilled out. Jennifer was busy helping Mrs. Carey prepare and serve the food as well as engaging the young ladies in lively conversation. For she, too, liked to be around this age group as it flattered her to be looked up to and admired for being older and wiser.

Michael and Pastor Bob were organizing games and entertaining the youth, while Mr. Carey was setting up the bonfire pit in a picturesque spot by his catfish pond to be used as the gathering place at the end of the hayride. After everyone had consumed all the hotdogs, hamburgers, chips, cakes, and brownies they could hold, Mr. Carey mounted his powerful tractor and pulled the flatbed trailer loaded with hay around and helped the kids climb aboard.

As Pastor Bob helped lift Jennifer up to the trailer, Michael jumped up behind her, trying not to let his eyes linger on her cute derriere, which her blue jeans so flattered. Controlling his eyes around Jennifer was becoming more of a challenge each day, as he was increasingly enamored with her feminine charms. He made a comfortable spot for her next to him on a small bale of hay and took her hand in his. The young people were all busy talking and laughing as the wagonload bumped its way slowly down the dirt farm road that led to the pond. Michael had to jump up and make a quick grab for one young lady as she was sitting a little too close to the edge and was in danger of falling when Mr. Carey ran over a large pothole.

"Whoa, there, Sally," he said as he clutched the fifteen-year-old's arm and steadied her. "Don't jump off just yet; not without your parachute, anyway. It's a long way down," and he winked at her. She grinned and blushed, telling him,

"My name's not Sally. It's Karen."

"You don't say, Karen! You look just like that cute little girl, Sally, I used to read about in my first grade reader. You know the one. Had a dog named Spot and a cat named Puff, or Duff, or Snuff or something like that," Michael flirted harmlessly with her. " And she had cute little dimples just like yours."

Karen could not think of anything else to say and just grinned in an embarrassed way and blushed some more, her dimples deepening.

Jennifer smiled broadly at Karen's awkward response to Michael's compliment. She would have behaved in like manner when she was Karen's age, though she would have dearly loved the careless affection and attention he gave. She knew he was trying to make each high-schooler feel special and desirable, though his time there was limited, and she loved him for it. Michael had such a good heart. He had told her several times that one day, he would like to start a home for wayward kids who had been discarded by the community. One day, after he had made enough money to finance it through his career in the music industry in Nashville, that is.

She placed her arm through his and hugged it against herself, smiling warmly into his eyes, soliciting a little kiss on the forehead and a tender smile from him in return.

"Hey, you two," chuckled Pastor Bob teasingly. "Enough of that kissy face. You're supposed to be the chaperones, remember?"

Pastor Bob had been observing the two young people together all evening, and they reminded him very much of his wife and himself not so very long ago when he was courting her, making him suddenly miss her very much. *Cute couple,* he thought.

As the group unloaded once more at the bonfire area and settled down on the ground by the pond, the stars began to shine and the first quarter moon to glow in the deepening purple and pink dusk of that lovely Alabama farm. The bullfrogs and cicadas were performing a free concert, with the fireflies, called "lightening bugs" in Alabama, putting on the fireworks display. It was as romantic a setting as any young woman could imagine, and that romance was not lost on Jennifer, who sitting next to Michael with her slender hand gently enclosed in his, was just about as happy as she had ever been in all of her brief life.

Pastor Bob stood up front in the center of the youth, read some scripture, and gave a brief talk about not succumbing to peer pressure, but instead being courageous enough to take a stand for righteousness. Then Michael came forward with his guitar and led the youngsters in some favorite campfire songs like *Kumba Ya, I Have Decided to Follow Jesus,* and *Amazing Grace,* after which he played and sang a few songs of his own making. His compositions were beautiful songs of God's love and grace, and had the same effect on this group of youth as they did back at Hillside. The young people were enthralled. He sang softly in his tender, clear, tenor voice as he gently caressed the strings of his acoustic guitar.

Michael simply was gifted. And he simply was all that Jennifer had ever wished for or wanted in a man, all that she had ever dreamed of. So kind and good. So strong, spiritual, and masculine. So talented and intelligent. So handsome and so much fun to be with. So at peace with both himself and the world. So assured of his own abilities, without conceit. He was in many ways her hero. And he was better than any literary lover she had read about in her classic romance novels—better than Mr. Rochester, better than Heathcliff, better than Maxim de Winter, and even better than Rhett Butler. For they were all make-believe and had no spiritual dimension. But Michael was real. And he really loved God.

As her eyes focused on him making such lovely, ethereal music that peaceful May night in 1975—sitting by a pond on a farm near Coburn, Alabama under the starry, moonlit sky, the blazing bonfire lighting up the darkness all around and reflecting its leaping, dancing firelight in her dark, impassioned eyes—her heart was filled with unabashed love and unquenchable longing for him. Suddenly, she knew that she wanted him more than she had ever wanted anyone or anything in her life! Wanted him to belong to her, and herself to belong to him. Wanted him desperately. Wanted him to be hers and hers alone, her husband and the father of her children. Wanted him forever.

And just at that moment, as she longed for him so powerfully that lovely night, she almost felt a physical sensation, as if her heart had left her bosom and in an instant had flown across that distance of five feet to where he was sitting, embracing him tightly, binding him with some mystical, invisible cord of love that was very, very strong, and then returning back into her own breast, forever uniting the two of them.

She could no longer withhold any part of her heart from him! This thought both frightened and thrilled her. Frightened her because she was not yet certain of his own affection. Thrilled her because, just maybe, he was the answer to the deepest desire of her soul. A desire for unconditional, overwhelming love, acceptance, and security. A desire to have a happy, fulfilling home life of her own such as she had never experienced, never to be abandoned or broken again. A desire for spiritual, emotional, and physical intimacy that would make her wildest dreams come true.

As she sat there, mesmerized by the magic of the moment, totally captivated and overtaken by the powerful emotions of true love, she prayed silently, *Dear Lord, thank you so much for giving me such a wonderful boyfriend as Michael. Please don't ever take him away from me!*

Chapter Four

"*N*ow, hurry up, Jen. Don't keep me waiting here forever while you doll yourself up," Michael half-jokingly instructed in the lobby of Dorm 10. "I think you look beautiful just like you are."

It was now about 9:20 p.m., and Jennifer had insisted that Michael bring her back to the dorm to change into her Roman gown before the party. She knew that the girls had worked too hard on her outfit and would never forgive her if she did not wear it to the dance. And in her vanity, she had also thought that she looked like a radiant bride while modeling it earlier and was curious to see Michael's reaction when he would first see her attired in such a fashion.

Katie had left two hours ago and was not in their room, and the other two of her friends were also out that evening, so she was alone for a few minutes. She broke her own time record in the quick shower category and touched up her makeup and styled her hair at an equally record-setting pace. She lightly sprayed on hers and Michael's favorite cologne, placed her dress over Sarah's borrowed long slip, tied on her pair of leather sandals, and lastly placed the laurel of English ivy on her head.

As she surveyed herself in the mirror before grabbing her purse, turning out the lights, and locking the door, she knew that she had never looked prettier. Her cheeks had a natural rosy glow so that rouge was unnecessary tonight. She was totally, whole-heartedly, completely in love and on her way to spend an evening with the object of that love. There is nothing more becoming to a young woman than that.

She immediately knew that the time she had spent in her room was worthwhile when she saw Michael's response as he first gazed on her emerging from the hallway. He was awestruck. His eyes widened and he took both of her hands in his as he looked her over in disbelief from top to bottom and back again.

"Wow, Jennifer," he spoke in an almost reverent whisper, "you look just like a goddess ... No, better than that ... You look like a princess ... like Cinderella ... like a beautiful bride!" And he warmly embraced her, loving the feel of her body next to his and the silky texture of her gown. "And you smell good, too. Like a flower garden." He kissed her affectionately, warmly, slowly and added, "Are you sure you want to go to this party? I know you don't usually like these fraternity shindigs."

"Of course, we have to go to the party," she responded, blushing more and reveling in his warm embrace and his appreciation of her beauty. "Katie and Joe will kill us if we don't show up, and I would certainly look pretty foolish all dressed up like this if we didn't go, wouldn't I?" she asked him flirtatiously with a twinkle in her eyes.

"Oh, no! You don't look foolish to me! Not at all. You look ..." and he broke off momentarily, searching for an appropriate word, as he took in her pretty face, shining dark hair, and darker still, large and beguiling eyes, and the soft, sensuous curves of her body that the dress so flattered, "Ravishing. That's how you look. Ravishing ... And sexy as the mischief," he added sincerely. "Is it getting warm in here?" and he pulled on his shirt collar and smiled.

"Then I guess we absolutely *have* to go to the party, now," she responded playfully, glowing and very pleased with his words as she gently pulled herself out of his arms. "We don't want to risk 'ravishment' or whatever the noun form of that word is, now, do we."

Jennifer was an English major and planned to become a journalist or a freelance writer. She loved words, and had used the correct one here even though it sounded strange to her ears.

"We don't?" questioned Michael, grinning in mock disbelief. "Speak for yourself, Toots. But on that note and on my word as a gentleman and a solid Roman citizen, please allow me to escort you to the Forum, Miss Jennifer."

And he offered her his arm, which she took in equal ceremony as they left for the *SAE* house.

The couple could hear before they could actually see the Sigma Alpha Epsilon house, so loud was the hired band scraping at their instruments and shouting out the lyrics to various pop songs of the day. Obviously to this band, as well as to most musical groups of that era, "loud" meant "good," and this band wanted to be the best. The uncomfortable volume of the music was one reason Jennifer did not care for these get-togethers. She would feel as though she had cotton in her ears and have a raging headache upon leaving such engagements. The band was attempting to replicate a Blood, Sweat & Tears' song that Jennifer used to like, but wondered if she ever would again.

"What goes up, must come down. Spinnin' wheel gotta go round. Talkin' bout your troubles, it's a cryin' sin. Ride a painted pony, let the spinnin' wheel spin."

As the attractive pair entered the house, much attention was turned towards Jennifer. Much male attention, that is. The females in the crowd had a difficult time disguising their jealousy while the males just gaped at her in appreciative, unadulterated lust and looked at Michael with envy. Jennifer turned slightly crimson, uneasy though flattered with all this attention, while Michael whispered loudly in her ear, "See, Jen. I told you. You look like a princess tonight." And he placed his arm more firmly around her waist and peered more sternly into the eyes of the brotherhood of the *SAE's* to signal to the guys that she was spoken for.

"Hey, Michael and Jenny! Come on up here!" called down Joe from the upper level balcony/loft of the fraternity house. " I saved you a beer, but you'd better hurry before Harry, here, wrestles it away from me."

At his first glance of Joe in a toga, Michael had a very difficult time controlling his laughter. His mental image of earlier in the day had been remarkably accurate. Joe—and for that matter almost all of the young men with the exception of one stocky guy with a classic aquiline nose who looked incredibly like Julius Caesar—appeared totally ridiculous in their thrown together togas, most of which had been made, like Joe's, out of old sheets, though not with as skilled a seamstress as Katie. And by this time, well into the third hour of the party, many of the outfits were much worse for the wear, large gaps in the "skirts" revealing, thankfully, swimsuit trunks which most of the young men had had the foresight to don before the evening's social.

But the funniest things to see were the laurel wreaths on the heads of these unfortunates. These headgears ranged from artificial plastic vines to chains of clover blossoms hastily strung together by their dates. Many had migrated down from their heads to their necks, worn more like a Hawaiian lei, and others were hanging sideways like the crooked halo of The Littlest Angel. The young women, however, all looked very lovely, adding weight to Michael's earlier statement to Jennifer that girls just plain look better in dresses that men do.

"Hey, ya'll!" drawled Katie when she saw her friends. And she hugged Jennifer. "Doesn't Jennifer look like an angel, Michael? Like an angel bride in her gown?"

"Oh, yeah!" he agreed enthusiastically, and he squeezed Jennifer close and gave her a kiss, causing those standing close by to call out both some decent and indecent remarks.

"Enough of that for now, Mike, my man. Pace yourself, buddy, pace yourself. There's still plenty of night left," observed Joe who then gave Jennifer a brotherly kiss on the cheek saying, "You do look beautiful, Jennifer. I'd say that you and Katie are the prettiest girls here."

Joe then handed Michael a mug of beer and asked Jennifer if he could get her a soft drink. He knew Jenny hated beer—said it tasted like carbonated horse urine or something like that, didn't she?

The two couples stood there for about ten minutes trying to converse over the blare of the band and the raucous laughter of the intoxicated crowd, sipping their drinks and looking around.

I don't know why people like to drink so much, thought Jennifer. *If they could see how silly and stupid they look and how much their behavior changes—for the worse, most times—they wouldn't do it.* There were several girls present who were her acquaintances and co-residents of Dorm 10 whom Jennifer had liked and admired. But the more tipsy ones hardly appeared like themselves. With glassy eyes, disheveled hair, and goofy leers, they were stumbling around the dance floor dripping their half-consumed beers onto the wooden boards. Every once in a while, one's coloring would turn a little green and she would beat a rather crooked path to the bathroom.

To Jennifer, staying in control of a situation was the highest good. So many bad things had happened beyond her control in her life—primarily the divorce of her parents with the subsequent removal of her father from her home, and the more recent remarriage of her mother to that boring Bill Miller—that she felt she must stay in charge of what was left to her, however small that might be. And having alcohol control her was unthinkable. Besides, she really, really hated the taste of beer! *Yuck!* she thought. *How can anyone like the taste of that awful, bitter stuff? I would much rather have a Coca-cola.*

Michael, on the other hand, did not mind the taste of beer so much. Especially the second one that Joe immediately placed in his hand after he finished his first. He saw no inconsistency between his faith and a beer or two. He did believe that it was wrong to become drunk, of course, but justified his one or two brews by reasoning that unbelievers thought Christians to be fuddy-duddy, holier-than-thou types enough, without adding to their false stereotype and caricature by refusing a friendly beer or two on occasion. *Besides*, he reasoned, *I am of legal drinking age, unlike many of the younger of Joe's brothers here tonight.*

He sometimes wished he had not promised his parents on a sacred oath that he would never have more than two in an evening. He had made that promise under duress at the funeral of his mother's favorite brother and, indeed, his favorite uncle, who had been killed in a head-on collision four years ago by a drunk driver going ninety miles per hour on the wrong side of the interstate just outside Birmingham. His heart-broken mother and his very somber father had asked him to place his hand on the Bible and swear to the two-beer limit. They would have asked him to be totally temperate and abstain altogether, but were more realistic than he gave them credit for at the time.

His father, especially, knew how difficult it was for a man never to have a beer with his buddies. So Michael had taken the sacred oath and felt as bound to it as any President had ever felt bound to the official Oath of Office on the Capitol steps. More bound, than some, he was sure. And, in principle at least, though it was so difficult to live out, Michael believed that the Lord could not honor a man who "lingered long at the cup." So he abstained from the third offered mug willingly, though, tonight at least, reluctantly.

As that second brew was making its way through Michael's system, he was beginning to loosen up a little. He had not eaten much at the hayride because he had been so busy working with Pastor Bob and horsing around with the kids. Although the effects of the alcohol were minimal on a man of his size and weight, still he felt a pleasant sensation, a little buzz that made him look at Jennifer with even more affection and desire. The band was attempting to play "Stairway to Heaven," and couples were now slow dancing, bodies pressed tightly together, gently swaying to the rhythm of the melody. Soon he and Jennifer, and Katie and Joe were among the couples on the dance floor.

If one could have invented a passion meter that measured youthful desires of the flesh, the needle would have been at the maximum reading, as the crowd of young adults burned with sensual longing for one another. For the former members of the Youth Group at the Hillside Church in Mobile, Alabama, who had made written pledges to remain chaste until marriage, the situation on the dance floor was less than ideal. Yellow caution lights were flashing in their minds, but the couples ignored them or told them, "It's okay. I have everything under control."

For Michael and Jennifer, who were not only embracing and swaying to the seducing tones of the song, but also were kissing each other with increasing fervor, time was non-existent and there were no other dance partners on the floor.

Jennifer, in particular, had never felt this way and was strangely emboldened to explore heretofore unknown territories of her innate sexual longings. Everything in her body and soul told her that Michael was the one and only man for her, the one God had ordained for her from the foundation of the world, her future husband, the future father of her children, the one she would love now and forever, the one she could fully trust and give herself completely to.

She was so certain of this immutable fact at that moment that she was unwittingly communicating it in some mysterious way to Michael through her ardent kisses. And also, she was unknowingly relaying that message to him by the soft, burning glow emanating from her eyes, the mirror of her soul, as she gazed steadfastly into his own clear blue ones. She loved him, and she loved being with him, feeling his strong, masculine arms around her, feeling so very close to him, physically and emotionally.

To Michael, standing there on the dance floor totally enthralled, Jennifer was the most alluring, intoxicating, exciting creature he had ever held in his arms. He loved the feel of her, the way she tenderly enfolded herself in his embrace, the softness of her lips, the very fragrance of her, the passionate fire in her large, dark, mysterious eyes, and especially the way she was responding to his natural desires, pressing her body so close to his. His own inborn radar was receiving the message she was sending him loud and clear.

And he wanted her desperately.

"Come on, Jen. Let's go. Let's get out of here," he whispered urgently, softly in her ear, his warm breath causing goose bumps to rise on her neck and arms.

"Okay, but we need to tell Katie and Joe goodbye," she murmured back to him.

The couple signaled a good-bye to their friends, who were also locked in a loving embrace, and made their way through the crowd toward the door while the band sang out of mystery, wonder, and a stairway to heaven.

While the dance floor of the *SAE* fraternity house had been dangerous enough for the young couple hoping to remain pristine until marriage, alone in Michael's car, the pair was in even greater peril of falling into the turbulent waters of premarital sex as they waded undaunted along its shores. Yet, flirting with these forbidden risks made the erotic nature of their sexual desires even more exciting.

What is forbidden always appears sweetest to the fallen nature of man, and the sweetness of sexual desire was powerful and seductive.

Michael had driven them to a secluded parking spot, a quiet country roadside place just a few minutes off the main highway leading out of town. His car, a 1972 Pontiac sedan, had belonged to his mother but had been given to Michael by his parents to take to college when his Mustang had been wrecked beyond repair by a woman who had run a traffic light one week before he was to begin his freshman year. He had chosen to take the insurance money to buy a new guitar, keyboard, and some other items, and his parents had never asked him to return his mother's car. They actually felt that he was safer driving a family sedan than he would have been with a new sports car, and had not mentioned his ever returning it.

Since the sedan had a bench seat in front, there was no console or gear shifting mechanism to separate the two of them, and they were engaging in very long, impassioned kissing and embracing, while the radio played softly. Roberta Flack was singing soulfully,

*"The first time ever I saw your face, I thought the sun rose in your eyes ..."**

All the good training that the young people had received about avoiding hazardous situations—such as being alone in parked cars on late, moonlit, Alabama nights out in the middle of nowhere, listening to romantic, sensual music—was ignored by Jennifer and forgotten by Michael as the couple became more and more engrossed in each other and in the exciting, pleasurable, God-given sensations of sexual foreplay.

This time, Jennifer did not push Michael's hands away. She had stopped thinking rationally a long time ago, and was instead allowing herself just to *feel* rather than *know* what was proper, healthy, and good.

Michael was equally attuned only to the present ... There was no past ... There was no future ... There was no right ... There was no wrong... There were only he and Jennifer ... Beautiful, exciting, desirable, sweet, soft, sexy Jenny. Jenny, who even now was responding to his passion with an equally strong fervor of her own. Jenny, who was his first true love and was about to become his first true lover.

"Sweet, sweet, Jenny," he murmured as he kissed her smooth, graceful neck and throat, his lips slowly moving downward. "You are so wonderful ... So very beautiful ... So wonderful."

"Oh, Mikey ... I love you ... I do ... I love you ... so much," she whispered softly, sincerely from her full, impassioned heart, experiencing powerful, thrilling sensations and emotions that were all brand new to her.

"The first time ever I kissed your mouth, I felt the earth move in my hand ..." sang Roberta on into that late Alabama evening.

But as he began to rearrange and then try to remove her clothing, something awakened in Jennifer's mind and brought her back to the reality of their situation. Suddenly, she knew that she was in real danger of losing what she could never regain.

Michael had not said that he loved her! Michael had made no commitment to her! She had just told him that she loved him, something she had never intended to be the first to do. But he had not responded with the expected, "I love you, too, Jenny." She was madly, totally, completely in love with him and, as such, had so much to lose, while he had little to lose here in this parked car, she thought clearly. The burden was always on the female, she knew, since the female had the most to lose. She was not stupid. She was not wicked. She was only very much in love.

She gently but firmly pushed his hands away and said, "No, Mikey, no. Please don't do that."

"Oh, Jenny, you don't mean that," he responded insistently, and kissed her warmly, making another effort.

This time she pushed him away with more strength and repeated, "Yes, Michael. I do mean it. Please don't do that again."

As he tried once more to remove the article of clothing and fondle her, she backed away completely from him, pushing him away with both arms.

"Michael, please stop it! You are scaring me!" she insisted loudly, with a slight tremble in her voice.

This time, he came out of his overpowering, passionate fog and looked at her face, finding a very real expression of fright and concern in her dark eyes which threw a cold, wet blanket over his libido. He knew instantly that this "session" was over unless he took her by force, which was unthinkable.

"ALL RIGHT, JENNIFER!" he barked loudly into her face in the midst of his own extreme disappointment and intense sexual frustration while he backed away from her. "BUT WHAT I WANT TO KNOW IS, WHY ... ALL OF A SUDDEN ... WAS IT SO WRONG? ... WHY ... DID YOU MAKE ME THINK THAT YOU WERE GOING TO—? ... OH, HELL!"

And with that expletive, he beat the steering wheel with both of his fists, started the motor, and spun the tires on the gravel as he drove the automobile off the shoulder of the deserted back road and onto the pavement of the highway with great speed, accelerator to the floorboard.

"The first time ever I lay with you ..." Roberta continued on, until Michael turned her off with a vengeance, pulling the knob off the radio and hurling it out the window.

Jennifer had started to tear up at his first verbal explosion, and was now crying a stream of silent, steady tears as she rearranged and refastened her clothing. She had never seen Michael angry before, much less use the word "hell" unless he was talking about not wanting sinners to go there. He was always so even-tempered and easy going. She had never seen him come even close to losing his temper at any one. And now he was very angry with *her*! She was confused and frightened at the thought.

He drove recklessly on, silently fuming, speeding down the streets, until he finally whirled up in front of Dorm 10. He slammed on the brakes, *just the way Jennifer did to me,* he thought ruefully, making the tires squeal and Jennifer grab the dash to keep her balance.

Turning toward her, he said shortly without ceremony, "I hope you don't mind if I don't walk you to the door this time." He did not look her in the eyes, though he could see that she had been crying. *Fine!* he thought unsympathetically. *I feel like crying, too!*

"Goodnight, Michael," she muttered through tears. Then she opened her own door, slammed it shut, and ran up the steps to the dormitory, bewildered and distraught.

"Great! Just great!" the frustrated young man vented angrily to no one, and he spun the tires again, making them sing, and sped out of the parking lot as fast as his '72 Pontiac would go.

As he raced and raged on, his car nearly ran into a group of girls walking along the crosswalk leading to a different dormitory. Looking at them in his rearview mirror, he saw them running away from his car as fast as they could, and he was brought back to reality and slowed down.

"Damn!" he exploded, hitting the steering wheel again as he stopped at a traffic light.

There was a couple in the car next to his in the left turn lane waiting for the light to change, and they were kissing with enthusiasm, their hands freely roaming all over creation. He didn't understand it. In his overheated state of mind he didn't really want to understand what had transpired just now between Jennifer and him.

What is it with women? How do they think? How could Jennifer think that I could just throw on the brakes and walk away from her like that? After she made me think that she ...

But as he waited a while for the light to change, he slowly began to cool down and to think more logically and calmly. After a minute or two, he acknowledged to himself that the fault was not Jennifer's... Not really.

Of course, she doesn't know what it is like to be a man! How could she? She could no more understand how a man thinks and feels than I know how a woman does! God sure must have a sense of humor, he thought, *creating men and women to be so different and so very baffling to each other. And yet with such a desire to be together, too. Yeah, it's just too funny!* he chuckled to himself in bitter frustration. As he drove on, he considered the truth of the matter.

I have to phone Jennifer and apologize when I get to The Cave, he told himself. *She was pretty upset. I shouldn't have yelled at her like that. She must think I am a raving lunatic! She was right to protect herself, and I didn't mean to hurt her feelings. And I know that I shouldn't have tried to make love with her ... It's just that ....*

Michael was at a loss as to how he should conduct himself with Jennifer. He cared very deeply for her, and he knew she loved him. She just might be the one he wanted to spend the rest of his life with. But what good did that do him now? He had one more year of college to complete and then try to make a living in the very insecure music business that he dearly longed to pursue. It would probably be at least two years before he would be able to take care of a wife. How could he be expected to wait so long to satisfy his very real sexual needs? Surely there was some acceptable outlet for his physical desires. God couldn't be so cruel.

He knew that he needed to talk to some older, more experienced man. Someone he trusted and admired. Someone who had made it through the struggles he was now experiencing with Jennifer and had emerged unscathed. He immediately thought of his father. His father had always been his hero, even from a little boy. His father was a man of integrity. He admired his father's wisdom, intelligence, strength, and athleticism, and yet he was also a very gentle, compassionate man. But how could he broach such a personal, embarrassing topic as his sexual frustrations with his father?

Yeah, right! he thought sarcastically. *I can just hear the conversation now. "Hey, Dad! I want desperately to sleep with my girlfriend, but I can't, right? And I think she wants to do the same with me! But we can't, right? So what am I supposed to do? Break up with her? But I like her; I like her a lot. And it would hurt her feelings, too, because she said she loves me. So what do we do?"*

"Oh, yeah," he acknowledged facetiously aloud to himself as he pulled into the parking spot at his apartment. "I can just see my dad's face now. Wouldn't that be a father/son moment to remember!"

Many years later, when Michael's own two sons were preparing to leave for college, he recalled that imaginary conversation with his father and knew that it was *exactly* the one he should have had then—that his father would have welcomed it, his father would have understood, his father would have offered good advice. And he had that conversation with his own boys before they left him ... and several times afterwards.

But now, he turned off the motor, and out of habit reached for the radio knob that was missing. *Great!* he thought ruefully. *I guess I can get another one from the Pontiac dealership. Just hope they don't ask me how I lost it.* And he laughed to himself in frustration as he entered his apartment.

He walked in, turned on the lamp, and picked up the phone, dialing Jennifer's number.

"Hello, Jen," he began gently. "I need to apologize to you for … you know …"

"Yes … I know, Michael," she replied softly so not to wake up Katie. She chose her words falteringly, carefully. " I didn't mean to… upset you so … I'm sorry, too."

He could tell from her voice that she had been crying the entire time he had been driving home. He felt even worse and continued, sighing,

"I know, Jenny. It wasn't your fault. You didn't do anything wrong … It's just that … I thought that ..." he broke off, falling silent as he twirled the telephone cord around his fingers. How in the world could he explain this to her?

"I think I understand, Michael," she risked. "You know … It isn't easy for me, either … But I couldn't—"

"I know that, too, Jen. Look, it's late and we're both tired. It's been a very full day … not to mention a very full night." He attempted a light-hearted chuckle which she attempted to return in agreement, and then he continued, "Let's talk about it tomorrow—No, wait. I can't tomorrow. I have a huge finance test Monday, and I haven't been studying at all, so I really have to work on it tomorrow. We'll talk one day next week, okay?" he asked.

"Okay." But she sounded disappointed. "We'll work it out, Mikey ... It will be okay? ... Right?"

"That's right, Jen ... We'll work it out ... Goodnight now," he responded wearily.

"Goodnight, Michael," she replied with a very slight tremble in her voice.

As she hung up the phone, she bit her lip to stop its quivering and prayed, *Please don't let it be "good-bye."*

Chapter Five

All Sunday morning, the day after the Roman party fiasco, Jennifer fumed and fretted. She knew that she should not be so worried; at least that is what her rational mind told her. What had she done that was so wrong to have upset Michael so much? Perhaps she did get a little carried away by her own physical sensations and emotions. Perhaps she did make him think that she was willing to make love to him last night. Perhaps the thought had entered her own mind, at least subconsciously. It had certainly never been her intention! She had not meant to tease him or to frustrate him so much.

I just don't know what to do! she worried *Do other couples struggle with this, too? I know that I love Michael so very much, but he did not say he loved me, too. I would be the most foolish girl on the whole college campus if I were to give myself to him not even knowing if he loved me! Why should I give myself to him if I have no assurance of his commitment to me? Besides, I know in my mind that waiting until marriage is best.*

On and on her troubled thoughts spun and circled in her weary mind that Sunday morning in May. *But he must love me. Why would he be dating only me and be so thoughtful and affectionate if he didn't at least have some kind of love for me? How do men think? What goes on in their mysterious minds?*

Since Jennifer had no brothers and no father in the house, men were a real enigma to her. She had never understood them and had been afraid of boys until she was almost eighteen. And even now, she was very aggravated at herself for feeling such a need for them in her life. *Why can't I just feel and think like those feminists we keep reading about in sociology class? Why must I feel that I "need" a man to make me think I am worthwhile? How I wish I didn't care so much about Michael! After all, who needs him!*

She tried and tried all that morning not to think about him. But deep down in that sacred, private place in her soul, that place that did not allow her to deceive herself, that place where she had to be honest with herself, she knew that *she* needed him. She knew that his love, or at least his kind attention to her, fulfilled some basic, instinctive longing in her heart, that his strong, masculine love was filling up some very real vacuum in her soul—a need for security, a need for safety, a need for permanence. And she hated that fact.

She hated that fact because the fulfillment of that need was beyond her control. How could she control the masculine spirit of the man to make him love her? She couldn't. How could she make her own need to be loved in that way disappear from her heart? She couldn't. *Why do life and romance have to be so difficult?* she pondered in a state of anxiety.

She had gone to church that morning because she always did and because she thought Michael might be there, too, even though he indicated to her that he would most likely be home studying all day. He had not been present, but the sermon had brought her some peace of mind. It was about the unconditional love of the Heavenly Father and about Jesus being the Good Shepherd, who lays down His life for the sheep and does not run away when the wolf comes like the hired hand does.

Jennifer had never been able to relate to God very well as a heavenly "father." The word "father" was almost meaningless to her, having grown up for all practical purposes, fatherless—or at least abandoned by her father when she needed him most. She used to try to imagine God as that perfect, make-believe father she had seen on television, like Ward Cleaver helping "the Beaver" solve some problem, or Michael Landon as Pa Ingalls in "Little House on the Prairie." That was about the best she could do with that word picture.

But she could relate to being a little, lost sheep that needed the loving, watchful eye of the Good Shepherd. When she was a little girl, she used to imagine herself as the lamb in Jesus' arms in the drawing of the Good Shepherd that was in her Sunday school classroom. And after her parent's divorce, when she was so distraught and felt so frightened, that picture would come into her mind at night and give her some sense of security. Jesus had been so real to her then.

But for some reason, lately, she was feeling farther and farther removed from His care. She had felt that she was now on her own, that the Lord expected her to grow up and get out there in the "real world," whatever that was supposed to mean, and make it on her own without being so dependent on Him. Just where she got this idea, she did not know. It certainly was not from the Scripture, but she had not been reading her Bible the way she used to, either. In fact, she seldom opened its covers any more.

But she had felt comforted by the reading of its sacred pages this morning at church. How she wished she could firmly fix in her mind and her heart the fact that she was indeed provided for and protected by the Good Shepherd! Then, maybe she would not worry so much about Michael or anything else. But heaven seemed so far away, and Michael's strong arms were so comforting right now, here, in the present. Like so many struggling pilgrims, she found it very difficult to transport heaven's promises to her present earthly situation

She was in her room now that Sunday afternoon, sitting on her bed with her English history book open, her pillows propped under her head and behind her back, and her knees pulled up to balance the heavy volume. She had twenty-five pages of very small print interrupted by only a few illustrations of some very homely British noblemen to read and outline before tomorrow's class. Katie, too, was seated on her own bed studying for a calculus exam. The two had made it a habit not to converse with each other at their designated study times, and were faithful to honor each other's need for quiet concentration in pursuit of the good grades they both desired and usually acquired. They had been hard at work for almost two hours when Polly, Beth, and Sarah burst into their room.

"Hey, ya'll," interrupted Polly, "Why don't you put down your books and take a break. We're all going to walk down to the End Zone for some ice cream."

"Well, *I'm* not going to get ice cream," argued Beth. "I'm just walking down there for the exercise and maybe a diet something-or-other soft drink." Beth was always concerned about keeping her figure perfect.

"Yeah, that's right, Beth," volunteered Sarah, teasingly. "You don't want those End Zone calories to show up on your 'end zone,' do you?" The girls all laughed in agreement.

The End Zone was a local fast food, hamburger, ice cream establishment about three-quarters of a mile from their dormitory just across the street from the football stadium. The girls liked to deceive themselves into thinking that the walk there and back would more than burn up the calories they consumed in ice creams, milkshakes, and the other *haute cuisine* served there.

"Sure," said Jennifer, glad to have an excuse to put her book down. She was having trouble concentrating on the Tudor kings. Her mind kept wandering back to last night in Michael's car, and she would have to re-read each paragraph a few times to make any sense of it.

"Yep, I'll go, too," Katie agreed, slamming her book shut. "I'm just about finished, anyway. I'm gonna ace that test tomorrow, for sure!" Katie was a whiz at math. Jennifer envied her that, because while she had never had trouble with math in high school, the theory of the higher mathematics had been quite a challenge for her. That was one reason she had switched her major to English.

The girls created a pretty picture as they made their way down the hill from Dorm 10, all of them dressed in attractive shorts and blouses. They received many complimentary horn toots from automobiles driven by bunches of young men, who also whistled and asked them if they needed a ride. Of course, their offers were kindly refused.

"Beth, you need to walk on ahead of us. You're attracting too much attention from the hormone-crazed males of the species," remarked Polly in jest. "By the way, did you have a good time on your date with that cute med student from Valdosta? What's his name ... Stud?"

"No, his name's not 'Stud!'" replied Beth in annoyance. "It's 'Spud.'"

As the girls all giggled at that revelation, Beth continued in explanation. " I know it's a stupid nickname. But he told me that he was such a fat baby ... I believe he said he weighed over eleven pounds when he was born ... Anyway, he was so fat and it had been such a tight squeeze to get him delivered, that his eyes and nose and all were squished and hidden in the rolls of fat, and his father took one look at him and said he looked like a potato ... You know, like a spud."

The girls were now all laughing uncontrollably, even Jennifer who had been rather quiet to this point.

"Wow, I've heard some funny stories of stupid nicknames before, Beth, but that one takes the cake!" Sarah commented, tears in her eyes. "The potato pancake, that is."

"Well, I don't think it's any dumber than most. And anyway, he sure doesn't look like a spud now, does he?" defended Beth, her brow wrinkled some in irritation at her friends' attack on her new conquest-in-the-making, the conquest she hoped would be her crowning achievement at that institution of higher learning.

And she knew she had them there. Despite his less than ideal introduction into this world, which had disfigured him temporarily, Lawton Davis "Spud" Thomason, III, was incredibly handsome now, they had to admit. And the fact that his father was the richest, most successful thoracic surgeon in Valdosta and was certain to pass his practice down to Spud made him even better looking to Beth.

"Oh, he's cute, all right," offered Polly, "but I don't think he's any better looking than Jenny's heart throb, Mikey-boo." She grinned at Jennifer. "By the way, I saw your beloved blaze into the parking lot late last night, tires screaming, dump you out at the curb, and then flash out of here like a bat out of you-know-where. In fact, he nearly ran me down! What's wrong? Did you two have a lover's quarrel?"

Darn you, Polly! Why do you always have to be so nosey? Jennifer thought in frustration, but replied coolly, "Well, we did have a small disagreement, but he phoned me later, and everything's okay now."

"Really, Jenny?" Katie asked in concern. She had been asleep when Jennifer came home last night and, being the sound sleeper that she was, had not awakened. "You seemed to be getting along so well last night at the party. What happened?"

"Yeah, I heard about your 'getting along well' last night, myself," Beth added. "My roommate, Kelley, told me that you and Michael were all over each other on the dance floor. She was at that party, too, you know."

"Oh, he probably got all liquored up and tried to jump her bones," smirked Polly again as she carefully observed Jennifer, digging for more information.

Jennifer was becoming aggravated now but had to try to hide it. Polly was the least favorite of her dorm buddies but seemed to know the most about her. It wasn't fair. She explained as calmly and with as studied an air of nonchalance as she could manage.

"I dare say we were not the only ones on the dance floor 'all over each other,' Beth. In fact, I seem to recall that your friend, Kelley, was making some pretty serious body contact with that Jimmy what's-his-name, herself."

"Evasion! Evasion! You're evading the question, Jen!" Polly continued her tactless probing. "Now, this plot really 'sickens,' as they say. Mikey must have been a really bad boy! Say, now that I think of it, you haven't returned my nightgown yet. Are you having to stitch it up after Michael ripped it off your quivering flesh?"

"Oh, Polly!" all the girls chided her at once.

"Polly Monroe, you are one sick puppy!" Sarah observed in disgust. "You ought to spend more time reading your text books and less time with those cheap, trashy romance novels of yours!"

"I think your doctor needs to change your medication," Katie offered sarcastically. She knew that was an unkind, insensitive remark, as Polly did have prescription medicine for her regularly occurring migraine headaches. But she had noticed a troubling change in her best friend's countenance after that last crude remark of Polly's, and she had attacked in defense of her buddy.

Polly seemed to take no notice of and no offense at any of the comments hurled at her. She pressed on relentlessly.

"So what about it, Jenny? Give, give! Spare us no steamy details! Tell us all of Mikey's misbehavior!"

"Polly!" the girls all cried at her again, to no avail.

Polly Monroe was usually a very helpful, considerate young woman. She had a boyfriend who had given her a promise ring at Christmas, and they were supposedly semi-engaged. But he attended the cross-state rival university, and though the couple talked on the telephone almost every day, they only saw each other once every four to six weeks. This gave Polly every reason to envy, and then to torment her friends whose beaux were constantly buzzing around Dorm 10. And when she was in the tormenting mode, she could be quite obnoxious.

"Don't be so absurd, not to mention so melodramatic, Polly," Jennifer responded in what she hoped was a disdainful manner. "Your gown and Sarah's slip are hanging perfectly whole, no rips or tears, in my bathroom shower. I washed them by hand this morning and am letting them air dry according to the instructions on the labels. You should have them by this evening. Nothing went on last night that is any of your concern, Polly, so you can rest your overheated imagination on my account."

By this time, Polly was beginning to wear down a little. She knew Jennifer could be as tight lipped as a CIA agent when she wanted to be, and anyway, her other friends were sending her looks as if to say, "Leave it alone, Polly. Jennifer doesn't want to talk about it."

"Okay, then, Jenny. I guess you really told me," Polly conceded. "But let me know if you need any strength training to bulk up so you can fight Michael off. I have the name of a great personal trainer." Then she winked and added wickedly, "Or, if you choose to give in to 'something that's bigger that both of you,' I want to hear all about that, too! I promise I won't tell a soul!"

Thankfully, with that last jab, Polly walked ahead about two yards to begin pestering Beth, saying,

"Now, Beth, this tuber that your intended resembled at his birth— was it an Irish potato, an Idaho russet, or more along the lines of a yam or sweet potato?"

As Polly left and turned her attentions elsewhere, Jennifer drew a very deep, cleansing breath and thought, *Finally, Polly! Please go bother someone else!*

Katie and Jennifer were now walking well behind the other three, and Katie purposely slowed her pace to put more distance between them. Then she turned her head toward her roommate and asked with concern,

"Are you really okay, Jenny? You have been quieter than usual today. Michael isn't trying to pressure you, is he?"

As much as she doubted Polly's sincerity, Jennifer trusted Katie with her feelings. She replied in confidence, "Oh,no! ... No ... Not really ... I mean ... Well ... Do you mind if I ask you a personal question? You don't have to answer it if you don't want to, you know."

"Of course not, Jenny," Katie responded warmly. "You know I will be as honest with you as I can be. You're my best buddy. Well, except for Joe, of course."

Jennifer smiled at Katie's honesty. Katie was such a good friend. She asked her quietly, "You and Joe ... Do you ever struggle with... you know, controlling yourselves ... when you are alone together, I mean?"

"I know exactly what you mean, Jen," said Katie with understanding. "Well, not too much, you see, because we try—or at least, *I* try—not to be alone with him too much. It's just too much temptation. And besides, I—no, we—are scared to death of my daddy!" And she giggled.

"You mean, your daddy would kill you if you ever 'got into trouble?'" Jennifer inquired.

"No! No way! That's not what I meant. Daddy wouldn't kill *me*! He is crazy about me, you know, and would always take care of me, no matter what. I know that for sure. No, what scares me is that Daddy would kill *Joe!*"

And both girls laughed together.

"It's true! I'm serious!" she continued as she could see Jennifer did not believe her. "You know my father is an excellent marksman. He always wins the turkey shoots at Thanksgiving time. And he has a collection of about five or six shotguns and hunting rifles in the storage room. Well, whenever any boy would come to the house to take me out on a date, Daddy would always be there at the door to let him in. He would then usher the unfortunate kid into the kitchen and sit him down at the table. He would have all his guns lying out there and he would clean them. Funny, that was the only time I ever saw him cleaning them," Katie recalled with a facetious twinkle in her eye.

"Anyway," she continued with affection, "while he would be cleaning them he would say to the boys --- Oh, and you have to get Joe to do his imitation of Daddy's little speech. It's so funny! Joe looks and sounds just like him, and he knows it by heart because he has heard it so many times --- So, anyway, Daddy says while picking up each firearm and rubbing oil or something on the barrels, he says, 'Young man, you know my wife and I have three sons and a daughter, my daughter Katie. Well, Katie came along as kind of a surprise after our last son's sixth birthday. She was a surprise, all right, but she was a delightful surprise at that. I never knew I could love any little girl as much as I love my Katie.'"

As Katie told this story, Jennifer could see how much she loved her father. And the feeling was mutual, she knew, because not two or three days would go by but Mr. McComb would phone up his "little girl" and talk with her for at least thirty minutes.

Katie continued warmly, "Then he would pick up a gun, all of them unloaded, of course. He keeps all the ammunition locked up in a safe always. But anyway, he would pick up a rifle, usually, point it out the window and pretend that he was checking the sights, and say, 'Yep, my Katie is my pride and my delight, and I just don't know what I would do if anyone, and I mean *anyone,* ever did anything to harm or hurt her. Do you know what I mean, son?'"

At this point, she had to stop the story, as both girls were laughing so hard. Then she continued,

"You can imagine that by this point the poor boy would be as white as a sheet and would usually mutter something like, 'Yes, sir. I understand.' Just about then, I would enter the room and Daddy would kiss me goodbye and say loudly, 'Now lassie, you let me know how this young man treats you, okay?' And then he would lead us out of the room. So you see what I mean, Jen, about being afraid for poor Joe's life if he ever were to meddle with Matt McComb's little girl!"

"Oh, Katie, that's just too funny. How sweet. How very sweet." Jennifer responded sincerely, a poignant smile still on her lips as her laughter died down.

How she envied Katie then! Although she envied Katie tremendously at that moment, she did not begrudge her for having a loving father, but only wished she had had one, too. But because Jennifer's own father, Bob Jacobs, had remarried and moved to Illinois two years after the divorce, and Jennifer and her younger sister, Susan, only saw him at Christmas and for three weeks in the summer, she felt cheated in a way she had no desire to explore much further because it hurt too much—cheated and sad and angry, all at the same time.

Her father, who had not been terribly close to either of his daughters before the divorce, was hampered even more in his attempts to know them by his own guilt over the breakup of his marriage and his long absences from them. And though he loved them, he was lost as to how to reach Jenny and Susie, and hoped, rather than believed, that his regular child support checks with extra money sent on birthdays and holidays were somehow communicating his concern for his girls.

Besides, they were doing very well in school and church and seemed well adjusted and happy. Everyone said that children eventually "got over" a divorce, and his daughters seemed to be getting along just fine. He even bragged on them to his co-workers and neighbors whenever he had the chance, showing them pictures of his girls receiving badges, medals, certificates, and making the honor roll.

And their stepmother, Helen, who was amiable and well intentioned, was proud of the girls, too, though she never knew how to make them feel comfortable and accepted in her home. She received little help from the children toward that end, as they had the typical resentful feelings of any girls whose father was now living with someone other than their mother.

Katie interrupted her roommate's imagining what it would be like to have a father like Mr. McComb by explaining further.

"*I* didn't think it was so very sweet, Jenny! Not at all! Not for a long time. Did you know that I never had a boy take me out on a second date? No, sir! Daddy scared them all to death." She laughed. "You remember the Senior Prom?"

"No, I didn't go. I didn't have a date, remember?" Jennifer replied matter-of-factly.

"Oh, yeah. Well, the boys were all too stupid to know what they were missing, Jen. Anyway, Jim Martin, the class president was my date, and I was so looking forward to going with him, but after Daddy's little speech, Jim was so scared that he wouldn't even slow dance with me. It's true! Every time a slow song would be played, Jim would take us over to the refreshment stand and we would have a coke. I think I drank about twenty cokes that night." Katie smiled at the memory. "Joe was the first boy ever brave enough to kiss me goodnight ... after he asked my permission, of course." Katie's eyes reflected her warm affection for Joe at that moment.

"Kate, I envy you that—" she broke off, searching for the right word. "Oh, that 'protection,' I guess. You know my own father never met any of ... *either* of my two boyfriends," Jennifer stated simply, smiling sadly at her own pitiful joke.

"That's too bad, Jen," Katie responded softly in sympathy, not knowing what else to say. They walked a moment in silence before she added, concerned, "But Jennifer, you never really answered my question about Michael putting the moves on you. If it's none of my business, just say so."

"Well ... Oh, Katie, I don't know very much about men. I mean I have no brothers or anything like you do. Can I ask you one more thing?" she queried.

"Sure, Jenny. Anything." Katie studied her friend's worried expression.

"Do guys have to love a girl to want to ... to be intimate with her? Or is it just fulfilling their own lusts or what have you? I know this sounds silly, but I honestly don't know. I mean, almost all girls really have to love a guy to engage in ... you know ... physical stuff. What do you know from your brothers about this kind of thing?" she asked, sincerely seeking knowledge.

"Gee, Jen, I don't know for sure. I mean, this isn't the kind of thing I usually discussed with my brothers, if you know what I mean," Katie began, her forehead wrinkled. "I do know that my oldest brother, Gerald, was awfully depressed when his girlfriend broke up with him two years ago. My parents were very worried. Took him to the doctor for a check up, even. Gerry thought that Cathy was going to marry him, but she turned him down. He took it very hard."

"What happened?" Jennifer asked.

"Well, the doctors told Daddy to give him Geritol or something and to go fishing with him as often as he could. Stop laughing! That was the prescription Dr. Haselett wrote out. Really! Funny cure for a broken heart. Anyway, it *did* seem to help. I think just talking to Daddy while they fished helped. But, he got the real cure when he started dating Missy Wharton. Oh, did I tell you? They are engaged. Getting married in September, I think," Katie finished, smiling.

"But that doesn't really answer my question, does it? I mean, your brother loved those girls. Do you think he ever wanted to ... get physical with them before they were engaged?" Jennifer inquired as they walked slowly on.

"Oh, Jenny, I don't know for sure. I used to see them kissing pretty passionately out in his car. The windows would get pretty foggy and all that. But to answer your question, I do think guys can sort of separate the physical from the emotional part of sex. More than likely. Yes, I'm pretty sure about that. But that doesn't mean that they don't care about their girlfriends. And it doesn't mean that they might not try to have a 'carnal,' shall we say, relationship with someone they like a lot or even love, before marriage, that is. I don't know if that helps any," the young coed faltered.

"Yeah, that helps. That is what I was thinking all along, too," Jennifer stated and sighed.

At this point, Katie stopped walking, turned and looked Jennifer in the eyes very seriously saying,

"Look, Jenny. All this is theoretical. But I am concerned for you. For you *and* Michael. If you are asking me if I think it is okay for you and him to sleep together, I would have to be honest and tell you 'no.' I don't think that is what is best for either of you. It may sound corny and old-fashioned, but I really believe that waiting until marriage is best. Especially for the woman. You know, our hearts are so easily broken as it is, and if you throw sex into the picture—"

Jennifer interrupted, stating firmly, "I agree with you, Katie. I really do! Believe me, Michael and I have not slept together, nor am I planning to."

"Good," replied Katie, smiling again. "That's a load off my shoulders."

And as they continued walking, now only a few yards away from the long awaited End Zone chocolate milk shakes, her good friend added,

"Just make certain that Michael knows that, too." And she smiled a teasing grin into her roommate's eyes before adding mischievously, "Or I'll get Daddy to drive up here and clean his guns in front of that Evans boy, seriously!"

Chapter Six

*M*onday morning at nine o'clock, Jennifer was sitting under her usual oak tree on the Commons waiting for Michael to meet her for breakfast, as had been their habit for over four months now.

But he did not come.

He had not phoned her Sunday night, either, though she had hoped that he would. Sure, he had told her on Saturday that he had to study all day for the big finance test, but still, she had hoped that he would have taken at least five minutes to call her. *I hope he is not still mad at me,* she worried. *After all, he was very, very upset that night.*

"What's wrong with you, Jenny?" asked Sarah, who had met her there to retrieve her world geography book that Jennifer had borrowed for a report. "You certainly do look blue today. Isn't Michael meeting you here for your morning breakfast run?"

"I don't know," she replied, and tried to smile. "Something must have come up. I suppose I'll find out sooner or later." *What could have happened to change his plans? At least he could have called me,* she fretted.

Sarah noted Jennifer's concern and patted her gently on her arm. "Don't worry, Jen. I'm sure there is a good explanation. Michael is crazy about you. Anyone who sees him with you knows that."

Jennifer smiled a weak "thank you" to Sarah for her words of encouragement. *Thank you, Lord, for good friends,* she prayed silently.

"Well, I've got to go to class now," continued Sarah. "Can you believe there are only two-and-a-half more weeks left in the semester? I can't wait to go home for the summer break."

With a "bye now," Sarah walked off to her class while Jennifer sat back down under the shady oak tree. She sat there for an hour, trying to study for her ten o'clock class and hoping that Michael would suddenly appear with some explanation. But still he did not come. So at ten, she walked to the Humanities Building by herself, something she had not done for a long time now. How she missed Michael's parting smile and wink at the doorway as she dragged herself into the classroom and wearily plopped down into the nearest desk.

Though she usually enjoyed this English history professor's lectures, that day Jennifer had a difficult time concentrating. She doodled in her notebook, chewed on the end of her pencil, and tried not to fret.

Surely, Michael wouldn't break up with me because I refused to make love with him. No, Michael wouldn't do that. He's not that kind of a guy. If he were, I wouldn't love him. Then what could it be?... *Oh, Jennifer, get a grip on yourself! Why are you such an insecure wimp?* Her self-talk continued on as she doodled some more.

About ten minutes before the class was to be dismissed, she caught some movement outside the door in the hallway with her peripheral vision and heard a "pssst, pssst." As she turned her head and focused her eyes in that direction, she saw Michael with a huge grin on his face motioning her to come out to him. As she was seated at the back of the large classroom not far from the door, she slipped out as inconspicuously as possible.

Michael, still grinning, grabbed her arm excitedly and led her down the hallway and out the door of the building. When they were safely outside, he picked her up in his arms and whirled her around a couple of times before placing her gently back down.

"Ahhhh! Jennifer!" he exclaimed joyfully. "I've just heard the best news. Actually three items of good news! I couldn't wait to see you and share them!"

Her own smile was equal to his. He wasn't angry with her! In fact, he had sought her out to tell her some good news. But what could it possibly be to excite him so much?

"Well, don't keep me in suspense, Mikey! What in the world is it?" she asked.

"I stopped by my advisor's office this morning, after I aced that finance exam, that is—And by the way, thanks for understanding that I needed to study all day yesterday—Anyway, my advisor looked over my credits and discovered that if I take only two more courses in music theory and fulfill one supervised practical work requirement, which I can do this summer in the summer session, I can have a double degree—you know, a major in both business *and* music!" he responded with enthusiasm.

Jennifer was somewhat puzzled and letdown as she had expected something more newsworthy than that, and it must have shown on her face because he explained further,

"Don't you get it, Jen? With a double major like that, my chances of getting that good job in Nashville that I want so much will be greatly increased. Oh, by the way, that's why I didn't show up for breakfast—I was at my advisor's office. Hope you didn't wait on me."

"No, that's okay," she lied and then continued. "That's great, Michael. But you said you had three newsworthy items."

"Well the other two things happened just at the right time, Jen. I know God must be in charge of this or something," he observed. "I got a call last night from Pastor Bob at the 'hayride church,' you know, and he asked if I could be their music director for the summer! Their guy is having surgery that requires a long recuperative period, and they needed someone for the summer only."

As he spoke they began walking back toward the Student Union. He continued his explanation, "It just so happens that the music director job would perfectly fulfill my practical experience requirement for the double degree—and it pays $75 per week, which is peanuts, really, but I only have to work for one hour on Wednesday nights for choir rehearsal and two hours or so on Sundays for the worship services. Can you believe the coincidence?"

"No, I can't," she replied. "That can't be a coincidence. The timing is too perfect. That is wonderful, Mikey," she smiled at him. "But those are only two items. What is the third?"

"Well, the third is something that may make you a little sad, you know, because I know how fond you are of my luxurious accommodations at The Cave," he teased.

"Yeah, right!" she agreed, sarcastically.

"Joe phoned me last night and said a fraternity brother of his is dropping out of school, actually flunking out, I believe, and he needs someone to sublet his new apartment not just for this summer, but also for all of next year. And it's a great apartment, too! Brand new, with a balcony view of that nice golf course the town is just completing. Can you believe the luck?" he asked rhetorically.

"How fabulous, Michael! The Cave never was the place for you. Your entire outlook on life will improve just getting away from that yucky place," she responded with a shiver.

"Well, that's where you come in, Toots," he smiled at her. "I was wondering if you could help me move my precious few belongings from The Cave to the new place Saturday—that's when I can take possession. You know, kind of help me spruce it up and get it organized and everything. Joe said this guy was pretty messy, and it may not be in great shape." As he made this request, he also had a playful, mischievous look in his eyes.

"Saturday ... You need me on Saturday ... Sure," she replied, tentatively at first, her brow wrinkled somewhat. "I'll be glad to help you, Michael; you know that."

"You seem a little concerned about Saturday. What's wrong?" he asked facetiously. But at the ambivalent expression on her face, he could not keep the ruse alive and laughed, stopping her in their walk and placing his hand around her shoulders.

"Jennifer, don't ever try to become an actress. You can no more hide your emotions than the man in the moon. Don't you think I remembered that Saturday is your birthday?" he laughed tenderly at her and kissed her forehead.

"How can you tease me so, you scoundrel," she replied, her cheeks reddening. "I didn't think you remembered."

"How could I forget something as important as that? I mean, this one is 'The Big-Two-0h,' isn't it? You will no longer be a teenager, Jen. I can no longer be accused of robbing the cradle," he played with her. "Hey, I'm not so sure I want to be seen with an older woman like that. Your flower may be starting to fade already."

"You're so terrible," she returned, pretending to pout and hitting him lightly on the chest. "I can assure you that my 'flower' is only *now beginning* to bloom, Michael Evans!"

"You don't have to tell me that, Jennifer. I know that very well. You are one gorgeous lady! In fact, you get more beautiful each time I see you." He said this instantly, from his heart, without premeditation, and he then placed her hand in his as they continued walking, loving the way she blushed at his compliments.

He continued, "I remembered your birthday, all right. How could I forget it with Katie reminding me every day? And I want to take you out to dinner at The Springs on Saturday evening. In fact, I've already made the reservations. Hope you'll pardon my presumption."

The Springs was the nicest restaurant in the small town. It was actually an old, antebellum home, and as such, had several small, intimate dining rooms decorated in the very elegant, classical Old South style. Not only were the chefs schooled in European cuisine, but also silver candelabras, vases of roses, fine linen, English bone china, and sterling silver flatware were the order of the day there. On Saturdays, the restaurant featured a pianist with a silky voice performing old love ballads and torch songs on a grand piano in the foyer by the spiral staircase. It was very romantic. And very, very expensive.

"Oh, Michael, that's so nice, but are you sure you can afford it?" Jennifer asked innocently, and then became embarrassed at the faux pas.

"Of course, I can afford it, Toots," he replied, chuckling, taking no offense. "What did you think I was going to have us do—stay behind and bus tables and scrape plates? Don't be silly."

Of all Jennifer's fine qualities, Michael appreciated her naiveté and innocence the most. He continued, "So we're on for Saturday night, then? Good. But I really was hoping you could help me get moved into the new apartment during the day, too. I thought if we loaded up my car and your wagon, we could get everything moved in one trip. Joe said he would help me with the furniture."

"Oh, I was serious when I said I would be glad to help," she replied. "In fact, it will be fun for me. I like to fix up apartments and such. And I think the Hulk has one more move left in her before she rolls over and dies," she laughed.

"The Hulk" was her nickname for her old, green, faded '64 Ford station wagon. Though terribly unattractive, it was mechanically sound, and was a better mode of transportation for long distances than walking, she had always rationalized. And it held boxes and boxes of stuff, so it was ideal for driving to college and back. And ideal for making a cross-town move, too.

"Great, then! That's all settled," he stated, and smiled down at her. "Then how about buying me lunch now. I skipped breakfast, you know."

"I did, too," she replied. "I wasn't all that hungry and I needed to study some more. Can you believe this semester is almost over? Sarah was talking just this morning about being happy to go home soon."

"Say, you're going home this summer, aren't you. I hadn't thought about that before. I'm really going to miss you." His voice sounded very disappointed, as he suddenly realized that fact.

Stopping in his tracks, he looked at her with a disturbed expression. He had become accustomed to spending so much time with her on a daily basis, that he felt very sad at the prospect of missing her. Taking one look at his disheartened countenance, she responded automatically,

"Well, you know, Mother told me that I could go to school this summer if I wanted to. It wouldn't hurt me at all to enrich myself in my major. I wonder if it is too late to enroll?" she questioned.

"No! Not at all!" he replied enthusiastically. "In fact, the deadline is not until next Tuesday, my advisor told me. If you could stay this summer, it would be fun. You know, just take a couple of courses. Then we could have all kinds of time to 'play,'" he grinned impishly, raising his eyebrows.

They had resumed their walking, and by this time had reached the cafeteria and were loading their trays. Jennifer blushed again, involuntarily, thinking immediately of their "play" time on Saturday night. He sensed her thoughts and added quickly,

"Look, Jen, what I meant by that was just hang out together ... Go swimming, golfing, play tennis, watch some movies. You know... 'Play.'"

"Oh, I know. That's what I thought you meant," she returned, still blushing. *Why do I have to blush so easily? It's not fair!* she thought. *Everyone always knows what I am thinking.*

They made their way to the table by the window and sat down. Her cheeks were still rosy red, and she could not meet his gaze.

"Jenny," he began awkwardly, feeling he must clear the air. "Please look at me. I know we said we would talk this week ... about what happened in my car, you know."

"Yes, I know. And I wanted to tell you I'm sorry—" she began very quickly, but he interrupted her.

"No, please. Let me say again that you did nothing wrong ... That I shouldn't have tried ... That I shouldn't have yelled at you... We just need to be more careful ...when we are alone and all," he stumbled somewhat, trying to be as straightforward as he could and communicate to her his struggle as he searched her eyes. "You know, you are very hard for me to resist, Jenny. I need ... *We* need ... to be smarter, I guess, and not think we can always pull the plug while the electricity is flowing, if you know what I'm saying."

"I understand, Michael," she replied honestly, now fully meeting his gaze. "Of course, you are right. Again, I'm sorry ... I didn't mean to—"

"That's okay." He took her hand and squeezed it, winked, and finished with, "Enough said, Toots. Let's eat. I'm starved!"

Bright and early on Saturday morning, as early, that is, as college kids will get out of bed on a Saturday, Jennifer and Katie hopped into the Hulk and drove over to the soon-to-be-evacuated Cave. There they met Joe and Michael, already hard at work loading the bed and chest of drawers onto a small, rented truck. The girls had stopped at a donut shop, and as they climbed out of the car, they held the box up for the men to see.

"Thanks, ladies," grunted Joe, as he wiped the perspiration from his forehead with his sleeve. It was going to be a warm day, that fourth day of June 1975. Summer, spring's oppressive, humid cousin, also arrives very early in South Alabama. "This will help a lot. And that jug of cold orange juice looks like an oasis to me. Boy, is it hot!"

"You girls are really something," Michael added, after downing his own juice which Jennifer had poured for him. "You even thought to bring paper cups. All my dishes are packed," he told Joe and Katie. "Can you believe I actually got Jenny to come over yesterday afternoon and help me pack? First time she ever spent more than three minutes in the poor old Cave. Gonna miss this place," he mourned in mock sorrow. "It's the quaintest little place I've ever lived in."

"It's the ugliest little place you've ever lived in," corrected Jennifer. "And I'm not going to miss it at all."

Katie grinned and looked at Michael saying, "Aren't you forgetting to tell Jennifer something, Michael? You know today is June fourth, a special day for one of us here."

"Now, let's see," Michael scratched his head and rolled his eyes upward. " It's too late for Groundhog's day ... and too early for Labor Day ..."

"It's Labor Day, all right, Mike. We've got a lot more work to do here, and I have plans for this afternoon with Katie, so please go ahead and kiss Jenny 'happy birthday' so we can get this thing over with," Joe commented cogently with impatience. Joe hated moving more than almost anything.

With the obligatory birthday kiss over and done—and Joe sneaking in a little brotherly kiss on the cheek, too—the men finished loading up the truck while the girls began carrying boxes to the cars.

While the two of them were in the kitchen area—actually just a small counter top with one crooked shelf above and one crumbling cabinet below—Katie gave Jennifer a mysterious smile, saying, "I know what gift Michael got you for your birthday. In fact, I helped him pick it out."

"You did? You've got to tell me what it is, Kate! I promise I will act surprised! I'm good at acting," appealed Jennifer, her eyes sparkling with excitement. She never could wait to open a present. As a little and even not so little girl, she would always sneak into the living room late Christmas Eve and peek inside the presents under the tree.

"Jennifer Jacobs, what a terrible lie! You're an awful actress and you know it! No way am I going to tell you," expounded Katie.

"Please, please, oh please!" Jennifer whined in imitation of a spoiled child wearing down a parent while she plucked at Katie's sleeve and danced around on the floor. "I promise I can act surprised! You know I can't stand to wait! Never have been able to. Tell me! Please, oh please!"

As Katie was playfully slapping her hands away and saying, "No! No way!" Michael and Joe walked in.

"What's going on?" Joe asked.

"Oh, Jenny is begging to find out what Michael got her for her birthday, but I didn't tell her, Mike," answered Katie.

"Good! And if she keeps up this whining, you and I can just go back to the jewelry store and return it!" joked Michael, slapping Jennifer gently on the leg.

"The jewelry store? The jewelry store, did you say?" repeated Jennifer, her eyes now dancing. "You've got to tell me now!"

"Not now. Later, Miss Priss! You must restrain yourself." And he kissed her lightly.

"Okay, ya'll," interrupted Joe, wiping his forehead once again. "Enough of that already. Let's load up the rest of the wagons and get outta here."

Working very quickly, they managed to remove all Michael's belongings within fifteen minutes and drove directly to his new accommodations across town.

When they arrived at the new apartment and Michael opened the door, noxious fumes greeted them immediately. The odor seemed to be emanating from the kitchen. They opened the refrigerator to discover strange growths, all of them assuredly toxic, pouring out of half-opened containers of cheese, tuna cans, pizza boxes, and various and sundry other unidentifiable receptacles.

As the foursome stared in disbelief and disgust, the girls holding their noses, Joe remarked slowly and ominously, patting his buddy on the back in sympathy, "Oooooo. This doesn't look good, Mike, old man. I told you Jack was a slob. The rest of the place doesn't look too bad, though," he observed, looking around.

"Doesn't look too bad?" exclaimed both girls in unison.

Obviously there was great gulf that could never be spanned between Joe's standard of housekeeping and that of the girls. The bathroom was unspeakable, and there were wads of dust and dirt all over the carpet. The counter tops had film on them at least an eighth of an inch thick, and the windows were all smudged with who knew what.

"Looks as though Jack liked to wipe his greasy hands on the windows instead of using his napkin like his momma taught him to," Katie conjectured.

Jennifer, having surveyed the whole job, walked into the middle of the living room, exhaled once quickly, clapped her hands together, and said,

"There's no need to fear! Super Maid is here! I'll have this place spic and span, ready for the white glove inspection, within two hours or my name's not Jennifer Elaine Jacobs."

"You don't have to do that, Jen," offered Michael.

"Don't worry. No problem. I like to clean up a mess like this. Gives me a feeling of great accomplishment when it's spotless," she stated sincerely. "And I know the exact location of the vacuum cleaner in the truck."

"If you don't want to make Jenny unload the truck with you and carry up your heavy furniture, Mike," began Joe impatiently yet again, "then we'd better get moving. Katie and I have to leave in about forty-five minutes."

Katie and Joe were going home to Mobile for the rest of the weekend. It was Katie's mother's fifty-fourth birthday tomorrow, and Mr. McComb had planned a surprise party for her. He had told Joe to have his daughter home no later than five o'clock this afternoon, and Joe wanted to make certain they had at least an hour to spare to allow for any unforeseen problems. He did not want to be on Matt McComb's bad side.

As the young men unloaded the truck and carried the furniture up one flight of stairs, Jennifer vacuumed the carpets, which immediately made a big difference to the room's appearance. Katie had brought up the cleaning supplies and was busy washing the windows.

By the time the last load of furniture was making its way up the steps, Jennifer had progressed to the very challenging refrigerator. As the men came in, she ran into the living room giving instructions.

"No, don't put that sofa there! Bring it over here, so when you sit on it you can see out the glass doors onto the golf course." And she pointed out the spot.

"I thought if it were here," Michael explained, "I could see the television better. But I'll do it to please you, Mrs. Clean."

"Augghh!" complained Joe, as he set the last piece down. "Well, that's the last of it. You owe me big time, Buddy. Come on, Kate. I've got to drop you off and then go by the house and shower and grab my bag, so we need to hit the road."

Katie walked over towards the door after she hugged and kissed Jennifer and Michael goodbye.

"Thanks so much, Joe. And you, too, Katie. Couldn't have done it without you," Michael said as he hugged Katie and shook hands with Joe, slapping him on the back. "And don't worry, Joe. I will definitely name my first born after you for all your help."

"Yeah, right," Joe chuckled on parting. "I was thinking more along the lines of a nice steak dinner and a couple of brews."

"Drive safely!" Jennifer called out as the couple left. "Thanks, Katie, and tell your mother 'happy birthday' for me!"

After they left, Michael began unpacking his boxes and putting his clothes away while Jennifer finished the kitchen and moved on to the bathroom. In less than an hour, the apartment looked bright and squeaky clean, and smelled fresh, too.

Then Jennifer walked into the bedroom where Michael was placing his clothes into his chest of drawers. "Ready for inspection, sir!" she called out, and gave him a salute, her eyes shining.

Grinning and taking her hand, he walked into the living area and looked around, remarking, "Wow, Jenny. You made such a difference! Thanks so much. I feel as if your dinner tonight will be payment for services rendered instead of the gift I meant it to be."

"Don't be silly. I really enjoyed it. Just wish I had taken a 'before' snapshot so we could see the improvement." She went on, " I think a couple of nice green plants would look real good here and here," she pointed to spots on the kitchen counter and the dining table. "And I placed your dishes and glasses in the cabinets, but we need to go to the store and get shelf paper to do the job right."

"Why shelf paper?" he asked, puzzled.

"Oh, you *have* to have shelf paper," she replied. "It keeps the shelves ... clean."

"But did you clean the shelves before you put the dishes away?" he inquired.

"Sure, I did!" she answered.

"Then, why in the world do I need shelf paper?" he persisted.

"I don't know, but you do," she stated, definitively.

The couple stared at each other for a few seconds very seriously, and then burst into laughter.

"I never will understand the strange workings of the feminine mind," Michael observed, "but if shelf paper will make you happy, then by all means we'll get some."

He then took her in his arms and hugged her tightly, saying,

"You've worked so hard all morning for me. I really do appreciate it. And for being such a good worker," he added with a grin, "I just may let you order dessert tonight at The Springs!"

She smiled demurely at him and murmured, "Hope they have chocolate cheesecake."

"If they don't, we'll drive around until we find some," and he kissed her, this time very slowly.

She suddenly realized that they were all alone and recalled their conversation at lunch on Monday. She pulled herself out of his embrace, blushing, and responded by changing the subject.

"Well, I think that's just about everything, except ... I guess you need to put sheets and blankets on your bed. Do you have clean ones? If not, we can try out this washer and dryer." And she opened bi-fold doors that concealed the compact, double-stacked laundry equipment. "They look brand new, although a little small. I've never seen a set like this before. Cute, but tiny. You'll have to wash one sheet at a time, I think."

Michael, too, was well aware that they were alone. He took his cue from her behavior, saying, "No, that's okay, Jen. I'll do my sheets and stuff after I run you back to the dorm."

"But I drove the Hulk, remember?" she reminded him. "So if everything here is finished, I'll head back myself. I have a little shopping to do and want to have time to rest some before dinner tonight."

"Okay, then," he replied, "I'll pick you up at seven."

He walked her to her car, carrying down empty boxes to throw into the dumpster along the way. As she pulled out of the parking lot, he called out, waving to her as she drove away,

"On second thought, I'll pick you up at six forty-five. Happy Birthday, Jennifer! Thanks, again!"

Chapter Seven

*T*he weather was hot and steamy that Saturday evening of June the fourth, 1975, and the forecast called for possible severe thunderstorms to move through the area later in the night. But it mattered not to Jennifer Jacobs. This was the night of her twentieth birthday, and storm or no storm, she was delighted to be spending it with the handsome young man she loved.

She had never dined at The Springs before, so she was overwhelmed as they drove up the lane toward the entrance. Double rows of great oak trees lined the long, winding, gravel driveway, obscuring the view of the old mansion until the last possible moment. Then suddenly, the graceful Greek revival structure appeared, stately, timeless, and venerable in its surroundings. Flowers spilled out of containers all around the mansion and in between the shrubbery plantings, and ferns adorned the walkway. As the parking valet opened the door for her, Jennifer had to blink her eyes to erase the almost indelible image of Scarlett O'Hara dressed in a floral hoop skirt descending the steps leading down from the wrap-around veranda, so picture perfect was the setting.

Taking her slender arm, Michael proudly led her up the steps and into the restaurant, thinking all the while that she was the most beautiful woman he had ever seen. Why had he not appreciated her rare, dark beauty before, he wondered? He had always found her attractive, of course, very pretty and well-proportioned. But he had not known until this evening, when she had almost floated into the lobby of Dorm 10 in her long gown, her deep brown eyes glowing, her dark hair shining, and her full lips luminous with some sort of new lipstick, he guessed, that she was so very, very beautiful. Like a Spanish countess. Almost like a painting that should be hung in a museum somewhere to demonstrate what a truly beautiful woman should look like, to his mind.

She wore a vibrant cobalt blue evening dress that exposed her pretty shoulders and upper chest in a draped, three-pleated, neckline, fitting tightly through the bodice and waistline, and then cascading softly down. She had borrowed the dress from Beth, who was very generous with her wardrobe, and who finally had to admit that it actually looked better on Jennifer, though Spud may have disagreed. She had experimented with her hair all afternoon and was wearing it up in a type of a French twist with small, wispy curls escaping around her face. This style was most flattering to her delicate facial features and large, dark eyes. Around her smooth throat hung a diamond and pearl pendant necklace on a delicate gold chain, and matching teardrop earrings dangled from her small, round ear lobes. But more appealing than her elegant attire was the warm, radiant beauty of a young woman in love.

Michael, dressed up in his best blue suit, looked very handsome, too. All eyes followed the couple appreciatively as they entered their small dining room that had once been the sun porch of the mansion. Its windows overlooked the Millwood Springs, for which the plantation had been named, and the beautifully landscaped formal gardens. A slightly raspy-throated piano singer was at work on the black Steinway at the foot of the sweeping staircase as Michael pulled out her chair, enriching the atmosphere with sweet love songs.

"It's not the pale moon that excites me, that thrills and delights me. Oh, no! It's just the nearness of you."

As he stood over her, he could not help but notice the shapely contours of her soft, full bosom as she bent over slightly to be seated. Already his thoughts were moving in the dangerous direction he was striving so hard to avoid. *Oh, Jenny,* he thought illogically, *why do you have to be so lovely and enticing?*

The singer continued, *"It isn't your sweet conversation that brings this sensation. Oh, no! It's just the nearness of you."*

"Well, what do you think, Jen? Is it all you expected?" he asked as he seated himself across from her, concentrating on her response. He wanted so badly for this evening to be special for her.

"Oh, Michael, it's so lovely here ... and so romantic. I would dearly love to live in a romantic old house like this one. Maybe this is what heaven will be like." Her soft, large eyes glowed warmly as she took in her surroundings.

The pieces of mahogany and hand-painted furniture were all antique or antique reproductions with Aubusson carpets on the well-worn, hundred-year-old plank flooring. Their table for two was located in an intimate corner and was adorned with a vase bursting forth with white roses, pink carnations, ferns, and baby's breath. The linen tablecloth and napkins had antique lace edging, and the cut crystal stemware sparkled. The reflected glow of the candles in their silver candlesticks made Jennifer's dark eyes shine. Tiny, white lights were twinkling in the many potted palm trees scattered around the room, softening its corners, while the piano played softly, romantically in the background.

Jennifer sighed as she drank it all in and added wistfully, "I wish I could stay here for the rest of my life."

Michael smiled and responded tenderly, "Then ... I wish I could, too." And he warmly enfolded her graceful hand in his, looking deeply into her eyes.

He realized then, just at that moment, how much he loved her. He had not known it before—had never stopped consciously to analyze his feelings for her. But now, he knew. Jennifer was the only woman for him! No one else could compare! This knowledge fell heavily upon him with a suddenness that made the air around him seem electric, and he began to marvel at the wonder of the young woman who sat before him.

She was beautiful, desirable, intelligent, sweet and good, and had a tenderness about her that melted his heart. She had worked her fingers to the bone for him all day for no other reason than her love for him. She would drop any of her own plans to be with him, to help him, to encourage him. Suddenly he wished he had bought her a ring instead of the bracelet that was wrapped up and hidden in his coat pocket. He wanted her to know how much he cared.

"I need no soft lights to enchant me, if you'll only grant me the right ... to hold you ever so tight ... And to feel in the night ... the nearness of you," sang the pianist to the end of the song.

Jennifer, who had met and kept his intense eye contact from the time he had responded so warmly to her remark, smiled a little and said,

"Isn't that a sweet love song. I wish they still wrote songs like that. Thank you for bringing me here, Michael. It's a magical evening already. I will never forget it."

"I don't think I ever will, either," he replied tenderly, still gazing at her intently, caressing her fingers gently. "You are so beautiful. I love you, Jennifer. Happy Birthday." And he reluctantly released her hand to pull her gift from his pocket.

To Jennifer, the three words he had just uttered were all the present that she had wanted, would ever want again. Her heart rate began to quicken and her cheeks to redden. Before she took the gift from his hand, she looked at him, her sweet, innocent spirit completely open, and stated softly from the fullness of her heart,

"I love you, too."

Just at that moment an insensitive waiter came to assist the young couple. They had not even looked at their menus yet, so they sent him away with their drink order. Iced teas all around, the house wine of the South. While Michael, at twenty-one, was of legal drinking age, Jennifer was not. And he was so intoxicated with her at this moment, alcohol was unnecessary.

"Go ahead, open your present. No more waiting," he teasingly instructed, anxious to know what her reaction would be.

She tore open the wrapping. It was from Fitzwater's, the most exclusive jewelry store on Main Street that made a killing selling diamond engagement rings in the small college town. Inside the black box lined with burgundy velvet was a gold bracelet. It had small, multi-colored, semi-precious and precious gems all around it except for one, flat gold segment that had *"Jennifer"* engraved in script on the front.

"Oh, Michael, it's so lovely! I will wear it always! Thank you!" burst forth Jennifer from the happiest place in her young heart, her eyes glowing brightly to rival the candlelight.

"I wish I could have done more, Jenny. Katie helped me choose it, as you know already," he explained somewhat awkwardly, carefully observing her response. "Turn it over. Look what's inscribed on the back."

Engraved on the back of her nameplate were the words, "With all my love, Michael." She clutched it to her breast, her face radiant, and exclaimed with eyes now glistening, "I couldn't have wanted anything else in the whole store, Michael!"

"Here, let me fasten it on for you," he replied in relief at her response.

Standing up, he clasped the bracelet around her delicate wrist, brought her hand to his lips, and repeated, once more gazing deeply into her lovely dark eyes, "Happy Birthday, my beautiful brown-eyed girl. I love you, Jennifer Jacobs. Very much."

"Some day, when I'm awfully low, when the world is cold, I will feel a glow just thinking of you ... and the way you look tonight," floated the lovely lyrics to their ears.

An older couple across the room had been observing the handsome pair for the past fifteen minutes and remembered their own courtship. They smiled at the thought and took each other's hands for a brief minute in remembrance, wishing this sweet young couple all the happiness of their thirty-five year marriage.

The evening progressed slowly, leisurely, but it seemed to fly by for Jennifer and Michael. It was indeed magical, and they wanted it to go on forever. The food was extraordinary, served in five courses.

They did not say much. This was not the time for small talk and idle chatter. This was the moment all women dream of from the time they first watched *Cinderella* as very little girls. This was the moment to simply gaze into the eyes of the one you have loved for a long time... when you discover that he loves you, too.

And Michael, though he never would have admitted it, felt a little like Prince Charming, only because Jennifer was the loveliest Cinderella he had ever imagined. He would have dearly loved to place the glass slipper on her foot and take her back to his castle to be his forever.

He could not take his eyes off her, and had very little idea what he was eating. He only knew that he loved Jennifer Jacobs ... very much ... and that she loved him, too. Nothing else mattered to him at that moment. Nothing at all.

Jennifer was simply in heaven. She had to keep reminding herself that she was not dreaming—that Michael Evans, a man she could not have created in her wildest fantasy, was actually in love with her, was holding her hand at every available moment and gazing at her with eyes full of adoration, warm affection, and deep desire.

"Wise men say, 'Only fools rush in.' But I can't help falling in love with you. Like a river flows surely to the sea, Darling, so it goes, some things are meant to be. Take my hand; take my whole life, too. For I can't help falling in love with you."

This classic Elvis love song was to be the last of the evening. Michael and Jennifer were the only people left in their dining room and were loathe to leave. How he wished they could dance! He wanted desperately to hold Jennifer in his arms and kiss her for a long, long time.

"Shall I stay? Would it be a sin? For I can't help falling in love with you. No, I can't help falling in love with you."

They left the restaurant at ten-thirty, strolled to his car, and were in each other's arms immediately, before Michael even placed the key in the ignition. All the passion and tension that had built up throughout the romantic dinner were released instantly as they embraced and kissed tenderly, gently.

"This will always be the best birthday of my life," Jennifer whispered. "Thank you."

"I'm so glad," he replied softly. "You are the most enchanting, beautiful, twenty-year-old woman that old mansion has ever seen. I'm so glad you're my girl."

"Am I really 'your girl,' Mikey?" she asked quietly, her dark, sweet eyes totally open and trusting as they peered steadfastly into his. "Do I really belong to you?"

"If you're ever in doubt of that, Jenny, just look down at that bracelet," he answered sincerely and kissed her again, his warm, strong hands on her soft, round shoulders. "Just look on the back of that bracelet. It says, 'with all my love,' and that is what I am giving you, if you will take it."

They continued their expressions of affection a little while longer. Then Michael sighed a heavy sigh as his passions began warring against his spirit again. How long this war would go on and how much resistance he could maintain, he did not know.

He resolutely moved himself back directly under the steering wheel, started the car, and drove them slowly back toward town. The predicted line of thunderstorms could be seen toward the west as lightening was flashing off in the distance.

"It's still early. Would you like to go to a late movie or something? Or do you think it would be better for me to take you on back to the dorm? We could sit in the lobby there and talk, and maybe just ride out that approaching storm," he suggested, trying very hard to win this battle with his flesh.

"I can't believe you forgot that I have those two plants on the floor in your backseat," she answered, smiling.

Part of Jennifer's shopping time that afternoon had been spent purchasing those plants for his new apartment.

"You know, you said you would take me back to your apartment after dinner so I could set them up. And I also bought the shelf paper while I was shopping this afternoon." And she giggled. "I know how badly you wanted that shelf paper. It will only take a few minutes to install it."

"Yeah, I'm so glad about that," he teased back. "I don't want to be the only guy in my building without shelf paper. That would be embarrassing."

So the couple headed back to Michael's new, perfectly clean apartment, barely ahead of the fast-approaching storm. As she was walking ahead of him up the stairs carrying one plant while he carried the second and the all-important shelf paper, he again was taken with her lovely shape, her slender waistline and the very sensuous, soft curves of her body that were accentuated in her dress. The yellow caution lights were flashing wildly. *This is not a good idea,* he thought. *We should have gone to the dorm lobby like I suggested.*

Unlocking the door, he walked into the dark space and turned on some lamps. The storm was now heavy upon them with sheets and sheets of rain beating against the west facing windows. He looked outside and tried to say lightly,

"Well, it appears as though we are stuck here for a little while, anyway. Unless you brought your swimsuit, that is. Now, where did you say you wanted to put those plants? One on the dining table, right? And the other one, where?"

"Oh, no! You put the wrong one on the table," she responded, concern on her face that he would misappropriate the interior appointments she had so lovingly and carefully selected to warm and beautify his new dwelling. "This one, the cute little pig, goes on the kitchen counter," she stated with authority, removing it from the table while handing him the one in her hand.

Then she walked over to the kitchen, placed it down, moved it over slightly, surveyed the position, moved it a little more, and finished with, "Yep, just about right there. That looks good."

Something about the seemingly illogical, irrational workings of her feminine mind went straight to Michael's heart, and he set the other plant down on the dining table, walked over to the kitchen where she was standing, and took her in his arms while laughing kindly.

"Jennifer Jacobs, you are so sweet and so funny," he spoke gently. Once more he looked deeply into her enormous blackish eyes, those eyes he already knew better than his own, adding warmly, "And I love you so much."

She said nothing but just drank in and returned his loving look, and kissed him ever so sweetly, and then with more fervor, her hands wrapped tightly around his neck, her body pressing more closely to his. Lightning, thunder, blowing rain and wind were howling outside.

"I love thunderstorms. They are so powerful and so cleansing," she murmured in his ear as she gently kissed his neck, loving the masculine smell of him. "And I love you, too … so very much." And she continued kissing him passionately.

Just then, the lights went out, as the storm winds pushed a tree down over some power lines, and they were embracing and kissing in the now darkened room.

He responded quickly, instinctively to her sweet, insistent ardor, adding to it all the passion and fire of his own love, desperate longing, and desire for her. He could no longer reason away his incredible, powerful yearning to express himself sexually with the woman he loved—the beautiful, thrilling, sweet, and sexy young woman he held in his arms. The young woman who was as fragrant as a rose, and was so soft and warm in his embrace. The young woman with the most tender, sweetest, fullest lips, and the softest, silkiest hair, and the largest, most mysterious, dark and glowing eyes. The young woman with the sensuous, soft, and shapely body that was pressing so closely to his, glorying in his touch. The young woman who was equally attuned to his own desires and longings at that moment in time, and was responding so naturally, wonderfully, and magically to his gentle, intimate caresses.

His own, lovely Jennifer, who even now was yielding, surrendering herself to him so sweetly and completely, responding to him so trustingly and beautifully, as if he were the conductor of an orchestra and she were the embodiment of all the musicians, allowing him to direct her in the glorious symphony he was composing. No. The beautiful symphony they were creating *together,* each one adding more richness and harmony to the main melody, as the full concerto sweetly, dramatically unfolded. Together, composing their own variation of the Creator's theme that has bonded man and woman together in life-giving love since the Garden of Eden—a richly resounding, magnificent symphony, so much the same and yet so individual and unique, as old as creation itself and yet always brand new. Their own timeless masterpiece, like none other ever heard.

While gentle and sweet, their composition was also fevered and intense, as electricity and sexual passion were flowing between them almost equal to the flashes of lightning that were the only illumination in the room. Somehow, they had moved to the sofa, and Beth's borrowed dress was lying on the floor next to Michael's blue suit. Again, time and place seemed meaningless to either one of them. There was no time ... No time except the present ... And no people in the world except each other.

Now that Jennifer knew beyond any doubt that Michael belonged to her and she to him, her reserve of the previous week was disappearing as she was giving herself to him, totally, utterly.

And Michael was lost in the wonder, the passion, the indescribable sensations of truly knowing her intimately, heart to heart and skin to skin, taking him into the mysterious realm of the yet unknown fulfillment of his own sexuality. And her physical loveliness, coupled with her soft, sweet moans of pleasure, thrilled him beyond measure.

But before he continued his discovery of her, he whispered earnestly in her ear, his warm breath tickling her neck, "Are you sure you want to do this? You must tell me now, Jenny! No teasing!"

To Jennifer's mind, giving herself to him at that moment seemed to be the logical conclusion of all her heart's desires. She wanted to belong to him. Forever. All of her. Nothing held back. She trusted him completely. She loved him powerfully. And the joyful elation of her senses as she reveled in his tender touch only reinforced her thoughts.

"Michael, I love you so very much! I want to be part of you always! How can this be wrong? I want to stay here with you tonight," she whispered back ardently. " I love you so much!"

"And I love you ... wonderful ... exciting, beautiful Jenny … my beautiful brown eyed girl," he murmured. "I love you, too. I do."

With those words, and with the symphony of the storm joining in dramatic accompaniment to their own thrilling concert and serving as their serenade, the two young people lost their battle for abstinence until marriage, and experienced prematurely that most awesome, enthralling, ecstatic, mysterious and mystical, holy bonding of sexual union.

Chapter Eight

C lear, bright sunlight was streaming in through the bedroom window of Michael's new apartment that Sunday morning, the fifth of June 1975. The sun rises early in June in south Alabama, and the squall line of thunderstorms that had swept through the region last evening had cleansed the atmosphere of its heavy oppression and left in its place cooler, less humid air and clear blue skies. It was not yet seven o'clock.

As the sun's rays found their way onto the bed where Jennifer lay sleeping, she began to stir. At first, she did not realize where she was, as she had never been a morning person and most days was not fully awake until at least eight or eight-thirty. As she took her first peek at the new day through sticky, morning eyes, however, the knowledge of her whereabouts landed heavily upon her. She was in Michael's bed!

But Michael was gone!

After calling his name out loudly but receiving no answer, she jumped out of bed. With her heart pounding, she peered out the window into the parking lot, lifting the slats of the mini-blinds to discover that, indeed, his car was not parked in the place they had left it last night.

Last night! The most profoundly romantic, fulfilling, and yet strangely fearsome night of her life! She blushed at the thought of it, blushed like a bride. It had been so wonderfully glorious to her, though she now felt more than a little guilty. But the guilt was slowly being replaced by a growing sense of panic in her spirit.

Where could Michael be so early? Why in the world did he leave? she wondered. *Oh, no! Maybe I did something wrong! Maybe he was not pleased with me or doesn't love me anymore! Perhaps he has lost all respect for me! Men do that—* she had been told—*lose respect for women who have given themselves away.*

She remembered the Old Testament story of King David's son, what's-his-name, who burned with lustful desire for his half-sister, what's-her-name, but after he had his way with her, despised her. She remembered the exact King James Bible words: *"So that the hatred wherewith he hated her was greater than the love wherewith he had loved her."*

It can't be! It can't be! she worried, her fevered imagination taking over her rational thought processes. *Surely Michael doesn't hate me!*

She recalled their exuberant, sensual, and yet gently sweet evening, and her mind told her that this thought was ridiculous. Why, just before they fell asleep last night under his freshly laundered blankets to the sounds of gentle raindrops on the roof and distant, rolling thunder, he had whispered in her ear as they cuddled so closely, "You are an awesome lover, Jenny, so beautiful and exciting. I love you. And I love having you here in my bed with me."

And had they made love again sometime very early this morning… hours before daylight? Or had she merely been dreaming? Her cheeks glowed fiery red once more as she realized that she had not been dreaming. He had taken her once more with the same passion and pleasure as before … as though he could never have enough of her.

But then, where can he be? she continued to fume and fret. *Why would he wake up and leave me here all alone? Why … other than this morning when he woke up and thought clearly about it, he was disappointed in me … in both of us?* And try as hard as she could, she could not erase the mental image of Michael taking a long, solitary walk around the campus, his head hanging, his hands in his pockets, muttering to himself, regretting what had happened last night and trying to think of a way to let her down gently.

Suddenly, she was made acutely aware of her nakedness, standing there alone in her lover's bedroom in the clear light of day. Her nakedness that had seemed so natural and so right last night while in Michael's arms, but now, in the morning, seemed so shameful and embarrassing, even though no one was there to witness it. No one but God that is, she knew full well.

Quickly grabbing the soft, white cotton blanket from the foot of the bed and wrapping it around herself, she walked to his closet, opened the doors, and found a large, old football jersey of his. As she pulled it over her head, it fell almost to her knees.

She padded into the bathroom and gazed at her reflection. She still wore her diamond and pearl teardrop earrings, necklace, and her birthday bracelet, which were now so incongruous against his football jersey. She automatically turned the bracelet over and read, "With all my love, Michael." He had told her if she were ever in doubt of his affection to read it, she remembered. She felt slightly comforted and continued with her morning grooming as best she could.

Her hair was hanging down on her shoulders and her makeup was all smeared. She washed her face and automatically reached for a toothbrush before realizing that hers was back at Dorm 10. Back where she should have been this morning. She compromised, using her finger as a toothbrush to get the awful morning taste out of her mouth. She wanted to shower but had no clean clothes to wear, so she washed up as best as she could, combed her hair, and began worrying some more.

She wandered aimlessly into the living room, still lost in anxious thought. Beth's dress was lying on the floor by the sofa, and next to it was Michael's best suit. She blushed yet again at the memory of their passion. The adults at church had been right! They had said that sex was a wonderful, powerful, pleasurable gift of God, intended to bond a husband and wife together. She had experienced the power, wonder, and pleasure herself last night—although it was slightly painful—and especially the bonding of herself to Michael. But had he felt bound to her? She sure thought he had! But then, where could he be? Why would he leave in such a hurry that he did not even bother to pick up his suit from the floor? It was going to be so wrinkled it would have to be cleaned and pressed.

She placed Beth's dress carefully over the back of a chair and smoothed it out with her hands. Then she carried his expensive suit and tie back to his bedroom closet. Before she hung up his coat, however, she hugged it tightly to her chest. It smelled like a combination of his aftershave/cologne and his own, unique masculine scent, an aroma that she loved, and she remembered how it felt to be in his arms. She draped the tie over the back of the coat, closed the closet door, sighed deeply, and walked over to the window again, looking out at the parking lot.

Still no Michael. *Why would he leave and stay gone so long?* she fretted.

She was thirsty, so she walked to the kitchen for a glass of water. She noticed some muscle soreness and tenderness around her inner thighs as she walked. And with each sensation of discomfort accompanying her steps, her mind cried out, accusing her, *Failure! Failure! You have failed!* As she reached for a glass in the cabinet, she turned on the radio.

"Tonight, you're mine completely. You give your love so sweetly. Tonight, the light of love is in your eyes ... But will you love me ... tomorrow?" Carole King sang.

She turned it off quickly and sighed again. Just about then, she heard Michael placing his keys in the lock. Not knowing why, she panicked and ran back to his bedroom, pulling the door almost closed but not latching it so not to make noise. She sat there on the edge of his bed, her heart racing, waiting for him to come open the door. But instead, she heard him fumbling around in the kitchen, opening cabinet doors and drawers.

What could he be doing? she wondered. She could hear her heart beating in her ears, and her palms were sweaty as she squirmed nervously.

In a few moments the bedroom door opened, and Michael walked in carrying in one hand a plate filled with eggs, bacon, hash browns, and toast, and in his other a tall glass of orange juice. Pinched under his arm was one long-stemmed, red rose. He was surprised to see her sitting there on the edge of his bed dressed in his old football jersey. He smiled tenderly while crooning softly,

"Good morning, Sweetheart. I see you're awake already. I was hoping to wake you up myself this morning with breakfast in bed."

Upon hearing this, she burst into tears, placing her hands over her face, her shoulders shaking.

Michael, totally confused and shocked by her reaction, quickly laid the breakfast plate on his bureau, the rose falling to the floor, and sat down by her side. He placed his arms around her shoulders and gently cradled her head against his chest.

"What? … What in the world is wrong, Jenny? Why are you crying?"

He was greatly concerned and immediately began to punish himself for what happened last night. *She must be regretting it terribly to cry like this. I should have taken her back to the dorm after dinner.*

"Sweetheart," he continued soothingly, "why all these tears? Why are you so sad?" His eyes searched her face.

She cried out brokenly between sobs, "Oh, Mikey! ... You are so sweet! ... So very sweet! ... When I woke up, and you weren't here ... I thought … I thought …" And she sobbed some more.

"What did you think?" he asked, momentarily at a total loss as to the cause of her anguish.

Then the light of understanding came on suddenly.   She was still crying uncontrollably.

"Oh, Jenny, you didn't think that I ... that I had left you, did you? That I was somehow ... not wanting you anymore, did you?" he questioned, grieved.

"Oh, yes! ... That's it!" she choked out. "I was afraid you didn't ... Didn't love me anymore! … Didn't respect me!" And her shoulders continued shaking.

"Jennifer! Jenny! How could you think such a thing? Not love you anymore? How absurd! I love you more than ever! You are my brown-eyed girl, remember?" he stated with emotion, and held her closer, kissing the dark, tumbled hair of her head that was on his shoulder.

At his comforting words and kind embrace, she wept all the more.

"Jennifer, you must learn to control that foolish imagination of yours! How could you think such a thing? After last night, I mean?"

He sat there with her head still on his shoulder and his arms wrapped tightly around her, his right hand gently caressing her dark, soft hair as she quaked with her tears and her fears. As he tried to comfort her, he thought in frustration,

This is not how the morning after is supposed to be! How I wish I could have married her last night! She should be reveling in the knowledge of my love for her, like a bride on her honeymoon, not sitting here crying her heart out because she thought I was tossing her aside after I had "conquered" her!

Consequences. The word came to his mind. He had been taught very well that there are always consequences for our wrong decisions and sins. Sometimes they come right away, and sometimes they are delayed. But there are always consequences. To see his girlfriend, now his lover, whom he cared for profoundly, this upset because he had taken her before they were married, before she was assured of his commitment to her, hurt him deeply.

For Michael was a good, kind, and decent young man. While he had experienced ecstasy beyond his dreams with her last night, glorying in her soft, sweet presence, "ravished with her love" as the Proverb stated, he knew that their progression into sexual intimacy was out of order.

And he, too, felt guilty.

"Jennifer, now stop this silly crying and look at me," he pronounced firmly but softly.

She complied as best as she could, trying to resume her normal breathing pattern and to stop the tears. He took her hands in both of his, gazed steadfastly into her tear-filled eyes, and stated slowly, urgently,

"I want you to know that I love you *very, very* much. I would marry you now if I could, if I were out of school and on my own. You must not ever think that I would use you this way and then ..." he broke off. He could not even vocalize the awful words that describe a cad, a scoundrel, and a reprobate. "How can you not know how wonderful you are? How can you not know how much I love you? Please believe me!"

"I believe you, Michael," she replied, much calmer now, managing a weak half-smile. "I didn't really think ... It's just that I couldn't imagine where you could have gone so early."

"When I woke up, you were still sleeping so soundly that I thought you'd be asleep for a long time, Jen. I wanted to go into the kitchen and make you some breakfast, but all that was there was a box of baking soda in the refrigerator and a roll of shelf paper on the countertop," he smiled.

Then they both laughed.

"Right. The good ol' shelf paper," she smiled back fully now, finally in control of her tears, as she blew her nose on the tissue he offered.

"There! That's better! I like your smile so much better than your tears, Toots." He brushed her bangs away from her eyes and embraced her warmly once more as he continued his explanation.

"So anyway, since there was nothing to make breakfast with in the kitchen, I thought I could run down to the diner over by the highway and get us some carry-out eggs and bacon and toast. I had no idea you would wake up so early. Now ... do you understand, silly thing?" he asked, his eyes teasing her again as he placed his hand under her chin and lifted her face to his.

She smiled and nodded her reply as he gently dried the last of the tears from her face.

"Good!" he went on, standing up and pulling her up with him. Then he lifted the rose from the carpet, placed it in her right hand, kissed her forehead, and smiled a slightly worried smile into her red-rimmed eyes, adding, "Let's go into the dining room and see if maybe we can somehow warm up this plate of food and continue our breakfast tradition. Then I'll take you back to the dorm so you can get ready for church. This afternoon, I thought we could study together at the library—finals coming up soon, you know. By the way, you look a whole lot better in my football jersey than I ever did!"

He had kept up the steady stream of conversation because he did not think he could handle any more painful tears from her right now. He was still troubled by her insecure reaction to his not being there when she awoke. It made him feel like a selfish jerk—like a sorry, contemptible, low life bounder who used women for personal pleasure and then cast them aside like last week's newspaper. *Surely she doesn't think of me like that, does she?* he worried.

Michael was also well aware of the still abandoned, frightened little girl that occupied part of Jennifer's personality due to her parents' divorce, though she had spoken of it only once to him through many swallowed tears, which she had bravely fought off. He wanted very much to place his arms around that broken child in her soul, to assure her of his devotion to her, to help mend the shattered places that fatherlessness had wrought in his dear lover's heart. And now, what had he done but cause her to think that he, too, had left her.

<u>*Consequences,*</u> he thought again, as they worked side by side in the small, bright kitchen, warming up the food and setting the table. She looked so sexy and fetching in his old jersey. Had they really been on their honeymoon, he would have liked to make love with her again, right now. But in her present emotional state, he would not even try to mention it.

She might think that's all I'm after, he thought ruefully. *And besides that, I shouldn't be "planning to sin," should I? I mean, what happened last night was not planned. It just happened. I should never touch her again like that—not until I can marry her.*

And how he wished he could do just that—whisk her off to the justice of the peace, place a ring on her finger, and take her on a long, long wedding trip to someplace exotic and beautiful! *But my bank account balance is practically nonexistent after the gift and the dinner last night. How can I marry her now—penniless, jobless, one-more-year-of-college me? Why does life have to be so very difficult now?*

Knowing what he should do and yet finding the strength to do it were two different things. He knew he should not plan to make love with her again but ...

But ... now that I know how wonderful she is, how can I resist her? <u>*Consequences,*</u> he thought.

They were at the library studying for finals that began on Tuesday. But Michael was having difficulty concentrating at all.

After the magnificence of last night, this day was totally miserable for him. Not only had it begun so terribly with Jennifer all upset and sad, and him feeling as guilty as Cain, but also when he had taken her back to the dorm, she had worn his jersey and a pair of his shorts which she could keep fastened around her slender waist only with the aid of a safety pin he had rummaged around for. He had not wanted her to go back there in her evening dress of last night. He was concerned for her reputation and did not want anyone slurring her name. He had thought that his clothes on her looked more like the sloppy attire some of the campus women wore anyway. *Maybe no one noticed, as it is still early and most of the girls are not awake yet,* he had hoped. And he was more than thankful that Katie was not there to question her whereabouts. More painful consequences were being thrown his way than he had ever given thought to.

Jennifer, too, was feeling uncomfortable around Michael today. She could sense that he was not happy, and that made her unhappy, too. *What a tremendous letdown after the rapture of last night,* she thought. And the sermon at church seemed to have been tailor made to make them feel even guiltier. It was about the hypocrisy of saying you have faith but then not backing it up with your actions. *"Why do you call me 'Lord, Lord,' but do not do what I say?"* was the scripture reference. Both of them felt a tremendous, unspoken guilt at that topic.

Now, at the library they sat, staring at their books and turning pages but not assimilating very much of anything. After about an hour of this, they left, holding hands but not making much conversation.

In the car, Jennifer felt like crying again. *How could everything seem so right one day, and the next so wrong again?*

Michael finally broke the silence with, "What do you say about going to see a movie? They are playing an old Alfred Hitchcock classic with Cary Grant at the campus theater. How about it?"

"Sounds good to me," she perked up some.

They were not the only students in denial about the upcoming exams, as the theater was jam-packed. He purchased a big tub of popcorn and two soft drinks, and as they settled into their seats, enjoying the suspense picture, they began to feel more relaxed and natural again.

When the film was over, they chose to walk instead of riding in his car. It was a lovely afternoon, and they strolled a long time on the campus grounds, holding hands and feeding the pigeons their leftover popcorn. Still, there was unspoken tension between them. They had not discussed either what had happened last night or Jennifer's tears this morning, and she knew this had to be talked over if they were to conquer this awkwardness that had settled over them today, making them both so miserable.

She began, tentatively at first, and then more boldly as they continued strolling, "Michael, I'm so sorry I cried this morning... Believe me, it surprised me as much as it did you ... I think ... if you had been there when I woke up, it would have been an entirely different day today. My 'foolish imagination,' as you so aptly put it, just got carried away when you weren't there, and then I turned on the radio in the kitchen only to hear Carole King asking, 'Will you still love me tomorrow?'"

"You're kidding," he said. "That was on the radio?"

Then he stopped walking, took her face in his hands, looked ardently into her sweet, trusting eyes and stated, "I hope you know the answer to that question is a great, big, YES!" He emphasized his statement by kissing her tenderly and embracing her.

"I still love you, too," she whispered quietly, warmly, her eyes beginning to glisten again.

"Then, why in the world are we so depressed today?" he asked as they continued walking slowly, shuffling their feet and holding hands.

"I suppose I feel a little ... No, that's not true ... *More* than a little... guilty," she began truthfully after contemplating his question. "I mean, I have been taught all my life to remain a ... to remain 'pure' until I was married ... And then last night ... It just felt so right, you know."

"Yes, I know. I know that very well, Jen," he spoke honestly, too. "And then the sermon this morning ... Ouch! Talk about guilt," he chuckled sarcastically and she joined him.

He stopped their walking again and suggested, "Come on. Let's sit down on this bench and talk some more."

They sat facing each other on a park bench beneath a huge, old maple tree, still holding hands. Two squirrels were chasing each other and chattering noisily as a blue jay was trying to scare them away, while a soft, light breeze was making pleasant rustling sounds in the leaves of the spreading shade tree and gently caressing the faces of the young lovers.

Michael continued, his eyes searching her face, "Look, Jen, I wish I could say that ... Oh, how can I word this? ... I wish I could say that I wish I hadn't made love to you last night. Truthfully, part of me *can* say that … but part of me can't."

"Yes, I know what you mean," she agreed, nodding her head, her eyes very seriously focused on his.

"You do?" he asked, curiously surprised, his eyes widening somewhat.

"Sure, I do," she replied sincerely, incredulous that he still did not understand a woman's sexual passions very well. *Weren't you there last night, Michael?* she thought, and the beginnings of a weak smile creased the corners of her full lips.

"Well, then ... I also wish I could truthfully say that it won't happen again if I am around you like last night, but … I can't say that either," he explained honestly, still concentrating on her reaction.

"Neither can I," she agreed, openhearted and totally truthful.

"You can't?" he asked again, still wide-eyed at her unguarded transparency.

"Michael Evans! How can you think I don't understand what you are talking about? I'm not a statue carved out of stone, you know! I have feelings, desires, and passions the same as you. And I love you so much! You are hard for me to resist, too. Very hard. I love you so much," she spoke from her heart, earnestly desiring that he understand what had motivated her behavior last night.

He sat there for a minute, taking in her remarks, just staring at her and loving her back with his eyes, his fingers gently caressing hers. Then he dropped her gaze, looked out into the campus park while seeing nothing, sighed, and said,

"Well … Then, what are we going to do? I can't marry you until I get out of college and have a real job, and I can't resist you when we are together. I don't even want to think about not seeing you again… So … what are we going to do?   I don't expect an answer, Jen. I'm just thinking out loud."

She sat there thinking, too, but getting nowhere. She knew that the chances of their seeing each other on a daily basis and not making love again were very slim indeed. He had mentioned marriage twice now these past few hours. That sounded like commitment to her. Real commitment. But was he serious?

"Are you asking me to marry you, Michael?" she asked a little timidly.

"Where have you been these past twenty-four hours, Toots?" he returned half-smiling, his eyes on hers again. "Don't you know I would marry you today if I could—if I were out of school and had a job?" And he gently brushed away a stray lock of hair that the wind had blown into her beautiful dark eyes, which were now glowing very warmly.

Wow! He really does mean it! she thought, and was thrilled. *But he has never actually proposed.*

"But you have forgotten one thing: I haven't said 'yes,' Mr. Evans," she flirted, now pouting coyly, her eyes sparkling playfully. "You are mighty presumptuous and full of yourself, Sir."

"Well, let's fix that right now," he rose to her challenge, playing along, his eyes twinkling with mischief.

He got down on one knee in front of her, took both her hands in his, and recited in his best elocution,

"Miss Jennifer Elaine Jacobs, even though you are now an old woman of twenty, and your flower is beginning to fade, I wish to be bold enough to inquire of you ... Would you do me the very great honor of becoming my wife?"

He had begun his proposal lightly, teasingly, but by the time he spoke the words, "the very great honor of becoming my wife," his eyes and his voice were dead serious. He meant every word, and she knew it.

She sat there for a moment barely breathing, mesmerized by the magic of this moment on this park bench in Coburn, Alabama, on the day after her twentieth birthday, June 5th, 1975, being proposed to by the man of her dreams—the man who only this morning had brought her breakfast in bed. The man who had calmed her fears and assured her of his love. The man she loved so powerfully. She wanted to freeze this moment and never forget it. Never.

Her eyes filled with tears, and she replied very softly, almost in a whisper, "Becoming your wife would make me the happiest woman in the world, Michael."

They were in each other's arms again, just holding each other very close. Wanting to stay there for a while and remain one in spirit, while the birds overhead sang out joyfully, as if on cue.

When they finally released their hold on each other, he remarked gently, taking her left hand, "It may be a little while before I can save up enough for a ring, but—"

"I don't care about that now, Michael! I have my bracelet!" she responded with emotion, smiling through her tears and fondling the piece of jewelry.

"That's right, Jen. You have a very original engagement bracelet," he replied smiling, touching the bracelet himself and twirling it several times around her slender, graceful wrist. Then he kissed her hand and gazed longingly into the dark recesses of her lovely eyes.

They began to walk again, silently, arm in arm, each one lost in the wonder of having discovered their future life's partner, the one who would stay by their side, for better or worse, for richer or poorer, 'til death do us part. Each one so very thankful for the other. Each one so much in love. Each one wishing the wedding could be tomorrow. Or even better … tonight.

"This brings me back to our original dilemma, though," he finally spoke again. "How am I ever going to be able to resist you? And for a whole year, too! Too bad we can't have the honeymoon first and then the wedding ... Or can we, Jennifer?" He stopped and looked at her questioningly.

"Well," she dropped her gaze and fluttered her eyes downward, her cheeks reddening as usual, "I'd say we had a pretty good start on the honeymoon part last night, wouldn't you?"

"Oh, yeah!" he agreed warmly, giving her bedroom eyes even now. "I'd say that was a pretty fair beginning! I'd say it was the most thrilling night of my whole life, Jen, beyond my wildest dreams. And I'd say you are the most exciting, sensuous, gorgeous, sexy woman in the world! And I'd say I love you. Very much."

She was blushing even more at his words, and her own passions were stirred at the memory of being with him.

He laughed, remarking, "You will never be able to hide your thoughts, Jenny. You blush so easily, more than anyone I have ever known, even though it must be unusual for someone with your beautiful olive skin." And he embraced her ardently, lingeringly with desire, and kissed her.

"Is it getting warmer again, or is it me?" he whispered.

"Hmmm," she whispered back.

They turned around and started walking slowly back toward his car.

"So how about it, then? Just between us … no one else knowing. Can we have our honeymoon this year and the wedding after my graduation?" he asked her hopefully.

"You mean, we can't tell anyone we're engaged?" she replied, puzzled.

"No, silly! I want everyone to know you are my intended. What I meant was, we need to keep the ... you know ... honeymoon part, just between us. Our secret," he stated as if the matter were settled.

"Michael, forgive me if my flirting just now misled you, but I haven't agreed to that," she began apologetically. "What you are suggesting sounds like pure rationalization to me. You know, like saying we're planning to rob a bank, but it's okay because we will pay all the money back plus interest in a year. And then asking the Lord to bless us in our venture," she reasoned logically.

He could not deny her argument. Sighing, he observed,

"I know you are right, but what about last night? Maybe I haven't repented entirely, even though today's sermon did make me feel very bad. But last night just seemed so ... Oh, I want to say, 'spiritual' to me. You know, like we were truly already married at dinner when I first realized that you are the only one for me, Jennifer, and ... it just somehow didn't seem all that wrong to me. I guess I believe that the Lord understands. I mean, it's not like it was a one-night stand with someone you don't even know. Do you know what I am trying to say?" he asked sincerely.

She wrinkled her brow a little and replied, "I know exactly what you mean, Michael. Obviously, it seemed right to me, too ... Last night, that is. But this morning ... Well, that was another story."

"Yeah, but this morning I was gone when you woke up, and you already said that our whole day would have been different had I been there," he maintained his rationale.

"That's true; it would have. But I'm still not sure that I wouldn't have felt guilty. We are going out of order, you know."

This time she stopped walking and turned around to look him fully in the eyes, to emphasize something important and vital.

"Michael, I know you very well. Sometimes I think even better than you know yourself. I know you love God, and I know you love being a leader and a role model for those kids at church. I do, too. How could you stand up in front of them and teach them abstinence and self-control when you weren't practicing it yourself? How could I? No, Mikey, we can't plan to sin like this. Even if it does seem good to us, and even if we think the Lord does understand. It's just not right."

Even as she was speaking, he knew she was correct, as much as he hated to admit it. And he was ashamed of himself for trying to lead her astray.

"I know you are right," he acquiesced, sighing again in resignation. Then he took her hand, kissed it, and finished with, "Please forgive me for trying to talk you into 'sinning' with me. You are right. It's just that it is so difficult for me to be near you, Jennifer, and not want to take you in my arms and ... you know."

"Yes, I know," and again she reddened. "It's not easy for me, either."

"It's like that song, that pretty love song, the one that was sung last night, the one you liked so much," and he took both her hands in his, looked around to make certain no one was paying any attention to them, and sang softly, romantically to his lover, now his bride-to-be.

"It's not the pale moon that excites me, that thrills and delights me. Oh, no! ... It's just the nearness of you. It isn't your sweet conversation that brings this sensation. Oh, no! ... It's just the nearness of you. When you're in my arms, and I feel you so close to me, all my wildest dreams come true. I need no soft lights to enchant me, if you'll only grant me the right ... to hold you ever so tight ... and to feel in the night ... the nearness of you."

After he finished, he took her in his arms again and kissed her once more. As she was still speechless, he added sheepishly, "I know that song. It's an old Frank Sinatra number that my parents used to play. Come to think of it, they would disappear from the family room about then, too." And he winked at her.

"Ooooo, Mikey ..." she murmured slowly, looking up into his face, her eyes glowing with passion. "Let's put down one ground rule right now. You can't *ever* sing me that song again! Not until our wedding night!"

He laughed and she joined him as they began again to stroll leisurely, arm in arm, back to his car. The sun was beginning to set in a glorious display of pinks and deep purples while the evening breezes brought a refreshing promise of fine weather for tomorrow.

"I guess we do need to set some ground rules, Jen, if we're gonna be able to resist," he agreed. "What else do you suggest?"

"We can't ever be alone in your apartment."

"Not ever?" he played along.

"No! Not *ever*!" she emphasized.

"Okay."

"Or in your car for more than two minutes ... No, better make that one minute," she added.

"Why not thirty seconds?" he toyed with her some more, grinning broadly.

"All right, silly! Thirty seconds, then. You know what I mean!" she defended.

"Just drive to where we're going, then get out. Right?" he clarified.

"Right."

"Okay. Anything else, Miss Manners?" he teased.

"Well, so far at least, that's where we have gotten into trouble, so let's at least work on those two and see how it goes. Okay?" she reasoned.

"Okay, Toots. Whatever you say. Maybe this will work out after all."

Chapter Nine

*B*ut it did not work out at all. Although they tried for a few days to keep their ground rules, soon the goodnight kisses in his car lasted well beyond the thirty seconds limit, and they were back to where they had been the night of the Roman Forum party. Still, Jennifer would somehow find the will to resist and pull herself away, leaving him not at all a happy man. But she, at least, felt relieved that she had escaped yet another temptation … for the time being, anyway.

When the semester was officially over on June the fifteenth, Michael decided to host a cookout at his apartment to celebrate. Joe and Katie were coming over to play a set of mixed doubles tennis with Jennifer and him, and then they were all going to grill steaks for dinner and go to a movie afterwards.

Michael and Jennifer had been at his apartment only a minute or two making preparations for the food and were expecting Joe and Katie any minute, when the telephone rang.

"Hello," answered Jennifer cheerfully while smiling at her fiancé, cradling the phone between her head and shoulder. She was chopping the salad and looked very pretty in her white Bermuda shorts and sleeveless, red knit sweater.

"Hey, Jenny, it's me," responded Katie. "I hate to tell you this, but Joe and I can't come today. He just phoned me and said that he was as sick as a dog. He has that stomach flu that is going around. So I guess I need to cancel, too."

"Oh, no, Katie! Sorry about Joe not feeling well, but you can come, can't you? I'll drive over to pick you up if you need a ride," Jennifer requested urgently, the smile instantly leaving her face, her brows furrowed in concern. She wiped her hands on a towel, took the phone in her hands, and began pacing in the dining room.

"Well … you two really don't want me to come by myself, do you? …You know, three's a crowd and all," Katie replied hesitantly.

Michael, who had overheard the conversation, was shaking his head while mouthing the word "no" and grinning impishly, more to tease Jennifer than to indicate disapproval of Katie's solo attendance.

His fiancée frowned even more, turned her back slightly toward him, and continued her conversation with her roommate.

"Don't be silly, Kate. We *really, truly* want you to come. Please say yes!" she begged.

"Aw, Jenny, to be perfectly honest, I'm not feeling too well either. I think I may be coming down with that bug, too. It would be amazing if I didn't catch it … from Joe, I mean." And she giggled as only Katie could. "So tell Michael I'm sorry. Maybe we can do it Monday or Tuesday before we head back to Mobile."

As Jennifer hung up the phone, she wrinkled her brows even more in consternation. She had been looking forward to this afternoon. She had not stepped even one foot into Michael's apartment since "that night," and had wanted to prove to herself that she could enjoy just being there with him and their friends without sexual tension.

"What's up, Toots?" he quizzed. "The Smothers' can't come? Too bad."

"They're not 'The Smothers'' yet," she stated, still showing concern in her expression. Katie and Joe had announced their engagement last week just as Michael and Jennifer had.

"And yet, somehow when I see them together now, I think of them as 'The Smothers'," he smiled, and her frown diminished somewhat. Walking over to her side, he placed his arms around her waist, drawing her close, and finished his thought. "And I'll just bet that they think of us as 'The Evans', too."

"But we're not 'The Evans' yet, either, and don't try to tell me we are," she teased him, hitting him lightly in the chest eight times to emphasize her last words, her eyes now smiling back into his. Then she pulled herself out of his embrace and walked back into the kitchen as she added flirtatiously, smiling slyly,

"Besides, I might just keep my maiden name. It's all the latest rage, you know. And I always liked the alliteration -- 'Jennifer Jacobs' -- But 'Jennifer Evans' doesn't sound too bad, either."

This was news to him, and he was not certain she was serious, but he loved the mystery of her feminine mind. He could not resist responding wickedly as he followed her back into the kitchen, barely missing her rear end with the expertly timed, repeated popping of the damp dishtowel he held in his hand.

"Well, you can keep your maiden *name*, Jennifer Jacobs, after we are married, but I can tell you one thing for sure: You *will not* keep your 'maiden*hood*'! … Oh, wait! …I forgot! … That's already been taken care of!"

Then he intentionally leered at her salaciously because such playful taunting would usually make her blush. And he loved her blushes so much!

Her cheeks did redden, indeed, and she began to chase him, hitting him playfully with the wooden spoon she held in her hand as he ran around the living area protesting, "Ouch, ouch! Put down that spoon!"

"How dare you throw that up in my face, Michael Evans! You are no gentleman, Sir!" she called out, her eyes narrowing but dancing just the same, not annoyed in the least at his teasing her. And she continued chasing him, hitting him lightly on his backside with the spoon as he ran into the bedroom. "No gentleman would *ever* recall such a shameful event in the presence of his lady friend!" she reprimanded him in jest.

Suddenly, his playful attitude vanished and he became serious. He grabbed her wrist gently, removed the spoon, and pulled her very close. He confessed solemnly, softly, ardently, his large, masculine hands encircling her slender waist firmly and securely, his blue eyes drawing her deeply under his masculine spell, making it difficult for her to draw breath.

"Funny, Jen. I don't remember it as a 'shameful event' at all." And he kissed her very tenderly, very leisurely, now running his hands slowly up and down her bare arms, his fingers lightly brushing the sides of her breasts. "No ... Not at all," he breathed softly.

His clear, blue eyes burned into hers with so much love, desire, passion, and desperate longing, and his strong arms embraced her so warmly, insistently, and amorously, that she could not resist him. Not at all.

And so it progressed over the next few weeks, on into the summer school session. Their sexual passion, once released, could no more be restrained than individual water droplets could be replaced behind the dam in the reservoir after the floodgates had been opened. Each time the couple failed to resist each other only made it easier to give in the next time. And each time was just as sweet and glorious. And each time they felt less and less guilty, and more and more comfortable. *After all*, they would tell one another, *we are just having the honeymoon before the wedding. We are going to be married by this time next year. We are in love. It has to be okay.*

They had even given his apartment a secret nickname, "The Honeymoon Suite," they called it, or "The Suite," for short. And they called what they did there, "honeymooning before the wedding," or "HBTW" in abbreviation. When they would be studying together in the library, sometimes he would pass her a note that read, "Let's go back to The Suite for some HBTW." And then he would lift his eyebrows and smile a mischievously seductive smile, his blue eyes twinkling irresistibly at her, until she would blush and smile back a "yes."

They played with their newfound sexuality as a child plays with a much desired and eagerly anticipated toy when it finally arrives on Christmas morning, taking it down from the shelf and enjoying it as often as possible, thinking about it constantly when forced to place it back on the shelf to go to school or do chores, believing they would never tire of the pleasure it gave them, and that no one else in all of history had quite experienced the secret joy they knew.

For Jennifer in particular, the pleasure of lovemaking itself, although exciting and thrilling, paled in comparison to the feelings of connectedness and oneness with Michael she sensed while lying in his arms. And the loneliness and fear that had grown in her heart from her broken, abandoned childhood would disappear as she held her fiancé and lover so close, becoming one with him forever.

She felt safe there with him. For the first time in over ten years since her daddy had left home, she felt safe in Michael's loving embrace. *"I am my beloved's, and my beloved is mine,"* she would quote to herself from Solomon's Song over and over again as she serenely drifted off to sleep in his comforting, masculine arms after their passion had spent itself so wondrously.

And Michael just plain enjoyed the sexual fulfillment he experienced with his sweet, soft, and sensuous, beautiful bride-to-be, lover, and friend, thinking he was the luckiest man alive to have found her and that no one else could ever compare to her. Though sometimes, usually at church, he would feel a little guilty at his lack of self-control and premarital gratification, he continually justified his actions to himself by choosing to believe that somehow the Lord understood—that it had to be acceptable because he was already married to Jennifer in his heart.

And as usually happens when consciences become seared, the young lovers added deceit and duplicity to their other shortcomings, to cover up their whereabouts when a parent phoned, or when Joe and Katie asked them where they had disappeared for so long.

They told no one of their intimacy, not even their best friends. They could not afford for anyone to know, and besides, it was nobody's business but their own, they reasoned. Michael might lose his summer job at the church and his double major in music and business would be lost, not to mention his reputation as a fine, young Christian man.

And he made it a priority always to have her back in her dorm room at a decent hour. He did not want her to be thought of in any light other than a positive one and at first, he guarded her reputation religiously.

But he always hated coming back to The Suite alone. Not seeing her lying in his bed, not listening to the soft rhythm of her breathing, not having her lovely head on his pillow, filled him with such loneliness and empty aching that he soon had her tell Katie that he was taking her back to Mobile on Friday nights, driving back early Sunday for his church commitments. In truth, they would stay in town, "honeymooning" all weekend.

And as they honeymooned, they would plan their wedding, choosing the right music, planning the reception, discussing whether to write their own vows or use the traditional ones or do a combination of both, deciding what would be the destination of their wedding trip.

Little did they know at the time, but they were already experiencing the glowing, warm, blissful sensations of a married couple's first year together, and the actual ceremony and events that followed would have been somewhat of a disappointment and a letdown to them. Like Jennifer's never experiencing the wonderful, thrilling surprise of Christmas morning because she had already opened the gifts the night before.

Nevertheless, now the couple was totally, completely enraptured with each other. Neither one had ever been this happy and contented in his or her life. Their future appeared so bright and the present so thrilling that each new day was viewed as an incredible gift that was to be enjoyed together—thoroughly enjoyed together in every aspect.

But as June gave way to July, and July to the first of August, the _consequences_ that had so haunted Michael the morning after Jennifer's birthday celebration were about to unfold in the most painful way yet—in a tormenting, dreadful way that would alter the courses of both of their lives forever.

Chapter Ten

*J*ennifer had a gnawing, gripping fear deep in her heart that at first she had refused to acknowledge, even to herself. As she sat in the waiting room of the Student Health Center on campus, she tried to hide a little more behind the column in the far corner of the old building's interior. She was deathly afraid that someone she knew might see her there and ask her what was wrong. And she knew it would be difficult to convince them that she only had a sore throat she wanted a doctor to look at, an excuse she had made up beforehand to give just in case she needed it. She was afraid that the deadly fear she had been harboring in her heart might betray itself in her countenance, and whoever it was that might have asked her the question would immediately know the real reason she was there.

She was that paranoid because she was that frightened.

"Jennifer Jacobs. You're next," the voice of the clinic nurse seemed to boom out at top volume to Jennifer's ears.

She looked around as she got up from her hidden seat and walked into an examination room. *Good,* she thought. *At least no one I know is here.*

The clinic nurse was a large, unattractive, unsympathetic, embittered old spinster who despised her job almost as much as she despised the young people all around her. She had taken the position because it was the only one she could find when the doctor she had worked with for over forty years had retired last May. And the school had hired her for the sole reason they had needed someone right away, and she was the only applicant because of the job's low pay. It was not a pleasant fit for either the university or the nurse.

"Well, what's your problem, Miss Jacobs?" the nurse asked bluntly, not even bothering to look at her patient but keeping her eyes on the form Jennifer had completed. "It says here on your paperwork that it is a 'personal' problem. That usually means either a venereal disease or a pregnancy or both. Which one is it?" she continued cruelly.

Jennifer was hurt, shocked, and angered by the old harridan's manner and question and just sat there, saying nothing.

"Come on, now. I have to know, young woman, if you want any service here, that is," she snapped impatiently, now glancing down at her patient out of curiosity and finding her pretty.

The nurse hated pretty young coeds more than all her other patients and loved to torment them if their problems had anything at all to do with sex. The hateful woman, herself, had never been tempted in the sexual arena of life, as she had been that dreadful combination of ill-tempered shrew and physical unattractiveness that men tend to avoid at all costs.

"I want to see a doctor," Jennifer replied with as much courage in her voice as she could muster. *I will go into town to find a private physician if I have to before I tell this nasty, mean old woman anything,* she told herself.

Just as Nurse Nasty was about to tear into her again, an old doctor walked into the office.

"What's the problem here," he inquired kindly.

He was a gray haired man of short stature with warm green eyes, wire-rimmed glasses, and an easygoing manner. His appearance reminded Jennifer of photographs in her history books of Harry S. Truman.

"Miss Jacobs, here, wrote down 'personal' on her form on the question asking about the nature of her visit," explained Nurse Nasty, barking out her words in a contemptuous manner, " and now she won't tell me what her problem is but insisted on talking to a doctor!"

"Well, maybe that's because her problem is personal," the doctor replied. He disliked Nurse Nasty as much as anyone else and would try to rescue as many young coeds as he could from her clutches. He finished with, "You may go, Miss Bates, and I will talk with Miss Jacobs. Just leave the door open slightly, and we will be fine."

The nurse left in a huff, the way she always did, and the kind doctor looked at his attractive but anxious patient, patted her hand paternally, and said, "Now there, young lady. What can I do for you today?"

The old doc liked the young women on campus. He had raised four daughters and two sons himself.

Relieved that the evil nurse was gone, Jennifer looked at the kind campus physician and stammered, "I need ... I am afraid ... I need to know ... if I am ... if ..."

"Pregnant?" the wise old man filled in.

He had been in this position more times lately than he would ever have dreamed. This was his third one this morning alone. *Blast and confound these young men!* he thought. In his eyes, it was always the fault of the male, for in his day, no man worth his salt would dare deflower the purity and innocence of a sweet, young virgin. And this lovely lass certainly couldn't have been at fault. She looked a lot like his youngest, Lisa, did at that age. *Dark and slender like her mother.*

Jennifer bit her trembling lip, dropped his eye contact, and muttered, "Yes."

She had determined before she went there this morning that she *was not* going to cry like a baby. Like a baby! And she started to cry.

"Now, now, Miss Jacobs," comforted the doctor calmly. "Believe me, it's not the end of the world, though you may think it is now. Tell me, just how late are you?"

"About ... about ... three weeks, I think, or thereabouts ... Maybe four," she replied, trying to stop her tears.

Walking over to the desk against the wall, he picked up a calendar and gave it to her.

"Can you recall the first day of your last menstrual period? Do you have regular periods, or do they vary a lot?" he asked as her worried eyes studied the calendar.

"Oh, no, they are very regular," she responded. "Every twenty-eight to twenty-nine days or so ... I remember now. It was June the seventh. That was my last one." And she blushed.

She remembered that vividly because her birthday 'celebration' with Michael had been on the fourth, and she had been so relieved to start her period on the seventh, even though she knew it would have been unlikely that she could have become pregnant at that late date in her cycle.

"Are you experiencing any other symptoms—tenderness of your breasts, more frequent urination, nausea, fatigue?" he inquired kindly while lining up the dates on his gestational wheel.

"Yes … a little of ... all of them." And she bit her lip again to try not to cry any more. But she began to tremble involuntarily.

Blast these lousy young men! the good doctor thought again. *It's not looking good for you, young lady.*

"Have you told your boyfriend?" he gently probed, his eyes now refocused on her face, his sympathy for her growing as he noticed the trembling and the brave attempt to squelch the tears.

"It's my fiancé ... and, no ... I haven't told Mi-... him ... I wasn't sure and didn't want to ..." she began, falteringly and stopped before she completed her thought.

"Worry him? Well, who in the world should worry along with you, Miss Jacobs, if not your fiancé?" the doctor reasoned, his voice becoming a little irritated at that young, irresponsible, poor-excuse-of-a-man.

But seeing the alarmed, ashamed eyes of his patient caused him to rein in his exasperation at the phantom fiancé and turn his attention back to the medical matter at hand. Looking down kindly at Jennifer once more, he continued in a professional but sympathetic voice.

"Now I need to get a urine sample from you to run through our little lab. If you can wait about twenty or thirty minutes, we can know for sure. According to the information you gave me, you could be eight weeks pregnant with a due date of about March fourteenth. If so, I want to start you on prenatal vitamins, and we can set up an appointment for you with a local obstetrician, if you'd like us to."

"Eight weeks? That far?" And she trembled even more, her eyes now wide with fear.

"Yes, dear. Eight weeks. You remember from biology class, conception usually occurs thirteen to fifteen days after the start of your last menstrual period, and delivery usually occurs forty weeks after. So you may be eight weeks along in a forty week pregnancy," he explained patiently. *Poor lass. I hope the young man really is her fiancé. I don't see any ring on her finger. She just keeps twirling that bracelet around and around on her wrist.*

"Try not to worry, dear. When were you going to be married?" he asked softly.

"Not until next June." And she began to tear up some more. "But I don't understand," she continued, drying her eyes. "We were using birth control … devices. How could this happen?"

"What kind of birth control?" he inquired, studying her worried face.

"You know … Mich- … My fiancé took care of that part … you know …" she stumbled, embarrassed, her cheeks rosy red, her eyes dropping contact with his once more.

"Condoms?" he asked, and she nodded. He then elucidated, "If you knew how many condom pregnancies I have seen over my many years of practice … Why it would populate a small town, my dear! Condoms have to be worn properly, applied early, and removed at once, or else there is a good chance of failure. And sometimes they rip or tear, or there may be defect. You just can't rely on them one hundred percent. And," he added with a playful, knowing sparkle in his eyes, "they do absolutely no good at all sitting in the box on the night table."

That was his favorite condom joke, but he regretted telling it to Miss Jacobs as she began to weep again.

A plague on that young man! he thought. *He should be here watching his fiancée cry her eyes out. Just bring him to me, dearie, and I will show him the light, all right!* thought the sweet old gentleman.

"There, there, young lady. We don't know for sure yet, and even if it is true, all you have to do is to tell that young man of yours to bump that wedding date up a bit. Are you okay?" he asked gently, his hand on her shoulder to comfort her.

She nodded and tried to dry her eyes. But more tears continued to form in their sad, dark depths.

"All right, then, just go into the bathroom over there and leave the urine specimen in the plastic cup on the window. Then you can come back in here and wait. I will come to tell you the results myself, okay?"

He really liked this Miss Jacobs. *How I'd like to kick that young man's sorry backside from here to Georgia!* he thought as he showed her the bathroom and went to see his next patient. *Better not be another pregnancy,* he thought. *This so-called sexual "revolution" is destroying so many innocent, young hearts. Damn and blast these lecherous young men!*

Of course, the test was positive. Jennifer was eight weeks pregnant. And she was frightened. More frightened than she had ever been in her young adult life. Almost as scared as when her daddy had left home for the last time before her parent's divorce.

She told herself not to be so frightened. It was like the kind doctor had said. All they had to do was to move the wedding forward a little ... Well, more than a little, but that would be okay, wouldn't it? Surely, that would be fine with Michael.

Michael! How was she going to break the news to him? This was Friday, August third, and Michael's parents were driving up from Mobile to visit him. Jennifer was due at The Suite to help him clean it before their expected arrival this afternoon, and they were all going out to dinner at The Springs tonight to celebrate, as a family, the engagement of their son to lovely Jenny Jacobs.

The irony of her being pregnant and Dr. Evans being an obstetrician fell heavily upon her. Dr. Evans had been a favorite of Jennifer's. He was the kindest deacon at Hillside and had always made her feel special. Mrs. Evans, too, had been so sweet and supportive of her. How she liked them both and looked forward to becoming a part of their family! A real, whole, happy, family—not the broken, dysfunctional one that she had known.

She knew she could not tell Michael the news until after his parents had left on Saturday afternoon. He would naturally be upset and would find it impossible to hide his emotions from his family. But how could she hide her own fears from them all until then? She would have to do the best acting job of her life, though all her friends told her she was a lousy actress. She would have to show them, all right, and herself that they were wrong! She could do this, for Michael's sake. She could do anything at all for Michael.

But still, try as hard as she might, she could not stop the worrisome, panicky thoughts from sweeping over her spirit like a tsunami overtakes a port city. As she drove from the campus to The Honeymoon Suite to help Michael prepare for his parents, the dire reality of her situation flooded her mind with problems heaped upon problems as she tried to think of a solution to her crisis.

What will happen to us now ... with a baby due March 14th? We will have to get married right away ... as soon as possible, and hopefully no one will guess our problem ... Not for a while, at least. She hoped for a millisecond, until her realistic, honest nature forced her to accept the truth.

Who am I kidding? Of course, everyone will know! Everyone will know, and Michael may even lose his job at the church. Oh, no! Lose his job? That $75 a week isn't really a job! He will have to drop out of school and get a real job! No! No! I won't let him do that! I can get a job and somehow we will manage. But who would hire me, knowing I am pregnant? No one would! Maybe I can just not tell the prospective employer of my "condition." But that wouldn't be fair or honest, would it?

I know ... I can work out of our apartment, typing reports, theses, and dissertations. I could get lots of work here doing that, surely! But could I earn enough money to support us both and pay Michael's tuition? Of course not! Maybe our parents will help us ... but how can we ask or expect them to pay for our mistakes? They will be so angry and hurt to begin with, so how can we ask them for help? Oh, Lord! What have we done? We have sinned and destroyed our lives! That's what!

She was in a state of true emotional turmoil at this point, and to make matters worse, felt a sudden wave of nausea sweep over her. Pulling the car over into a gas station lot, she ran to the bathroom and vomited, crying all the while. When the episode was over, she washed her mouth and splashed her face with cold water, trying to compose herself.

I can't think like this ... not now. I must not allow myself to dwell on any of this until after Michael's parents have left tomorrow evening. Then I can indulge myself with thinking these kinds of thoughts ... and it won't be so bad then, because Michael will be there with me. Michael will figure something out to make things work somehow. And we will have each other, so together we will be able to conquer this crisis.

Using all the willpower at her command, she ordered herself not to think anymore about their problem until Dr. and Mrs. Evans pulled out of the parking lot tomorrow evening. She got back into her old car, found a breath mint in her purse, and drove the rest of the way to The Suite with a firm resolve to win an Academy Award for the next thirty-six hours. *I can do this! I can do this! It's just until tomorrow evening. Then Michael and I will make our plans together.*

"Hello, Toots," her handsome fiancé grinned at her as she entered The Suite. "Thanks for coming over to help me clean up the place a bit. Though it really isn't too bad, because you're a such a good housekeeper, Jen." He walked over to her side and gave her a hug, looking at her curiously.

"Hey, are you all right? You look like you've been crying. Is everything okay?" he added, concerned.

"Oh, yeah," she replied and smiled. "I think I just have some allergies ... you know, hay fever ... It's that time of the month ... of the year, I mean."

"I didn't know you had any allergies," he responded as he began to load the dishwasher.

Thank heaven you didn't notice my Freudian slip, she thought.

"Oh, not many. Just a few little ones. Not much," she lied. She then took a deep breath, asking, "What can I do to help?"

"Can you check the clothes washer for me? I put in the sheets and stuff. I think they're ready to be thrown in the dryer now. Mom and Dad are staying at a hotel because I only have one bedroom, you know, but I wanted them to think I wash my sheets and towels even if I don't have overnight guests ... Well, no one but you, that is, and I'd hardly call you my 'guest,'" he added, a playful smile lighting his face.

As she put the clean clothes into the dryer, she returned, "What, then, would you call me, Mikey?"

He walked over to her side and helped load the machine, saying,

"Oh, I'd call you my lover, my bride-to-be, my heart's desire, my better half ... You know, something along those lines. But by this time next year, I'll be calling you 'the old ball and chain' or 'the old battle axe,'" he teased.

As she did not smile or hit him playfully the way she usually did, but only stared straight ahead and wiped her eyes with her fingers, he stopped and asked,

"Hey, Jenny. Are you really okay? Stop that a minute and look at me. You're not nervous about this engagement dinner with my parents tonight, are you? You know they are crazy about you, don't you?"

She knew she had to win that Oscar now or the whole weekend was sunk. With all her self-control and resolve, she turned and looked him in the eyes, waving some of her clean, damp undergarments in his face.

"Just look at this, Michael! You washed my underwear in with this load! Just think what your parents would say if they saw *these* in your clothes washer! You really need to be more careful. Why, what might they think then?" And she smiled a coquettish, seductive smile at him, trying to throw him off track.

"Ooo, that's right!" he acknowledged quickly, his eyes widening. "And your toothbrush and some of your cosmetics are in my bathroom, too. Let's both have a quick walk through to make certain there are no clues as to our honeymooning before the wedding. You check the bathroom, and I'll check the bedroom."

As Jennifer dutifully obeyed his request and removed her personal hygiene products from his bathroom, he called out to her from his bedroom as he rummaged through his chest of drawers,

"Oh gosh, I'd better hide the condoms, too. Where could I put them? ... Say, could you take them back with you and just lock them in your car's glove box or something?"

"Sure," she replied flatly. *Fat lot of good they did!* she thought bitterly. Yet forcing herself not to think any further on the subject, she asked him, "But what makes you think your parents are going to rifle through your underwear drawer in search of them in the first place?"

He paused a minute and looked in her direction thoughtfully before replying.

"Good question ... A guilty conscience, I guess?" he laughed ruefully. "I can just see myself, sitting on the sofa talking with them, beads of perspiration forming on my forehead as I am thinking, 'Don't look in the sock drawer! Don't look in the sock drawer!'—You know, sort of like that poor guy in Poe's story, 'The Tell Tale Heart'—until they both read my thoughts, march straight into my bedroom, dump the contents of the sock drawer onto the floor, and yell, 'Aha!' as they expose the condom box."

He threw his arms up in victorious emphasis to his parents' daydreamed discovery.

" 'Aha?' I can't see either of your folks ever saying 'Aha!'" she responded, smiling very weakly at his imagination and histrionics. *But, what would they say if they knew the whole truth, Michael? No! I can't think of that now.*

"You're right, Jen." And he frowned a little, walked over to her, placed his arms on her shoulders and continued seriously, "It's just that ... My dad has always had this uncanny ability to see right through me and—"

"Your dad? That's usually the mother's job, isn't it?" she interrupted, her eyes avoiding contact with his.

"I know. It's backwards at my house. I could always maneuver my way around my mom pretty easily. You know, turn on that masculine charm and everything," and he winked at her before growing serious again. "But with my dad ... Well, he somehow always knew what I was up to ... and ..." His eyes grew very solemn before he finished. "I wouldn't want to disappoint him for anything. It sounds hokey, I know, but I really want my dad to be proud of me, Jen."

She pretended to pick some lint off his shirt collar so not to have to look him in the eyes, sighed deeply, and replied, "I'm sure that both of your parents are very proud of you, Michael."

"Well, they will be now that I am fortunate enough to be marrying you, Toots! They have always loved you, Jenny, you know. Mom always said you were the prettiest girl at Hillside and couldn't understand why all the boys weren't fluttering around you." And he placed his hand under her chin, raised her lips to his, and kissed her sweetly.

She was glad for the kiss, because she could close her eyes. She could not allow him access to her eyes at that moment. He would know right away that something was terribly wrong.

"Let's get finished here, because I have some things I need to do back at the dorm," she said while pulling herself out of his embrace, and she quickly busied herself in another room.

They finished cleaning the apartment in record time, and it was time for her to leave. While walking her downstairs to her car, Michael took her hand in his and requested,

"Can you wear that blue dress again tonight? You know, the one you wore on your birthday? I will never forget it. You had on that dress, sitting at the dinner table across from me, when I first realized how much I love you. You look so pretty in it. My dad will think I am the luckiest man in the world to be engaged to you, Jenny. You are so beautiful." He kissed her good bye and said they would be there around seven o'clock to pick her up.

As soon as she drove out of sight of his apartment complex, she burst into tears again. *O Lord, please, please help me stay calm and happy tonight! Please let me know everything is going to be all right!*

Sadly, it was the first real prayer she had prayed in several weeks now. And she was not certain that it made it all the way up to heaven.

The dinner at The Springs was a big success. Everyone seemed to enjoy themselves immensely. Dr. and Mrs. Evans welcomed Jennifer into their family with open arms and did not cease to tell her how very beautiful she looked in her vibrant blue gown.

Mrs. Evans kept up a steady stream of conversation with Jennifer concerning the wedding. She was so glad they had chosen June. She and Dr. Evans had been married in June, also, and they would be following in a happy tradition. And no bride was lovelier than a June bride. She asked Jennifer all kinds of detailed questions about how she wanted the ceremony to be, and told her she would be glad to help in any way, but she would gladly stay out of the way, too, whatever Jennifer wanted her to do. She chided her son gravely for not having purchased an engagement ring yet and did not like the idea of an engagement bracelet. She knew that many of hers and Dr. Evans' friends would want to throw them engagement parties and bridal showers next spring. She was very, very kind.

And Jennifer, although she managed to pull off another Academy Award winning acting job, was very, very miserable.

Beth's borrowed dress was fitting her tighter around the chest and the waist than it had two months ago, and she was worried that Michael might notice. She need not have worried, though, because all he noticed was that she looked so absolutely gorgeous, like a rose that was in full bloom. He did observe that the bodice of the dress appeared tighter, showing off her lovely bosom better, but that only made him enjoy gazing at her all the more.

He and his dad were talking about how his double major in music and business should indeed help him find a good job next June. Dr. Evans had some business contacts in Nashville, too, and was already putting out feelers to get a good job lead for his son. He congratulated Michael on his choice of Jennifer to be his bride, saying that she was very lovely and intelligent, and had always possessed such a sweet vulnerability and softness that had touched his heart when she was a young girl at Hillside, adding that he expected him to take good care of her.

Toward the end of the meal, Dr. Evans offered a toast "to their happy lives together, blessed with health, joy, and the sound of children's laughter ringing up and down the hallways of their future home." At this toast, Jennifer blushed tremendously, and Michael playfully pointed it out to all at the table saying, "You can always tell what Jennifer is thinking by her very enchanting blushes."

As they all rode back in his luxury car to take Jennifer to the dorm, Dr. Evans addressed both of them from the front seat.

"I had a conversation with a patient of mine who happens to be the sister of Pastor Bob at the church you are working for, Michael, and she told me what a grand job you are doing there. And you, too, Jennifer. She said that all the kids really look up to you both and admire you tremendously, and that you are terrific examples to them of good, upright morality and virtue in this permissive age. She wanted me to pass that along to you both. Your mother and I are very proud of you, Son, and of course, you too, soon-to-be Daughter."

Both young people were glad that it was dark in the car, as they had trouble responding properly to that compliment both in their countenance and in their demeanor. Jennifer, especially, began to fight back tears.

I'm almost home. I'm almost home, she repeated over and over to control herself. *I can make it through this evening. I'm almost home.*

When they arrived at Dorm 10, Jennifer thanked the Evans' so much for such a lovely evening and asked them if they cared to come into the lobby to visit. They declined kindly while kissing her goodnight and saying everyone appeared tired, and that they looked forward to seeing her tomorrow for lunch at Michael's apartment. He had plans to grill out steaks and make his famous Caesar salad for everyone.

Walking her to the door, Michael took her cold hand in his and asked seriously, trying unsuccessfully to make direct eye contact with her,

"Do you feel as bad as I do about that last remark from Dad?"

When she nodded, he rationalized, "By this time next year we will have already been married two months now. We have to keep that in mind, Jen. The Lord must understand, don't you think?"

She nodded again, only because she desperately needed to be alone in her room to cry and cry her tensions and anxieties away after the charade of this dinner with his dear family. He took the tears forming in her eyes to mean that she agreed with his own guilt, and offered on parting, as he kissed her good night,

"Don't worry, Jennifer. You are my beautiful, brown-eyed girl. And I love you very much. Everything will work out all right. Just wait and see."

Chapter Eleven

"Good-bye, now!" called out Dr. and Mrs. Evans as they seated themselves in their car in the parking lot of the apartment complex late the next afternoon. "Be careful, you two! Watch yourselves now. We know how difficult it can be to control yourselves until the wedding, you know. We're not *that* old and over-the-hill yet," Michael's dad observed with a sparkle in his eyes but still with dead seriousness as he shook his son's hand and patted him on the back. "Remember, Son, you want to start your marriage out on the right track by honoring God and each other."

"Oh, Rick," Mrs. Evans smiled to her husband upon hearing his remark as she gave Jennifer a parting hug and kiss. "Must you talk so to these two? Just look at Jennifer. You've made her blush again. Pay no attention to him, Jenny, dear. He gives this little speech to all young couples. It's the nature of his business, you know. Bye now, kids, and Michael, try to pick up that telephone of yours and call your mother sometime, okay? I like to know that you are still alive. Jennifer, make him call me every once in a while. He'll listen to you. Bye now!"

With those words of warning, wisdom, and guilt, Michael's parents pulled out of the parking lot, smiling and waving until they were out of sight.

"Well," he began after they left. "That went very well, don't you think? My parents are crazy about you, Jen, and so am I!" he stated with feeling and squeezed her shoulders tightly.

He had been standing there with his arm around her shoulders the whole time his parents were talking. And he felt Jennifer tremble slightly when his dad gave them his "official" warning about controlling themselves. He had had a difficult time, himself, maintaining eye contact with his father during those few words of instruction, so he thought he understood the reason for her trepidation.

But now that his parents were well out of sight, Jennifer's trembling only worsened. He turned around to look into her face and was surprised to see that she was crying.

"What in the world is wrong, Jenny?" he asked, his eyebrows knitted in concern. "My parents simply adore you. Why are you crying?"

"Oh, Mikey!" was all she could say as she covered her face with her hands and shook with still more tears.

"Come on, Sweetheart, let's go inside and talk," he instructed, gently leading her back into The Suite. "What's wrong?"

He was not all that concerned at this point, thinking it was just the strain of the official engagement dinner that had made her nervous, or something along those lines. Women cry so easily, he knew, and over the silliest things. When they walked into the living room, Jennifer collapsed upon the sofa and cried even harder. He sat down beside her, placing one arm around her shoulders, and cradled her head against his chest, gently stroking her soft hair with his other hand.

"Don't cry, Jennifer," he said soothingly. "Tell me what the trouble is. What is it?"

As the seconds and minutes ticked off the clock on the wall, and she still was having trouble articulating her sorrow, Michael began to feel a little uneasy himself. *What could make her cry and shake like this? This isn't nerves. This is something more serious than that.*

A terrifying thought entered his mind, but he quickly discarded it. Why borrow trouble? He asked her again what the problem was. Finally, after a few moments she calmed herself enough to speak and explained, still through tears,

"Oh, Michael ... I went to the Student Health Center yesterday morning ... you know ... before I came over here to help you clean up The Suite ... and ..." she faltered. She could feel his arm muscles tighten and his hand stopped stroking her hair.

"And ... What, Jen? Go on. What happened there?" he questioned, tensing even more.

"And ... I talked to a very kind doctor ... But the nurse was so mean and hateful! So very nasty! ... She made me feel so ... awful and cheap ... and dirty!" she cried more at the memory of Nurse Nasty.

"Go on, Jenny ... Why did you go to the health center? What did the nice doctor say?" his voice was anxious and insistent though still calm and tender.

"He said ... He said ... That I'm ... That we're ... Oh, Michael! We are going to have a baby! I am pregnant!" and she sobbed even harder.

"Oh, no! No, Jennifer, no! That can't be true!" He removed his arm from around her shoulders, sat directly in front of her, one hand on each shoulder, and looked her squarely in the face, his own face white. "How can that be true? Did he do an exam? What kind of test did he use? It can't be true! We have been taking birth control measures!"

Suddenly, Jennifer was scared to death. This was not the reaction she had needed or expected from him. His panic only added to her growing anxiety, and she looked him fearfully in the eyes and responded with emotion,

"The doctor said that condoms are not fool proof. He said that the condom pregnancies he had seen over the years would populate a small town. He said they could rip or tear—"

"Yeah, yeah, I know all about that, Jennifer," he interrupted her. "But we didn't have one rip or tear, did we?" he asked. He was standing up now, pacing back and forth in the living room, pulling at his wavy blonde hair, his blue eyes worried and extremely troubled.

"No ... but remember that night ... several weeks ago ... you know... the time ..." she began. They both recalled that evening when there had been a slippage and possible leaking because of it.

"Oh, yes, I remember now! Oh, Lord! ... Oh, God! ... How could this happen? Why now? ... And to us, of all people on this campus?" he asked rhetorically.

"Michael! Please stop that pacing! You are making me nervous! I am pregnant. And so we are going to have to be married earlier than we had planned. Right?" she pleaded for his comfort.

"Oh, yeah! I whole hell of a lot earlier than we had planned!" he replied in frustration.

"Don't swear at me, Michael!" she responded. "It's not my fault, you know! I didn't plan this. I certainly don't want to be pregnant now. Not now!" And her tears began to flow once more.

He stopped his pacing, suddenly feeling very guilty. If he was fearful, how much more must Jennifer be. And she had known about this all weekend and had kept it a secret in front of his parents. His parents! Oh, no! He sighed, sank back down on the sofa by her side, and held her in his arms.

"I'm sorry, Jennifer. It's just such a shock ... Such a shock ... So unexpected, that's all," he tried to sound comforting, but his mind was racing. "Was the doctor sure? What test did he use?" he asked, hoping that some type of miraculous error had occurred to make the test results false.

"He used a urine test that he said was over ninety percent accurate," she answered.

"Then there is a chance of an error," he stated, still in denial, grasping at straws.

"Yes, I suppose so. But there are other symptoms I am experiencing," she began.

"Such as ... ?" he asked.

"Such as morning sickness, swollen, tender breasts, more frequent urination, I'm very tired all day, my clothes are fitting tighter ... And haven't you noticed that I haven't had a period since June the seventh?" she wondered.

He was up again, pacing the room, "No, Jen, to be honest with you, I haven't noticed. Oh, no! ... Not since June seventh! ... And this is August fourth ...That means—" he broke off, panicking even more.

"The doctor said I was eight weeks along in a forty week pregnancy, starting from the first day of my last menstrual period... That the baby will be due around March the fourteenth," she completed his thought.

"March the fourteenth? That's just great! Before I even graduate from this damned, hell hole of a university!" he expounded angrily and pounded his fist on the doorframe. "Yeah, that's just great!

There I'll be … a penniless student with three more months of school, a wife to support, and a new baby! Damn! Of all the damned, rotten luck!"

Jennifer hated it when Michael swore because he so rarely did it. It was out of character for him, and it made her more afraid than ever. Suddenly, she felt extremely ill. She ran into the bathroom, slamming the door behind her, and vomited as quietly as she could into the toilet she had cleaned so well yesterday just about this time.

At the sound of her illness, Michael came back to the reality of her suffering all this time, all by herself, for these many weeks now when she must have suspected she was pregnant. And he felt the guiltiest he had ever felt in his entire life. Even guiltier than when he had skipped school and deliberately taken his dad's car without permission, driving a couple of friends to Panama City, Florida, one Friday during his senior year in high school. He would never forget the look of disappointment and distrust on his father's face when he returned late Saturday evening. That day had been miserable for him.

But it in no way compared to this one.

He sighed deeply, composed himself, walked over to the bathroom door and gently knocked on it. As he walked in, he turned on the faucet in the sink. Squeezing out a clean washcloth, he knelt beside his fiancée and tenderly wiped her forehead and face with its cold, damp surface. He then flushed the toilet, took her in his arms, and spoke comfortingly.

"Oh, Jenny, please forgive me. I am behaving like such a jerk when you must be scared to death. And sick, too. Please forgive me."

At his kindness and out of her own embarrassment at being sick in front of him, she began weeping again.

As they knelt there together in front of the commode in The Honeymoon Suite, he stroked her hair again and told her over and over, hoping to convince both her and himself, "Don't worry, Jenny. Everything's going to be all right. Just wait and see."

He took her back to the dorm early that evening. She looked very tired from all the emotional strain of the past two days, and he needed some time to himself, time away from her disturbing tears, time to think long and hard. After he had deposited her safely at Dorm 10 with a goodnight kiss and more verbal assurances, he ran to his car and took a very long drive out into the surrounding countryside. There was a full moon in the cloudless sky and many stars were out, all twinkling merrily, oblivious to his extremely painful dilemma.

He pulled over off the main road and stepped out of his car. A barn and a farmhouse stood just up ahead, and several cows were standing around chewing their cud behind a barbed wire fence, not paying any particular attention to him, as cows are wont to do. He pulled out a long blade of grass and chewed meditatively on it right along with the cows, sat down on the hood of his car, and began thinking in circles, trying to discover a way to "make everything all right," as he had promised Jennifer he would. His troubled thoughts were warring against the peace of that warm, moist, August night in Alabama in 1975.

Well, I guess we just have to get married right away. There is simply nothing else to do. The longer we postpone the wedding, the more obvious it will be that we had to get married, he thought. *"Had to get married!"* How he hated that phrase! How he remembered the snide remarks people would make about such unfortunate couples. People could be so cruel. Especially the self-righteous, holier-than-thou types that seemed to flourish so well in this climate. *And the stigma will be on Jennifer, sweet, sweet, vulnerable, still innocent Jennifer,* he knew. *How unfair!* he reasoned. *After all, I was the one who seduced her into believing the honeymoon before the wedding bit! It's all my fault, but everyone will blame Jenny.*

At this point in his reverie, he got up from his car and began walking down the dirt farm road, still chewing on that blade of grass. The crickets and cicadas were almost deafening, and there was a soft breeze blowing as he rambled on, lost in thought.

How foolish of me to buy into the "HBTW" thing myself, he reasoned. *Well, I guess there are newlyweds who get pregnant on their honeymoons, too. And now there can be no formal wedding like the kind we had planned.* Michael had always enjoyed weddings.

They were such happy events. He was asked to sing at so many, and paid handsomely for the brief work, too. *And now, Jenny and I will have to sneak off somewhere to some God forsaken justice of the peace to be married. It isn't fair!*

His thoughts became more embittered and contorted the longer he walked down that moonlit road out in the middle of nowhere. *No, it's not fair. Jennifer deserves to have a wonderful wedding, all dressed up like Cinderella in a beautiful, white gown with flowers in her hair!* He remembered how lovely and enticing she looked in that simple white gown the night of the fraternity party. *She deserves to have all her girlfriends as her bridesmaids and be the center of attention, loved and admired by everyone in attendance. Oh, what have I done to you, Jenny?* he punished himself.

Stopping, he picked up a rock and hurled it angrily into the woods on one side of the path. As it landed, he heard the scurrying sounds of some animal that it had frightened, perhaps a raccoon or an opossum, or even a skunk. *A skunk,* he thought bitterly. *That's just what I feel like ... a stinking, miserable, lousy skunk!* But at the sounds of the animal fleeing in fear, he immediately felt somewhat better. At least he was not the only creature in these woods tonight who was frightened!

He also remembered his father's instruction to him last night at dinner, to take good care of Jennifer. *Yeah, I've taken good care of Jennifer, all right.* Last night at dinner! It seemed like a million years ago. How bright his future appeared to him last night! And poor Jennifer knew all along, and had to sit there listening to his mother talk on and on about teas and showers and parties next spring. *Now, there'll be no teas and showers and parties,* he thought angrily. *None, that is, unless it's a baby shower given by someone who "feels sorry for the poor dears."*

Baby shower! Baby! No, I'm not ready to be a father, he worried. *I know nothing at all about babies, nor do I desire to be anyone's daddy yet. Not yet! Not for several more years! I'm still young myself, and so is Jennifer. We should have at least a couple of years to ourselves to enjoy each other without waking up tired and grumpy each morning because the baby cried all night. It's just not fair!* he whined on to himself.

And won't my parents be proud of me ... of us! Yeah, they'll be proud, all right! Again, he remembered his father telling them both last night how proud he was of them. *I wonder if Dad will even continue to pay my tuition after he finds out. He may think that since I am a "married man" now with a wife and a baby on the way, it's time I started acting like it ... and he wouldn't be far off base in that assessment either. Will I have to drop out of school my senior year and get some dead end, low-paying job just to pay for diapers and baby food?* he wondered bitterly.

He also recalled his father's comments about how the church looked up to and admired them as sterling examples to the youth. *I'll be lucky to keep that so-called "job" now. No, that's not so. We can probably hide the pregnancy until the end of the month, and I will be finished there by then, anyway. But they will eventually know. And my future employer in Nashville will know, too, if word gets around. Would they still hire me in the Christian music business if they discover that my bride and I "had to get married?"*

A tight knot began to form in the pit of his stomach, and he hit himself over and over again on his right thigh with his tightly balled fist as he walked on and on, giving full vent to every troubling thought that entered his mind, framing every problem that would face him in the worst possible light.

Jennifer's words of just a few weeks ago came back to haunt him. She had reminded him of his commitment to the young people to be a good example and to practice what he preached. *I should have listened to you, Jenny ... But, then again, you gave in to me pretty easily, too ... No! That's not fair of me! I am not going to blame Jennifer for any of this! She tried to resist me in the car those times and tried to get Katie to come to the apartment that day. It's not her fault. I'm not going that route. What a miserable marriage we will have if I convince myself she "made me" marry her. That's a lie. But how in the world am I going to be able to support both her and the baby and stay in school, too?* he fretted.

Just where in his thought process his faith fit in, he was unaware. For Michael had kept the Lord at arm's length since he had become physically intimate with Jennifer. Without his conscious knowledge, he had distanced himself from that sweet, spiritual communion that was once the core foundation of his life. Self-deceived, he had placed his relationship with God on a back burner on slow simmer so that he could fulfill his own desires and longings to be with his lover, his bride-to-be, knowing subconsciously that were he to be totally honest and forthright with his Creator, he would not find approval for his current behavior. He had justified his actions to himself by believing that he was already married to Jennifer in his heart, that surely God must understand his love for her. And hadn't God created the powerful emotions of sexual passion anyway?

How long he continued walking that calm, clear night, he did not know. He wanted to walk and keep on walking until perhaps he had walked away from his problem. But there was no distance, however great, that could relieve him of his responsibility and duty to his pregnant fiancée. *I could never walk that far,* he reasoned. *Men who walk that far are the scum of the earth, are bottom dwelling, low-life rascals, rogues, and reprobates. No, I must take care of Jennifer now. That is my top priority. How I wish I had thought of all this before I lusted so much for her beautiful body! I just had to have her now! I couldn't wait.* <u>*Consequences.*</u> <u>*There are always consequences for our mistakes and sins.*</u> He knew it of a certainty, now. It was not just a meaningless aphorism implanted in his brain since childhood by the teachings of his religion.

As he continued on and on, forever walking late into that August, Alabama night, walking and pondering, walking and worrying, walking and hoping for a solution to erase this dreadful mistake of "outrageous fortune," somewhere in the very back of his mind, a sly, tiny, little voice was calling him to consider another alternative, a choice he had not given any thought to before now. A solution to his dilemma that only a very few at that time in 1975 had ever taken and that had always been anathema to him before now suddenly appeared and spoke to his mind. The little voice in his head began to reason with him.

"Come now, let us reason together," imposed the wily, subtle voice, urging him on. *"Perhaps you can avoid those painful consequences you feel are so inevitable right now. Why put Jennifer through all this suffering and humiliation? Why make her the laughingstock of all the hypocrites back at Hillside? Why disappoint your parents and*

the church and ruin your career on top of everything else? One little car trip to Atlanta on one afternoon next week will put everything right again. And everyone will be happy. And the future will look bright again instead of so foreboding and uncertain."

Seemingly out of nowhere, he was made aware of a conversation he had with Joe just last week. Joe had told him in confidence, as they were playing a round of golf on the new course by his apartment, of a fraternity brother of his who had gotten his girlfriend pregnant and had driven her to Atlanta to a women's clinic there for the termination of her pregnancy. Joe and he had both paused briefly and looked at each other, wondering if that was a bad mistake on the brother's part, or a wise move to alleviate a very troubling situation. Initially, they had thought it was cowardice on the guy's part and had left it at that, as just then, Michael had hit a tremendous drive off the tee of the twelfth hole, and the topic had quickly been forgotten.

But now, the cunning, crafty little voice was telling Michael in soothing, comforting tones that perhaps this would be the best thing he could do for Jennifer and himself—not to mention for their families, the church, their friends, and just about everybody in the whole state of Alabama.

"It's perfectly safe and legal now. Not like it was back in the old days. No back alleys. Respectable doctors and nurses in nice, clean, safe clinics could take care of your problem in just a few minutes. Then you could go back to the way it was."

Well, not quite, he thought cautiously. *I will make certain Jennifer gets on the birth control pill, even though she had refused to go to the clinic for them before all this happened because she had been afraid she might have had them discovered. And I'll use protection, too. That way, this can never, ever happen to us again!*

The more he rationalized and reasoned to himself, the better this plan appeared, and his walking pace quickened as this idea took root in his thought processes, bringing hope to circumstances that had appeared so hopeless just moments before. Why had he not thought of this option before? It made such good sense given their current situation. In fact, it was the only solution that made any sense at all to him now, and his mind began to throw off some of the tremendous burden of worry and confusion that had been pressing down on him so heavily.

After all, it's not a baby yet. It's just tissue—unformed, shapeless tissue. And Jennifer can still have her good reputation and her wonderful wedding, and I can finish school and everything will be back to the way it should have been. And we can always have lots and lots of children after a few years of marriage. We can have eight or nine, if she wants to! Yeah, this idea sounds like the best solution to our problem. And my parents won't be disappointed and neither will Jennifer's, and no one at all will need ever know. It will be our secret.

As he turned around on that country road lit by the full, round moon and the shining stars, and headed back toward his car, he thought, *I told Jennifer everything will be okay, not really believing it myself. But now, I truly can see the light at the end of this tunnel we're in. Yeah, everything <u>really</u> will be all right now.*

He ran all the way back to his car, so much relief did this plan bring to his troubled mind.

Chapter Twelve

M ichael was up bright and early Sunday morning. He woke up by himself, alone in his bed, a break in the usual pattern of the past few weeks, as Jennifer had usually spent both Friday and Saturday nights with him at The Suite. Although he missed her, he hoped that she had experienced a good night's restful sleep, sleep that would "knit up the raveled sleeve of her care," a phrase he remembered that Shakespeare or some other famous author had once said. He had been terribly concerned about her yesterday.

The constant worry she had carried by herself coupled with the nausea of her pregnancy had left her with the beginnings of dark circles under her eyes last night, and a tired, weary lethargy that was so unlike her had enveloped her as he drove her home. She had told him that the nice doctor had given her some prenatal vitamins to take and that she hoped they would make her feel more energetic. *Prenatal vitamins,* he thought. Soon she would no longer need those, he hoped. Soon she would be feeling fine, back to her old self, back to the Jennifer he knew and loved. Warm, vivacious, Jenny, with those large, dark, sparkling eyes and that enticing, sweet smile.

He wanted to phone her but it was still so early. He hoped she was still asleep. So he decided to go for a refreshing morning swim, then come back, call her, get ready for church, and ride over to pick her up from the dorm on his way.

How he wished that this pregnancy had not occurred! Though he had made the decision last night that it should be terminated, this morning he had a nagging uneasiness and concern that perhaps it was not the thing to do after all. And what if Jennifer did not like the idea? What would he do then?

Hoping the swim would help him overcome these new doubts, he plunged into the cool, refreshing depths of the clear water and peered up at the early morning, summer sky. *Surely, this is the only thing to do,* he persuaded himself as he swam lap after lap in the deserted pool. *By this time next week, everything will be back to where it was before this tragedy happened to us,* he reasoned. *Jennifer will be here with me at this very pool next Sunday afternoon, as she has been, wearing that great looking black bikini and looking as sexy as the mischief, and we will swim and sit in the pool chairs, drinking a soft drink and planning the wedding like we have been. There really is no other solution to this crisis that makes as good sense as this one. This will effectively erase our mistake and quickly make things right again. Yes, by this time next week everything will be okay.*

Jennifer had not felt like going to church that Sunday morning. Michael had phoned her as planned, but Katie had told him that she appeared to have a stomach flu or something, because she was sick in the bathroom. She had asked Katie to relay the message that she was going to skip church this morning, but could he please come by the dorm after the service. She hoped she would be feeling better by then.

Michael's uneasiness only increased upon hearing this. All during the church service as he led the choir and the congregational singing, he missed seeing Jennifer's face—her sweet, adoring face always smiling encouragement to him, always full of love for him. And he worried. *Was she still sick, her head hovering over the toilet? Was there anyone at the dorm to look after her if she needed them?* Katie and Joe were in the congregation, as Katie had told him that Jennifer had insisted that she go on to church, telling her that she was already feeling better. He could hardly wait until the service was over to go check on her, but he had to wait. He could not leave until the closing hymn was sung and hands were shaken and hugs were given to various members of the flock.

And he hated the lying, too. Everyone kindly inquiring after Jennifer and hoping she would soon be feeling well. He felt that he had the word, *"HYPOCRITE,"* tattooed on his forehead as he told them all she was sick with a stomach bug. *Yeah, it's a stomach bug, all right!* he told himself sarcastically.

All of this reinforced in him the truth that the trip to Atlanta had to be the best solution to their trouble ... really, the only solution. Inwardly he shuddered in shame and disgrace when he thought how disappointed and disillusioned all these good church people would be with him if they knew the truth. The true believers would vicariously partake of his painful downfall and suffer with him, while the hypocrites and cynics would laugh at and mock Jennifer and him behind their backs. How could he deal with that? How could that benefit anyone at all? No! He would not allow that! The termination of the pregnancy was the only viable solution.

By this time next week, all would be well again. And Jennifer would be feeling fine again, too. Yes, and he would have his sweet Jenny by his side again and everything would be okay. *Next Sunday, next Sunday,* he thought. *It will all be over by next Sunday.*

Racing over to the dormitory right after the service, he was relieved when Jennifer walked into the lobby, smiling a hopeful little smile and dressed in an attractive pair of slacks and a new blouse, apparently feeling much better. Her eyes, though worried a little, were shining, and she appeared rested and calm. So different from last night.

"Hello there, Toots." He embraced her gratefully while whispering in her ear, "I love you."

"I love you, too," she replied very quietly, her anxious eyes beginning to glisten again as tears were forming.

"No ... No more of that," he warned her gravely, shaking his finger in her face. "We are going to have a fantastic day today, Jenny. No more sadness ... okay?"

"Okay, Mikey. You're right. No more sadness. What's done is done, and everything will be fine," she responded resolutely, taking courage from him, and she smiled a real smile into his eyes.

But his eyes did not smile back at her. They quickly averted and his brow involuntarily wrinkled. Immediately, her smile left, too, and she felt suddenly uneasy as her finely honed, feminine ability to read subtle non-verbal nuances detected uncertainty and dissonance from his body language.

"What is it?" she asked with concern. "What's the problem, Michael? Everything *is* going to be okay, isn't it?"

He took a quick breath, smiled a crooked smile and responded firmly, "Sure, Jen, I told you I would take care of it ... take care of you, didn't I? Come on. Let's go get some lunch, and then maybe later we can sit out by the pool, if you feel like it, that is. How are you feeling? Can you eat some lunch?" And he led her out the door and down the steps toward his car as she replied.

"Yes, I think so. I am feeling better. Much better than this morning, I can tell you. Some vegetable soup and crackers sound real good to me. And I brought my vitamins with me. I'm supposed to take them with a meal—" she began as she pulled the bottle with the bold letters proclaiming "PRENATAL VITAMINS" from her purse.

But he interrupted her, asking quickly, "Jennifer, you didn't let Katie or anyone else see those vitamins, did you?"

"No. Of course not, Michael! Why are you so jumpy? I guess I can hide my condition for a little while longer, but Katie is not stupid, you know, and neither are any of my other friends ... That is, maybe with the exception of Tricia, the air-head … But we are getting married very soon, aren't we? Like maybe even this week, aren't we?" she questioned urgently, her eyes trying in vain to meet his. "I would really like to go ahead and do it, the sooner the better, Michael. Wouldn't you?"

They were in his car now, driving down the main road to their favorite family restaurant that was their traditional Sunday dining spot. It boasted a very good soup and salad bar in addition to delicious family style entrees. He pretended that he did not hear her question, so she repeated it.

"Michael, I said I would like us to get married as soon as possible, maybe even this week, wouldn't you? I don't want to have a bulging tummy before I have a wedding ring on my finger, do you? My pants are already getting harder to fasten," she demanded an answer both in her tone of voice and in the way she was tugging at his sleeve.

I don't want you to have a 'bulging tummy' now, at all, he thought as his eyes narrowed, but he replied,

"Let's talk about that after we eat, okay, Jen? Let's just try to have a pleasant lunch and then go to The Suite to talk about this, all right? Then, like I suggested, maybe we could go swim—"

"No! Michael, no! I want us to talk about it now! Why are you not wanting to talk?" She paused before adding, "Have you changed your mind ... about marrying me?" and her voice began to quiver slightly.

Suddenly annoyed at her insecurity and apprehension—perhaps because it mirrored his own—he quickly veered off the road and into an empty parking lot, turned to her, and stated with authority,

"Jennifer, of course I haven't changed my mind about marrying you! What kind of a jerk do you think I am? You are my responsibility, and I am not going to abandon you!"

"Your *'responsibility?'* What do you mean by that? Your *'responsibility?'* Do you mean you don't love me anymore?" she quizzed him, fear knocking on her heart's door again.

"No! That's not what I meant at all! Why are you trying to put words into my mouth? Of course, I love you! What I mean is that I am going to marry you ... Of course. I am not going to walk away from you like ... like a sorry bastard would!" he replied forcefully, his blue eyes blazing.

"Well, then, why are you not wanting to talk about the wedding... the marriage ... you know?" she persisted, peering very studiously into his eyes, trying to understand his thoughts.

He sighed deeply, avoiding her questioning eyes, and tried again, "Look, Jen. Can't we just eat lunch and then talk about this later this afternoon? I would just as soon not have this conversation here in this parking lot or in the dining room of the restaurant with strangers all around us!"

"Neither would I!" she returned, her own dark eyes now snapping right back at him. "Let's just skip lunch for now and go back to your apartment and talk! I want to discuss this now, Michael!"

"Okay! Fine with me! I've lost my appetite now, anyway!" he barked right back at her, and put the accelerator to the floorboard, spinning the tires as he catapulted out of the parking lot.

Neither one of them said one more word until he pulled into his parking spot at the apartment complex. Jennifer had been thinking, *No matter what he has said, he must not want to get married this week or he would have agreed with me. Then what could he be suggesting? What is left for us to do if not to be married as soon as possible?*

She did not wait for him to come around and open her car door as he usually did, but instead leapt out herself and walked very quickly, almost ran, up the steps to The Suite, not even glancing his way.

"Oh, great!" he remarked aloud at her irritated reaction. "Just great." *This is going to be a very rational, logical, composed conversation,* he thought.

As soon as he unlocked the door, she strode angrily in and plopped down on the sofa, her impassioned eyes challenging him as she stared resolutely into his face.

"All right. Now that we are here in the privacy of your home, please tell me why you don't want to get married this week," she demanded.

This was *not* the way he had planned to broach this subject with her. Nevertheless, he stood in the middle of the living room and began nervously, yet with determination, trying to choose his words very carefully.

"Jennifer, I don't know why you are so defensive about this ... why you are so adamant about getting married this week when we haven't really discussed all the ... ramifications of ... all the problems associated with ... all the options ... available to us to choose a wise—"

"What 'options?'" she returned, rudely interrupting him. "What 'options,' Michael? I am pregnant. I am expecting *our* baby on March the 14th of 1976. It is now August 5th, 1975. What 'options' do you have in mind, Michael?"

He would not meet her gaze.

"Jennifer, look, I *do* want to marry you! I wanted to marry you the night of your birthday party. But I am broke! I have one more year of school left, and I want to wait until June to marry you, like we have been planning all along! What's so wrong about that?" he asked her.

He realized the stupidity of his rhetorical question immediately, but she did not wait for him to explain himself. She shouted loudly, waving her arms as she spoke,

"'What's so wrong about that'? I can't believe you, Michael! 'What's so wrong about that' is that I suppose you mean you want me to be pushing a *baby carriage* down the aisle in front of me in June instead of carrying a bouquet of white roses! Is that what you mean?"

The pregnancy hormones that had been making her weepy were now kicking in but finding a new expression, causing her to display anger in a way Michael had never seen in her before. But he was up to her challenge and was angry, too.

He shouted right back at her, "No, of course not, Jennifer! Don't be such a jackass! You know that is not what I meant!"

He had allowed their anger and frustration with each other to escalate to that point, but upon observing the hurt expression on her face when he called her a 'jackass' and recalling her condition, he quickly repented and added more patiently, sitting down by her side, sighing deeply, and taking her hand.

"I'm sorry, Jen. I didn't mean to call you a name. We both need to calm down a little and discuss this more rationally and not read into each other's comments things that are not there ... Please?" he requested gently, peering into her wounded and fearful eyes.

"Okay ..." she sighed too, not liking to argue with her lover, her future husband. This was the first argument they had ever experienced. And over such a topic, too! It wasn't fair. She went on, more calmly but with an urgent, troubled tone, "Okay, Michael, but I need to know what options you are talking about. How can we wait until next June to be married when the baby—?"

He stood up again, began pacing, and broke in on her thoughts.

"It's not a baby yet, Jennifer. Not yet. You are just barely ... you know ... expecting ... and it's not a baby yet. There are ways that we can ... Things we can do to ..." he faltered, searching for words that did not sound so horrible to his own ears, much less to Jennifer's.

As he tried to explain, her face turned white with comprehension and she stammered softly, somewhat in shock, "Oh ... no ... no ... no, Michael ... You can't mean? ... You can't want me to have ... to get rid of the baby? ... Of *our* baby? ... Don't you want the baby?" Her voice trembled, and her right hand automatically, instinctively caressed her abdomen while her dark eyes were wide with unbelief and fear.

He could not look at them. He continued pacing and concluded brokenly, trying to use just the right words and phrases, not allowing himself to look at her until he was finished explaining.

"Please quit calling it a baby, Jen. It's not a baby yet ... Not yet ... And if we go to Atlanta this week ... to a clinic I found out about ... we can ... just not have a baby now and wait until after we have been married a couple of years ... and then have lots and lots of kids if you want to, and ..." he stopped, both pleading for her to understand what he had said thus far and because he did not know what else he could say.

Still white, Jennifer replied quietly, seemingly while standing outside herself, "I can't believe you want me to have an abortion, Michael. I can't believe it at all. The only girls who have abortions are the ones who have bad reputations ... Who are trashy and cheap ... Who sleep with boys they don't even care about ... and lots of them, too. And now you want me to ...?"

While she was speaking, she tried to look into his eyes to understand what he was saying. Surely he was not saying what her ears thought they heard.

He was seated back by her side in a moment, looking into her face, taking her hand in his and stating emphatically,

"No! That's not true, Jen! Not anymore, anyway! Maybe it used to be that way ... You know ... back before it was legal and all ... but not now! How could you even think I would suggest it if I thought it was still that way, Jennifer? You must believe me."

She was still in shock and said nothing, but stared at him in disbelief.

He continued, trying to explain how he arrived at his decision, still holding her hand tightly, his fingers nervously caressing hers, his eyes alternately meeting her own worried ones and then glancing quickly away, as if he could not fully afford to hold her gaze.

"If we ... don't have this ... Terminate the pregnancy now ... then we can be back to where we were before this weekend, don't you see? Remember how proud my parents were of us and how we were all excited about planning our wedding in June? Jen, I want you to have a beautiful, unforgettable wedding, all dressed up in a flowing white gown--"

"You want me to have an abortion now ... and then in June wear a flowing white gown?" she interrupted, her expression incredulous.

"Why do you want to make this so ... difficult and so ... so ... bad, Jenny? It is happening more and more these days. Why, I'll bet half the brides that walk down the aisle nowadays ..."

But he did not finish. And he could not look into her eyes.

They were both silent for a minute or two, as the clock on the wall ticked on.Jennifer's coloring was now returning to her cheeks, and the realization of what he was asking her to do flooded into her mind. She shook her hand free, the hand he had grabbed when he was begging her to terminate her pregnancy, and looked him squarely in the eyes.

"And what will you do if I don't agree to this, Michael?"

"What do you mean?" he requested.

"If I refuse to have the abortion, what will you do? Abandon me? Tell everyone it's not your baby?" she replied, her eyes at once both hurt and hard.

"Don't be so melodramatic, Jennifer!" he responded sarcastically to her challenge, also hurt and angry at her insult to his character. Standing up in front of her, he stated vehemently in frustration and anger, "Of course, I will go ahead and marry you now if you force me to and –"

She did not let him finish his thought, but jumped up and pushed him away with both of her arms and all of her strength, shouting loudly,

"IF I *'FORCE'* YOU TO ?!"

"Jen—That's not what I meant!" he tried to interject.

"IF I *'FORCE'* YOU TO?!" she continued screaming at him at the top of her lungs. "YOU don't have to worry about THAT, Mr. Michael Patrick Evans!! No, you don't have to worry about that AT ALL!! Because now that I know what you are really like, I WOULDN'T MARRY YOU IF YOU WERE THE LAST MAN ON THE PLANET!!"

And with those angry words emanating from a broken, disillusioned heart, she stormed out of his apartment.

"Jennifer! Jenny! Come back here and talk like a rational person!" he called out after her, trying to grab her hand and calm her down so she would listen to reason, but to no avail.

Her car had been parked at his apartment since yesterday, and she jumped in it, started the motor, and made the tires scream and smoke as she sped away from him as fast as she could.

"Damn!" he cried out loudly and hit the drywall with his fist, making a small indentation. "Damn it, Jennifer! Why won't you listen?" he spoke to a phantom and kicked at the unforgiving wall of The Honeymoon Suite.

Chapter Thirteen

*J*ennifer was pushing The Hulk as fast as its eleven-year-old engine and chassis could make it go down Interstate 85 on her way home to Mobile. She had stopped by the dorm only long enough to pack her toiletries and a change of clothes, telling Katie she needed to go home to pick up some items she needed for a project due next week. That had been a weak excuse, and Katie had not bought it, but at this point Jennifer neither cared nor worried about it.

She had to get out of this town! She had to get away from her former fiancé! She had to talk to her mother. Her mother, she knew, loved her unconditionally. Her mother, even though she was not the strongest woman in the world, would somehow comfort her and tell her she would take care of her now that Michael had abandoned her. Yes, even though her mother and she were not the closest of friends, the divorce having changed their relationship forever, Jennifer's instincts were now drawing her home like a magnet.

Jennifer and Susan's mother, Betty, had been totally surprised and completely unprepared by her husband's demand for a divorce those ten years ago, never guessing that his long silences and longer absences from home, supposedly "on business," had been covering up an on-again, off-again affair that had begun not long after Susie was born. Betty had been exhausted and ill-tempered by the end of each and every day, having cared for a newborn and a two-year-old by herself, and her husband was coming home with needs of his own that she had neither the energy nor the desire to meet. She had suffered with postpartum depression after Susie was born that was not taken seriously at the time because it was just not recognized in that day. The emotional and sexual distance between the two young parents had widened until Bob Jacobs was easy prey for a pretty, sexy bookkeeper at work.

And Betty had been completely distraught when the divorce was finalized. She had struggled with each new day, only surviving them with the aid of Valium, and had failed somewhat at the important job of raising her daughters, though she badly wanted to be there for them and help them through the unfair circumstance their father had brought upon them.

The girls, especially Jennifer, had experienced a premature role reversal, feeling that it was part of her responsibility to take care of her badly wounded mother and to make everything all right for her. The irony of the situation was that the ten-year-old would fall asleep each night to the sound of her mother's semi-stifled sobs as a lullaby and awake from her own nightmares to find her mother trying to soothe her tears.

And now, ten years later, new tears that Jennifer had repressed in her rage—tears she so desperately wanted her mother to wipe dry—were flowing freely down her pale cheeks as she put more and more miles behind her, well into the three-hour drive from Coburn to Mobile. How could Michael have lied to her so yesterday? How could he tell her he would marry her and then tell her he wanted her to have an abortion? How could she ever have believed him? He said that he loved her, and then this! She could not understand it! ... Not at all!

She looked down on her wrist at the engagement bracelet. *"With all my love, Michael,"* it read, cruelly mocking her. Impulsively, she tore at the clasp while still trying to steer the speeding old car which was weaving slightly on the nearly empty freeway. Finally, she worked the fastener loose and flung the bracelet out the window in fury, crying even harder.

"Oh, Michael! How could you do this to me? How could you offer me 'all your love' and then do this to me?" she cried aloud, totally broken-hearted and disconsolate.

In her pride, she had taken his offhand remark about her "forcing" him to marry her as the deepest cut of all. *Forcing you to marry me! Who do you think you are, Michael? Who do you think you are to believe that I would ever want to marry you not knowing if you loved me? That I would somehow like to trap you into an unhappy marriage because you are so wonderful that I just had to have you at any cost?*

All the emotional turmoil coupled with her pregnancy and the empty stomach she had never filled today made her suddenly extremely ill. She pulled The Hulk onto the shoulder of the interstate and vomited onto the pavement, only throwing up stomach fluids and nothing else. After the wave of nausea passed, she drove on more slowly, still crying all the while, and stopped at the next gas station. She filled up the gasoline tank, purchased some crackers and a soft drink, and drove herself the rest of the way home. Home to her mother.

Not quite an hour after Jennifer had raced out of his apartment, Michael figured that maybe now he could try one more time to talk with her logically and reasonably. Surely she had calmed herself down by now and would allow him to explain what he had meant. *Why is she always reading negative thoughts and intents into my every word?* The workings of her mind lately were a real mystery to him, and it was as frustrating as everything to try to make her understand him. But he had to try. He had to try and keep on trying until she understood that he only had her best interests at heart. *Can't she see that this is the best solution for her own happiness?* he wondered. *And of course, I didn't mean that she would 'force' me to marry her! It just came out that way. I will marry her, all right, if she refuses to ... if she can't make herself ... I'll marry her, all right. She must know that!* he reasoned.

He picked up the telephone and dialed her number.

"Hello," said Katie.

"Oh, hi, Katie. It's Michael," he began, his voice somewhat agitated.

"Yes, Michael, I recognize your voice by now, you know, as many times as you call for Jenny," replied Katie somewhat flirtatiously.

"Can I speak to her?" He sounded concerned and impatient.

"Didn't she tell you? She's headed back down to Mobile. Said she needed some something-or-other from her mother's garage for a project due next week. Didn't she tell you?" she asked, incredulous. "I tried to talk her out of it, you know, because she was so sick this morning and all, but she wouldn't listen and—"

"What time did she leave?" he interrupted urgently.

"Oh, I guess a little less than an hour ago ... maybe more, maybe less but—" Katie responded.

"Thanks, Kate." And he hung up on her.

After hanging up the phone, Katie started biting her fingernails, as she always did when worried or troubled, and paced up and down in her room. Something was very wrong between Michael and Jenny. *What could it be? Could Jennifer be ...? Surely not! Then what could it be?*

Pulling the faded, slightly rusted Hulk into the long driveway of her old house, the house she had not really lived in for over two years now, Jennifer felt numb and very weary. She had stopped crying over an hour ago and was now experiencing a vague emptiness, a low-grade, distant ache with which she could somehow cope. For Jennifer had never been a quitter. Though broken and bruised by the senseless misfortunes of her past, she had always found the strength to fight back. She had always been a fighter. No opponent was going to take her down without engaging in a fierce, bloody battle to the death. Although she was sensitive and tenderhearted, she also possessed a strong resolve and a stubborn, persistent spirit that she could tap into whenever circumstances placed her with her back against a wall facing a monster. Life could do cruel things to a person, she knew, and sometimes fighting selfishly for survival was the only way to make it through.

As she stopped her car and switched off the ignition, the sight of the towering old maples and oaks that kept the house shaded from the hot, Alabama summer sun brought a small measure of peace back into her hurting spirit. How she loved those old shade trees! She used to climb up in them when she was a little girl, climb as high as she could, nestled in their sheltering branches. There she created her own private sanctuary where she would pray and sing hymns to God. Especially after her parents' divorce, she would find a quiet place of refuge and peace up there, as close to heaven as she could get, crying and pouring out her heart to her Creator. And she would see bird's nests up there, too, and be reminded of how Jesus had said that not even one sparrow fell without the knowledge of God. And she would feel comforted back then.

She opened her car door and slowly stretched out her legs and arms. Looking up at the treetops, she felt a sudden urge to climb up there again. She walked over to an old oak, rubbed her hand along its coarse, rough bark, and looked up. The tree had grown so much since she was little, and it was very difficult for her to hoist herself up to its bottom branches, but after a few clumsy attempts, she managed to get herself firmly established in its lower levels. She climbed carefully upward until she was about as high as she could safely go and found a relatively comfortable place to sit, her back resting against a very sturdy, thick branch.

As she sat there, she remembered her sad childhood, remembered how much she had longed for a happy home with a mother *and* a father, remembered how she had promised herself that when she married, it would be for life, so that her children would never, never have to know the pain of their parents' divorce. Tears began to flow silently down her pale cheeks as she sat there and contemplated both her painful past and her uncertain, frightening future.

"O Lord," she began to whisper her prayer, her tear-stained face pointed heavenward, "what have I done? I have always wanted a happy home for my future children—a home with a good father. And now, this baby may not even have a father! What have I done?"

She was just beginning to address heaven. There was so much more she wanted to say, but her prayer was interrupted as her mother's sedan began to pull into the driveway.

Upon seeing Jennifer's car, her mother quickly exited hers and began walking toward the house with two bags of groceries. Jennifer hurriedly dried her eyes, composed herself, and called out.

"Hey, Momma! I'm up here!"

Betty Jacobs Miller, a trim, tall woman of forty-four with graying, dark hair and eyeglasses covering dark eyes like Jennifer's, strode over to the oak tree, looked up and questioned,

"For heaven's sake, Jennifer, what are you doing up there? Be careful, Sweetheart! You might fall and break your neck. Whatever possessed you to climb this old tree? Please be careful. There may be some rotten branches, you know. How long have you been home?" She had a concerned frown on her face but was delighted, though somewhat surprised, to see her first-born daughter.

As Jennifer was cautiously making her way down, she replied,

"I just got here about five minutes ago. I don't know why I felt like climbing up here, Momma. I guess I just want to relive a childhood memory, that's all."

"Well, darlin', you're still very much a child … at least to me, your old, broken-down mother, that is," responded Betty with a failed attempt at humor. "Here … let me help you. That's right, just grab my hand." And Betty assisted her beautiful, eldest child down from her former haven, giving her a maternal hug and kiss.

"What are you doin' home? I wasn't expecting you, though it's a wonderful surprise. But you look tired, Sweetheart, and pale. Are you okay? Did Michael drive you?" her mother quizzed, gently brushing a strand of hair from her daughter's forehead and caressing her cheek lightly.

"No … He had a ... big exam that he needed to study for. I drove down by myself. And I'm fine, Momma. Just a little tired, like you said," Jennifer lied as she stooped down, picking up a bag of groceries and leading her mother into the kitchen.

She did not want her mother to gaze too deeply into her eyes just yet. Not yet, though she did not know why.

And she also did not know why she was suddenly lying to her mother. After all, she had driven all the way home to pour out her heart to her, to tell her of her grievous trouble and of her lover's betrayal. But now that she was standing in the kitchen that was not really her kitchen anymore, putting away groceries that she would not be there to eat, she felt strangely out of place, like a man without a country. Her mother's house was not really her house anymore, and she was no longer a child that could break a favorite toy and expect Momma to either repair it or buy her a new one. It was very disconcerting to her troubled soul.

"Is Bill out playing golf again?" she inquired, putting away a jar of peanut butter and closing the pantry door. She had driven home knowing that she and her mother should have a long time to converse, as Bill played golf every Sunday afternoon, rain or shine, and should be gone for several hours.

Betty did not say anything at first, and Jennifer immediately sensed that something was wrong. She turned to face her mother and saw that she was crying, her shoulders gently shaking. She walked over and placed her arms around her mother.

"Momma, what's wrong?"

Betty, trying desperately to control her tears led Jennifer to the kitchen table, sat down across from her, took out a tissue from the box, dabbed her eyes, and replied,

"Jenny, I had not wanted you to know ... had not wanted to worry you at all ... had not wanted to intrude in any way on your happiness. You have so much going on at school and with planning your wedding... but ... but ... Bill and I have filed for divorce."

"Oh, no," responded the daughter flatly. "I'm so sorry, Mother."

Jennifer had never liked Bill Miller, anyway, and had thought he was the most boring man in the universe not to mention the most insensitive and selfish. But if her mother had loved him and wanted to be his wife, that was her business. She felt sorry for her mother, though not sorry that Bill Miller was now out of the picture. She reached across the table and squeezed her mother's hand in sympathy.

Betty stared out the window seeing nothing, her eyes now dry, and continued brokenly.

"We had not been communicating well at all ... not since before your sister's graduation from high school ... not since Christmas, really ... And we were disagreeing about money and expenses and... other things ... And then he came in about a month ago and said that... that he wanted out of the marriage ... that I wasn't meeting his needs and he, mine ... And so ..." she trailed off. There was really nothing more to say.

After a considerable silence, Jennifer stood up from the table, hugged Betty's shoulders absently, and walked over to the kitchen sink, her back to her mother, turned on the tap for a glass of water, and thought, *Why did I ever think I could bring this problem home to Mother? How did I expect her to fix it? I can't even tell her now... not with her own heartache to deal with. This would likely just finish her off.* She sighed an exhausted, hopeless sigh.

Betty, thinking the sigh was for her, responded immediately.

"I don't want you to think that this is *your* problem, Jennifer. I am fine. Really, I am. I have seen this coming for a long time now. And it is for the best in the long run, I believe. Bill and I never were suited to each other ... Not really. I had only married him because... Well, I hoped that I could somehow piece together a ... a family for you girls. I felt I owed you a real family ... But ... I guess it just wasn't meant to be," she finished as best she could.

As her engaged daughter still said nothing and did not turn around, Betty changed the subject to a happy one, saying in what she hoped was an excited, upbeat tone of voice,

"Enough of that. Let's talk about something better, something good. Now ... Come sit down here and tell me about you and Michael. About your wedding plans. I saw Dr. and Mrs. Evans at church this morning, and they said they drove up to Coburn this weekend and took you both out to dinner. They said you looked so beautiful in a brilliant blue gown or something, and that the two of you were very much in love. Come here and tell me about it. I guess we need to start making some initial plans, anyway, even though it is a way off yet. Time flies, you know. Is that why you came home, by the way? You never told me."

Jennifer could no longer stem the tide of her rising, turbulent, and fearful emotions. She turned around, tears streaming down her cheeks, ran over to the table into her mother's arms, and cried out,

"Oh, Momma! ... Oh, Momma!" she sobbed, just as she had done a decade ago when she had discovered that her daddy had left home for good, sobbed her broken spirit out in her mother's loving arms, shaking and trembling.

"Jennifer! What is it? What's the matter, darlin'?" Betty called out, alarmed, as she embraced her daughter, rubbing her back as she had done so often in the past when she had awakened from her nightmares.

"Oh, Momma! … I'm so scared! … I'm so scared!" was all that she could choke out as she continued crying from her desolate heart.

"Tell me what it is, Sweetheart! Did you and Michael have a fight? Did you break off your engagement?" Betty guessed.

Jennifer still said nothing but stayed locked in her mother's arms, grasping her tightly, as if she were a life raft and Jennifer was caught out in a raging, stormy sea. As she shook violently in Betty's embrace, there was a brief knock on the kitchen door …

And in bounded Michael.

He immediately ran to the table and threw his arms around the two of them.

"Thank God you are all right, Jennifer!" His face was ashen as he explained breathlessly, "When I phoned Katie about an hour after you had left, I was so worried! I didn't want you driving all the way down here by yourself when you were so upset …and in your old car and all. Anything could have happened! And with you still sick and with no breakfast or lunch … I was so worried! I drove down about ninety-five to a hundred miles per hour the whole way! You had me so worried!"

Betty had no idea what was going on between the two of them. She thought it was perhaps a lover's quarrel or some misunderstanding that had been blown out of proportion. She simply backed away as he knelt down beside them and handed her daughter over into his arms where she now was, still crying.

"Jennifer! You must promise me you will never do anything like this again! I was so frantic! I don't know what I would do if anything were ever to happen to—"

He stopped speaking, and stroked her hair, kissing her head and hugging her very tightly against himself. He had been terribly distraught and troubled the entire drive down from Coburn, searching every mile on the freeway up ahead, expecting to find her old car rolled over in a ditch. He knew that in her emotional state and her condition, she was capable of very dangerous driving, and her tires were slick, too. One blow out at a fast speed could have finished her.

Betty, embarrassed now to be witnessing such a baring of her future son-in-law's soul, walked quietly out of the kitchen, leaving the two of them alone and closing the door behind her.

After a few minutes, Michael managed to calm his lover. He gave her some tissues from the same box her mother had needed only minutes before, sat down by her side at the table, and began to explain more calmly and slowly, looking her fully in the face, his eyes full of quiet passion.

"I want you to know that I love you very, very much ... I didn't mean to make you think that I felt ... trapped ... or forced, or anything like that, Jennifer. Lately you have been so sensitive to anything I say ... And I guess I understand that, because of the pressure you are under ... But—"

She interrupted him, "I think I understand ... and I ... I ... I am beginning to see what you meant about ... the options."

She had immediately forgiven him when he had rushed into the room, full of love and concern for her safety. And now that she was home and had spoken briefly with her mother, she felt that she could not add one more burden to Betty's already heavy load. *To deal with a second divorce coupled with my being a pregnant bride in a shotgun wedding might just be too much for her to bear,* Jennifer thought. She had always been her mother's favorite, truly her pride and joy. She knew that the shame and disgrace of this out-of-wedlock pregnancy would break her mother's already deeply wounded heart. The trip to Atlanta appeared to be best, just as Michael had said.

He stopped her with a finger over his lips. "Does your mother know?" he whispered conspiratorially.

She shook her head, "no."

"Come on. Let's go outside for a walk," he suggested.

"All right," she replied softly, and to her mother she called out loudly, "Momma, we are going outside for a walk. We will be back before long, okay?"

"All right, dear," came back her response. "Take your time. I'm not going anywhere." Betty had never been the kind of nosey, prying mother so many daughters have. She had always been a private individual herself, and respected her daughters' needs to own their own thoughts and lead their own lives without her interference.

When outside, the emotionally drained couple strolled slowly, arm in arm for a while, not speaking. Jennifer was very relieved that he had followed her home. She did not know what she would have done had he not appeared in her kitchen when he did. She knew now that he truly loved her. She had shouted some very cruel things into his face only three hours ago, but he had realized that she did not mean them. He had worried about her as no man had ever done before, not even her own father. He had pursued her as no man had ever pursued her. She would do anything for him now. Even the thing she did not want to do.

She broke the silence with, "Michael, I want you to know that I think I understand now ... what you were talking about earlier ... about ...about the trip to Atlanta."

"Look, Jen, I don't want you to think that if you don't want to... do it ... that I will not marry you right away. I will. It's only that... Well, it just seems to be the ... solution to our dilemma that makes the most sense for us right now. This way we could go ahead with our plans for school and the wedding in June and not disappoint our families or—"

She interrupted him, "Yes, I know what you mean ... I don't know, really, why I didn't want to think about it ... Except that it just somehow seems ... unnatural and ... not quite right for some reason... I mean I know it's not a baby yet or anything ... But still..." she left off, not knowing herself how to complete her thoughts or why she felt so uneasy.

They walked on in silence for a few more minutes, both of them thinking but not verbalizing their own doubts about the exact nature of the procedure used to terminate a pregnancy. Even to Michael, it did not seem "quite right" for some unknown reason, but it seemed to be so practical and rational a solution to their crisis that he could not ignore it. It would quickly make things right again.

"Well, I don't want you to think that I don't love you or don't want to marry you, Jennifer." He stopped walking and took her in his arms again, peering steadfastly into her tired, dark eyes. "If this... this trip to Atlanta makes you feel that way, then it's not worth it." He held her very tightly again. "You don't know how very worried … how panicked I was when Katie told me. Oh, Jenny, I could just picture you lying dead on the highway, and I would blame myself forever! I want to take good care of you!"

"I was so angry, Michael ... because I thought you said I was forcing you to marry me … that you didn't really want me … And I just overreacted, I guess," she whispered in his ear while they embraced.

Then they kissed, their first kiss since noontime in the lobby of her dormitory. It seemed like a very long time ago, that Sunday noon. More like a year had passed and not just a few hours.

Suddenly, Jennifer realized it was late Sunday afternoon. "But what about the church service tonight, Michael. There is no way you can make it back in time."

"That's right! I had forgotten." He glanced down at his watch and finished stoically with a sigh, "Oh, well, let me just use your mother's telephone and I'll explain … something to Bob. Let's go back there now, if you're ready. And have you eaten anything?" he asked.

"Just some crackers. I wasn't hungry. But I am now. I'll fix us both a sandwich, and you can use the phone. We can talk with Mother some, and then go back to Coburn, okay?" she asked, looking back into his very handsome face, feeling safe once more in the strength of his masculine arms, thinking she was so lucky to have him and how much she loved him.

He had pursued her. She had shown him her worst side that afternoon, and still he had pursued her. He was very worried about her. He must love her very much.

"Okay, we'll just drive back in my car and leave The Hulk here. It deserves a rest, I'm sure," he agreed with a rueful chuckle, smiling into her weary but less troubled eyes.

And the pair walked back to Betty's house, arm in arm, now of like mind.

They were about three-fourths of the way along their journey back to Coburn, Michael's eyes fixed on the road, one arm on the steering wheel and the other down on Jennifer's shoulders as she had her head on his lap resting, he hoped, even sleeping. After the emotionally draining weekend, she had been so tired and sleepy that she had rolled up his sweatshirt to use as a pillow as she had lain down. Her quiet, rhythmic breathing let him know that maybe now her worried mind was at peace, when suddenly she sat bolt upright and cried out, looking frantically around her at the interstate highway.

"My bracelet! My engagement bracelet! Michael, where are we? Oh, Michael, my engagement bracelet! Stop! Stop! Stop the car and turn back one more exit! I've got to find it!"

Her sudden outburst, after the peace of the silence in the car, made his heart skip a beat and caused him to almost wreck the automobile, sending adrenalin coursing through his veins.

"What are you talking about? What about your bracelet?" he asked, his heart thumping wildly in his chest.

"Oh, Michael, I threw it out the window this afternoon ... when I was so mad at you and I thought … Oh, we've got to find it! I've got to find it!" she cried out hysterically.

"Okay, Jenny, okay ... Just calm down now. We can turn around here and go back to look for it, although the odds of finding it are pretty slim," he replied compassionately.

Even though it was only five thirty in the afternoon and still bright daylight, he knew the odds of finding a small piece of jewelry thrown out of a speeding car somewhere within a half-mile radius were very poor, indeed. But the desperation in Jennifer's eyes and voice made him know he had to try at least, for her sake. *She must have really hated me to throw away her bracelet like that. No, she didn't hate me. She was just so hurt and angry,* he reasoned.

"Michael, I've just got to find it!" she cried. "I'm so sorry! I shouldn't have ..." and tears were flowing once again so that she could not complete her sentence.

All I seem to be able to do is to make her cry nowadays, he thought in frustration. *By this time next week, everything will be back to normal.* He took her hand and said comfortingly,

"It's okay, Jennifer. I understand. Try not to worry about it. It's just a bracelet, that's all. I can get you another one."

"But I don't want another one! I want the one you gave me the night of my birthday! I want to find it! I've got to find it!" she moaned, refusing to be comforted.

He slowly pulled the car onto the shoulder of the interstate highway and walked over to her door. But she had not waited for him to open it and was already out walking up and down the median of the roadway, her eyes carefully searching in the tall grasses of the August summer. Bees were buzzing in the flowering weeds, and every minute or so a car or truck would whiz by.

"Please be careful, and don't walk so close to the road," he instructed. "Do you remember exactly where you were when you tossed it?"

"I think somewhere right along here. I threw it out on this side, and it should have landed here in the median," she replied, her eyes still searching frantically. "Please look hard, Mikey. Please help me find it! I want it back so badly!"

They searched and searched, walking slowly up Interstate 85 for about a quarter of a mile, and then back down it. A few kindhearted good Samaritans traveling down the road that hot August day stopped their cars and inquired if the young couple needed any help. Michael would tell them they were fine but were looking for a lost bracelet. Most would give him a sympathetic, puzzled expression, then travel on, but one nice old gentleman actually walked alongside them, carefully examining the ground at his feet, looking diligently for the lost item. His heart went out to the dark young lady as he observed the brokenhearted expression of her countenance. His dear, departed wife had once lost a necklace he had given her for their thirtieth wedding anniversary, and he remembered her own heartache over it.

But try as hard as they could, they did not discover it. One time, Michael yelled out encouragingly, "I think I see it!" as something bright and shiny caught his eye, reflecting the late afternoon sunlight. As he reached it, however, it was only a discarded piece of aluminum foil. Finally, after about thirty minutes of searching, he called Jennifer over to his side.

"Look, Jenny, it's just impossible to find something so small in this high grass, and especially since we can't pinpoint the specific area to search. You said you were driving over eighty miles per hour.

It could have flown anywhere. Even across the highway over there." He pointed to the other two lanes of the four-lane freeway. "What I can do is contact the state highway department and put in a request to the grass cutting crews to save it for us if by some miracle they find it."

"Yes … You're right, of course," she began in resignation, her lower lip trembling. Then she cried out with great emotion, new tears falling down her weary face, "Oh, Michael, I wanted it back so badly! I am so sorry! Please forgive me!"

He very tenderly enfolded her in his arms, caressing her dark head against his shoulder, reassuring her.

"It's okay! It's okay, Jen! Like my mother said on Saturday, an engagement bracelet is stupid anyway. I want to take you to Fitzwater's tomorrow as soon as they open and buy you the prettiest engagement ring they have in the store. I can open up a charge account. They are used to poor students buying diamond rings on time. I can even get you an identical bracelet to the one you … to the one that's lost, if you like. But please stop crying, Sweetheart! You are breaking my heart, and I can't take much more. Okay?"

Still crying, she nodded her head "okay" and dried her eyes with the back of her hand. "I love you so much, Mikey. So much," she spoke softly.

He took her tear-stained face in his hands, peering into the dark depths of her sad eyes, and responded earnestly, "I love you, too, Toots!" Then he added playfully, "But tomorrow, you must promise me that no matter how angry you become with me, you won't throw your engagement ring out any windows. All right?"

When she gave him a half-smile at his facetious request, he knew he had his sweet Jenny back.

Yes, by this time next week, everything will be back to the way it was, he thought confidently. *No more tears. No more sadness.*

Chapter Fourteen

*T*rue to his promise, Michael was standing in front of the largest showcase displaying the diamond engagement rings at Fitzwater & Sons Jewelry Store on Main Street in Coburn, Alabama at ten o'clock Monday morning, the sixth of August 1975, Jennifer by his side. He had one hour between classes, thinking that would be plenty of time to choose a ring, and had arranged to meet Jennifer out front.

As they had walked into the store together, he had told her again of his intent to purchase the best ring in the establishment for his beloved bride-to-be.

"That's a pretty one, don't you think?" he pointed to a setting on the back row featuring a large, brilliant cut center diamond with a grouping of three smaller stones on either side. "May we try that one?" he addressed the salesman, a middle-aged man with stooped shoulders and a lopsided toupee who had been fussing and clucking around the couple since they first walked through the doorway. He could smell a big sale here—and a large commission.

As Michael slid the jewelry on her finger he asked her, "What do you think, Jen?"

Surveying it carefully, she moved her hand slightly from side to side before replying honestly, "Well … It's pretty, all right, but I was thinking of something simpler. Maybe just a plain solitaire. And I've always liked the oval cut better than the round, brilliant cut. Maybe like that one over there," she pointed out.

"Ah, yes … The oval cut is quite stylish to so many of today's young ladies," stated the salesman solicitously. "There. Let's try it on your hand, Miss Jacobs."

All three observed the golden bezel cut band with the one and one-half carat oval diamond on her slender hand and thought it looked quite at home there.

"And it's a good quality stone, too. High in both color and clarity, with very few imperfections," offered the salesman diplomatically. "And since you are here so early, we can have it sized by this afternoon, ready for you to pick up."

"Then, if she wants it, that's the one we will take, because Jennifer is high in both color and clarity, and has very few imperfections, too," Michael winked at the salesman and smiled at his fiancée, his arm around her shoulders, giving her a squeeze and a quick kiss on the forehead.

She smiled back at him briefly, and then moved her eyes immediately back down to the ring. It was so pretty, its facets brilliantly reflecting the light from the strategically placed track lighting fixtures above.

She sighed as she said, "It's so beautiful, Michael, but are you sure you can afford—"

"Say no more about that, Toots, because I am certain I can sell my soul to Fitzwater's here, as their bondservant for the next few years or so to pay for it. And it will be small price, indeed, to win your hand," he interrupted her, his eyes twinkling merrily, and he lifted her hand to his lips, kissing her ring finger.

"Oh, sure you can, son," replied the salesman, chuckling. "We have all sorts of 'painless payment plans.' You should still have some of your soul left, even after the last installment is made."

He liked this young couple, although the bride-to-be wore a slightly worried expression around her eyes. *Maybe she's not quite certain of the young man,* he speculated.

"So when are the nuptials to take place?" he inquired curiously as he locked up the jewelry case and led the couple towards the sales desk.

"In June … Early in June after my graduation," replied Michael abruptly, the smile quickly leaving his face. "If we can go ahead and get the paperwork ready, that would be good because I have a class in about twenty minutes," he finished hurriedly while glancing at his watch, intentionally avoiding Jennifer's questioning face.

They left the store just in time for Michael to catch his eleven o'clock class, agreeing to meet at noon in the Student Union for lunch. The anxious expression around Jennifer's eyes only intensified after he kissed her goodbye and turned the corner, leaving her alone in front of the jewelry store on Main Street.

The wedding is definitely not until June, she now knew for certain.

At seven o'clock that evening back at The Suite, the pair was sitting on Michael's sofa, looking down at Jennifer's hand, admiring the costly engagement ring that sparkled and shone in the late summer sun whose rays were glistening in through the sliding glass doors of the living room.

"Do you really like it, Sweetheart?" he asked her, nuzzling her head with his and kissing her on her temple.

"Yes, I do. I really like it a lot. Thank you so much, Michael," she said, still not taking her eyes off it.

An awkward silence followed her statement. This Silence had separated them all afternoon, like an unwelcome guest, following them around from building to building as they picked up her ring from Fitzwater's and did some shopping, staying with them as they entered his apartment and prepared a spaghetti dinner that both of them merely picked at, keeping them company as they cleaned the kitchen and were now seated on his sofa, his arm around her shoulders. The Silence was daring one of them to introduce the dreadful, monstrous topic that must be discussed—and be discussed soon.

Eight weeks along … Eight weeks and counting … Eight weeks and moving into the ninth. The clock on the wall, ticking, ticking, ticking away the minutes and the hours seemed to be taunting them. "Eight weeks leads to nine … Nine weeks to ten …Ten weeks to eleven … When are you going to do it? … When are going to do it?"

Finally, Michael challenged the Silent intruder.

"Jenny …You must know how I hate to bring this up … Especially today, when we picked up your engagement ring and everything … But … But we need to make the trip … You know …the trip to Atlanta … one day this week, I think."

She did not say anything, but kept her eyes focused on her shining diamond ring, the symbol of his love and devotion. The Silence hung heavily over them again, laughing at them, jeering at them, daring them to defeat him.

"I mean … the longer we wait … the more difficult it will be … And the more dangerous—" he tried again. "Not that it's dangerous at all! I didn't mean that! But … it is just better to go ahead and … do it, now. You know, before you get any farther along," he valiantly fought the ghastly Silence.

Still, she said nothing. And she did not lift her eyes from her hand.

The clock ticked on, calling out the seconds, shouting out the minutes.

"Please talk to me, Jenny. Tell me what you are thinking," he begged her to join forces with him to defeat their common enemy, trying gently to turn her head up to make her look at him.

"What do you want me to say?" she asked quietly without emotion, still looking down at her ring, not cooperating with his attempt to force her to meet his eyes.

"I want to know what you are thinking, like I said," he replied, even more imploringly. *Why won't you talk to me, Jennifer? We have to talk!* his soul cried out silently.

This time, she heard the silent, desperate plea of his heart, as only a woman can do, and out of compassion for him, turned her face to look at him.

"Michael … I don't know exactly what I am thinking. I don't know … I feel … sort of like I am in a cage or prison or something… of my own making … bound up inside myself but not wanting to break out … Not yet anyway … Like the cage is where I am supposed to be for now … I don't quite know how to explain it. I know in my head that what you have suggested we do … about going to the clinic in Atlanta … sounds like the best thing now. I knew that yesterday when I saw Momma in Mobile. But in my heart, I am afraid and…

and not certain that it's the right thing to do at all. I feel trapped inside myself ... That's the only way I can explain it," she answered him sincerely, searching his eyes to see if he understood her questions and her dilemma.

"Oh," he said simply, contemplating her words for a few moments. Then he continued, "But I don't think you will feel 'trapped' anymore after the ... after we get back from Atlanta. The dilemma that is 'trapping' you will be over and done with then, don't you see?" he explained from his understanding of the intent of her words.

"Yes, I can see logically what you are saying ... But somehow part of me ... a very large part ... is welcoming, even embracing the trap. I know it sounds foolish," she responded, looking somewhere over his shoulder out into the distance, out into the future.

She had dropped eye contact with him because she could see that he did not understand what she was saying. But then again, how could he ... when she did not fully understand it herself?

But he certainly understood the trap metaphor. That was exactly the way he felt. Trapped. Trapped by an unwanted pregnancy. Trapped by the unfortunate circumstance that had fallen upon him out of the clear blue.

"How in the world can you welcome a trap, Jenny? Traps are something you want to get away from, aren't they?" he asked, seeking knowledge of her heart.

"Yes. They are. They are. I don't understand it myself, Michael. But you asked me what I was thinking and there it is," she replied honestly. "I'm just not at all sure about this ... decision. And I am afraid of making it while I feel this way."

She responded softly and strangely without emotion, making eye contact once again, as if she wanted him to piece together the puzzle of her own thoughts and concerns and come up with a positive course of action that was somehow different than the one he had proposed. What that course could be, though, she did not know.

He replaced his arm around her shoulders more firmly and hugged her closer to himself, rubbing her arm, as if trying to protect her from her own doubts and fears. Then he stated, firmly, with authority,

"Well, then, let me be the one to release you from the trap, Jenny, to make you sure about this decision. To take away your fear. Because I know that you don't belong in this trap. Not now. Not now."

As she still said nothing, but dropped his gaze once more, he added with assurance, "Let's go ahead and make the trip tomorrow. Postponing it will only make you more fearful. You don't have any classes after nine o'clock, and I can skip the only one I have in the afternoon. We can leave at ten and be back by late afternoon. Everything will look a whole lot better by this time tomorrow. You will see. Okay," he stated, rather than asked her.

Still, she did not reply but looked down at her diamond ring, moving it around from side to side, examining the way its prisms made little rainbows form on the opposite wall.

"Jenny, please look at me," he pleaded.

She turned her head and peered into his eyes, into his strong, protective, resolute blue eyes.

"I want you to trust me on this one. I love you, Jennifer, and believe that this is the best solution for us. This will make everything all right again and will take us back to where we were before this weekend—with no more worries and sadness. Okay?"

His confidence, coupled with the strength of his masculinity, made her believe that perhaps he was right after all. He seemed so convinced of the validity of this solution to their crisis that she acquiesced, her dark eyes pouring out both her trust and her fears as she looked at him.

"Okay, Michael. I will trust you. I know that you love me. Okay." And she put her head on his shoulder, her arms around his neck, adding, "But I want to stay here with you tonight. Please don't make me go back to the dorm. I need to stay here with you tonight."

"Sure, Jennifer, sure! Of course you can stay! I want you with me always. You know that. I am only concerned for your reputation, that's all," he stated emphatically, while rubbing her back with his strong hands and kissing her dark hair. "But I'll make up something to tell Katie and your friends at the dorm. It's going to be okay. Everything is going to be okay. Just trust me."

Everything is going to be okay. Everything is going to be okay. This mantra was playing inside Michael's head throughout the two-and-a-half-hour drive from Coburn to Atlanta that hot, hot day, on August 7, 1975. The weather forecast called for record high temperatures, close to one hundred degrees or more, but the air-conditioning in his car was pumping out cool, comfortable air as he kept his eyes fixed on the asphalt interstate highway, observing the wavy heat radiating from its surface as he continued driving relentlessly on, on toward that woman's clinic in Atlanta that would soon make everything okay.

Jennifer was seated as close to him as she could be without actually being in the driver's seat herself, her cold hand on his bluejeaned leg, her frightened eyes also staring straight ahead, not looking to the right or left, staring out straight in front of her, and yet seeing nothing. Neither one of them spoke much as the Silent monster was now riding in the backseat of the '72 Pontiac, stretching himself out luxuriantly, making himself right at home, mocking them the entire trip, challenging them to speak what was on their hearts.

They had left Coburn at ten fifteen, after her nine o'clock class, a class that could just as well have been missed, as she had heard nothing the professor had said. Their last evening together had been one of tenderness and intimacy, with Jennifer clinging desperately to her lover, her future husband, as if she feared she might never see him again, might never make love to him again, might never embrace him nor be embraced by him again for the rest of her life. And Michael had tried to communicate to her in their lovemaking his unparalleled, powerful, overwhelming love for her, a love that he believed he could not adequately express to her verbally, as his words sounded so insufficient and trite when he spoke them.

Afterwards, she had lain in his arms, gently weeping, her tears wetting his chest as he stroked her soft hair. And he had asked her why. She had replied that she did not know, except that she loved him so much, so very much. He had never felt closer to her than at that moment. She was truly flesh of his flesh and heart of his heart, and by this time tomorrow night, everything would be all right.

About ten minutes outside of Atlanta, Michael stopped the car at a gas station to fill up the tank. He knew instinctively that after the procedure was over and they were back in his automobile heading home, he would not want to stop. He would want to leave there as quickly as possible and not come back to that city for a long, long time, if ever again. This would be a closed chapter in their lives, never to be reopened.

Jennifer walked inside the station while he attended to the car. She had become suddenly aware of the fact that she needed to talk to some man other than Michael, needed to confide in another male figure, someone more removed from their problem than he was. A growing sense of fear and panic was beginning to envelop her, and she knew beyond any doubt that she needed the presence of a strong masculine figure very desperately at this most fearsome point in her journey through her brief life, at this most dreadful juncture of her life's story.

This impression had hit her heavily about half an hour ago and had not left, but had instead grown stronger and more insistent as the skyline of the city ahead loomed larger and larger. She took out her change purse and dialed the only number she knew to call at that moment.

"Bob Jacobs," the long distance voice traveled absently through the pay phone line.

"Hello ... Daddy?" she questioned timidly. Mysteriously, she had always known his work phone number from memory though she had rarely used it, maybe just one other time in her life that she could recall, and yet it was indelibly etched in her mind.

"Hello ... Jenny? Is that you?" responded the now-focused voice of Robert Jacobs, CPA, at his desk in southern Illinois. "This is a pleasant surprise, Jennifer. You sound tired. Are you okay?"

"Yes ... yes ... Daddy, I am okay ... How about you?" she replied weakly, tears beginning to form for some unknown reason at the sound of her father's voice.

"I'm fine, darlin'. But are you sure you're okay? You sound like... Are you crying, Jennifer? Where are you? Is Michael there?" asked her father, so far removed from her and yet always her provider and protector, at least in his mind.

Oh, Daddy! I'm so frightened! Michael is taking me somewhere I don't want to go! Please come and get me, Daddy! her heart was crying out.

But her mouth responded, trembling somewhat, "Yes ... Michael's here. I'm fine, really ... We're fine. We're taking the afternoon off and heading down to Atlanta ... to a Braves game ... I just wanted to... I just felt like I needed to ... hear your voice ... That's all," and she choked back the tears.

"Well, you know you can call me anytime, honey. You know that. I've always told you that. Told you and your sister that, too," he offered, still uneasy. "So you're going to a Braves' game, huh? Who are they playing?"

She could hear the clacking sound of office machines and other telephones ringing in the background at the busy accounting firm's office. She tried to stay focused on his question, although her heart felt as if it was about to explode.

"I ... I don't know ... I'm not sure, Daddy ... And I don't mean to bother you at work ... It's just that ..." she trailed off, swallowing a large lump in her throat.

Robert Jacobs, CPA, was at a loss as to what was really happening here. He would have to make a note of it and mention it to Betty the next time he phoned her about their daughters.

"You're not bothering me, sweetheart. Not at all ... Do you need anything, Jennifer? ... Do you need any money?"

No, Daddy, I don't need any money. I need you, Daddy! I just need you! I need you to come rescue me, Daddy! I need you to take care of me! I need you to love me, Daddy! I just need you! Her soul continued longing for what she had never possessed.

But she replied, "No, Daddy ... I don't need any money ... I ... I... just want you to know ... that I love you, Daddy. That's all." And her voice broke.

She placed her hand over the mouthpiece of the phone so he could not hear her softly sobbing.

"I love you, too, honey ... I love you, too ... Are you sure you are okay? Are you sure you don't need any money?" he insisted.

What could this be? he wondered. *She is definitely upset about something. Why won't she tell me? Should I ask to speak to Michael?*

"No, Daddy … No thanks … I'm fine ... I'll ... I'll … talk to you soon ... Okay?" she managed to reply.

"Okay, darlin'. Soon. I wish you and Susie had come to see me this summer as usual. I really miss you," he added sincerely.

"I ... I miss you, too, Daddy ... I do ... I have to go now, Daddy, so ..."

"Okay, darlin' ... Tell Michael to take good care of you, okay? Goodbye now, Jennifer. Have fun at the ballgame," he finished, still greatly concerned and perplexed but not knowing what else to do.

"I will," she lied once more with quaking voice. "Goodbye, Daddy."

And she hung up the telephone, that miraculous means of communication.

Chapter Fifteen

A Woman's Clinic. Michael pulled the Pontiac around to the back of the large brick building that had once been a private residence. He had been told by Joe's fraternity brother, whom he had sworn to secrecy, its exact location and the amount of cash needed for the procedure. "Make sure you take cash," he had been told. "They won't accept any other type of payment." And he had also been told to drive to the rear where the security guard would let them in the back door, away from the protestors who usually picketed the clinic.

But there was only one, lone picketer today, an older woman who looked like someone's grandmother. She carried a homemade sign fashioned with magic marker and dime store poster paper that read, GOD HAS A PLAN FOR YOU AND YOUR UNBORN BABY.

He found a parking spot close to the door and turned off the engine. Heat waves were radiating from the surface of the lot, and the relentless sun was beating down heavily upon them. It was twelve forty-five.

He put his arm around his fiancé's shoulders and hugged her saying,

"Look, Jenny, I will go in with you and pay the ... fee ... and make certain everything is set up and you are taken care of. And then I want to come back out here to the car to wait for you. I won't go anywhere! I will wait right here for you, okay? They will not allow me to go back into the … procedure room with you, anyway.

And I think I would go crazy pacing in that waiting room. Okay?" he told her.

She could not say a thing. She felt that if she opened her mouth just once, she would scream hysterically and not be able to stop. She numbly nodded her head.

Seeing the extreme fear in her face, he embraced her even tighter and said,"This is the worst part, right now. Once we go in and everything is ... begun ... and then over with ... everything will be fine. It will be just fine, Jenny! Believe me! And then, when we get home, we will be back to where we were before all this. Okay? And Jennifer, I love you very much! You are my beautiful brown-eyed girl, remember?" and he kissed her forehead.

True to his word, he walked her in, paid the fee, checked to make certain she would be taken care of, and then kissed her lightly saying, "I'll be right outside … right out there in the parking lot ... if you need me."

Then he opened the door and left her there in the reception area. All alone.

He left the motor running in his car for as long as he could to keep the air-conditioning working out in that hot, miserable parking lot that August 7, 1975, that record breaking, searing, scorching day in Atlanta. The radio, too, was turned on, playing song after song that made him feel like a wretched scoundrel and a sorry good-for-nothing. The songs of that day were either about love or sex, occasionally about the two combined, and he felt he had let Jennifer down on both counts. That he loved her, he knew full well, but the fact that his actions and behavior did not match up with that love, he could not escape. He knew he never should have placed her in this predicament to begin with. That his beloved fiancée should be eight weeks pregnant and still ten months away from her wedding day both broke his heart and made him feel very, very guilty.

All of the conversations he had experienced with his obstetrician father came back to his memory now in full force. What contempt his father had for young men who impregnated young women and then failed to marry them, failed to take responsibility for their own children! How his father felt about abortion, Michael did not know, except that he knew he did not perform them. This topic had just never been discussed at home in front of Michael and his two younger sisters. It was too shameful and off-limits, he guessed. He was equally ignorant of exactly what went on in the procedure to terminate a pregnancy, except in the vaguest terms.

Joe's fraternity brother had told him that his girlfriend had come through "with flying colors," other than being a little scared beforehand and sad afterwards. He had assured him that the clinic was safe, and the doctors were reputable. What he had *not* told him was that his girlfriend, who previously had only consumed a couple of beers on weekends, was now drinking several times as much, getting drunk just about every Friday and Saturday nights to the point of passing out, and angrily ordering him to either get her another beer or else "get the hell out of my way and I'll get it myself, you worthless s.o.b." when he would protest that she was overindulging. And she had never sworn before or called him names, either. In fact, he was having a difficult time being around her at all anymore, and they were on the verge of breaking up. But, no, he had not thought to tell Michael about that because that was not in any way related to the abortion, was it? That was just them.

So now Michael sat in his car, listening to the radio while drumming his fingers nervously on the dashboard and wishing with all his soul that this day were over—wishing that the need for this day had never arrived in the first place. As the minutes and then the hour passed by, as slowly as when he was a little schoolboy in the first grade waiting for the dismissal bell to ring, the young man began to feel very uneasy.

What is taking them so long? Shouldn't she be all finished by now? It's been an hour and a half. Surely it can't take that long. What if something went wrong? Women used to die from these things.

Stop it! Stop letting your imagination run away with you! Of course, women don't die from abor--... from this medical procedure anymore, now that it's legal. Get a grip! ... Still.... What could possibly be taking them so long?

As his mind fumed and fretted, worried and obsessed, panicked and accused, his shirt first became sticky, and then soaked through with sweat. He had to turn off the motor as he was using up his precious gasoline and also overheating the engine. As he sat in his hot, steamy car and then stepped out for a while, he thought hell could not be hotter or more torturous than this moment. How he wished he could ride around the block to a convenience store for something cold to drink! But he couldn't leave.

What if Jennifer were to walk out that door and find my car gone? No, I have to stay. Please, dear God, let Jennifer be okay! Please let her walk out of that door right now!

Others walked out, one after another. But no Jennifer. And still the minutes dragged by, one after another. Time lagged and dragged and almost stood still, not cooperating at all with his wish that this all be over and done with, not caring a lick that he desperately wanted Jennifer back by his side once more, safe and sound, healthy and happy. Not giving a damn that he was anxious, troubled, and very uneasy.

Suddenly, his acute uneasiness turned into Fear. A Fear that pounded on the very door of his soul. Terrible Fear such as he had never experienced before in his life, for Michael was a fearless man. He had never been truly afraid of anything, even as a small boy. Not even of evil monsters on television or film that sent most children running for the shelter of a parent's lap. But now, he could not control this dreadful Fear. Fear of losing his precious Jennifer. Fear of his being the cause of her untimely, unnecessary death.

<u>*Consequences.*</u> <u>*There are always consequences.*</u> *Take good care of her, Son*, his father had told him. *Oh, God, if You will just make her okay, I promise I will never, ever place her in danger again!* he prayed desperately in his hellish emotional turmoil and torment.

As an hour and a half stretched its way slowly, almost imperceptibly into two hours, and still she did not appear at the door, he began to pace in the parking lot, pace back and forth like a caged, nearly crazed animal, hands pulling at his hair, sweat pouring down his forehead and into his eyes, shirt clinging to his wet, tense torso.

Girl after girl, young woman after young woman, walked out the back door, some of them greeted by a young man, some escorted by an older adult, but most of them all alone. Some of them drying wet eyes; others staring out into the bright daylight defiantly.

But still no Jennifer. No lovable, beautiful, dark-haired Jennifer. No precious, irreplaceable Jenny. Where was his sweet fiancée and friend? His enthralling, thrilling lover? His Jennifer? Was she okay? Was she in pain? Was she now in the operating room? Had something gone wrong? Was she bleeding to death?

Fear cried out, accusing him, *"Yes! She is bleeding to death! She is dying! You won't see her again, and it's all your fault! You're the one to blame!"*

No! That's not true! She is okay! Get a grip on yourself, man! he told himself. *Oh, God! Please, please!*

At this point in his misery, he could not even articulate a prayer. He could only beg God. He could only beg God for mercy. *Oh, God! Please! Lord Jesus, please!*

He finally decided he could wait no longer and must now go into the clinic to inquire after her—the clinic he had avoided so much just two hours before. But the door opened yet again ... And out walked Jennifer!

A pale, white Jennifer. A Jennifer whose eyes were glazed and absent. And yet a Jennifer who was alive. His Jennifer!

He ran quickly up to her and hugged her tightly, so tightly that his sweat made the front of her blouse wet, and breathed his prayer into her ear.

"Oh, thank God you're okay! Thank God! Thank you, God! I was so worried ... so worried!" And still he held her, held her as if he feared she would run away if he released her, held her until his own trembling had stopped.

She was as icy cold as he was hot, and although her arms were around his shoulders, she felt stiff and remote in his embrace, not the soft, pliable Jenny that he knew, the Jenny who melted into his arms so sweetly, so trustingly.

Finally, he released his tenacious, suffocating hold on her somewhat, and with his hands still on her shoulders, he looked into her face and asked earnestly,

"Are you all right? Do you feel okay? How did it go?"

Looking deeply into her eyes, he found there a strangeness that he could not define. Was it hurt? Was it shock? Was it betrayal? What was it? These were eyes he had never seen before in his Jenny. Distant. Confused. Cold. Vague.

"I want to go home," she stated simply without emotion, dropping his gaze, looking over his shoulder.

"Sure! Sure! I want to go home, too!" he agreed, leading her over to his car and opening the door for her. "Would you like something to drink? It's so hot, so miserably hot."

She shook her head, "no" as she slid unto the front seat.

"Okay, then, let's get you home as soon as possible." He sat down in the driver's seat and placed the keys in the ignition. "Please come over and sit next to me," he pleaded as he closed his car door. She was not in her usual spot right next to him, but was sitting in the normal passenger position. "I was so worried, Jen! I want you right here next to me so I can make sure you are okay ... Please?" he requested, patting the seat beside him.

Funny, I've never had to ask her that before, he thought. *She always snuggles up right beside me. Is she angry with me?*

She automatically complied, scooting herself over to the middle position of the front seat of his car, but said nothing nor looked at him. Her eyes were staring straight ahead, fixed, almost unblinking. Her hands were in her lap, not over on his knee or through his arm as usual. And she was so pale. And so cold.

As he pulled out of the parking lot, he was relieved that it was all over and done with, that he had his sweet fiancée safely back by his side with no pregnancy to worry about. And yet ... what was wrong with Jennifer? She would not even look at him. She appeared to be in shock. *What did they do to her in there?* he wondered.

He drove on for a mile or two, his right arm around her shoulders as his left arm steered the automobile through the three o'clock traffic, pulling her close to him. He remembered the day after her birthday when she had told him that she was not a statue carved out of stone, and yet that was exactly what she felt like now. His arm was around a statue carved out of stone as she sat by his side—rigid, cold, staring straight ahead, barely breathing. And so pale, so deathly pale. A new fear gripped him suddenly. He asked her hurriedly, urgently,

"Jennifer, did the doctor give you any instructions? I mean ... Is there anything we need to watch out for? Any symptoms to be concerned about?"

She did not reply, but continued staring straight ahead, trancelike.

"Jennifer! I am talking to you! I am concerned about you! Are you okay?" he demanded with more passion.

"I am fine," she replied again automatically, not changing her facial expression, not looking at him.

Not satisfied with her response, he pulled the car into a convenience store parking lot, put the gear shift into the park position, turned both his shoulders around to face her while taking her shoulders in his hands, and stated firmly with grave concern,

"Please look at me, Jennifer. I want to know if you are all right. Are you feeling ... anything that might not be ... expected. Any... pain? Did the doctor tell you to watch out for any … unusual bleeding or anything like that?"

She looked at him vaguely, as if she did not quite understand what he meant and repeated, "I am okay."

"Are you sure?" he asked, not believing her fully, trying to look down in her lap for any signs of hemorrhaging. But the shirttail of her blouse was covering her. *Why the blank look in her eyes? What happened to her in there?* he asked himself.

She nodded her head and stated without animation, "I just want to go home. Please take me home."

"Of course, I am taking you home, Jenny, but I want to make certain you are okay. You are so pale and cold, so ... unlike yourself," he tried to break through her fog. "If we need to have you checked out by another doctor to make sure you're all right, I will gladly do that. I am worried about you!"

At that, she pulled herself out of his arms and stated firmly, a small spark in her dark, vacant eyes,

"You don't have to worry, Michael! I am not pregnant anymore."

"I didn't mean it that way, Jen. You know that! I just want to be sure you are all right," he pleaded with her to understand.

Instead she continued, "Now please take me home. I just want to go home. And Michael," she added emphatically, her large brown eyes cold but dead serious, focused directly into his for an instant, "I want you to promise me on a sacred oath that you will never, never tell *anyone at all* about this. Not *anyone! Ever!*"

"All right, Jenny. Of course. We won't ever tell anyone. It will be our secret. On my sacred oath, I promise. But, please, please tell me if you start to feel ... anything at all that might not be ... right. If you feel dizzy ... or faint ... or anything? Okay?" he begged her, deeply troubled.

She merely nodded, her eyes distant and remote once more.

"Okay. Look, I am so thirsty. I must have sweat about a gallon out there in the parking lot while waiting for you. I am going to run in here for just a minute or two, real quick. Can I get you something to drink ... or to eat?" he asked, trying to calm his own fears at least momentarily. *Perhaps it is just shock. She must be all right or she would tell me ... Surely.*

She shook her head "no." Then she moved over to the door of the passenger side of the front seat and turned her back toward him, placing her head against the window and closing her eyes.

"Please take me home ... back to my dorm room," she almost whispered.

Oh, Jenny, what did they do to you? he thought, but said,

"I will, Jenny. In just a minute. I've got to get something to drink. Now, I'll leave the motor running so it won't get hot in here. I'll be right back, okay? ... Okay, Jen?" he asked twice before he got another nod from his lover, his bride-to-be, and he ran into the convenience store.

He was back in two minutes as he had promised with a large soft drink, a bottle of orange juice, and a packet of her favorite peanut butter crackers, though she had said she did not want them. She was still hunched over in the passenger corner of the car, shivering, with her eyes tightly shut. How she could be shivering on such a smothering, hot day, he did not know. But he walked around to the trunk of his car and grabbed a picnic blanket and a towel that he kept there. Closing the trunk, he got back into his Pontiac and gently placed the blanket around his sweet, trembling Jenny, tucking her in as best as he could, and he folded the towel to fashion a pillow, placing it between her head and the window. Still, she kept her eyes closed and did not speak.

"Jenny, I got you some juice and some crackers," he said tenderly, softly. "Do you want them? ... Jenny?"

She shook her head, "no."

"Okay, then. I will place them right down here on the floorboard, just in case you change your mind. Why don't you put your head on my lap and lie down and sleep? It would be much more comfortable," he offered protectively.

Again, she shook her head "no," and said wearily, mechanically, her eyes still closed, "I just want to go home. Back to my dorm. Please."

"Okay, sweetheart. Okay. But I want you to stay with me tonight, though, at The Sui-- ... at my apartment, so I can make certain you are okay," he said matter of factly, as though it were settled.

She opened her eyes wide and looked at him with a stubborn resolve saying, "No! I don't want to go there! I want you to take me back home ... back home to my dorm room."

This response from her elicited an immediate, unexplained stabbing pain to his heart, much like the raw, gaping wound that total rejection brings to a lover. And it was completely unexpected.

How different from last night, he thought. *Last night she begged me to let her stay with me. Last night she could not stand to be out of my sight or out of my arms. Last night was so sweet. We were so united in spirit, soul, and body. And now she wants to have nothing at all to do with me. Wants to be as far away from me as she can. Oh, Jenny, what happened to you there?*

Chapter Sixteen

*H*e was back at The Honeymoon Suite by himself, his bride-to-be in residence at Dorm 10 at her insistence. They had ridden along the two-and-a-half-hour journey home mostly in silence, though Michael had not stopped trying to engage her in conversation for the first forty miles or so. She had stayed pressed against the passenger door, her back turned towards him, clutching the armrest, as far away from him as she could get while still remaining in the front seat of the automobile.

About half way home, she had asked him to stop so she could use the restroom. The whole time, he was very confused and frightened by her response to the clinic visit and had even toyed with the idea of confessing all to his dad, of driving on past Coburn, driving down to Mobile to get his father to examine her thoroughly to make certain she was not in any danger, to ascertain if the pregnancy had been terminated properly.

What if she has sustained internal injuries? he worried and tortured himself. *What if she bleeds to death tonight in her bed? Why won't she stay with me so I can take care of her?*

When she had returned to the car from the restroom, he had reached out to her and tried to embrace her, but she had pulled away, repeating her same request, the ubiquitous request to "go home." He had asked her again, if she was experiencing excessive bleeding, but she had insisted she was "fine." She did drink the bottle of orange juice and nibble at a cracker, and her coloring was much better, so he decided not to drive down to Mobile to his father's office.

After that, she had opened the back door and crawled into the back seat, had lain down, blanket around her, towel under her head, lying on her side in the fetal position, to ride the rest of the way "home," home to Dorm 10. Home in silence. She had not even told him goodbye when he had walked her to the dormitory, but had brushed right past him down the hallway.

Now back in his apartment, alone, Michael was totally exhausted, completely drained, and excessively confused. Physically, emotionally, and spiritually spent. He had dropped down on his sofa and stared vacantly into space, much as Jennifer had done when she first sat down in his car in the clinic parking lot. He knew he should shower, as his shirt was smelly and uncomfortable with dried perspiration, and he had not eaten anything at all today since breakfast. Breakfast! His and Jenny's daily meal, their unchanging breakfast date.

He glanced around the room in the late afternoon sun and recalled how just about this time yesterday he had thought everything would now be back to the way it was before the crisis pregnancy occurred. How wrong he had been. How abominably mistaken. What had he thought they would do afterwards—go out to dinner and celebrate? How does a couple react to the willful termination of their pregnancy, he wondered? What had he thought her response would have been? Joy? Elation?

Suddenly, the realization flooded into his mind that he had not *thought* at all. He had *reacted,* not *thought.* He certainly had not thought it through enough to determine how his pressuring his fiancée to terminate her pregnancy would affect her emotionally and psychologically. He had not really thought about that at all. He had *assumed* that she would be as relieved as he was that the problem was solved. He had not thought that maybe her reaction would be very different.

He stood up from the sofa, the same sofa that just two months ago had been their first honeymoon bed, where he had experienced such ecstasy and bonding with the beautiful, exciting woman he wanted to marry, the woman he wanted one day to become the mother of his children. But not now. Not yet. And yet ... Why did he now sense, somewhere deep within himself, that he had sustained a great loss today? Why did he feel so hollow and empty inside?

He walked over to the telephone. He had to make certain that Jennifer was okay, that she was not going to die tonight.

"Hello," said Katie softly.

"Katie, I need to talk to Jennifer. Please," he pleaded abruptly.

"Just a minute, Michael. She is in bed sleeping. Do you want me to wake her up?" Katie sounded worried.

"Yes, if you don't mind. Tell her I need to talk to her ...badly," he continued, trying in vain to disguise the agony in his voice.

There was the sound of feet on the linoleum floor, some muffled conversation, and then Katie returned to the phone.

"Michael, I am afraid that she won't ... She said she is very sleepy and that she will talk to you in the morning," Katie relayed, her voice anxious. He heard the door open and Katie step out into the hallway before continuing hesitantly, her hand over the mouthpiece of the phone for privacy, "Michael ... is Jennifer ... all right? Please forgive me for this ... You may think it is none of my business ... but she isn't... isn't ... pregnant, is she? I am only asking because I love her ... love you, too ... and I want to help if I can," she finished boldly.

He took a quick breath and responded shortly, "No, Katie, she isn't ... She isn't. Look, I need you to do me a tremendous favor, if you will."

"Sure, Michael ... anything I can do," she replied, worried.

"Just please ... look after her tonight ... Make sure that if she stays in the bathroom a long time ... that she is all right. Check on her, if you will. Can you please do that for me, Katie?" he begged her earnestly, his heart in his voice.

"Sure, Michael, certainly. You know I will ... Are you okay? You sound so tired and ill yourself," she inquired, more concerned than ever. "Can I get Joe to go over there to see you?"

"No, no. No thanks, Kate. I am fine. I just need you to watch after Jennifer tonight. That will make me feel better. Okay?" he requested urgently.

"Okay, Michael," she stated comfortingly.

"Thanks so much. Goodbye," he finished.

"Goodbye ... and call Joe if you need to ... talk or anything," she instructed anxiously as he hung up the telephone.

Michael then walked wearily over to the refrigerator to get something to drink, moving slowly, stiffly, dragging his feet as if he were an old man. He passed the pig planter that Jennifer had bought him for his housewarming gift two months ago, the night of her birthday party, the night she had truly become his. And, recalling how she had lovingly placed it just so on the counter, he caressed it briefly. And then he wept.

"Oh, Jennifer! ... Jenny! ... My sweet lover! ... What did they do to you?"

That night, Michael slept fitfully, awaking every hour or so with fear on his mind. *Please, please, oh God, make Jennifer all right. Please don't let her bleed to death.* Worry churned the waters of his troubled mind, making sleep impossible. He thought again that he should have taken her to the emergency room in town to have her examined. Something must have gone wrong in Atlanta. Surely this was not the common reaction to a pregnancy termination! Had it been painful? He knew she had been very much afraid. He could not rid himself of the memory of the strange, haunted look in her eyes and her cold paleness as she exited the clinic. Maybe it was just shock.

No. It was more than shock. She had been angry with him. Now, alone in his room with time to reflect, he knew that without a doubt she was very angry with him. But she had not said so. She had not told him how furious she was with him. She had not said anything… anything other than how badly she wanted to go home, and how he must not ever tell anyone else about this dark secret. Why wouldn't she talk to him?

I should have insisted that I go back there ... in the room with her. Maybe then she wouldn't be so angry with me. Why didn't I insist? Hopefully, she will be a different person today.

As these thoughts tumbled one upon the other as he tried to rest his weary mind and body, his bed linens became a tangled heap, and he tossed restlessly all night like a patient suffering from chronic pain who cannot find release even in sleep. Whenever he closed his eyes, he would see that grandmother walking up and down the sidewalk outside the clinic, crying and praying as she carried her homemade sign. GOD HAS A PLAN FOR YOU AND YOUR UNBORN BABY. He awoke from a short nap with the dawn and had to get out of bed. It was too early to phone her, so he again went for a swim in the deserted swimming pool.

There were already a pair of golfers on the course adjacent to the apartment complex pool, out for an early round before going to work or class this morning, he figured. He remembered his conversation with Joe on that course, about the clinic in Atlanta. He wondered briefly what might have been different had Joe never mentioned that option. He did not believe he would have thought about it on his own. But then, what would he and Jennifer be doing now? Getting blood work done and making application for a marriage license, he presumed, and then driving ... somewhere ... to a justice of the peace for a secret marriage ceremony. Surely that was not what Jennifer had wanted ... Or was it?

He waited until seven-thirty to phone her, and was thrilled when it was she who answered the phone and not Katie. She was okay! She must be all right!

"Jennifer? Good morning, Sweetheart! How are you? I miss you so much! I hardly slept at all," he whispered fervently into the phone.

"Oh ..." was her reply, her voice blank and tired.

"How did you sleep? Are you feeling ... better?" again, spoken earnestly.

"Yes ... I am okay," she replied, her voice still lifeless and flat.

"Listen, I've got to see you, Jenny. I am on my way over there now. I want to take you to breakfast," he said quickly.

There was no reply, so he stated again,

"Jennifer, I am on my way right now. You will be ready, okay? I've got to see you. I am so concerned, okay?"

"Okay ... all right ... I will be ready," she replied weakly.

"Good! See you in a couple of minutes. I love you, Jenny!" he stated passionately.

"Okay, goodbye," she replied absently and abruptly hung up the phone.

That was the first time she had not responded with the usual, "I love you, too," and he noticed it immediately. Noticed it forcefully. *Surely she is not still angry with me? I did not force her to do anything, did I? I told her I would marry her if she did not want to-- ... Why is she still so angry with me?* he pondered.

Sadly, over the next few days and weeks he had to ask himself this question over and over again. That first morning after the trip to Atlanta, she had seemed almost as vague and vacant as the day before, though she would allow him to hold her hand, and she responded to most of his questions the first time he asked them. But she was distant, very distant, and still stiff and cold towards him, not the warm, loving, adoring Jennifer of his past. Whenever he would try to draw her out as to the change in her behavior, she would just stare at him uncomprehendingly and tell him she did not understand what he meant. If he dared to attempt any reference to the clinic visit, she would look away abruptly and then become angry, insisting that she was "fine." That was all forgotten, anyway, wasn't it, never to be discussed again?

The Sunday following the clinic episode was one Michael would later recall with bitter irony. He had remembered that the previous week, when she was in her dorm room suffering from morning sickness, he had known everything would be "back to the way it was" by today. He remembered how before the termination, she would sit there in the church service literally beaming at him, glowing, radiating love and passion. But today, as he led the congregational singing, looking at her sitting in her usual place in the choir loft, he saw the same empty, blank look about her countenance that had not left her since Atlanta.

It was as if she was a paper doll—flat, one-dimensional, no animation at all, a robot—as if someone had robbed her of her soul. That "divine spark" that the poets all wrote of had been snuffed out of her. *Surely, she will snap out of this ... whatever it is ... in time.*

Maybe it just takes time, he chose to believe. *Surely I will get the Jennifer I know back, the real Jennifer.*

But it did not happen. The Jennifer he knew did not come back. Slowly, over the next three or four weeks, she seemed to improve somewhat, becoming more animated and more responsive to him. She continued to go to class and even to make fair grades. She would sit out by the swimming pool with him on Sunday afternoons, but not in her swimsuit, looking at bridal magazines as she had done before. Instead, she would wear her shorts and a blouse and study for her classes. She had not spent the night with him at The Suite since the night before Atlanta. He had been too afraid to even mention it to her, as her response to his physical touch had remained cold and lifeless.

And her eyes—those deep, dark, lovely, mysterious, beguiling eyes that he had loved so much, that had sparkled, shimmered, and danced in his presence, that had glowed warmly, ardently, passionately in his arms—though not as vacant as they had been, were now becoming guarded, shallow, and hard, with all the tenderness, trust, and vulnerability gone.

He knew in his heart that whatever had happened to her in that clinic was the reason for the sudden change in her personality. And he felt responsible. Responsible, and as guilty as could be. He would try to get her to talk about it, but would be chilled by the return of the vacant stare and questioning look she would give him, asking him what he was talking about, saying that she was "fine." Then she would become suddenly angry, asking him to take her home – home to her dorm. But the blank, vacant look concerned him more than the coldness and anger. The anger, at least, he could understand.

Worst of all, however, she was becoming increasingly cold towards him. She would with growing frequency skip their standing breakfast dates, simply not showing up nor offering explanation when he would question her. And sometimes when he phoned her at the dorm, he would hear her instruct Katie to tell him she was not there. When she was with him, she would not meet his eyes, but would instead focus her gaze somewhere in the vicinity of his nose. And she still felt like a statue in his arms. When he tried to kiss her, she would turn her head away from him and then pull herself out of his embrace.

But he kept on believing, kept on hoping that in time she would recover her loving tenderness towards him. For he loved her still, in spite of her change, and felt that the real Jennifer was somewhere just beneath the surface of this shadowlike, lifeless imposter. He believed that in time, he could somehow tap into the true Jenny and recover her, rescue her, bring her back to life—and himself back into her heart. In time. And he was willing to wait. Wait for as long as it took, because he loved her still with the same passion as before. He could bring her back to life, he knew … In time.

But he ran out of time.

On Saturday, September 7, 1975, the first weekend of the college football season—an almost sacred ten-week period in the state of Alabama, which is eagerly anticipated by its adult citizens in much the same way small children look forward to Christmas—there was a knock on the door of his apartment. Michael was wearing his pajama bottoms and was in the last stages of shaving, preparing to go pick up his fiancée from the dormitory and meet Joe and Katie for the big game. He ran to the door, hoping it was not his new next-door neighbor again, a semi-attractive but pesky blonde who always wanted to "borrow" something.

"Oh, Jennifer! Hi, Toots! What a nice surprise! Come on in. I thought I was going to ride over and get you, but traffic is so bad, this will work out even better," he smiled warmly.

This was the first time since Atlanta that she had come on her own to his apartment. *Maybe she is getting better.* He tried to kiss her lightly but missed as she walked on ahead of him into the living room.

She looked as beautiful as ever, dressed nicely in attractive slacks and a sleeveless cotton sweater that showed off her lovely figure. And she smelled sweet, too, wearing some new cologne, not his favorite, but still nice. As she said nothing but just stared at him strangely, still with inscrutable, though slightly haunted eyes, he continued,

"I just have to knock off a couple more whiskers and then change clothes, and we can go meet Joe and Katie. Why don't you help yourself to some juice and donuts that I picked up yesterday? They are over there in the kitchen."

Ignoring his offer, she addressed him, beginning slowly, choosing her words very carefully, and looking at him with an odd mixture of sadness, discomfort, and stubborn resolve.

"Michael ... I have something I ... Something I need to say to you... Something important ... Something more important than the football game."

At last, he thought, *maybe she is willing to talk about the trip to the clinic and everything. Maybe we can clear the air and finally get over it.* He looked at her studiously, trying to discern her expression before replying seriously.

"Sure, sure, Jen. Let me just wipe this shaving cream off my face. It won't take a minute. Just wait here a second," and he walked quickly to the bathroom, expecting her to sit down on the sofa.

But she followed him and stood in the hallway by the bathroom door as he made two quick strokes with his razor and wiped his face off with a washcloth.

Good! She followed me back here. She used to like to just stand there and watch me shave, he figured optimistically.

"Michael ... I don't know how to tell you this ... I don't even understand it all myself," she stammered, "but I have come here to return your ring ... and to tell you I don't want to ... I can't ... I can't see you again."

And with those unexpected words, she held out to him the one and one-half carat, oval cut diamond ring—high in both color and clarity, and with very few imperfections—in its original box, the box she had said she was planning to keep and place on their future Christmas tree each year.

This time it was Michael who just stared blankly ahead at her, not believing the words that he heard. This idea had never entered his mind, because he knew how much she had loved him. He knew it better than he knew his own name. She had loved him completely, as no one ever had to his mind, not even his parents. She had loved him mightily and had given herself to him fully. They had been bonded together, spirit, soul, and body. He knew that. And he could somehow resurrect that Jenny who had loved him. He knew he could. In time. This could not be happening.

He did not take the box. He did not move at all. So she placed it wordlessly on the bathroom counter beside him. As neither of them spoke for what seemed an eternity but just looked at each other, she with slight confusion and yet unyielding determination, and he with disbelief and distress, the telephone rang.

As if on autopilot, he walked numbly over to the kitchen and she followed.

"Hello," he said absently. "Oh, hi, Joe ... Listen, can I call you back in a few minutes? ... Oh, okay ... Yes ... We'll ... I'll ... We'll meet ya'll there ...Yeah, okay ... Bye."

"That was Joe," he began to mumble as he turned towards her, replacing the phone on its cradle, still in shock at her statement. "They are going to meet us at the stadium by the center gate ... They are meeting us there by— ... Jennifer, you didn't mean what you just said ... You didn't mean it, did you ..." he stated firmly, still refusing to believe her, his eyes desperately searching hers.

His face appeared so stricken and so dazed that she felt she had to offer some explanation.

"Michael ... I am sorry. I really am. I don't know why or ... how this has happened ... But I do know that I don't love you anymore. I can't marry you," she tried again, her voice flat and emotionless, her eyes falling away from his face.

"No, Jennifer! That can't be true! You are just ... confused and still ... upset ... about what happened in Atlanta," he offered an explanation, his eyes begging her to understand, his voice pleading.

But she interrupted him angrily, placing her hands over her ears at his mentioning Atlanta and shouting out emphatically,

"NO! ... Stop it! ... Why do you always bring up—?! I don't love you anymore, and I can't marry you! That's all there is to it!" She removed her hands from her ears, and then added more calmly while only glancing briefly into his eyes, "I am transferring to the Montgomery campus next week. I can't see you anymore. I am sorry... That's all I can say."

And with that, she turned her back to him and walked towards the door.

"Wait! Jenny!" he strode over to her side and grabbed her arm, holding it tightly. "Please, don't do this! We just need more time, that's all! We can work this out in time!" His eyes were full of love and agony, desperately imploring her. "Jenny, I still love you! I love you, Jennifer, and I want to marry you! Please don't do this!"

"Let go of me!" she shouted at him, fiery-eyed, as she pulled herself away from his grasp. "Can't you see that it's hopeless? It's hopeless, Michael! I am sorry. Goodbye."

This time he let her walk out the door. And walk out of his life, leaving him desolate. He fell down on the same, sad sofa that had witnessed so much love, passion, and heartache, placed his head in his hands, and cried out into the emptiness of The Honeymoon Suite,

"Jennifer! What did I do to you? … Oh, Lord! … What did I do?"

Chapter Seventeen

J. *E. Jacobs*, read the name above the mail slot of her new, one bedroom apartment just one-half mile from the Coburn University at Montgomery campus. It was September 14, 1975, and Jennifer's last box was unpacked while The Hulk was pulled into her assigned parking spot.

Leaving the main campus in Coburn as quickly as possible, impatient for change, Jennifer had decided to switch her major courses from English and journalism to business, thinking that she would have more opportunities for a successful career in the business world. With her quick mind and the extra classes she had taken over the years, she could graduate in just fifteen months. She felt that she needed a fresh start, a clean slate, a new beginning. Her heart had been badly broken, but she drew on her reserve of hidden strength and inner resilience, proving once more that she was a fighter.

She had felt compelled to get away from Coburn and from Michael. She had known down deep in her soul that she had to break away from the past. Why, exactly, she and Michael had drifted apart, she stubbornly refused to admit. But she was certain that she had loved him once with all her heart, soul, and strength, and that he had failed her. No, more than that, he had betrayed her. She had trusted him completely, and he had violated that trust in the cruelest way. She knew that much. But that was all she would allow herself to recall or even to think about. What was past could not be revisited. It was done. No use thinking about it at all.

Even years later, with the aid of compassionate, professional counseling, she was not able to recall very much that had occurred during the four-and-a-half weeks immediately following the trip to Atlanta. It was as if that memory bank in her brain had been completely erased. But she did know that she had to leave Michael, had to get away from the places that reminded her of him, had to get a new perspective on life somewhere else, if she were to survive. And Jennifer was a survivor. She had survived her parent's divorce. She had survived terrible heartbreak and bitter disappointment. She could survive. And, subconsciously, extreme denial concerning the clinic visit was her method of survival.

At this point in her life at least, survival was the goal. Happiness was not the issue. She would get the strength she needed for survival from the only source she could truly trust—herself. *I am woman, hear me roar!* she often repeated to herself. She knew she was intelligent. She knew she was attractive. She knew she could be stubborn and tenacious. She knew she could depend on herself, just as she knew now that she could never depend on anyone else. Not anyone. Especially, not any man. Not her father. Not her former fiancé. No, she could not depend on anyone else, but that was okay. Because she could depend on herself, on good old reliable Jennifer Jacobs.

Her broken engagement, she had explained to friends and family, was due to the fact that she suddenly realized that Michael was not the man for her. That was all. No hard feelings. No further explanations. It was better to discover this now than later, wasn't it?

She filled her class schedule as full as possible, concentrating all her energies on her studies. She wanted to graduate at the top of her class, and then begin work on her master's degree. If she had to depend on herself now, and no one else, then she knew she must succeed in a man's world, playing by a man's rules. Achievement, the accomplishment of tangible goals, producing results in the marketplace, these were the new priorities of her life, her new life here in Montgomery.

She worked part-time in the school library to help pay her living expenses, a job she enjoyed because she could study during the many breaks in work activity. And with her days packed so full with activity and busyness, with school and work, with light housekeeping, meal preparation, and laundry, she had no time to think. No time to feel. And that was just fine with her.

Courage, strength, and determination are what were needed to succeed in this rotten world, she knew. The weak, tender, frail, and vulnerable are cast aside like trash and garbage, are trampled under the feet of the strong, courageous, and determined. She was strong. She was courageous. She was determined. She had learned the hard lessons of life early. She could survive.

Not only could she survive this fierce, hard world, but also she began to believe as the weeks and months passed and she accomplished her many academic goals, that she could actually succeed. Her professors all loved her, as she was one of the few students in their classrooms who took her lessons seriously, who was not there to party and find a mate. They enjoyed her quick wit and her thought-provoking questions. They gave the attractive brunette coed high marks and much praise.

She had not made any new friends, however, not because she did not value friendship, she told herself, but because she was much too busy. She occasionally spoke with Katie on the phone, with the call usually being initiated by Katie, and there were a few acquaintances at work and in class with whom she enjoyed light conversation and small talk, but she shunned and discouraged anyone who tried to take a real interest in her. Especially any young men.

A few brave men had asked her out but had quickly been denied the presence of her company. The more insecure and passive of the male gender, however, could not even broach the topic of a date with her, lovely though she was, as the cold, challenging look in her dark eyes and the stubborn, unyielding set of her jaw sent them quickly scurrying to another desk in a different part of the classroom. All this was just fine with Jennifer. She did not need men, and anyway, she told herself, she needed to concentrate on her studies. Her grades were better than any of the young men's, and she felt she could compete with them on any intellectual level that they chose and win the contest nine times out of ten.

As the autumn gave way to winter, though, after Christmas and New Year's celebrations were over and the cold grayness of the skies fell heavily round about her, she began to feel an unexplained loneliness, a gnawing emptiness, a great sadness—an empty longing that her accomplishments and active schedule could not fill and which would make her cry herself to sleep.

So she began to accept a date every now and then to go to a basketball game or a movie, to fill up a lonely evening. She was very picky about the movies she would see, though. Nothing sad or romantic. Nothing violent or scary. Comedies were fine, but that was all. She would not go out with a young man more than twice, however, though they would continually phone her and ask again, and she would not allow them to even hold her hand. If she felt she might be attracted to her date, she would not accept a second invitation.

She no longer attended church services, although she still believed in God and knew that He was real, and she still occasionally prayed subconsciously. But God had never seemed so far away from her as He was now. Although she would never have admitted it, she did not like the way God had unfolded her life up to this point, and she felt that she could not trust even Him. She had to trust herself. No one else. Not even God.

One February day after seeing an advertisement on the television sponsored by the Humane Society, she impulsively jumped in The Hulk and drove to the animal shelter, returning with two kittens, brother and sister, neutered and vaccinated. The male was gray and white striped, and the female, mostly white with a black spot on her forehead, black ears, and a black tail. Always the history buff, she named them Ferdinand and Isabella, or Ferdie and Izzy for short.

She had always liked cats, and they were much more suited to apartment living than dogs. Why she had wanted a pair of them, she did not know, except that she reasoned they would keep each other company during her long absences. With their entertaining antics as they chased one another around her apartment, pouncing on and attacking each other playfully, purring softly on her pillow at night, the loneliness in her heart would abate, and she felt she could very well become an old maid with a cat family and be happy about it. And be much happier than most families. A truly happy family was a myth, anyway. A television program. Pure fiction. She did not need a family to be happy.

So she cruised along through the rest of the short Alabama winter, applying herself fully to her academics, working, and taking care of her new feline family, staying too busy to think—too busy to feel much of anything but fatigue.

March waltzed in like a lamb that year, and she was outside one very warm, lovely, late winter Saturday, March the fourteenth to be exact, washing her faded old car. She was aggravated at herself because she kept forgetting things that day, which was so unlike her as she was usually well organized and meticulous. She knew she needed some towels and a bucket to put the soap in, but she had forgotten them again, already making three trips up the stairs to her second floor apartment for various items needed for the car-washing chore.

"Oh, Jennifer," she quizzed herself aloud as she ran up the steps for the fourth time, "what in the world is wrong with your head today? Why are you so forgetful and distracted?" When she exited her home, she unknowingly left the front door slightly ajar.

She took her time washing The Hulk because it was such a beautiful day, unseasonably warm, with the daffodils, tulips, and azaleas blooming and birds flitting around, refurbishing their nests. The temperature was in the upper seventy's, and she wore cut off blue jean shorts and a favorite old tee shirt. Spring had always been her favorite season, and she enjoyed just staying outdoors on days like this.

After she finished the job at hand, she sat down there on the curb and stretched out her bare legs into the warm sun, resting a while, in no hurry to take her things back up the stairs. She had planned to drive down to Mobile to visit her mother and sister but was postponing the trip a little while longer when a neighbor, a young man named Mark, pulled into a parking space nearby, walked over, and greeted her. He was stocky and well built with dark hair like hers and pale, gray eyes.

"Hello there, Jennifer. I see you decided to rid the old Hulk of its outer coat of dirt and dust. Just let me know, and I will be glad to help you get it *really* clean, you know," he teased, sitting down next to her on the curbing and grinning at his last remark.

Mark owned a late model, convertible sports car and fussed and clucked over it as though it were his first-born child, washing and polishing it almost daily. He would often write the words, "Wash Me," in the dirt on Jennifer's old station wagon with his finger, but then deny that he had done it.

"That won't be necessary, but thanks so much for the offer," she replied, smiling a little. "And I think I saw a butterfly land on your radio antenna yesterday, so you might want to borrow my bucket and soap right now and attend to it before it gets any worse."

This was the closest she had come to flirting since last summer, and initially she was surprised at herself for encouraging the handsome young man. But for some mysterious reason, she felt that she needed to flirt today, to be admired by an attractive man today, to be distracted today. Today, March the fourteenth, 1976.

Mark was tremendously heartened by her coquetry. He had taken her to the movies once in February and had thought she had enjoyed herself. But she had refused his subsequent invitations for an evening out with him.

Playing along, he replied, "I appreciate your concern, but I ran it through the touchless car wash just before I came back home for my golf clubs." He smiled back at her, his eyes taking in her long, slender legs, before asking, "Do you play golf, Ms. Jacobs?"

"No, not really. I mean I have walked around the course several times pulling a bag of clubs behind me and taken a few misguided whacks at that tiny white ball, plowing up real estate as I went along... but you could hardly call that 'playing golf,' could you?" she responded, pulling her knees up to her chest, wrinkling her nose, and smiling at him from the corner of her eyes. *Why does it feel so right to flirt with him today, when I have been avoiding him like the plague all winter long?* she wondered.

More emboldened than ever, he risked rejection from her one more time and asked, "Would you be interested in playing a round— no pun intended there, let me assure you—with me this afternoon? It's such a gorgeous day."

And he averted his eyes from her, preparing himself for another refusal. But it was worth the try. She was so pretty and mysterious. It was worth the try.

"Well ..." she began, "I had told my mother that I would drive down to Mobile this afternoon, but ..." she did not finish.

Better and better, he thought. *She didn't say, "no."*

"But what? Come on, now. You can drive down to Mobile tomorrow," he offered.

"No, I can't. I have to work tomorrow. No fun for Jennifer," she pouted playfully, her lips pursed and a half-frown creasing her forehead. *What am I doing here? I don't want to go with him, do I?* She doubted herself. *Why do I feel I need to be distracted today ... today of all days? It must be spring fever.*

"Well, then," he persisted, "you can drive there next weekend. Momma can wait one more week, can't she? Jennifer needs to have *some* fun. 'All work and no play,' you know."

He looked back at her face and lifted his brows, teasing her again, noticing how the sun's rays brought out the rich sheen and golden highlights of her dark hair. She was beautiful, all right.

"Oh ... all right, then. Okay. But just nine holes. I have a big exam on Monday that I need to study for. And after you see me play, you will be sorry, I guarantee it," she relented, still not knowing why.

She had not meant to get involved with another man ever again. That was why she had the two-date rule. One date if she really liked him. Oh, yes, they were gentlemen at first, all politeness and good manners, acting as though they really lov—cared for you. But then, of course, the truth finally emerged. All they really wanted was—

"Great! Nine holes sounds just fine!" Mark jumped up and held his hands out to try to help her from the curb. But she ignored them and stood up without his assistance. He continued with the energy of optimism, "Here, I'll help you carry all your car washing paraphernalia upstairs, and then we can maybe go grab a hamburger or something before we go to the course. All right?"

He was enthused at the prospect of another date with her after all her previous rebuffs.

She smiled a "yes" at him, and they started up the steps toward her apartment. As they neared the front door, however, finding it open at least twelve inches, Jennifer cried out, alarmed,

"No! Oh, no! I hope my kittens have not run away!" She dropped the bucket at the threshold, her face contorted in fear, and ran through the dwelling calling, "Ferdie! Izzy! Come on out! Come to Momma! Ferdie! Izzy! Here, sweet kitty, kitty, kitties!"

He placed the items in his arms down on the floor and observed, unemotionally,"Even if they ran out, they'll be back when they're hungry. Once you feed a cat, it never stays away."

"No! You don't understand! They are only kittens and they don't have any claws! They couldn't defend themselves or climb a tree to get away from a dog or ... Oh, no! Why didn't I make sure the door was closed? It's all my fault!" she explained with a hint of hysteria in her voice, her eyes wide with dread and apprehension.

Mark wanted to be the proverbial knight in shining armor here to gain her favor, so he suggested, "Let's just try to calm down and search the apartment systematically and thoroughly, and if they aren't here, we'll go outside and look around the grounds. They're bound to turn up. They couldn't have gone very far."

So they checked under the sofas, chairs, and her bed. They looked in closets and cabinets. Jennifer even opened all the drawers in her bureaus because she told Mark that Izzy had been accidentally closed up in a drawer one day last week while she was in class. But the mischievous, adventurous felines were not there.

She was now at the point of panic.

"I've just got to find them! They are only babies, and they are completely defenseless!" she wailed, tears forming at the back of her dark eyes.

"Let's go outside then, and look. Don't be so scared, Silly," Mark replied in what he hoped was a comforting voice as he gently touched her hand to try to calm her.

He could never understand why some girls liked cats so much anyway. He used to tie tin cans to their tails when he was a little boy. But obviously Jennifer adored those two, furry fleabags, so he would help her search. *She will so grateful to me if I help her find them,* he reasoned to himself, *and then she can't help but want to see me more.*

They began their odyssey in search of the animals around the immediate grounds of the apartment complex. Jennifer never ceased calling out their names. All around the grounds of the dwellings she called, "Here, Ferdie, kitty, kitty! Come on back Izzy, sweet kitty cat!"

But still no cats.

Even Mark, embarrassed though he was, began to vocalize with half-hearted, "Here kitty, kitty, kitty's," hoping that no one he knew was witnessing him. He had always been a dog man, himself.

Other sympathetic neighbors upon hearing of the missing pets joined in the hunt for a few minutes at least, before they bowed out, claiming a pressing errand to run. All the diligent efforts to recover the brother/sister pair proved to be futile, however, and after about thirty-five minutes, Mark was ready to surrender to the fact that they would not be found until they were good and ready. That is just the way cats are, he knew. That was one reason he did not care for them.

"I'd say we have looked for them just about everywhere, Jennifer, and that they have either wandered off to greener pastures, or else they are hiding from us out of spite," he offered logically. "But don't worry, because as I said earlier, cats always come back at dinner time."

"But I can't stop trying to find them!" she replied, anxiously wringing her hands. "You don't understand. They are my … my family ... my … my companions and my responsibility. And they are helpless and totally dependent on me! I've got to keep looking!"

"Oh, I'll help you search some more later," he added quickly, noticing the intense worry in her face and touching her kindly on her arm once more. "Look, let's just go and have some lunch and then we can come back before we play that nine holes, and I'll just bet that by then they will be waiting here on your doorstep," he explained his reasonable, generous plan.

But she turned fierce, angry eyes on him, pulled her arm away, and exclaimed,"No! I will *not* go to lunch with you! Or play golf! You are just like a man! Totally selfish and unfeeling! Just go away! I will find them on my own!"

And with that, she turned her back on him and walked rapidly in the direction of the housing development across the street, still calling out for her cat family.

"Well, all right then!" he snapped back at her retreating form. "And don't bother thanking me for the hour I have already wasted!"

"Don't worry! I won't!" she called back over her shoulder, still walking away.

"Gees!" he said aloud to himself, throwing his arms up in frustration and resignation. He then turned away and strode back to his own home, shaking his head and muttering under his breath, "It's a good thing those stupid cats ran away when they did, or I might have wasted a lot of time and money on that woman before I knew about her! She's good-looking, all right ... But what a nut case!"

Jennifer wandered all over the neighborhood for the rest of the afternoon, calling for her precious little pets until her voice was hoarse, asking all the people she saw if they had seen them, tacking up posters with their descriptions and her telephone number around the area, offering a reward for their safe return. And all the time her growing sense of panic and fear was making her more and more irrational. She even phoned the police department to ask for their assistance and was surprised at their lack of interest in her problem.

She had completely forgotten about driving down to Mobile until her concerned mother telephoned her. Explaining her predicament, she had broken down in heaving sobs while talking with Betty Jacobs Miller, and she would not be comforted by her mother's assurances that the cats were bound to turn up, and that by this time tomorrow everything would be okay.

Everything is never okay! Never, ever is everything okay! Everything is a dirty, rotten, gut-wrenching disaster! she told herself while still sobbing.

And still the fugitive felines did not return home.

Late that afternoon, a thunderstorm began to blow across the city, dropping heavy rain and small hail onto the grounds of the apartment complex. By this time Jennifer was lying down on her sofa, crying, and blaming herself over and over again for her carelessness, thinking she would never see her kittens again. As she lay there, she heard a scraping sound at the door and an insistent meowing. Jumping up, she flung open the door to see a very wet, skinny, bedraggled Ferdinand on the porch area followed by an equally disheveled, shrunken Isabella climbing quickly up the steps. They ran as fast as they could into the living room with wild, frightened eyes, still meowing loudly as a lightning flash and subsequent thunder roll filled the space.

"Ferdie! Izzy! Oh, you bad, bad kitty cats! How could you have run away from home like that? You had me so worried! And so frightened! But it's okay, now. I'll take care of you, just wait and see. There, there, stop crying. I will take good care of you now," she both scolded and comforted her little, furry ones.

She brought out two clean towels and rubbed as much moisture as she could off them. Then, she got out her hairdryer, turned the fan setting on the low position, and got them both totally dry and fluffy, looking more like themselves than the tiny scarecrows they had been moments before. All the time she worked on her wayward charges, she spoke kindly and comfortingly to them, apologizing to them for her negligence, and crying softly—now tears of relief and joy.

When she had placed a bowl of warm milk on the kitchen floor and opened up a can of their favorite cat food, she felt that all was forgiven among all parties concerned, and her heart began to beat at its normal pace again. She sat on the floor there beside them, stroking them and loving their purring as they partook of the feast spread before them.

Thank you, dear God, she prayed involuntarily from her heart, sighing deeply. *Thank you, so much.*

She spent the rest of the evening studying for that big economics test on Monday. As she was totally exhausted from the intense emotional strain of the day, she went to bed about nine-thirty that evening, knowing that she would feel much more rested and content tomorrow morning.

Why this day had been so strange she did not know. She had felt oddly uneasy, depressed, and restless all day long, even before her cats had run away, and she was very glad it was over. "Tomorrow is another day," was her favorite line from *Gone With the Wind*. She repeated it to herself as she turned out the bedside lamp, stroked her purring charges, who were stretched out contentedly on the blanket beside her, and placed her weary head on her pillow.

The next thing she knew, it was morning again. The sun was shining, clear and bright, and the robins in the tree outside her window were singing joyously. The cats loved to sit on her bedroom windowsill and look longingly at those birds, so she pulled open the blinds so that they could sit on the ledge for a better view.

"There," she said, smiling to herself, apparently addressing the cats, "now you can sit here and lust in your hearts for those birds all you want to." Then she looked around her bedroom for the twosome.

But they were not there.

She ran down the hallway and into the living room, frantic, heart pounding, and discovered to her horror that the front door was open again. Wide open! And the helpless, defenseless Ferdie and Izzy had escaped again!

"Oh, no!" she cried loudly. "Oh, no! No! No! Not again! How could this happen again? Oh, Ferdie and Izzy, how could you run away again? Why didn't I close the door? It's all my fault! How could I leave the door open again?"

She ran outside, barefooted and still in her nightgown, calling out hysterically, "Ferdie! Izzy! Come here! Come back home to Momma! Come back home! I will take good care of you! I promise! Come back home!"

Suddenly, the clear, sunny skies began to darken. A terrible, awful, impenetrable blackness that choked the atmosphere rolled across the sky out of nowhere, and thunder and lightning accompanied by an icy cold, tremendous, sucking wind that pulled at her body, trying to rip off her nightclothes, blew heavily upon her. And all the while she was running ... running ... running for her life and for the lives of her sweet kitty cats, calling out,

"Ferdie! Izzy! Please come home! Please come home to Momma! I promise I will take good care of you!"

Then she heard them! Heard them meowing, howling, crying out in fear! Crying out for her to save them!

As she made her way over toward their desperate cries, fighting her way through the wind and the blackness and the thunder and lightning, the grass at her feet began to grow taller and taller. Up to her knees, then up to her armpits it grew! Now she had to fight her way not only through the cold, sucking wind but also through the tall, thick grass, pulling her way through it, fighting her way through it with all her strength, as it bogged her down, as it slowed down her progress almost to a standstill. All the while, the cats kept up their terrified, distressed howling, and she kept calling out to them, telling them she was on her way. She could save them!

"I'm coming! I'm on my way! Don't give up, Ferdie, Izzy! I am on my way to rescue you!" she called out plaintively.

Suddenly, the cats became children. Children crying out! Children hidden somewhere in the tall grass, crying out, calling out for their mother to come get them!

Where is the mother of these children? Jennifer thought, in a panic. *These children are crying out for their mother! Where is she? Why would she leave them out here in this tall grass and this storm by themselves?*

"Don't worry, kiddies!" she called out to them. "I will find your mother! I will find her and tell her where you are! It will be all right! Just hang on! Just hang on! I will find your mother!"

As she continued her arduous, valiant battle against the storm, the wind, and the tall grasses, fighting her way, tearing her way, struggling with each and every slow, labored step, the frigid wind pushing her backwards while she pressed on with all her strength, with leaden legs, towards the wailing of the infants calling out for their mother, she heard a new sound.

What was it? It wasn't the wind. Oh, no! It was the sound of the tractor-pulled lawn mowers, cutting down the tall grass in ever widening swaths! Cutting down the grasses close to where the babies were lying!

"STOP! STOP! STOP MOWING THE GRASS! STOP IT! THERE ARE BABIES OVER THERE! OVER THERE CLOSE TO WHERE YOU ARE! AND I CAN'T FIND THEIR MOTHER! YOU MUST HELP ME FIND THEIR MOTHER! OH, STOP! PLEASE STOP!" she cried out at the top of her lungs to the grass cutting crew, slowly, inexorably making their way toward the hidden infants trapped in the tall, concealing grass.

But the men on the tractors could not hear her voice over the sound of the wind and the mowing machines.

"OH, GOD!! MAKE THEM STOP!! PLEASE, PLEASE MAKE THEM STOP!! AND SHOW ME HOW TO FIND THEIR MOTHER!!" Jennifer screamed out in excruciating pain and emotional turmoil as the cold, relentless wind blew all around her, buffeting her, taunting her, torturing her.

She awoke with a start, sitting bolt upright in her bed in the darkened room. Her heart was pounding and her body soaked with perspiration, her tear-filled eyes wide open and wild with fear, her breath coming out rapidly, heavily. She looked around the room to get her bearings. The clock on the night stand read two forty-five a.m..

"Meow," murmured Isabella sleepily, as Jennifer's jerking movements had awakened the cat.

Presently, her breathing and heart rate slowed down to normal and she regained her composure, drying her eyes. She stroked Isabella a few times as the creature settled back down beside her and began the comforting purring sounds.

"There, there, Izzy, it's all right. It was just a bad dream, a nightmare … That's all. Now go back to sleep," she spoke softly to her cat.

But Jennifer could not go back to sleep. Not right away, at least. She could not recall all the details of her nightmare, but she knew it was horrifying and that she had felt powerless to stop the approaching evil, completely powerless to change the course of the disaster. And so terribly frightened, alone, and despairing.

She walked quietly into the kitchen and poured herself a large glass of wine. She had begun to drink one glass of wine before bedtime a few months ago, as she was having trouble sleeping and someone in her class had recommended it. "Just one, mind you," the classmate had told her. "Just one is all you need to get your tense muscles to relax and your mind to let go of some of its worry."

And although Jennifer had not liked its taste at first, she had begun to tolerate it more and enjoyed the warm, comforting, blurry feeling it gave her as it slowly made its way down her throat and into her stomach. It seemed to fill up the empty place inside her well enough to allow her to drift off into the land of much needed rest. And though this would be her second glass this evening, she drank it down in desperation while standing in front of her open refrigerator door, its light being the only illumination in the kitchen, drank it down quickly as though taking medicine.

There, she thought. *That should help me go back to sleep. I have to get some sleep so I can work and study tomorrow, with that big test and everything. I can't let one little nightmare keep me from resting.*

But as she softly padded her way back down the short hallway towards her bedroom, she still felt panicky and hopelessly despondent and prayed with all her heart that she would never again experience that dreadful dream.

Chapter Eighteen

S pring of 1976 became summer very quickly for Jennifer, always staying so busy that the days and weeks seemed to flash by in a blur. There was a two-week break between the spring and summer sessions beginning on June tenth, and she was headed down to Mobile for two days, and then on to the sandy beaches of Gulf Shores, Alabama, located on the Gulf of Mexico. Her younger sister, Susan, had invited her to come vacation there with her and a friend named Cindy at the oceanfront cottage of Cindy's parents, who were away on business in Europe. Although the parents were hesitant at first, they had agreed to let the girls stay there for a week if Susan's older sister would supervise them and serve as chaperone.

This was an ideal situation for Jennifer because she had always loved the beach and the gulf and would use any excuse she could find to escape there. Something about the warm, lovely, emerald green gulf waters and the feel of the fine white sand between her toes would bring some measure of peace into her longing, questioning soul—her soul which was now in a quandary as to the exact career path she should choose. This was the questioning segment of her unsettled soul. But the restless longing that was intensifying with time was not about a future job—it was for something she did not know. Maybe after walking miles and miles on the beach and staring for long periods at ocean sunsets, she would be able to make some sense of it. That was her hope, anyway.

As she drove the aging, creaking Hulk into her mother's long driveway, Ferdie and Izzy began circling the interior again, yowling and demanding to be released from its confinement. Like most cats, they were vocally opposed to riding in cars, always associating the vehicle with unpleasant visits to the veterinarian that usually involved painful injections and thermometers in uncomfortable places of their anatomy.

"Settle down, you two. You have been very bad kitties, you know," Jennifer gently scolded them. "We're home now."

She carefully opened and closed the car door, not allowing the animals even to think of escaping, and walked to the back door, finding her mother's open arms greeting her warmly with a big, maternal hug.

"So good to see you again, Sweetheart! I was just beginning to get a little worried," Betty offered.

"Oh, Momma, when will you stop worrying about me all the time?" questioned her now twenty-one-year-old daughter as she kissed her mother on the cheek.

"Never, I guess, Honey. It's just the curse of motherhood. You will know all about it one day, yourself," she smiled at her firstborn.

Jennifer quickly dropped her gaze and turned her back to her mother as she headed for the automobile, saying over her shoulder, "Thanks so much for agreeing to watch the cats for me while I am at the beach. By the way, when is Susie going to be here?"

"She should be here any minute now. In fact, I am beginning to worry about *her*, too," and Betty laughed at herself, joined by a small chuckle from Jennifer as she opened the car door, carefully grabbing Ferdie, and then closed it expertly before Izzy could leap out.

"Well, let's see if I can get the Hulk unloaded before Susie pulls in here with all her stuff, too," Jennifer explained as she released Ferdinand into the laundry room, closed the door, and went back for Isabella.

"My, but those two cats have really grown! What do you feed them? Antelope?" inquired Betty facetiously, admiring the beautiful creatures' glossy, sleek coats and muscular, agile bodies.

"Yeah, that's right Momma. Antelope … and wildebeest … when it's on special, of course," Jennifer teased back.

Betty, like her daughter, had always liked cats and would like to own one now except that money was tight. She gladly poured every penny she could save from her salary as an executive secretary into her daughters' living expense funds. Their father paid for their tuition and books in addition to slipping them some extra cash on the side when he was able, but Betty also wanted to contribute. And she worked hard so that her girls could have whatever material possessions their hearts desired. She knew, however, that the deepest longings of their hearts were for things that all the gold in the world could not provide. And for those things, she prayed.

Just then, Susan's car, a 1970 Chevy, began its trek down the driveway as Jennifer was depositing Isabella in the laundry room beside Ferdinand. The car had barely stopped before Susan jumped out with a squeal of delight and ran up to her hero of a big sister and hugged her tightly, saying with youthful enthusiasm,

"Eeeee, Jenny! It's so good to see you! I have missed you so much, and I can't wait for us to meet Cindy at the beach house day after tomorrow! We are going to have so much fun!"

Jennifer broke out into a huge grin at her kid sister's *joie de vivre* and hugged her back with equal affection. She had taken the role of big sister seriously, Susan being two years younger, and had always felt responsible for her baby sister's happiness, trying to shelter her as much as she could from the pain of their parents' divorce and walking circumspectly before her to provide her a good example to follow.

"So, I guess that means you are ready to let you hair down and throw away all those textbooks, Sis. Mom told me you made the dean's list last semester," Jennifer returned, beaming in pride at her young sibling's accomplishments as Susan embraced and kissed their mother.

"Yeah, that's right! I guess I just take after my big sister, that's all," replied Susan, wrinkling her nose at Jennifer. "Well, not quite. I mean, a made a "B" in chemistry, but a little bird told me you made straight "A's" again, Jen. That's great!"

"Come on inside, you two," instructed their mother, grabbing a suitcase and overnight bag. "We can talk over dinner, and these mosquitoes are about to drive me crazy. I made both your favorite dinners, spaghetti and stuffed pork chops, and I expect them to be eaten. You both are looking entirely too skinny … especially you, Jennifer. And I bought you your favorite cake at the deli, the triple fudge deluxe, as a belated birthday cake. I've got candles and everything."

"Thanks, Momsie! Sounds good to me. I think I will indulge myself tonight. I've worked hard this semester, and I deserve it." Jennifer kissed her mother on the cheek before closing the door behind them.

The three of them talked all through the delicious, home cooked meal, enjoying each other's company, singing 'happy birthday' to Jennifer, and laughing at the same old family jokes of the past, deliberately forgetting all the painful memories. For there was an unwritten law, never spoken aloud, but understood by all three: It does no good to bring up pain from the past. What is past is past. There is no changing it. Dwelling on it only makes matters worse. We must try to forget it, walk away from it deliberately, resolutely, and live only in the present.

This rule had brought them through many heartbreaks and trials over the years, seemingly unscathed. At least on the surface. Jennifer and Susan, both, were beautiful, poised, self-assured, intelligent young women, admired wherever they were. And Betty, too, had managed to convince all who knew her that she was strong, capable, and self-sufficient, able to bounce back from many disappointments, ready to take on the next challenge with courage and determination, wasting no time on self-pity.

In light of this established principle, however, each of them was emotionally estranged from the other two, soul strangers, all three, choosing to believe that they were all "doing fine," progressing quite nicely, thank you very much. Not confiding in each other their secret fears and insecurities. Not even acknowledging that such things existed. The Jacobs' women were all "fine," in need of nothing.

They spent the next day, Saturday, shopping at the new mall, trying on the latest fashions and admiring the way each looked in them, eating salads at the new restaurant to make up for last night, and then going back home to do laundry and prepare for the next week's beach vacation. The girls were leaving tomorrow to meet Cindy at noon at the cottage. They had told Betty that she was welcome to come along, too, but she had declined. She was needed at work that week, and she could not imagine that they really wanted her there the entire time. She said she might drive down Friday evening, though, if they did not mind too much.

So, smiling and waving goodbye to Betty at the end of the long driveway, the two girls drove off in Susan's newer Chevy about eleven o'clock Sunday morning after attending the early service at church. After church for Susan and Betty, that is, as Jennifer had said she would rather stay home and say goodbye to the cats and pack the car. Betty had not pressed the issue. She believed that she understood. Jennifer simply did not want the discomfiture of seeing Dr. and Mrs. Evans there.

To this day Betty had not completely understood why Jennifer had broken her engagement to Michael. She had taken her explanation at face value—that she simply had discovered that Michael was not the man for her—and had not probed the matter more deeply, for that was not Betty's personality or belief system. And the tough, hard look Jennifer had given her when she broke the news to her mother had served as a warning not to pursue the topic further. Her daughters had a right to their own thoughts and opinions and an inalienable right to lead their lives in the manner they saw fit. She knew that. But still, she was concerned about her dark-eyed, beautiful, firstborn daughter. What had happened between them, she wondered?

She knew Jennifer had loved him tremendously. And she remembered Michael's own reaction, right here in her kitchen less than a year ago, when Jennifer had fled Coburn after a lover's quarrel. Michael had been completely distraught. She knew he had loved her daughter that day. What could have happened to separate them just a few weeks after that event?

And she had heard through the gossip grape vine that he had been devastated by Jennifer's refusal of him. The breakup was all on her daughter's part, she knew, and for that reason the general acquaintance of the two had disapproved of Jennifer, thinking she was foolish to cast aside such a fine, talented, handsome young man as Michael Evans. This had irritated Betty more than a little as she believed that Michael was the fortunate one to have won her daughter's heart, even if fleetingly.

But she had noticed changes in Jennifer after the breakup. Changes for the worse. A cynicism creeping into her words and actions. A growing hardness in the depths of her dark brown eyes. A remoteness that she could not define.

What could have been the problem? Another woman? That seemed unlikely, but that was the only reason she could imagine. Either that, or some kind of problem with an addiction of some type, although that had seemed unlikely, too, given Michael's character. It was a mystery that she could not solve, that kept her awake nights. For Betty was not blind. She knew her Jenny was unhappy, even with all her academic achievements and her goals for her future. A great deal of sparkle had gone out of her eyes, and her heart seemed more distant and fiercely guarded than ever. Surely, in time, she would conquer whatever the problem was, Betty thought. *Please Lord, in time, restore Jennifer's joy and make her heart tender again*, she prayed as the girls drove down the driveway and out of sight.

Hutton's Haven was a "beach cottage" in name only. It was actually a two-year-old immaculately decorated, luxurious, four-bedroom, five-bath residence that Cindy's parents had designed and built as a weekend retreat and vacation home located just one hundred yards from the beach. Mr. and Mrs. Hutton owned and operated an engineering business in Birmingham and also possessed a mountain cabin that could sleep twelve comfortably in the foothills of the Appalachians in Tennessee, in addition to their primary residence, a Tudor style mansion in a wealthy suburb of Birmingham.

Cindy had befriended Susan at Coburn University this past year, both girl's freshman year, and the two had visited each other's homes quite often during holidays and long weekends. Cindy was an only child who had found in Susan's easygoing, encouraging, friendly personality the sister she had always wanted.

And Mr. and Mrs. Hutton had immediately taken a liking to the well brought up, unassuming yet charming, very pretty Susan, unofficially adopting her into their little family. Upon meeting Jennifer one weekend while all of them were in Mobile, the Hutton's had felt very safe leaving their only offspring in her capable hands for the week while they conducted business in Europe.

It was now early evening on Tuesday, and the three vacationers were in the kitchen preparing sandwiches and salads for dinner and nursing sunburns from their two full days splashing along the shores of the Gulf of Mexico and lying out on blankets reading dime store novels. At least the two young charges had been reading the romance novels. Jennifer had been studying, preparing early for her next semester courses. Mathematics had never come as easily to her as the language arts or history, so she wanted to get a head start on the tough accounting course she had been warned about in advance. This led naturally to her kid sister's comments as they chopped up a salad and spread mayonnaise on slices of whole grain breads in the state-of-the-art beachfront kitchen that evening in June.

"Why don't you take a break from your studying for the rest of the week, Jen," Susan began. "I don't think you will fail any courses if you give yourself three days' rest, do you?"

"But I am resting. I have thoroughly enjoyed myself here in this gorgeous house at my favorite beach, Silly. Look out … you dropped a cucumber slice on the floor over there. See?" And she pointed it out. "Thanks so much, Cindy, for inviting me here," she finished as she began to cut the three sandwiches into halves. "I really needed this."

"Don't mention it! I'm so glad you agreed to babysit us, or my parents wouldn't have let me stay. And then, I would have been forced go with them," Cindy explained.

"Right! How terrible for you!" said Susan with feigned exasperation. "That would have been one tough assignment, all right. Trekking around Europe all week. Ugh! How disgusting!"

Cindy then picked up the dropped cucumber and tossed it playfully at her friend saying, "You don't understand, Sue. I wouldn't have been allowed to 'trek around the block' by myself, much less 'trek around Europe' like you said. Are you kidding? My mom would not have let me out of her sight for one minute, and that means they would have made me follow them around from meeting to meeting in the most boring offices with the most tiresome businessmen on the continent. This week is definitely more fun, believe me! If we do get to go to Europe sometime soon on pleasure, though, I will see if we can take you, too, Susie. Maybe with you along, they wouldn't treat me like such a baby."

The three sat down to begin the meal at the kitchen table overlooking the water, watching the sea gulls and sandpipers cavorting along its sandy shores and two pelicans gliding gracefully just above the waves, witnessing the beginnings of a glorious red, orange, pink and yellow setting sun tucking itself in between the covers of some deep purple, billowing clouds low on the horizon.

"I, too, would dearly love to spend some time touring Europe one day. But I must agree with Cindy that for now, at this moment, there is no other place I would rather be. Just look at that glorious sunset. What could possibly top that?" commented Jennifer philosophically, drinking in the awesome beauty she was fortunate enough to witness before her.

The other two gazed at the majesty of the miraculous sky momentarily, listening to the comforting sounds of the surf gently lapping up on the shore, and meditating on Jennifer's words, before Susan added, lost in romantic reverie,

"Yeah ... You're right, Jen. The only thing that could make it better would be to feel the arms of your boyfriend or husband wrapped tightly around you about now."

And she sighed, a wistful, winsome, longing, dreamy sigh, as only a virginal nineteen-year-old girl can do.

"Talk about ruining a perfectly good sunset, Sue," broke in Cindy with a slightly wicked gleam in her eyes. "Why did you have to remind us that we are, all three, temporarily male-less? That's just too cruel. And, anyhow, with all of us sunburned, any arms wrapped 'tightly around us' would send us into screams of agony."

Jennifer, however, took that comment as the time to turn her back to the other two and walk to the refrigerator for the pitcher of iced tea. As she returned to the table, refilling all of their glasses, she lectured sternly, forcefully,

"For heaven's sake, Susan, why do you think you must have a man's arms around you to enjoy a sunset? What possible addition to the beauty and wonder of nature does 'a man' bring into the picture? Have you no soul of your own?"

Susan, rather than taking offense at her beloved sister's reprimand, immediately felt bad that she had been so insensitive to her feelings. She knew that Jennifer would by now have been on her honeymoon had she not broken her engagement to Michael. *How could I have been so thoughtless?* she fretted. She replied quickly, her cheeks reddening slightly,

"You're right, Sis. Of course. You are right. I only meant ... I just meant that--" she stammered trying desperately to think of something to say to ease what she suspected was her sister's suffering.

"And I seriously think that you need to spend your time reading more worthwhile literature than those ridiculous, fantastic, escapist romance novels of yours!" the elder sibling added vehemently, sitting back down at the table, glaring at her kid sister in ill-disguised contempt as she gently scolded her. "No wonder you are so boy-crazy! Really, Susan, I had always hoped that you had more sense than to think that 'some man' is going to appear out of the clear blue one day and 'sweep you off your feet,' solve all your problems for you, and take you back to his 'castle' somewhere to 'live happily ever after!' You do have more sense than that, don't you? Lord knows, you should have, anyway! Growing up in our 'happy' home!"

By this point in the diatribe, Susan had lost most of her sympathy for her big sister and was on the defensive. She met Jennifer's disapproving glare with some fire of her own saying,

"Why become so cynical and bitter, simply because our own parents didn't have enough sense to stay married? Why become a man-hating, resentful old shrew because of a few disappointments?"

"I am not bitter! Nor cynical! I am realistic! That's all. It's not just our parents I am referring to, but to the institution of marriage in general." Here she paused for a brief second to take a deep breath and calm down before continuing, "But what could you possibly know about anything at all, Susie-cuesie? You are only a baby. I just want to warn you to be more careful with your romantic notions. Those ideals of 'true love' and a 'knight in shining armor' are just make believe and will only leave you bitterly disappointed," she finished.

Susan, you don't know how rough it can be out there ... out in 'the world,' she thought.

Cindy had been both surprised and embarrassed by the vociferous exchange between the two sisters over something so personal. Surprised, because they had gotten along so well up to this point and she knew how much Susan revered and admired her big sister. Embarrassed because she knew they were talking, at least somewhat, about their own unhappy childhoods. As she had had no sibling of her own to grow up with, to disagree and argue with, she did not know the proper response in this situation, so she just sat there gazing down at the table and let the sisters finish their fight.

"Don't call be a baby, Jennifer! I am only two years younger than you, and you are by no means a woman of the world, yourself! Why do you feel you still have to tell me how to think and what to believe?" rejoined Susan, resentful of her sister's superior air.

Now that the unspoken rule—refusing to discuss the heartbreak of their parents' divorce—had been violated so blatantly and in front of Cindy, too, all the previous reserve was lost between them as they vented some of their frustrations to each other.

"You are deliberately misunderstanding me, Susan! I am *not* trying to tell you how to think! And though I am only two years your senior, believe me, I know what I am talking about. I want you to think real hard and be totally honest. See if you can name more than two married couples that you know who are truly happily married," Jennifer challenged her naïve sister. She wanted to protect her little sister from the heartbreak of disillusionment and betrayal, and maybe this would work, she thought.

"That's easy!" retorted Susan, still annoyed at her sister's condescension. "Let's see ... There's Aunt Pauline and Uncle Bob." She referred to her mother's sister and her husband, married for over twenty-five years.

"Glug, glug, glug, glug, glug," interrupted Jennifer while pantomiming her uncle's downing a bottle of liquor. "Good try, Sue, but that one doesn't count. Why Aunt Pauline has stayed with that loser for so long, I'll never know. Probably because he still has good earning's potential, saving all his drinking for *after* work hours. Go ahead. Try again," she taunted.

Flushing in anger at her mistake, Susan thought for a minute before replying.

"I know! What about Mr. and Mrs. Prescott, you know, your old friend Emily Prescott's parents. They are happy. They still hold hands and make eyes at each other." *There! You can't deny that, Jen! You used to love it when you spent the night at Emily's house,* she thought confidently.

"Okay. I'll grant you Mr. and Mrs. Prescott. You are correct about them. Now, name two other happy pairs," Jennifer conceded.

She had truly loved Mr. and Mrs. Prescott. Their daughter, Emily, had been her dearest friend and bosom buddy during junior high and part of high school before they had drifted apart. And she had spent many evenings at the Prescott home and had even gone on vacation with them a couple of times. They were a delightfully kind, mature, unselfish, and generous couple, she had to admit.

But she felt certain that Susan could not authoritatively name more than one other couple. So many of Jennifer's friends over the years had confided to her their own parents' unhappy unions, she guessed because they knew her parents were divorced, a rarity in that day, and had assumed she would understand their own sadness, fear, and resentment as they related to her the many arguments, affairs, apathetic silences, and emotional disconnects in their homes.

"How about Cindy's parents? Your parents are happy, aren't they, Cindy?" Susan begged for her affirmative answer.

"I'm out of this one! Don't get me involved in this, Sue," responded Cindy wisely, waving her hands in front of her in protest. "This is between you and Jennifer."

She was forgetting her former embarrassment now and was beginning to enjoy this real life drama. *This is better than television,* she thought. *And anyway, Daddy eventually gave up his 'thing' with that young blonde at the gym. Mother received a new diamond necklace after that one, didn't she?*

"Good answer, Cindy," encouraged Jennifer. "Are you ready to throw in the proverbial towel, Sue?"

"No way! I just thought of one. Mr. and Mrs. McComb. You know, Katie's parents," Susan rejoined.

"I can't give you any details because of my friendship to Katie, but they don't count, Susan. I know it. You'll just have to trust me on this one. Come on now, think of any parents of *your* friends, Sis," Jennifer instructed.

Katie had told Jennifer in confidence one evening, when all the lights were out in their dorm room and they were talking seriously, that her parents argued often, seldom talked, and usually spent most of their evenings in separate rooms, her dad occupying the recliner in front of the television and her mother in the sewing room or in her bedroom reading. They even had separate bedrooms, and she never saw them padding back and forth between them for any romantic rendezvous.

Jennifer strongly suspected that Susan's friends had also trusted her with heartbreaking secrets about their family lives because her forehead was wrinkled in serious concentration, and she had not replied to her latest challenge. She took no pleasure in forcing the unpleasant realities of modern family turmoil and deterioration upon her younger sibling but felt that Susan must possess such knowledge to be strong and courageous, not naïve and vulnerable as she had once been, and with disastrous results. *No, Susie, you must learn these hard lessons now, before your heart is also broken,* she projected.

While Jennifer was ruminating in this manner, Susan was involved in her own internal conflict. She knew she had a winner in Dr. and Mrs. Evans, Michael's parents, who were very happily married. But even as angry as she was with her older sister for trying to destroy her faith in the wonder and mystery of a good marriage, to try to make her hard-hearted and distrustful of men, she could not bring herself to open up the already festering, septic wound located somewhere down deep in Jennifer's soul. *No, Jenny, I can't do that to you. Not even now, as disappointed as I am in what you are trying to make me believe. I love you too much to do that,* Susan thought.

"Look, Susan, I'm not trying to disillusion you—" began Jennifer, beginning to regret on some level the bind she had put her sweet, innocent sister in, even if it was for her own good.

But Susan interrupted her angrily.

"Funny, Jen, but it appears to me that is *exactly* what you are trying to do! But I've got another one: Pastor Warren and Delores. He practices what he preaches, I know, because their daughter, Wendy, has told me as much. She said he is not perfect, but that he always apologizes when he makes a mistake and is very quick to admit it. And that he is kind and good to her mother all the time. And I'm certain there are many, many more." As she put forth this last happy couple, Susan got up from her chair and began to clear the table, still casting passionate, wounded eyes at Jennifer. " I don't know why, all of a sudden, you feel the need to think the worst about marriage. Don't let our parents' poor decision poison you, Sis, and don't try to poison me, okay?"

"Susan, please believe me. I am not trying to poison you! I only want you to guard your heart carefully! That's all. And I guess if you take the word 'disillusion' literally, meaning to erase or eradicate an 'illusion,' then maybe you are right. Maybe I am trying to get you to believe in reality and not some Hollywood, fairy tale, pipe dream of a deep, abiding romance that lasts a lifetime. It just doesn't happen that way ... not often enough to take the risk, anyway," Jennifer finished, grabbing Susan's arm and imploring her to be reasonable and admit the truth.

The younger sister paused and took a long, hard look into her hero of a big sister's face, sighed deeply, and concluded,

"But, Jen, if we don't take any risks in life, if we always choose the safe, dull, unexciting path, how very boring and lonely life would be. Don't you agree? And if we choose wisely to begin with—"

But she did not finish her thought. Instead she bit her lip and wished for the hundredth time that she would learn to think before she spoke. Who would have ever thought that Michael Evans was a poor choice? He was the most eligible bachelor they had known, and Jennifer had been madly in love with him. How in this world could he have wounded her so, embittered her so?

Jennifer released her hold of Susan's arm and turned around to begin clearing the table, summarizing her previous words of wisdom for the baby sister for whom she felt so protective.

"You don't always know about a person, Susan. And even if you do ... people change. It is best to trust your own heart, to try to make your own way in life, and not to depend on anyone else to make you happy. I am sorry if I upset you with this conversation, Sue, but I would just like to spare you some of the pain. Anyway, you're right about one thing," and she turned around, managed a crooked smile, and said, looking her little sister squarely in her eyes, "We do all have to take risks. That's a given." Then she reached both arms around Susan and squeezed her tightly while still holding some forks in her hand and finished, "But, sweet, sweet, Sue, just promise me you will be careful in choosing the risks you'll take. Just be careful... Okay?"

"Sure, Jen. I think I know what you are saying. Sure. Okay," Susan acquiesced, giving Jennifer a light kiss on her cheek.

Cindy, who had not budged from her chair at the table the entire conversation, now got up, walked over to the pair, stretched her arms around them, and asked,

"May I, the only, lonely child in this room, have a little of this sisterly love, too, and a nice, tight hug? Ouch! Not that tight! Remember the sunburn!" she added as the sisters complied. And their laughter was interrupted by a knock at the door.

"Oooo! That's our beach neighbors, Mr. and Mrs. Talbot," explained Cindy excitedly, looking through the glass in the French door. "They must have just arrived. And it looks like they brought their new grand baby."

She waltzed quickly to the door and embraced the Talbots with enthusiasm saying, "Look who's here! It's so good to see you again! And just let me look at that precious little granddaughter!"

Earl and Ruby Talbot entered the room beaming with pride at their first grandchild and smiling at the two strangers.

"Oh, let me introduce my friends to you," Cindy exuded. "This is my roommate at Coburn, Susan Jacobs, and her sister, Jennifer. Ladies, these two sweethearts are my adopted aunt and uncle, Mr. and Mrs. Talbot."

After greetings had been exchanged, Susan exclaimed, "What a beautiful little baby girl! Look, Jenny. Look at all that dark hair already. Looks a lot like your own baby pictures."

"Yes, she does have a lot of hair for only four months, doesn't she?" agreed Mrs. Talbot, still glowing with pride.

"Yep, she's got more hair now than I do," said Mr. Talbot, rubbing his bald head and laughing.

"How long are you going to have her here?" inquired Cindy, who was now holding the bundle of joy.

"We're babysitting for the rest of the week so Sam and Debbie can go away for a few days. Sort of a second honeymoon, you know," replied Ruby Talbot, still smiling. "And we are having the time of our lives, aren't we, Earl?"

"Is that right, Mr. Talbot?" asked Cindy facetiously, flirting with Earl. "And just how many diapers have you changed?"

"You'd be surprised, young lady. I've changed quite a few diapers in my time. And cloth ones at that, not these disposable kind. Much rougher in the old days," he related to Cindy, tickling the baby's cheeks as he spoke.

The Talbots visited for about ten minutes, inquiring after Cindy's parents and making polite small talk with the Jacobs girls, who each took turns holding the baby, though Jennifer's time was very brief as she was suddenly overcome by a sneezing attack and had to relinquish the infant to Susan right away. As they moved back toward the front door, Ruby said in parting,

"Now ya'll come over and visit us any time, and let us know if you need Earl's shotgun to chase the young men away, all right?"

"Oh, Mrs. Talbot, don't rub it in," moaned Cindy playfully. "There haven't been any young men around here to chase away, except those high school boys across the way who keep ogling Jennifer. She has a fantastic figure, and I hate her."

"At my age, young lady, all the girls have fantastic figures," joked Earl, winking mischievously at his wife.

After they had departed, Cindy and Susan ran to their bedrooms to freshen up before going to the movies as they had all planned. Jennifer, though, begged off, stating she would rather just stay there and walk along the beach because there was a full moon tonight. Besides, the movie in question had received bad reviews.

"Come straight back here after the show, or else call me!" she called out to her charges as they climbed into Cindy's new sports car. "I am acting *in loco parentis*, you know. Don't get me into trouble!"

They waved an acknowledgment and were gone.

Jennifer gave a very deep sigh and sat down on the front porch steps, gazing out on the white caps of the gulf reflecting the brilliant moonlight and listening to the lulling, hypnotic symphony of the waves meeting the beach, a gentle breeze softly caressing her face, arms, and legs. There was a young couple out walking hand in hand, their golden retriever running slightly ahead of them barking at the moon and chasing away the remaining sea birds. They waved a greeting to Jennifer and she returned it.

One day, I am going to own a place like this myself, right on the beach. Maybe not as large or as fine as this one, but nice. And I can do it by myself, too. I don't have to have a man to buy it for me. I can earn just as much money as any man and not have all the hassles that go along with marriage and child rearing, she thought confidently. *I can be my own best friend. I enjoy my own company. I don't need anyone to make me happy.*

After a while, she stood up, kicked her sandals off, and walked along the beach, letting the water come up and bathe her feet and ankles. She walked and walked and walked until she felt an ease in the lonely ache that had arisen somewhere in her mid-section shortly after the Talbot's visit. The moon was full and bright, low on the horizon, and she stared at it as she walked, inviting it to shine its fullness into her empty places and illuminate her soul.

I must be longing for a meaningful career. It is not far off now. I will graduate before Christmas. Then I can start to make a life for myself. A meaningful life. I can help mother, pay her back for her many sacrifices for me. I can give money away to charity. I can volunteer ... somewhere. I can be successful. I know I can. And I can have my own beach house. And I don't need a man to enjoy a sunset, the way Susan does.

She walked on and on along the moonlit path created by the reflected light playing with the foam of the breaking waves at her feet. The warm gulf waters were comforting to her sunburned skin, and the moon seemed to be beckoning her on, enticing her to pursue it, to reach out and up for it and for the stars all around it.

And as she walked on for two hours that June evening, declaring her dreams and aspirations to herself, staking her claim for her own piece of the American dream, little did she realize that she was slowly but surely hardening her feminine heart, silencing her real need for love and affection and for the hope of a family of her own. She was, without her conscious knowledge, becoming an expert in repressing and denying her soft, feminine nature, choosing rather to belittle that side of her character, to conquer and subdue it, to despise and distrust it, to put it to death, so that she could raise up the more masculine aspects of command and control, of acquisitions and power, of fortune and worldly riches.

Climbing up the front porch steps as she completed her solitary meandering, Jennifer said aloud, "One day, not so very far off into the future, I will have my very own beach cottage. And I will do it all by myself. I don't need a husband like Susan does. I don't need any man. I am woman, hear me roar." And since no one was around, she let out a little "rraarrr" into the soft gulf breeze before she entered the house.

The girls came back not long after the movie was over, agreeing with the critics about its lack of merit, and then retired to their respective rooms. They were tired and wanted to arise early in the morning to exercise along the beach before it became too hot. All the lights at *Hutton's Haven* were out at ten-thirty that Tuesday evening under the very full, very bright moon on the graceful shores of the Gulf of Mexico.

Jennifer drifted off to sleep without the aid of her wine that night as the long walk along the beach had totally relaxed her. *Everything here is so peaceful and quiet and lovely,* she thought, as she fell soundly asleep to the lullaby of the ocean. *I wish I could live here forever.*

Then the nightmare returned. Returned with a vengeance. The exact same dream. No variation. *The mowers were getting too close to those hidden, crying babies and where was their mother? Don't worry, kiddies! I will find your mother! Some one! Help! Please, oh God! Please, stop them!* And her reaction was much the same, except this time she cried out and awoke finding Susan sitting beside her on her bed.

"Wake up, Jennifer! Wake up! Everything's okay. It's just a bad dream. It's all right," she implored, concern in her sleepy eyes, her sobbing big sister in her arms.

As before, Jennifer was wet with perspiration and her heart was pounding in her bosom so fast and hard that Susan could feel it in her comforting embrace.

"Wha … What's up?" mumbled Cindy, not fully awake as she stumbled into the bedroom, rubbing her eyes. "Is anything wrong? Do we need Earl's shotgun?"

"No, Silly," replied Susan calmly. "Jennifer just had a nightmare, that's all. And she didn't even see that sick-o movie you and I did," and she smiled into her Jenny's eyes that had lost most of their terror by now. "She was calling out for help and kept saying, 'Stop, stop!'"

"Sorry … I'm sorry, ladies. It's a recurring bad dream … but I can't remember much about it except—" She broke off, pushing her hair out of her eyes and smiling a sad smile back at Susan. "My missing cats turn into children somehow. It's just one of those crazy, mixed up dreams. You can both go back to sleep now. I'll be good. I promise. No more screaming. Don't worry."

Cindy responded with a sleepy, "Okay. See you in the morning," and padded off to bed again, still half-asleep. Susan, however, remained seated on the bed, gazed into her hero of a big sister's moist, flushed face, pushed some more hair out of her eyes, and said with concern as she patted her hand comfortingly,

"Are you sure you're okay, Jen? You were screaming pretty loudly. Do you want to tell me more about that nightmare? I will be more than happy to listen, you know."

Susan was still trying very hard to piece together the mystery of Jennifer's sudden, unexpected, broken engagement and all the changes that had occurred in her personality since last September. And she somehow suspected that this nightmare was in some way related to this puzzling enigma.

"No, don't be silly, Susie. You need your rest, and I am okay now," Jennifer replied, refusing to look her little sister in the eyes. But she returned Susan's pat on her hand and finished, "As I said, I don't remember much about it. It is frightening but all mixed up, and is just one of those stupid dreams that we all have from time to time. Now, you just go back to bed and I will be fine. Okay?"

Not satisfied with her reply but knowing it was useless to try to pry information from her big sister that she was determined to conceal, Susan acquiesced, commenting wickedly upon leaving,

"All right, Sis. I hope you can get back to sleep. Just let me know if you see an escaped convict with a chain saw outside those French doors, however, and I will run get Earl's shotgun."

And she stepped very quickly out of the room, skillfully dodging the pillow that Jennifer threw at her in pretended disgust while calling out, "Thanks a whole lot for that mental image, Sue! I love you. Sorry I woke you up."

"I love you, too, Jen," came back the voice from Susan's bedroom followed by the sound of her door shutting.

Twenty minutes later, after she was certain the others were asleep, Jennifer was in the kitchen, pouring herself her saving glass of wine, swallowing it down quickly, allowing herself to enjoy the warmth and comforting burning sensation it provided though she still hated the taste. Then, for good measure, she filled her glass a second time and downed its contents with even more haste, holding her breath and shaking her head at its bitter taste. Closing the refrigerator door quietly, she tiptoed stealthily back to her bedroom and slid under the covers.

After ten minutes, the blurry, drifting sensation, which the alcohol provided and upon which she had come to rely to fall asleep most nights, overtook her consciousness. Just before falling to sleep again she thought, *I hate that dream. Maybe this is the last time for it. It must be an anxiety dream connected with school or something. Soon I will be graduated. Soon no more bad dreams.*

Chapter Nineteen

*A*nd graduate, she did. *Magna cum laude.* With highest honors. Just ten days before Christmas, 1976, she walked across the stage in the gymnasium to receive her diploma amidst the enthusiastic applause of Susan alongside her mom, and her father, who was there with Helen. Both of her parents were in attendance, all right, but were seated in opposite corners, which Jennifer thought ruefully was very symbolic. Some aunts and uncles and cousins were also in the very small crowd, as the main graduation would be held in June. She had even been named valedictorian and had given a very smart little speech about always giving one hundred percent to whatever challenges were presented in life. Her mother, and her father, too, had tears in their eyes as she spoke, both of them thinking that they did not deserve such a special daughter, both of them feeling guilty about raising her in a broken home, both of them hoping for a bright, happy, fulfilling life for their little girl. Their little girl, now all grown up and so mature and self-sufficient.

For self-confidence and assurance exuded from Jennifer now, as she had been listening to motivational tapes and encouraging herself daily since the week spent vacationing at *Hutton's Haven*. She had discovered then, quite without knowing how, that she wanted material success in this world. That she and she alone could work long enough and hard enough to prove herself invaluable to any employer, climb to the top of the ladder, and perhaps one day start her own business. That she could one day own her own vacation beach house and much more. All without the aid of any man. She did not need any man. She did not want any man. She could do this all by herself.

She had already interviewed with three large firms, applying for openings in managerial positions—openings which were rare in that decade of economic downturn, high inflation, high unemployment, and high interest rates. But in spite of, or perhaps because of those challenges, Jennifer shined brightly like the diamond that she was to prospective employers. She was intelligent and attractive, presented herself well in interviews, and perhaps most important of all, was a female.

The businesses of that day were subtly and not so subtly being pressured to hire more women in positions of management, and Jennifer fit that bill perfectly. She played her trump card expertly, dressing conservatively in modest business suits that were feminized by a slight slit in the skirt, showing off her pretty legs, and a nicely tailored jacket that flattered her womanly curves. She had mastered the art of acceptably flirtatious phrases and glances that made the older men who usually interviewed her feel suddenly young and virile again. As she smiled into their eyes and laughed at all their stale jokes, clean and slightly off color, depending on which she felt would help land her the job, they were quite smitten with her. And she had recovered her old blush, too, but this time she had learned to control it, taking it out of her toolbox to use at her discretion and replacing it with another implement when necessary.

If flirting with these old geezers will get me where I want to go, then flirt I will. I still remember how, she told herself while sitting in the reception area of MedTech Enterprises awaiting her final interview. MedTech manufactured high technological medical and dental equipment that it sold to hospitals and dentists all over the world. They had flown Jennifer up to Indianapolis for a second interview this January 9, 1977. There she sat, confidently dressed in her favorite navy suit with the softly ruffled cuff of the white blouse peeking out from the end of her tailored jacket sleeve and her large pearl earrings glowing just behind her dark hair. Her long, shapely legs were swathed in silky smooth stockings, and her skirt was just the right length to show them off. Not too long, and not too short. She looked good in that suit—and she knew it.

"Ms. Jacobs, Mr. Moyer will see you now," smiled the pretty, young receptionist as she ushered Jennifer into the sanctum of the Vice President of Sales, Tom Moyer. "Go ahead and have a seat. Mr. Moyer will be right in. He just rang me from downstairs," she finished and then closed the door to the plush office suite.

Jennifer could not help but be impressed with the lavish appointments of this office located on the nineteenth floor of the downtown building, and instead of sitting down, she walked slowly about the room. A wide panorama of the city spread out before her in floor to ceiling windows along two walls. The carpeting was thick and plush, the furniture appeared to be solid mahogany, and there were polished brass and marble accents on the granite flooring of the seating/coffee area of the suite that boasted comfortable leather chairs and a sofa. There were exquisitely framed pictures of his family on the credenza behind his desk alongside snapshots of him dressed in formal attire, cocktail glass in hand, standing next to similarly impressive-looking men. In the far corner across from the desk, there appeared to be a private bath just for the use of Mr. Moyer. The entire office suite had the rich, clean aroma of furniture polish, fine leather, and huge success.

If I work very hard and win the approval of the top brass in this company, one day this office will be mine, she coveted in her heart. *"If you can dream it, you can achieve it. There is no limitation on the human spirit other than our own fear of failure. Who deserves success? Those whose hearts and minds are sold out to attain it."* She repeated her favorite motivational mantras to herself as she awaited Mr. Moyer's arrival. These aphorisms had become ingrained in her mind and heart over the past year and were quickly entwining themselves with her soul—with the new soul she had been creating since she left the main campus in Coburn a year-and-a-half ago.

"Well, hello Ms. Jacobs!" Tom Moyer called out enthusiastically as he nearly bounded into his office.

He was a tall man approaching fifty, she guessed, trim and fit with brown and gray wavy hair and hazel eyes. He was wearing a very expensive, custom tailored suit and status symbol gold watch, and he was energetic, confident, positive, and quite an imposing presence. But he had a kind, disarming smile, which broadened as she returned it warmly, looking him squarely in the eyes and giving him the firm handshake that she had practiced so many times in the past six months.

I like him already, she thought. *I bet I could learn a lot about this business from him and get his job when he retires in ten years or so.*

"So nice to meet you, Mr. Moyer," she said sincerely. "Bob Brandon told me so many good things about you at my last interview."

"And he told me the same about you, Ms. Jacobs. Said that you were his pick out of all the interviewees if I approved," he returned her compliment. He pointed to a chair saying, "Please, have a seat."

She is very attractive and personable, all right, like Bob said. Love the Southern drawl. And I can't believe she is blushing. How charming, he thought.

He walked around the expansive desk to his chair and picked up her personnel folder, donned a pair of wire-rimmed reading glasses and said, "It appears as though you made straight "A's" ... Oh, no ... Wait just a minute ... I see a "B" ... in accounting, is it? What's wrong, Ms. Jacobs, don't like math?" he teased, peering at her over the top of his spectacles like a disapproving schoolmaster.

"Now, wait just a doggone minute," she blushed again, smiling, turning on all the Southern Belle charm that she could as she sensed that he liked it. She could turn it off just as quickly if the occasion warranted it. "I had a ninety-two average in that silly class! Just one point away from the ninety-three I needed for that 'A'. But that mean ol' professor had absolutely no pity at all! I'll remember him, all right, when I am rich and famous," she threatened facetiously.

There's that enchanting blush again. How could that 'mean ol' professor' not give her one measly point? he thought. *He should be dismissed.*

"So you want to be rich and famous, huh?" he asked, expertly.

"Well ... If I may be perfectly frank ..." she began demurely, fluttering her eyelids somewhat.

"Please do," he instructed.

"I wouldn't mind at all being rich. The famous part, I could do without," and she grinned at him, a practiced twinkle in her eye.

"Too much publicity and loss of privacy, huh," he played along.

"Yes. That's right. Like a fish in a glass bowl. Not for me," she finished, a playful pout creasing her full, red lips.

"But the riches are?" he questioned, his eyebrows raised in good-humored probing.

"Yes. The riches definitely are," she continued. "I want my own vacation beach cottage on the Gulf of Mexico to repair to, to refresh my soul, after working so long and hard for your company here, increasing your sales significantly and making a good impression on your customers. I am not afraid of hard work, Mr. Moyer. In fact, I want to be challenged. And I know in my heart I can succeed," she stated simply from her heart, now dropping the smile, the pout, and the blush. She wanted him to know she was serious.

"You know you can succeed *here*? Do you know anything about the equipment we sell, Ms. Jacobs?" he explored further, thoroughly enjoying this interview.

"Yes, sir. I have been reading and doing research on it for the past ten days or so, and Bob Brandon gave me more information when I saw him last week. But with medical technology changing almost daily, the trick to selling it—it appears to me—will be keeping abreast of it all as it evolves. And I am a fast learner, Mr. Moyer. I know I will succeed. Either here ... Or with one of your competitors," she finished with aplomb, with a serious face but with smiling eyes focused directly on his, holding his gaze.

He was silent for a dramatic moment, returning her steady gaze as in a contest to see who would blink first. She sensed the challenge and determined it would not be her, as she peered steadfastly into his face.

"By golly! I like your style, Ms. Jacobs!" he then exploded loudly, hitting her folder on his desk in emphasis and laughing out loud as he rolled his chair back away from his desk somewhat, leaning back in it and placing his hands behind his head, still looking at her in wonder and approval. "Yessir! I like your style just fine! I think you could sell raincoats to desert dwellers, by golly! You've got this job, Ms. Jacobs! Full, maximum salary for this position, plus commissions, of course, and full benefits. We have a great retirement package, you know. Plus a company car. Now how about it!"

The Southern Belle from Mobile, who had involuntarily jumped slightly back in her seat at his resounding initial outburst, was now restored to her original composure.

She smiled back broadly and stated with enthusiasm, "When can I start?"

She started work as a sales manager trainee exactly two weeks later, giving her barely enough time to move her belongings, at company expense, settle her accounts in Montgomery, say goodbye to her family in Mobile, and have the old Hulk tuned up and checked over for the ten hour drive to Indianapolis. This would be the old '64 Ford's last purposeful journey en route to the junkyard, and though Jennifer was eagerly anticipating the new company car—the first new car she would ever drive—she felt strangely sentimental and nostalgic about replacing the old clunker. It had taken her so many miles with very few mechanical problems and had been part of her identity since high school. *Oh, well,* she thought, *it's definitely time to rid myself of the last vestiges of my old life. Out with the old, in with the new!*

And as she drove along on the highways through her beloved state of Alabama, past what was familiar and into the unknown, on into Tennessee and Kentucky, and finally, crossing the wide Ohio River into Indiana in the deadness of winter, her two cats keeping her company, she was warm inside with excitement and anticipation of the future.

The future! That's where I belong! What's past is past. Over. Dead. Done with. I can't change the past. But, by golly, I sure can make my future bright! The future is where all my fortunes lie. And I can control it myself. Not depending on anyone. I am woman, hear me roar, she repeated to herself over and over again during the ten hour drive.

Her brain had been washed from negative patterns of thought during the past twelve months as she had spent at least an hour each day inundating herself in every positive-thinking, motivational, self-help tape and book she could beg, buy, or borrow from libraries, friends, or bookstores. She listened to the cassette tapes in her headset as she walked an hour each day or rode the stationary bicycles at the gym. She talked to herself encouragingly, positively now, instead of critically, as she had often done in the past She knew she must be her own cheerleader if she were to make it in this world. No one else would cheer her on, she thought, so she must do it herself. *Rah, rah, rah! Go, Jenny, go! You can make it! You can have good success! You've got what it takes! Rah, rah, rah!*

And so far, at least, all the effort to redirect her thinking had produced tremendous victories. She had continued to excel in her studies, conquering even her most challenging academic subjects, such as calculus and complex mathematics that had been her dreaded nightmares in the past. She felt very proud of the ninety-two in her fourth-year accounting class, the really difficult senior class that had left many of her former classmates one subject shy of their graduation requirements. And she had almost aced it!

In addition to this, she had been offered every job that she had applied for, far out-shining the other applicants. She had gone into the interviews knowing that none of the other hopefuls was as well prepared, as talented, as smart, or as good-looking as she was. She felt that the sky was the limit, and maybe she could even pierce the sky and conquer the upper reaches of outer space with the world at her feet.

So, as she neared her new temporary living quarters, a fully furnished apartment near the office that her company had arranged for her, the workings of her heart were in direct contrast with the dull, gray coldness of that winter day. The winter may have represented her past—cold, empty, dead, and lonely—but there was a warm, bright, glorious spring to be had tomorrow. Tomorrow. In the happy, hopeful future.

Chapter Twenty

"*E*xcuse me, but could you please give me directions to the Mercy Memorial Hospital?" Jennifer asked the gas station manager somewhere in downtown Cincinnati in February as she jumped up and down slightly, rubbing her gloved hands together to try to stay warm.

An icy blast originating in polar Canada but racing headlong down toward the warmer, more inviting regions of Florida, as if trying to blow as fast as it could away from itself, whipped around her, making her suddenly homesick for the mild, south- Alabama winters of her youth.

Jennifer, who had by now completed her rigorous training courses in Indianapolis, was on her first ever solo sales call. She had driven to Cincinnati in her new company car instead of flying, as it was only about a two-hour drive away. She thought she had mapped out her route to the hospital perfectly but somewhere along the way had made a wrong turn, and rather than drive around aimlessly for a while as many a man might do, she thought sarcastically, she did the reasonable, feminine thing. She stopped and asked for directions.

As it happened, she was not far off course and pulled into the hospital parking lot in plenty of time for her scheduled appointment. She had allowed herself an additional thirty to forty-five minutes, as was her habit, always wanting to arrive early instead of risking tardiness.

This sales call was in answer to a request for new, state-of-the-art diagnostic machinery, and Jennifer had been up until late in the evening preparing herself to answer any and all questions the purchaser might have. As she entered the hospital lobby, she thought about the irony of her situation. She had always loathed hospitals and dental offices. The sight of blood made her queasy, and all the sick people depressed her. But she felt she would become desensitized to it in time and that hospitals would become just other buildings to her before long.

She walked into the ladies room first to freshen up, then made her way to the administrative offices of the large Catholic hospital. At her scheduled time, she was shown into the offices of Sister Mary Margaret, the kind but no-nonsense, sixty-ish, heavyset nun in charge of purchasing new equipment.

"Hello, Sister," the new sales manager began, extending her hand, wondering if that was the appropriate form of address for a nun.

She wished she had thought to research that beforehand as she hadn't a clue, growing up in Alabama, a bastion of Protestantism, where she had only known one Catholic in her entire life, a sweet girl named Mary Beth.

"I am Jennifer Jacobs, new regional sales manger for MedTech."

"Hello. Welcome," returned the Sister, looking her over from top to bottom. "You must be half frozen, with that vicious cold front bearing down on us. Help yourself to a cup of coffee. And just how old are you, dear? Excuse me for asking, but you look like a teenager. And I was expecting a mature, good-looking *man*, despite my being a nun. Drat!" And she winked ever so slightly at Jennifer, her face still stony.

"I'll take the teenage thing as a compliment," Jennifer smiled back into the wrinkled but vibrant blue eyes of Sister Mary Margaret. *I like her,* she thought. *A down to the brass tacks type. Honest. No pretense.* "I am actually twenty-one. Will be twenty-two the fourth of June. And I am replacing Tom Collins, who has taken a position with another company."

"That's right. Tom Collins. Always liked that name. In fact, I could use a good stiff drink about now, myself. Would warm me up better than that cup of coffee you have," the nun continued her repartee, this time allowing a slight smile to crease the left corner of her upper lip as she still fixed her stare on this pretty, young sales manger. "But since it's still working hours, pour me a cup of coffee, too, please dear, while you're over there. Three shakes of sugar, no cream."

Jennifer complied cheerfully, while saying, "I know you are wondering how long I have been selling medical equipment and machinery. To tell you the truth—" but she was interrupted by the intrepid nun,

"Please do, dear. Always tell the truth. It saves so much trouble in the long run." And her eyes twinkled very slightly.

I really do like this nun, thought Jennifer. *Perhaps I should have been Catholic like Mary Beth.* She placed the foam cup into the Sister's hand, sat down, and continued, still smiling.

"You're right about that, Sister Mary Margaret. And it comes in real handy for salesmen, too, in the long run. I was raised a Baptist—"

"Humph!" broke in the nun again, her face dead serious, her eyes now twinkling merrily.

Jennifer now was fully participating in the joy of verbal interplay with this witty, sage woman and continued playfully and yet seriously, too.

"As I was saying ... I was raised a Baptist in Mobile, Alabama, and we were always taught that 'Whatsoever a man soweth, that shall he also reap' and 'Be sure, your sins will find you out.' So I want you to know that I value honesty, myself, and I will deal honestly with you and with any other of my clients. You may rest assured about that."

"Of course, dear. I expect honesty from all the MedTech people. They have never tried to cheat us in any way. And I'm sure they did a thorough background check on you before hiring you, too," the Sister set forth.

"Really?" Jennifer asked involuntarily, her brow wrinkling. She had never thought about that before. "A background check? On me?" *That was illegal, wasn't it?* she thought.

"Certainly, sweet innocent," replied the wily nun, searching Jennifer's countenance carefully as she rocked back in her chair, finger tips pressed together doing mini-pushups. "You didn't know that? There are many businesses that provide background checks for employers on any and all prospective employees. You're not concerned about it, are you, dear? You haven't concealed a criminal record, have you?"

"Good heavens, no! Of course not!" responded Jennifer, now blushing against her will at her own naïveté. *Darn this blush of mine! And I wanted to present myself as a mature professional to this hospital, too!* she castigated herself. She tried to regain her composure, cleared her voice, and spoke with what she hoped was assurance.

"Anyway, what I was going to tell you earlier was that you are my very first, solo sales call, and—"

"Oh, so you were a sales 'virgin,' as it were, until this meeting," questioned the nun, still observing Jennifer's face carefully.

"Yes, I suppose you could word it that way if you want to, though it seems odd to me," she began, her face reddening again, "but as I was saying ... with you being my first solo sales call, I was up half the night preparing to answer any questions you might have ... about the equipment and all ... So if you have any ... questions that is ... about the products, you know, and not about me ... please fire away," she stumbled and stammered, wondering why in the world she said the 'and not about me' part while dropping her eye contact with the Sister, suddenly becoming uncomfortable and losing her professional air under her steady gaze.

Darn it! she thought. *Why do I suddenly feel as if I am guilty or something? As if this nun can see into my soul and discern my past? We're talking about medical equipment here—not my virginity or lack thereof, for heaven's sake! Besides, this is certainly none of her business.*

The Sister did not say anything at all for what seemed like an hour to Jennifer, but just sat there, concentrating on the young sales manager's discomfort, silently entreating Heaven. *Oh, God, You who search all hearts and souls and who appointed me in this position to help sinners, not just purchase equipment, please help this pretty young lady, this Jennifer Jacobs, with whatever it is in her past that is troubling her at this moment. Remind her that You are a God of mercy. They teach that in the Baptist church, don't they?* The nun never lost her dry sense of humor, even in her conversations with the Lord.

Jennifer, however, was not addressing Heaven just now, nor was she feeling too kindly towards the once lauded Sister. *I can't believe she is just sitting there watching me squirm like this. Why did I ever like her so much? No wonder most kids hate Catholic school!*

Finally, after what seemed an eternity, Sister Mary Margaret felt impelled to speak.

"May I see your brochures and data on the new ultrasound technology, dear? We are very interested in purchasing those. They are so helpful in diagnosing illness and in tracking the progress of the developing fetus, you know. One of our surgeons even performed surgery on one of God's precious little ones *in utero* a couple of months ago. Poor little fellow had a blockage in his ureter or kidney or something that was diagnosed on one of your machines. Marvelous inventions, those," the nun continued as Jennifer gratefully spread out the requested information before her.

Now back on track, she continued with her presentation, answering all pertinent questions, comporting herself in a very professional and yet amiable manner, and closing her first ever sale. Sister Mary Margaret did not make any further personal references, but was kind and supportive of the young professional saleswoman. After the paperwork had all been signed and placed in Jennifer's briefcase, the nun remarked, looking directly into her eyes again,

"Now. That wasn't too bad for your 'first ever solo sales call,' was it? You survived it very well, dear, and I predict a bright future for you at MedTech." And a smile that lasted one-quarter of a second flitted across the Sister's face.

"Thank you, Sister. It certainly has been a pleasure to meet you. I look forward to many more meetings with you here, and if you are ever in Indy, please phone me. I would love to take you to lunch," Jennifer returned sincerely, smiling warmly, her feelings of affection for the nun returning after closing such a good sale. *Tom Moyer will be pleased, as well as my supervisor,* she thought joyfully.

"I may take you up on that, dear. Lunch is my favorite part of the workday, and I know you will take me somewhere nice and expensive with part of your 'very first' large commission check," returned Mary Margaret before continuing. "Now dear, I will walk with you out to the lobby as I always did Tom Collins, past our new neo-natal intensive care unit. Everyone always likes to see the new little ones when they visit our hospital. Makes them feel better about visiting all the old, sick folks, you know."

They walked out and took the elevator down to the lobby, turned down a hallway to the left, and stood in front of the glass window of the neo-natal unit.

"There he is … that's little William … the one I told you about who had the corrective surgery while still in his mother's womb. He was born six weeks early but is progressing quite well. His parents should be able to take him home next week. Hey there, little William. Yes that's right, son," cooed Sister Mary Margaret whose face was transformed, now beaming with pride and joy, her usual deadpan expression gone for the moment. "You will be home by this time next week, Lord willing."

Jennifer, out of politeness, looked momentarily at the scrawny, premature infant, squirming and contorting his facial expression and thought, *I guess he's got a face only a mother could love, poor thing,* before looking away.

Sister Mary Margaret then turned to face the new regional sales manager from MedTech and stated passionately, "Whether they know it or not, your firm is doing God's work, dear—at least here, in this hospital—by creating and manufacturing the technology that is saving the lives of these precious babies. You should be proud that you work for them, Jennifer. I wish you Godspeed, dear."

And she patted her cheek in a maternal way, trying unsuccessfully to look into her eyes, as Jennifer, red-faced, was focused on her briefcase, fumbling with its clasp.

"Yes, well … thank you, again, so much, Sister. I've really got to be going now. I have one more appointment and then a two-hour drive back home. Thanks, again. Will see you soon, I hope," and she managed a weak smile, shook hands formally, and turned to walk back to her car and away from this nosey nun.

As the nosey nun stood there staring at Jennifer's back as she strode quickly away, she pondered the young woman's previous, guilty discomfort while back in her office, her reaction to seeing little William, her avoiding her eye contact with a flushed face, and her now beating a hasty, awkward retreat, not wanting to look at the premature babies. And she prayed, sadly, from an insightful, broken heart, *Oh, no, Lord! Not another wounded one. Not sweet, pretty, little Jennifer, too. Please comfort and heal her, Lord Jesus.*

"Get out of my way, you stupid jerk!" Jennifer blew the horn of her brand new company car at the driver of the automobile who was unfortunate enough to be in line ahead of her as she fought her way selfishly through rush hour traffic. She was trying desperately to get out of Cincinnati quickly enough to arrive home in time for her night course at a local university where she was working on her master's degree.

The other driver apparently was having none too fine of a day himself. He blew his horn right back at her, waved an angry fist, and shouted inaudible obscenities as she turned her car fiercely in front of his, tires screeching. She pushed the accelerator to the floorboard and raced around him, weaving dangerously in and out of traffic, making her way toward the last traffic signal before the on-ramp to the interstate highway.

"If he can't drive, he should have his license revoked! Stupid man!" she spoke into the interior of her blue sedan. "Some men just think they own the road, that's all!"

Finally, she was headed down the freeway still thick with traffic but with no more traffic lights to deal with. Her heart rate was slowly returning to normal, and her hands no longer gripped the steering wheel as though it were a lifeline and she were overboard in shark infested waters. Her heavy breathing returned to normal also. She turned on the radio, flipping through the dial to find an easy listening station which she hoped would help calm her some.

"Someday, when I'm awfully low, when the world is cold, I will feel a glow just thinking of you ... and the way you look tonight," the Lettermen harmonized.

She quickly changed the channel.

"I need no soft lights to enchant me, if you'll only grant me the right to hold you ever so tight, and to feel in the night the nearness of you," Frank Sinatra softly crooned.

"Sorry, Frank. Not today," Jennifer spoke irritably to the radio.

She hit the channel selector button once more.

"I'd like to know if your love, is love I can be sure of, so tell me now, and I won't ask again. Will you still love me ... tomorrow?" Carole King implored plaintively in the pop classic.

She turned off the radio and placed a motivational tape in her cassette player.

But she did not hear the first few paragraphs of the speaker *du jour*. She was fuming again, *I sure hope this traffic thins out. I have to make it to that lecture tonight because I didn't understand the concept set forth in the textbook. If that blasted "Sister Double M" hadn't kept me in that stinking hospital for so long, I would now be well ahead of all these nasty people in their hateful little cars!*

She then blew her horn again at a driver trying to pull out into the left lane in front of her and cut him off, glaring at him as she drove past.

"Idiot!" she shouted loudly, unaware that her anger was totally out of proportion.

Anger had been her constant companion and roommate for the past six or seven months, moving in quite unexpectedly and making himself at home. Seething, fomenting, just beneath the surface Anger that would materialize in moments when her guard was down or when any type of stress or frustration would cross her path. She had not seen him coming, nor had she invited him consciously into her personality. In fact, she was quite unaware of him most of the time. But, nevertheless, Anger, being the rude houseguest that he is, was taking up residence in her heart and soul, invited or not. And she was using his energy to attain greater and more far-reaching goals, such as her desire to earn her master's degree in business. She was pushing herself, constantly straining and extending herself, staying very busy with virtually no free time to relax and recreate. No time to think. No time to reflect. But that was the way she wanted it.

Yes, it's all that nun's fault, all right! She monopolized my time and made me late for my next appointment. Luckily, I got that next sale, anyway. I should be happy now. A hugely, successful day. My first two solo sales calls come back with big, big contracts signed. Why am I not happy? she wondered.

"Happiness is all created by you, by how you choose to look at life, by how you choose to respond to the challenges life is constantly throwing at you," responded the motivational speaker from the cassette tape.

"Thank you!" she addressed the cassette player, now laughing to herself. "I needed that."

"That's right! You and you alone determine each day whether or not you will be happy," continued the tape player. "If you can control your attitude, your outlook, your orientation to seeing challenges as mere obstacles that you are overcoming to make you stronger and more able to be successful, then you can be happy no matter the circumstance," the recorded message finished with confidence.

Traffic was definitely thinning now, as most of the daily commuters were pulling off the freeway onto the main arteries of the suburbs that would lead them to their subdivisions and finally their streets and driveways. Jennifer was relaxing more and more, and Anger was once again relegated to the nether regions of her subconscious, awaiting the next minor incident that would again call him to the foreground to wreak havoc and bring chaos to her emotions and perhaps hurt feelings to her friends, co-workers, or family members. He was patient. He knew he would not be idle for very long.

She drove the rest of the journey back to Indianapolis and the much-anticipated evening business class in silence, listening to her life-saving motivational tapes and making herself "happy."

It was late that same evening, about eleven thirty, when Jennifer was finally able to turn out the lamp in her room. Her long day that had begun at five o'clock had been an exhausting one. Winning all the battles presented to her, not to mention fighting the bitter cold, frigid elements of nature, had left her completely drained. She had done her grocery shopping after her university course, arriving at the supermarket about ten o'clock, as was her habit. She preferred to stock up on supplies late in the evenings when the stores were emptied of most of the housewives and their squalling, whining infants and toddlers. Pulling the heavy covers up to warm her through the cold winter's eve, she snuggled up to the cats, who also liked the warmth of the down comforter, and she stroked them alternately as they purred her to a much needed, deep sleep.

Oh, No! No! Stop them! Please stop those mowers! Help me find their mother! There are babies, helpless, little babies over there! Hidden in the tall grass! Oh, God, please stop them! And the cold, relentless wind was blowing, ripping, tearing at her all the while as she fought her way over to where those children were.

"NO! … STOP! ... Oh, Lord! ... Oh, no! … No! …" She was sitting up in bed again, sweat running down the sides of her face, her pulse pounding in her neck, her breath again labored and heavy, tears in her eyes.

"No. Not again. Not that same terrifying nightmare again," she spoke to herself despondently as she brushed her hair from her damp forehead and tried to slow her breathing. She had not had that bad dream since leaving Alabama. She had thought it was associated with the pressures of graduating with honors at the top of her class and finding a good job, but now ...

As her adrenalin abated and her system returned to normal, she slipped from under the covers so not to awaken the cats and shivered as the cold air in the room met her perspiration-soaked nightgown. She threw on her bathrobe and walked to the kitchen, still shivering. She poured out a large drinking glass full of wine, a container that held at least sixteen to eighteen ounces, and downed it. The clock on the stovetop read three fifteen. And she had a very important meeting in the morning with Tom Moyer! She walked to the bathroom, opened the medicine cabinet and swallowed an over-the-counter sleeping pill, ignoring the warning on the label about taking the medication with alcohol. She had to get to sleep, but she was still wide-awake and slightly frightened of going back to bed. What if the nightmare should come back?

She padded into the living room, turned on the television set, covered herself with the hand-crocheted afghan her aunt had made her, and settled down on the sofa, watching an old, black-and-white movie about some gold miners in the Yukon as the cold, arctic wind whistled outside her window. After twenty minutes or so, the drugs she had consumed made her feel drowsy enough to go back to bed.

As she pulled the covers back over her tired body, she thought, *I probably was just over-stimulated today with my first sales calls, that's all. This bad dream will not recur. Surely.*

Chapter Twenty-One

"*N*ow, to present the award for the Salesperson of the Year, is our highly-esteemed, greatly feared, and most notably avoided in the parking garage at quittin' time, our very own Vice-president of Sales, Mr. Thomas Moyer!" quipped Bob Brandon, roasting his affable boss in good fun at the annual MedTech Enterprises Awards Banquet being held in the posh ballroom of the most elegant hotel in downtown Indianapolis at eight o'clock, the evening of March 14, 1978.

The crowd was applauding and chuckling appreciatively at the reference to Tom Moyer's driving habits in the multi-storied parking garage that abutted the office building. Tom was a huge racing fan, a local, vocal supporter of the Indianapolis 500 Race each year, last year being honored to drive the pace car at the annual Memorial Day weekend competition. And the frustrated, repressed race car driver existing in his alter ego would often express himself in the evenings, as he would speed his high performance sports car down the ramps in the garage. Twice, the local police had ticketed him, but this had put no damper on the middle-aged executive's spirit. He could easily afford both the fines and the increased insurance rates.

Mr. Moyer was now standing in front of the microphone at the podium, beaming his winning smile down upon the MedTech personnel and shaking a friendly fist in mock anger at his underling, Bob Brandon, who was seated at the head table and functioning as the master of ceremonies.

"It had better not be you, Bob, who phoned the local authorities and complained about my driving in the garage, claiming reckless endangerment or something."

More laughter followed as Bob was shaking his head 'no way' and looking back at his boss in exaggerated, wide-eyed innocence. "I need this job too much, Tom," he said, playing along with his superior.

Jennifer was seated at a table to the right of the speaker's podium and was laughing along with the others. She was dressed impeccably in a classic, cocktail length, dark emerald green, satin evening dress, short-sleeved, form-fitting, and with a relatively low neckline that was flattering but not too provocative. The back of the gown was cut in a deep v-line and featured a long row of buttons instead of a zipper, which she had experienced difficulty buttoning by herself as she had prepared for the evening's festivities. She wore matching green high heels and had her hair fashioned in an upswept style that displayed her graceful, slender neck and throat to perfection and flattered her high cheekbones and large eyes. She looked beautiful... and she knew it.

But what was more becoming than the twenty-two year-old's face and figure was the flushing anticipation of something good about to happen to her, the excitement of achieving another hard won goal, of fulfilling the next step in her overall plan for success in her life.

Because Jennifer knew beyond a doubt that she was going to receive that award. She had out-performed all the men in her region, had been praised the most of all the other sales managers, and had even read some of the letters clients had written to Tom Moyer commending her excellent work and careful attention to their needs. And she had only been there one year!

Why, I can own this company in ten years! she thought. Her commissions and bonuses had doubled her salary, and she had more money than she knew how to spend and invest wisely, though she was carefully researching it. She withheld no reasonable luxury from herself with the money she had budgeted for personal spending, and was feeling thoroughly elated at her year's successes.

So her heart was racing and her fingers were clasping and unclasping on her lap as she awaited the award's presentation. She was seated next to her escort for the evening, another MedTech employee named Jim Smithson, a thirty-year-old divorcee who worked in the accounting department. Jim had been denied her company more times than he could add on his calculator, but he possessed a bulldog determination to keep on trying. His persistence had finally been rewarded with her acceptance of his presence by her side tonight. And he was having difficulty focusing on the program, as he could not take his eyes off her. She was so lovely and feminine seated so close to him, her face attractively blushing, her large, dark eyes reflecting the overhead accent lighting and the candles on the table, the corners of her full lips turned up in an eager smile. He believed he was the luckiest man in attendance. He had already received his award. Now, if she would only say more than three words together to him. She was more distracted than usual tonight, he noted.

"We are so fortunate, here at MedTech, to be able to recruit the most intelligent, the most hard-working, the most dedicated, and—I might add, the best looking—sales team that this industry has ever seen," effused Tom Moyer, flattering himself and his staff narcissistically as they all applauded themselves. He involuntarily directed his eyes briefly at Jennifer when he said that last part, and her blush deepened.

"You all clean up real nice," he continued as the polite laughter lingered in the ballroom. "And you all worked your tails off last year, producing record sales, exceeding our own optimistic projections by fifteen percent. I want each and every one of you, salespersons and sales support staff included, and all you wives who allow your husbands to be gone four days a week—You are a part of our success, too. A very big part …"

And he paused here, as the room burst into spontaneous applause for the long-suffering wives, many of whom were relieved when their spouses were gone during the week because their lives were much simpler then.

"I want each of you to know how very proud I am of you, of your dedication and determination. Without you, I certainly would not be looking so good right now."

More laughter.

"I want you to know I that realize that. It is each of you who makes me successful. It is each of you who makes MedTech successful, and I wish I had an award to present to each of you," Mr. Moyer elaborated.

Then, for dramatic effect he paused to pick up the large plaque in anticipation of the actual presentation. He held it up high for all in the large ballroom to see, the bright lights reflecting off the engraved, brass surface and shining down into the crowd like a spotlight.

Jennifer's heart was really racing now, and her breath was quickening.

"But, unfortunately, I only have one of these Salesperson of the Year plaques to present. This year, the winner is a man who not only exceeded all my expectations, but also surpassed his own region's projected sales by a whopping twenty-five percent. Our Salesperson of the Year for 1978 is none other than Mr. Charles Graves of the Seattle region! Help me welcome him to the podium, guys! Come on up here, Charlie, and take this thing," concluded Mr. Moyer, smiling broadly at Charles Graves as he made his way forward from his seat near the back of the room to the applause of the MedTech faithful.

Jennifer's smile had become fixed and frozen from the moment the word "man" had escaped Tom Moyer's lips, and she was clapping her hands automatically and turning her head to view Charles receiving *her* award with the rest of the group. But she felt as though a mule had kicked her hard right in the chest. The inflated balloon of her hope had been burst suddenly and unexpectedly, leaving just a hollow, empty feeling in her heart.

She could not believe it! How could she have lost out to someone else? She was the newest, brightest, shining star at MedTech. Why Tom Moyer had told her as much only weeks ago in his office as he read her another flattering letter he had received about her! It was from Sister Mary Margaret, wasn't it? It wasn't fair! But how often had she been told that life was seldom "fair?"

While Charlie Graves was giving a few words of acceptance and appreciation, her date, Jim, leaned over and whispered encouragingly in her ear,

"Don't feel bad, Jennifer. You will win it next year. You're the best, you know." He had noticed her disappointment immediately, as his eyes had never left her face the entire time Tom Moyer had been speaking.

She did not even acknowledge his kind words with a look as she kept focused on the podium and Charlie Graves, feigning interest in his remarks.

What do you know about it, Jim? she thought angrily in her bitter disappointment. *What do you know about anything at all, you being just another "man!" Why do men get all the breaks in life? That is probably why Charlie got the stupid award in the first place. Why did I ever think that they would give this award to a female, anyway? The stupid jerks! I, indeed, worked my tail off, as Tom said. But what good did it do me? And I didn't hear Tom thanking any of the "husbands" for letting their wives be gone four days a week! It's not fair.*

She had already forgotten the large amount of money she had earned and her brand new, fully furnished condominium, so great was her disenchantment at that moment.

After the awards were all presented and the final words of gratitude and exhortation were spoken by the President and Chairman of the Board, chairs were pulled out from the tables and polite conversations were occurring as the MedTech family made their way slowly toward the exits. Tom Moyer and his wife of twenty-five years were shaking hands with the other officers and their wives, when he caught Jennifer in his peripheral vision and called out to her to please wait a minute before leaving.

While she waited, Jim commented, "It's only ten fifteen. Still so early. Would you like to walk over to the lounge to have a nightcap and talk for a while?"

Before she could reply, "No, thank you," Tom walked up and kissed her lightly on the cheek. Taking her hands in his as he looked at both of them, he said with teasing eyes,

"I see you've lowered your standards, Jennifer, and finally decided to go out with Jim Smithson. Really, dear, you could do so much better than this bean counter, you know. You're one lucky man, Jim."

And he released Jennifer's hands to slap Jim on the back.

"You've got that right, Mr. Moyer," responded Jim diplomatically while thinking, *Thanks a lot for the insult, you egotistical old wind bag.*

Tom Moyer was hoping he could get Jennifer interested in his eldest son who should be graduating from Brown University in June, if he could conquer that tough economics course, that is. She would be perfect for him. And what handsome, intelligent grandkids he would have!

Jennifer just smiled crookedly and looked inquiringly at Tom.

He continued, "I just wanted you to know that it was a very close race between you and Charlie Graves. Charles has been with the company for five years, you know, and his numbers were mighty impressive, even better than yours, Jenny, so I felt he deserved the award."

He paused here expecting a reply from her. But she remained silent, only looking at him with a slightly wounded expression around her eyes, although she was trying to smile. So he concluded,

"You are a great salesman ... salesperson, Jennifer, and I know that you will win this award sometime very soon if you keep up the good work. And I fully expect that you will. The sky will be the limit for you, Ms. Jacobs, here at MedTech ...That is, if you keep away from scoundrels like Jim Smithson here." And he winked at them both.

"Thank you, Tom," she replied simply and smiled more fully.

Yeah, thank you, Tom. Thanks a whole hell of a lot for the second insult, old buddy, thought Jim. *I have a hard enough time getting Jennifer to go out with me without your help!*

After the boss left them both, Jim turned toward his attractive date once more and questioned hopefully, "So, how about that nightcap? I'd like to talk quietly with you for just a few minutes, anyway. We never get to talk at the office. Not really."

She had intended to tell him "no," but now that she was so downcast, Tom's words not making her feel much better, she thought she might as well say "yes." *What is left to do?* she reasoned. *Go back to my condo and feel sorry for myself? I might as well have my glass of wine here with Jim than at home with the cats.* So she merely nodded her head, and they walked over to the hotel lounge.

Jennifer had been feeling ill at ease all day today, borderline depressed and anxious, forgetful again, as she had been that day two years ago when the cats had first run away. She had reasoned that the cause was all the stress and excitement associated with winning the award tonight. So that now, in light of Mr. Graves walking away with *her* prize, she was feeling more than a little despondent. And like that day two years ago, she felt she needed to be admired by a man today, as much as she hated to admit it. She needed to feel desirable and lovable today, although she could not explain why.

It was dark in the Rendezvous Lounge with soft candlelights flickering on the intimate tables. A woman with a low, throaty voice was singing melancholy love songs at the piano bar.

"Every now and then I cry. Every night you keep stayin' on my mind. All my friends say I'll survive. It just takes time. But I don't think time is gonna heal this broken heart. No, I don't see how it can if it's broken all apart. A million miracles could never stop the pain, or put all the pieces together again. No, I don't think time is gonna heal this broken heart. No, I don't see how it can while we are still apart. And when you hear this song, I hope that you will see ... that time won't heal a brokenhearted me ..."

There was polite applause for the talented singer who managed to croon a whole lot of hopeless heartache into the number. Jim and Jennifer had been seated as the song was well underway and had not said anything at all until the last note was played.

"Well, that's certainly a depressing song, isn't it?" began Jim while looking at his lovely date and managing a grim smile.

"Yes, you can safely say that without any fear of contradiction, I think," Jennifer rejoined, trying to return his smile, but not succeeding very well.

"Since they're playing 'crying in your beer songs,' how about a beer? Or would you prefer something else," he inquired politely.

"I hate beer," she began, wrinkling her nose. "Tastes like carbonated horse pee to me. But I would like a nice glass of red wine—a nice tall glass, if you please." And she did smile this time, really looking at him for the first time this evening.

Jim Smithson was five-feet-eleven inches tall, a nice match for her five feet eight inches, with thick, light brown, wavy hair that was already beginning to gray a little, wearing wire rimmed glasses over light, golden brown, kind eyes, and sporting an attractive, neat mustache. He had a broad, strong chest and muscular arms along with a slender waist despite his love of a beer or two, as he worked out regularly at the company gym during lunch hours. He was very handsome, exuding a sort of physical, sensual magnetism that was almost palpable, and had no trouble getting dates—except for Jennifer, that is.

"Then red wine it will be," he replied, smiling into her eyes, more optimistic now as he felt he had her full attention for the first time this evening. "A nice tall glass, too. But I will have the beer, if that's okay. It doesn't taste much like horse pee to me anymore, although when I first started drinking it … well, maybe." And he made a back and forth gesture with his hands to illustrate.

He placed their order with the waitress, who flirted shamelessly with him, as the singer at the piano began playing love songs from show tunes starting with *State Fair.*

"I'm as restless as a willow in a windstorm. I'm as jumpy as a puppet on a string. I'd say that I have spring fever. But I know it isn't spring. I am starry-eyed and vaguely discontented, like a nightingale without a song to sing. Oh, why should I have spring fever, when it isn't even spring?"

"That's how I feel," Jennifer blurted out suddenly, involuntarily. "I have been so … Oh, how can I explain it? … So jumpy and discontented all day. And I don't know why."

"Maybe it's because you knew you had that award in your pocket… But then, you knew that it wasn't a done deal yet, either," Jim volunteered, taking a short pull at the foam of his brew.

"Maybe," she pondered, her brows knitted together in concern, though she was still not persuaded. And then, playfully, "Hey! How did you know that I thought I had won that award?"

"Easy. It was written all over your face this evening … All over your very lovely face," he added, staring longingly into her dark, mysterious eyes as if he were drawn there by a magnet.

"I keep wishing I were somewhere else, walking down a strange, new street. Hearing words that I have never heard, from a man I've yet to meet," continued the show tune lyrics.

"Oh," was all her reply, and she felt her cheeks reddening again as she was finding it very difficult to drop his gaze.

But she had to. She was not interested in becoming emotionally attached to Jim Smithson—or to any other man. With some effort, she pulled herself out of his eyes, vowing not to allow herself to fall into them again, and took a sip of her wine.

She did not know why she was here with Jim, this evening of March 14, 1978, listening to love songs with a handsome, desirable man she had been avoiding for over a year now. She did not trust men. She did not need men. She did not want any man in her life. So why was she here with him, feeling strangely attracted to him, feeling that tingly, exciting sensation that made her want to kiss him, want to feel his strong arms around her and to run her fingers through his wavy brown hair? She had not felt that way in such a long time. She drank down more of her wine, refusing to look into his eyes again, trying desperately to resist the need to be admired and loved by him tonight.

No! I will not do this! I will not allow Jim ... or any other man ... to affect me this way. Why should I give up my power and control of my life to some man?

"I hope that didn't offend you, Jennifer," Jim broke in on her thoughts. "I'm sure you must hear all the time how very beautiful you are. I'm not trying to flatter you or anything. I just can't help myself. You are the prettiest, most enticing woman I have ever seen, and I would have to be blind not to notice it," he explained sincerely.

Again, Jennifer felt the warmth of his attraction pulling her away from her resolve to never again allow herself to desire a man's presence in her heart and her life. *I will just finish this glass of wine and ask him to take me home, dropping me off at the curb,* she planned.

"Wasn't your ex-wife pretty?" she asked, hoping to deflect his attention from her.

His expression changed dramatically, a look of remorse and bitterness sweeping across his countenance. He averted his gaze to the wall behind her, as if looking back a few years into a painful past.

He answered very gravely, "Oh, yeah, Alicia was pretty all right! Not as beautiful as you are, but pretty enough. We were high school sweethearts and were married when I was only nineteen. Not long after that, I received my 'Greetings from the President' informing me that the honor of my presence was 'requested' in that lovely Southeast Asian nation of Vietnam. Alicia was brokenhearted, and I was none too happy about it, either."

He paused here and took a long drink from his mug, draining it quickly and motioning to the waitress to please bring him another. He continued, as Jennifer said nothing.

"So, to make a very sorry, long story short, while I was up to my waist wading through the rice paddies and swamps of 'Nam, swatting at mosquitoes the size of Omaha, looking for 'Charlie,' and trying my dam— ... darnedest ... not to get my as— ... head blown off, I received a very nicely worded 'Dear John' letter from my wife telling me that she wanted a divorce."

He paused, receiving his new mug from the waitress and telling her "thanks."

"I'm sorry, Jim," Jennifer responded sympathetically.

"So was I. At the time, me a naïve nineteen-year-old kid, having lived a fairly sheltered middle class life until 'Nam, thinking about coming home to Alicia was what had kept me going ... kept me focused on staying alive and surviving that hell."

He paused again and took a long pull at his beverage before continuing.

"As it turned out, when I did come home eighteen months later, the no-fault divorce having been finalized while I was still over there, I discovered that Alicia had been pursued and overtaken, as it were, by a big wig in the, guess what? ... 'Sales' department at the manufacturing firm she worked for. They had been carrying on for quite some time, and she had convinced herself that she loved him. Of course, he was married and had no intention of leaving his family for her. It was a very pitiful, sick situation from the beginning. But... anyway ... 'That's life,' as they say."

He took one last, long drink from the golden fluid, finishing it and coming back into the present with a heavy sigh, looking back at Jennifer's face.

"So that ... in a nutshell ... is the story of my divorce. Unfortunately, it was pretty common back during 'Nam. Happened to quite a few of us, actually. And I guess I should be thankful I returned from that hellhole with only a broken heart," he finished, trying to smile stoically.

They were both silent for a moment.

Then Jennifer offered softly with no emotion, staring at him without really seeing, "My parents divorced when I was ten ... But their marriage was over many years before that, I think. I will never forget the day that Daddy came home from work, packed his bags, and ..."

She paused, her expression very somber, her eyes now more fully focused on her handsome escort's.

"I remember thinking he was packing to take us all on a vacation... to the mountains, you know ... like we used to do. I never thought that Daddy would just pack up and …"

And she trailed off, not meaning to stir up such a sad memory, although for some strange reason she did not feel as sad as she used to when recalling such things. She only felt oddly numb now when remembering the pain of her parents' divorce, an emotional numbness that was slowly, almost imperceptibly creeping into more and more of her heart these days, gaining ground almost daily without her conscious knowledge.

Nevertheless, she had not intended to reveal herself so intimately to Jim. No man could be trusted with such intimate knowledge of her, she knew. No man.

But Jim responded with sympathy, his eyes searching hers, saying, "Oh, too bad, Jennifer. I am sorry. At least Alicia and I had no children. I can't imagine forcing that kind of pain onto an innocent child." And he comfortingly placed his strong, warm hand over her cold, graceful fingers.

She withdrew them quickly, sighed, and averted her gaze, saying abruptly, "Look, Jim, it's getting late and I am so tired. Thank you for the lovely evening, but could you please take me home now?" she almost begged him.

"Sure, Jenny. I hope I didn't wear you out with my long, sad story. But it's not fair, you know. I bared my soul to you, but you haven't returned the favor. Next time, I'd like to hear all about your dark romantic past," he teased, his kind eyes twinkling mischievously.

But he knew he had said the wrong thing as a heavy veil covered her large, brown eyes, making them suddenly cold and forbidding.

She turned away from him and said shortly, "I'm going to the ladies room for a quick minute. Do you think you could be ready to leave when I get back?"

"Certainly. I'll pay the check and meet you by the front door," he returned as she left. *Why all of a sudden is she in such a hurry to get home,* he wondered, *just when she appeared to warming up to me?*

In the ladies room, as she straightened her hair and applied some fresh lipstick out of habit, her mind was racing. *I will not, will not allow myself to be attracted to Jim! He is probably nice enough; hopefully is a fine man, but I do not need him or any other man! I do not want to need any man. I can only count on myself. No one else.*

Her Head was warring against her Heart, engaged in a desperate duel to the death. Only one part of her was going to survive, she knew instinctively. How she hoped and prayed with every ounce of her being that her Head would stand victorious at the end of the day! But she could not deny the very powerful tugging at her Heart, the frantic yearning for masculine love that caused so much distress to her feminist sensibilities.

She knew she was a crazy, jumbled, mixed up bag of contradictions and inconsistencies. She wanted to have her cake and eat it too, as the proverb stated. But her Head said that was impossible. She could not be independent and strong and courageous, while at the same time, soft and sweet and vulnerable, and most of all, trusting, could she? How was it possible for those two warring neighbors to ever reach a lasting peace?

The two sides of her nature were relentlessly bombarding each other, with the real Jennifer caught in the crossfire as Jim was driving her home to her new condominium. Neither of them spoke as the radio was playing a sweet love song sung by Anne Murray.

"There's a wren in a willow wood, Flies so high and sings so good, And he brings to you, what he sings to you ... Like my brother, the wren, and I ... Well, he told me if I try, I could fly for you, And I

want to try for you, 'cause ... I want to sing you a love song. I want to rock you in my arms all night long. I want to get to know you. I want to show you the peaceful feelin' of my home."

As the soft, soothing, clear alto voice of the talented singer resounded richly into the interior of Jim's car via his state-of-the-art stereo system, tears began to form in Jennifer's eyes, but she valiantly fought them off.

"Summer thunder on moonbright days; Northern lights and skies ablaze and I bring to you, Lover, when I sing to you. Silver wings in a fiery sky show the trail of my love, and I want to sing to you. Love is what I bring to you, and I want to sing to you. Oh, I want to sing you a love song; I want to rock you in my arms all night long. I want to get to know you. I want to show you the peaceful feelin' of my home."

The tears were trying very hard to fight their way out of Jennifer's eyes now. She knew she once had a love song that she had sung to her lover, and he to her. It seemed like a million years ago. But the love song was so sweet, so powerful and mighty and rich, like a large, flowing river, bringing life to the parched, dry, empty places in her soul. The love song had made her feel so happy and fulfilled, and it had seemed that it was eternal. An eternal, never-ending love song that she would sing from her heart until her last breath and beyond.

What had happened to silence it? And was there another love song she could sing? Or was the song of love never to escape her lips again? How empty her life would be, she knew suddenly, if she never sang another love song. How cold and empty and meaningless her life would be without the sweet melody and harmony of love playing—ever playing—fully, richly, warmly, in the background of her life, a sweet, necessary accompaniment to the grinding everydayness of her existence, bringing beauty, peace, and joy to her needy heart.

As Jim pulled up to her home, the song was finishing, evoking such a longing for love as Jennifer had not experienced in over two years.

"Oh. ... I want to sing you a love song. I want to rock you in my arms all night long. Oh, I want to get to know you. I want to show you the peaceful feelin' of my home. I want to show you the peaceful feelin' of my home."

He opened the car door for her and walked her to the front door, both of them still silent. He was hoping for a kiss good night, though he would have gladly settled for a warm handshake and a sincere smile that reached her veiled eyes, telling him that she really enjoyed his company this evening—because the powerful love song had affected him, too.

Jim wanted to fall in love again, marry, and have a family. It had taken him quite a few years to recover from Alicia and Vietnam. But he thought he was fully restored at this point, and he felt he could now become a good husband and father ... if he could find the right woman, that is. And wouldn't it be lovely if Jennifer were that elusive woman! She was so beautiful and intelligent, and he somehow suspected that there was a tender, loving side to her nature that she was trying very hard to conceal from him and from the world for some mysterious reason. She was trying desperately to conceal her soft, feminine side to play hardball with the boys, he thought. But if he could somehow find it, then ...

Although she had not planned on anything other than a polite handshake and a "thank you for a lovely evening," Jennifer welcomed his desire for the kiss goodnight there on her doorstep under the moonbright sky as she turned around to shake his hand. She even met his desire with a passion that surprised them both, her arms reaching around his shoulders and her hands gently caressing the back of his hair as she kissed him longingly, lingeringly, over and over again, loving the feel of his moustache brushing her lips as she tenderly caressed his lips with hers. Loving the feel of his strong, muscular arms wrapping tightly around her. Loving the masculine smell of him and, for some unknown reason, even loving the lingering taste of beer on his lips.

Her passion surprised them both but frightened Jennifer terribly—both frightened and excited her, as this was the first kiss since Michael. She had never intended to kiss another man, ever. The heart in her chest was pounding loudly into her ears.

The Heart in her soul was crying out equally loudly, *SEE! I AM NOT DEAD! I am still here, very much alive! You have not killed me yet. Not yet. And I am very, very strong! Much stronger than you think. I am not dead yet. Far from it!*

When the lengthy, passionate kissing was finally over, she unlocked the door and murmured, almost involuntarily, as if standing outside herself and watching herself from another room, observing but not fully participating in her own life, wondering what would happen to her next,

"Would you like to come in?"

He was inside before the last words were spoken, and they were in each other's arms again before the door was closed, embracing and kissing with fervor, with purpose, striving towards a goal. Her overcoat was on the floor with his eyeglasses beside them.

The tears she had fought off were now flowing down her face as she welcomed back her Heart. *I still have a very strong, very powerful love song to sing!* she rejoiced.

But as Jim tasted her salty tears, he paused, wiping them gently from her wet cheeks with his fingers, and asked her, in a soft whisper, his blazing eyes penetrating hers briefly until she closed them,

"Why are you crying, Jennifer? What's wrong?"

She did not reply, but found his lips again and pressed her slender, shapely body even closer to him, kicking off her heels to make him appear taller. She was alive again! That was all she knew! She was not dead ... not yet! Her Heart was taunting her Head, claiming at least this one victory.

But as he began to fumble with the buttons at the back of her dress, something snapped inside her Head. *You have been in this position before, remember? And look where it landed you! Why do you want to torture yourself again in this way? Think, Jennifer, think! Do you want to be heart broken and abandoned again? Totally shattered and broken to bits? Stop this! Stop this, now, before it's too late!*

With sudden, unexplained physical force and power, she pushed herself away from him with both arms and shouted,

"STOP IT! STOP IT RIGHT NOW!"

And her eyes were now filled with rage, as her old buddy, Anger, showed up to have his say.

"Okay, Jennifer! All right!" Jim complied, totally shocked and taken aback at this apparent schizophrenic turn around. He backed away from her, concerned at the expression of outrage and anger in her dark eyes now, the same eyes that seconds before had burned with desire for him. He continued quickly, "I won't hurt you, Jenny, or force myself on you. You know that. I was just responding to you... To what I thought you wanted, too."

"What I want is for you to *please leave! Please leave now!*" she barked into his face in fury, adding, "And don't tell me what I want! But I know very well that all you *men* ever want is *one thing*! And one thing only! Well, you're not going to get it from me, Mr. Jim Smithson!"

As he reached down, grabbing his spectacles and picking up her coat from the floor, offering it back to her, he peered deeply into her very angry eyes and stated emphatically,

"Look, Jennifer. I don't know who you think I am, or how you may have been mistreated in your past, but I can assure you of one thing ... I am not like that! I did not plan this, nor do I want to take advantage of you in any way. I hate to see our evening end like this. Perhaps I can call you tomorrow after you have calmed down and..."

"No! You can't call me! I don't ever want to see you or speak to you again! Now, please leave!" she screamed at the poor accountant and Vietnam War veteran, who, knowing that it was useless to try to reason with her in this state, complied, saying upon parting,

"Goodnight, Jennifer. I'm sorry."

As soon as he left, rage, disappointment, confusion, sorrow, and frustration all fell down heavily upon her, making her want to tear down the building, to blow up the condominium complex, to destroy something!

She picked up a decorative plate from its easel on her side table, a plate that she had purchased while on business in Chicago at an unique antiques store next to her hotel last month, a plate that she dearly loved, whose colors matched the décor of her new living room perfectly. She flung it in fury at the fireplace mantle, and it immediately shattered into a dozen pieces. But that was not enough to assuage her fierce wrath. She then removed the vase from the same table and hurled it violently against the same innocent mantle, finally receiving some emotional relief as it, too, lay irreparably broken beside its former tablemate.

Then, she collapsed onto the sofa, placed her head in her hands, and wept bitterly. Wept in extreme disappointment and disillusionment. Wept in heaving, wrenching sobs that originated in the very core of her soul and seemed to shake and rock every fiber of her being in painful wails of inexplicable grief. Wept in a profound, unexplained sorrow and sadness, for what, she did not know.

But she did know that she had lost her award. She had lost her calm reserve and dignity in the company of Jim Smithson. She had almost lost her heart and given her body to a man she hardly knew. And she had lost respect for herself, or at least for her ability to control herself.

But even worse than that, she was so desolate ... so cold and lonely and empty ... inside.

The cats, who had been milling around her and Jim from the moment they had come through the door, and who had wisely run for cover when the ceramics went hurtling through the air, now emerged from their respective foxholes under the chair and the coffee table, jumped up on the sofa, and began to rub their soft bodies against their caretaker's arms, purring in what seemed to be an attempt to console her grief.

"Oh, Ferdie and Izzy!" she sobbed as she stroked them absently, her tears falling freely onto their silky fur. "What in the world is wrong with me? What in the world?"

And she cried even harder as the cats purred louder, on into the evening of March 14th and the early morning of March 15, 1978.

Chapter Twenty-Two

*T*he year of our Lord 1978 passed on into 1979, 1980, and 1981 much the same as the years have always passed, each one different and yet so much the same, the seasons of the calendar arriving and then moving on, making way for the next one, sometimes reluctantly, yet acquiescing just the same. Work and play, play and rest, rise up to work again. Time marches on, taking the people right along with it, seemingly indifferent to the heartaches and trials, joys and dreams of the mortals forced to live within its intransigent bounds.

For Jennifer Jacobs, the three years between her twenty-third birthday until now, just days after her twenty-sixth, were highly successful ones. She did indeed earn the Salesperson of the Year Award in 1980, just two short years after her first disappointment. She had been promoted and was now a director of sales responsible for training and helping the six people under her, taking a cut of their commissions, making her wealth increase steadily.

And while the years and time seem to be always the same, technology was changing very rapidly, and MedTech's research and development engineers and creative geniuses were keeping the company on the cutting edge of their industry. Demand was great for their products, and Jennifer was busier than ever. She had earned that Master's Degree in Business as she had planned, feeling that it was one of the reasons she received her promotion, beating out a very talented man who did not have his advanced degree. She had not ceased to pat herself on the back for her ambition and foresight in that area.

In her personal life, she was in the process of building herself a house. The old condo was fine, but she wanted the peace and quiet of her own house with her own yard. Besides, her accountant had told her she needed a bigger mortgage payment for tax purposes. And there was still a restless longing in her heart, a longing for permanence and security that owning a real house in a real neighborhood might give her. So she enthusiastically plunged ahead with her home building plans.

Fulfilling the promise she had made to herself to give generously to worthwhile charities, Jennifer had volunteered as a mentor, becoming active in a home for abused children until she decided her frantic schedule would not allow it. At least, that was her excuse not to go for her weekly visits there. Actually, she experienced severe depression whenever she would entertain the little children, so she bowed out of the physical appearances and instead sent regular gifts of money to the Christian home.

Earnestly desiring to help her mother with her financial needs, Jennifer had tried sending her regular gifts of cash but was kindly rebuffed by Betty, whose pride would not allow it. So instead, she purchased her expensive gifts, luxury items Betty would not have bought for herself, to try to repay her for the many sacrifices she had made for her and Susan through all the difficult years of single parenting.

She rarely talked to her father—perhaps once a month or so in a brief telephone conversation with the call always originating from him. And she saw him in person much less, maybe once a year when forced to do so at Christmas or at Susan's birthday celebration.

And as far as young men were concerned, she still accepted a date occasionally, if she was extremely lonely or bored, which was seldom with all her busyness. But she religiously stood by her one or two date rule—one date if she liked the man, or two if she did not. She would never fail to violate that tenet of her self-preservation code, because she had learned a very hard lesson about herself with the Jim Smithson episode of three years ago.

Jim had phoned her on the morning after their date, as he had told her he would, and was surprised to hear contrition and apologies from her immediately. He had thought she would still be angry. But instead, she had told him how very wrong she had been to scream those harsh words at him—that she had overreacted in the extreme. She had further asked him to please not hold her poor behavior against her, not to remember her that way. She had said that she was just overwrought with disappointment and frustration at having lost the award, had taken it all out on him, and had very kindly asked him to forgive her. But she had finished by saying she could not go out with him anymore. It just wasn't a good idea to date someone from the office, she thought. It could ruin perfectly good work relationships, didn't he agree?

Of course, he did *not* agree and continued to pursue her for several more weeks. He knew that it must have been some cruel mistreatment or betrayal in her past that had wounded her so and had made her so suspicious of men and their motives. Perhaps she had even been molested as a child. There was certainly no shortage of sicko's out there! But he felt he could persuade her to trust him in time, if she would only allow it. He was still very much attracted to her and had experienced a taste of the warm, inviting, sensual and exciting woman who still lived somewhere down deep in her soul—if she would only let her out. So he pursued her for a while longer. Until she finally wore him down with refusals and he gave up... reluctantly... but gave up just the same, as he grew tired of banging his head against the same wall of rejection.

As it turned out, not long after that he had met a very sweet young lady through a friend, had courted her, and was now contentedly married with a baby on the way. His dreams were coming true. And Jennifer was happy for him and wished him the best. She even bought him a very nice wedding present. She still saw him at least once a week at work because he was the man who tallied her numbers and authorized her commission checks.

For her own part, Jennifer had learned that evening of March 14, 1978, that she could not afford to listen to her Heart. The risks were much too great. She could not take counsel of her Heart because she knew that some measure of faith and trust in someone else is needed to take the risks that obeying her Heart would invariably bring. And she knew beyond any doubt at all that she did not trust men, could not trust them.

And she also knew it would have been wrong for her to sleep with Jim that night, even if she had been attracted to him. That she had nearly given herself to him sexually that evening frightened her more than anything else. She knew intuitively that her desire for him that evening had *not* been at its core a desire for sex. That was not her struggle. Rather, the sexual passion she had experienced while in his arms had simply pulled from her memory a time in her not too distant past that she had experienced complete, abiding love. True love. Powerful love. Physical, emotional, and yes, spiritual love.

Although she never thought consciously about Michael—as for years now she had mastered the art of rejecting even the first *hint* of the thought of him, using all the energy of her soul to forget the past and all its pain—still, deep in her subconscious, she stored the memory of the joy of *feeling* loved and giving love. And she had felt loved once. Truly loved. And had returned that love, multiplied, into the heart of her lover. Just what had happened to change that love, she refused to recall, working tirelessly to erase all that from her conscious memory. But still, the empty aching of once having lived out a very forceful, passionate love in her heart that was somehow cruelly taken away, would haunt her. That empty aching would haunt her as it had that night in Jim's car, listening to a beautiful love song... And recalling, subconsciously, a beautiful love.

Her dilemma that night in March of 1978 was that she might have developed a serious relationship with Jim over time that could have led her to commit herself to him, to her desiring to be part of his life and wanting him to belong to her. And this, she could not afford. She could not afford to lose control, offering her Heart to any man. That was intractable and unchangeable, she felt. That was just who she was, and she could no more change it than she could change the color of her eyes or her height. It was an integral part of her nature. She could not trust men, so she could not love one again. Period. Case closed.

She accepted this fact rather reluctantly at first, but as time wore on and she witnessed the many heartbreaks of her co-workers and friends because of unwise romances, she began to feel slightly superior. And she was so very successful at work, received so much praise and reinforcement from Bob Brandon and Tom Moyer, not to mention increased earnings, savings, and investments, she felt she was more than compensated for her lack of a husband or boyfriend.

She would marry her career where at least she and she alone was in control. Why should she sacrifice her life to try to please some man, she thought? Men are too hard to please, anyway. And they mostly are very selfish beasts, wanting to marry only to fulfill *their* needs and to have a wife do all the housework. She heard the married MedTech women complaining constantly about having to work full time *and* do all the housework and child-rearing jobs on top of that. Those women were tired and worn out all the time. Who needs all that, she reasoned? Not her!

And occasionally, more often than she would have believed, when she would travel on business with married salesmen or technicians, one or two of the scoundrels would try to put the moves on her! At first this shocked her, though she did not know why it should. *I mean, this is pretty stereotypical, isn't it? The traveling husband who is unfaithful to the little woman back home,* she would think. But what would infuriate her was the fact that they thought she was stupid enough, or immoral enough, or both, to comply!

Do they think I don't know the Ten Commandments? Or that I am so frustrated and desperate, I would degrade myself for the opportunity of sleeping with them? she would reason. *Do they think I would enjoy the role of 'the other woman' who breaks up a marriage, leaving little children crying in their beds at night because Daddy has gone?* This would make her so angry that sometimes, when she was bored or in a bad mood anyway, she would pretend to play along with their little schemes. She would flirt back and tell them she would meet them in their room that night. And she would laugh and laugh as the phone would ring when she did not show up for the tryst. She would laugh even harder, always into her pillow so not to be heard, if they should show up at her door, knocking urgently and whispering her name repeatedly.

The next day, if they should ask her what happened, she would feign ignorance and tell them she had no idea what they were speaking of. In a sad, sick way, this would give her a sense of revenge against the lust-filled male gender, a gender for which she had a growing contempt.

All this only added to her belief that marriages just were not made for the late twentieth century. What fools women were to marry some man, thinking he would truly love and cherish her like the vows said he would! That he would remain faithful to her, forsaking all others. No, she reasoned, she was much better off than sixty percent of the poor, hardworking, longsuffering wives she knew. The other forty percent were just plain lucky, she thought, or else heartache was awaiting them just around the corner. In any case, the more she saw of the world, the more hardened and cynical she became. And unbeknownst to her, her once soft, sweet, vulnerable, tender feminine heart was becoming as hard as stone.

It was against this backdrop of her skeptical, suspicious worldview that she had received a telephone call from her sister a few months ago, telling her of her engagement to a "simply wonderful, nearly perfect" young man named Paul Whitfield. Susan, who was now an elementary school teacher living back in her beloved Mobile, had met Paul over a year ago at church, and they had been "just friends" for a while until a romantic interest had developed between them. He had been in the Navy for a time, but was now an engineer for an electronics firm.

"Oh, Sis, you've got to meet him! He is the kindest, funniest, most intelligent and talented man I have ever known! You're going to love him! He is so magnificent!" Susan had told her enthusiastically.

"He'd better be," Jennifer had responded from her protective, big sister's heart, "or he'll have to answer to me."

As soon as she had been able to work it into her schedule, Jennifer had flown down to Mobile for the weekend to meet her future brother-in-law. In many ways, she felt that the traditional father's role of checking the young man out and ascertaining his suitability for marrying Susan had fallen into her lap.

But surprisingly, she had been well pleased with Paul Whitfield. She had looked for any possible character flaw she could find, and had, without anyone's knowing it, paid for a background check to be run on him. She dearly loved her little sister and wanted only the best for her.

But Paul checked out very well indeed. Other than a couple of non-sufficient funds checks returned while he was still in college and one drunk and disorderly charge during his first shore leave when he was only eighteen, a charge that had later been dismissed as he had become involved in a fight to defend his buddy against some local thugs, his record was flawless. He was now twenty-six, and his drinking, fighting days were all behind him, he had told her as he showed her the scar just above the hairline of his forehead where one of the miscreants had hit him with a bottle. That experience while he was still very young had taught him that "discretion is the better part of valor," and that it is extremely difficult to be the soul of discretion while one is inebriated. Hence, he was now a confirmed tea-toteler.

Jennifer had to admit to herself that she liked Paul very much. He was, as Susan had said, kind, intelligent, talented, and possessed a dry wit and a sense of humor that reminded her of Sister Mary Margaret. He was also attractive, with neat sandy brown hair, a handsomely chiseled face, and a lean, muscular physique that paired nicely with her beautiful sister. A little shorter than she would have liked, but tall enough.

More importantly, she liked the way he treated her sister with respect and courtesy and extended those behaviors to her mother, and indeed, to Jennifer herself. And he was a devoutly Christian man, too, who shared Susan's faith, so there should be no disagreements about that important aspect of their relationship. So before she had boarded the jet for the return flight to Indianapolis as she hugged her sister goodbye, Jennifer told her that Paul had earned her official seal of approval. She hoped and prayed that Susan would be among the forty percent of good marriages.

She had arbitrarily arrived at the forty percent figure on her own, based upon one unscientific survey in a women's magazine she had read once coupled with her own powers of observation and the fact that it just sounded right to her ears. Forty percent are happily married. Sixty percent are not. With these numbers firmly fixed in her mind, the odds were still in her favor. Whether they were accurate or not was of little importance to her. Her mind was made up. She did not want to be confused with the facts.

So now as June 10, 1981, the date of Susan's wedding, was only two days away, Jennifer was trying her best to get out of the office, back to her condominium, throw a few more items into her suitcases, and hurry off to the airport to catch the flight to Mobile. But the office was not cooperating, and her flight was in two hours and fifteen minutes.

"Sarah! How often have I told you not to file these invoices in with the brochures? Why don't you ever listen?" Jennifer exploded into the face of the young sales secretary, who by the end of this tirade was blinking back tears. "You are way too busy mooning over that boyfriend of yours instead of concentrating on your job. You talk to him too much on company time, and it's got to stop!" Her dark eyes blazed as she threw the stack of papers down on Sarah's desk with force. "If I don't see some improvement from you, and pretty quick, too, I will have to file a complaint with human resources. Now sort these out, and double quick! I've got a plane to catch, or don't you remember? Honestly, Sarah, you make all those dumb blonde jokes seem all too real!"

What a stupid incompetent! She was fuming still. *I'll know better than to trust that employment agency again!* Anger was now enveloping her personality with a vengeance.

"And Mike, just where the hell are my airline tickets to Pittsburgh for Monday? You did get the damned things, didn't you? You do know I am leaving from Mobile early Monday morning to fly directly to Pittsburgh, don't you? Or have you forgotten, too?" she turned her fury on her new sales trainee, a recent college graduate from Duluth, as she fumbled through the paperwork all stacked up on her disorganized desk.

Normally she did not swear. Being raised in the Deep South, she knew that proper ladies did not swear, and she considered herself to be such a lady. And from her good training in church, she also knew that "no corrupt communication" should ever "proceed out of her mouth, but that which is good to the use of edifying." However, during the past five years, her close work association with so many businessmen who could not speak more than five or six words without profanity and other "corrupted communications" and cuss words, had initially changed her language thought patterns and then inevitably, her speech. But usually only when she was angry. However, she was angry so often now. Especially as the days narrowed moving towards Susan's wedding.

She had just arrived home from a three-day sales trip late last night and had not had time to catch up on her correspondence. Her personality was deteriorating rapidly as her frustration was mounting, and Mike and her other staff could not send her on her way quite soon enough.

"They're right there, on the credenza behind your briefcase," Mike, rather red-faced, replied momentarily after he searched the general vicinity of her desk thoroughly.

Man, won't we all be glad when she is gone! No more Ms. Jacobs until next Wednesday! Hurray! he thought. "Is there anything else I can do to get you ready for your trip?" he asked toward that end.

"Yes, Mike, thanks for asking. Can you please run down to Jim Smithson in accounting and determine whether he has the calculations I need for that presentation in Pittsburgh?"

She tried to calm herself and behave more professionally, even managing a half-smile at Mike. But as he quickly left to fulfill her every desire, her thoughts became agitated again, as she aimlessly shuffled papers around on her desk in a huff.

How inconsiderate of Susan! Choosing to get married right in the middle of by busiest season at work. Just because she isn't really interested in advancing in her chosen career path, choosing to marry instead, why should I have to be the one to suffer?

Finally, with the combined efforts of Mike and the hapless Sarah—who had received many kind, sympathetic, though furtive, glances from all within a fifteen-foot radius of Jennifer—the young sales executive from Mobile was on her way to her car in her assigned parking spot, leaving her just enough time to drive home, grab her things, and catch that flight.

Unfortunately, as so often happens when things aren't going well, there was an office supply delivery van illegally parked behind her, blocking her exit from the garage.

"That's just great! That's all I need!" Jennifer complained loudly with great frustration. She frantically searched the general area hoping that the driver of the van would suddenly, magically materialize, but to no avail.

Fuming with rage, she barged back into the building, into the outer lobby by the elevator bank, grabbed a telephone that connected to a building-wide speaker system, and said in what she hoped was a calm but very firm voice, though she could hear her pulse pounding in her ears,

"Will the driver of the Office Stuff delivery van, who left his vehicle *illegally* parked behind my car on Level D of the parking garage, please get down here *on the double* and *move it* so I can please catch my flight? Please! I will give you *three minutes* before I call the police and have it towed the h-... *towed away!*" And she slammed the receiver of the phone back into its cradle so hard that it jumped out again.

Jennifer's staff, back upstairs in her office, all stared at each other with large, open eyes as soon as they recognized her voice on the intercom interrupting the music and smiled uneasily. Then Mike said very slowly, in a low, dramatic voice,

"Oooooo! Poor deliveryman!" And they all erupted into riotous laughter. But Dan, another sharp sales trainee, with sudden inspiration and insight, exclaimed,

"Poor *us* if we don't *find* that delivery man! Quick! Everybody! 'On the double,' as JJ said! Find that deliveryman! If we don't want her back *in here*, that is! 'Hell hath no fury!'"

This last quip was a private joke understood by all Jennifer's underlings. They had originally changed the old proverb, "Hell hath no fury like a woman scorned," to "Hell hath no fury like Jennifer Jacobs," and then shortened it further to "Hell hath no fury," or HHNF for short. They had used this as a sort of code language to signal to each other for use on days that their boss was in a very bad mood, ready to take someone's head off. They would write the initials, "HHNF," on self-adhesive notes and affix them to desks, papers, or telephones on Jennifer's "bad" days to warn their co-workers. And lately, her bad days had been outnumbering her good ones.

They all scattered frantically to search for that outlaw of a deliveryman, all except Sarah who stayed behind to answer the ringing phone.

"*Please, please* don't let it be Ms. Jacobs!" she earnestly entreated Heaven before lifting the receiver, her eyes focused above, her hands folded in prayer.

She need not have worried. It was her boyfriend.

"So, what is your reason for flyin' into Mobile?" asked the kind mother of twins seated next to Jennifer on her non-stop flight.

The sister of the bride had barely made it to her seat before the jet door was closed, as she had been forced to wait for twelve minutes for that pig of a deliveryman to move his big, fat truck out of her way. By then, traffic had started to back up, her suitcase clasp had broken, and she had discovered she was out of cat food to leave for her pets. Tonight she would have to phone Mr. Tomlins, the kind, old gentleman who lived on one side of her unit and who took care of Ferdinand and Isabella while she was gone, and ask him to please purchase some food. She would have to reimburse him when she returned, and would buy him a nice gift to compensate for all his trouble, she thought.

Needless to say, she was in one of the worst moods of her life, and then, *Wouldn't you know it?* she mused in irritation. *Now I have to be seated next to a young mother and her two squealing, sticky-fingered toddlers for the entire two-hour flight! This has to be one of the unluckiest days of my life. Susan owes me big time for this one.*

She tried to smile at the young woman, a rather large *faux* blonde with dark roots about her own age who was very friendly and chatty. She had a thick, south Alabama accent and was just the type Jennifer wanted to avoid for this flight as all she wanted to do was put her head back, close her eyes, and try to rest.

"I am flying down for my baby sister's wedding the day after tomorrow," she replied tiredly, trying to sound as though that was all she wanted to say about it. But it did not work.

"Oh, a wedding! How wonderful! So I guess you are the maid of honor then?" the young mother asserted.

"Yes. That's right," The weary saleswoman again tried to finalize the conversation. *Maybe if I put my head back and close my eyes, she will understand I don't feel like talking,* she hoped. Unfortunately, that did not work either.

"I just love weddings, don't you? Such happy occasions. Is it going to be a large, church wedding?" persisted the mother of twins, and then she added excitedly, directing her words at one of the twins. "Oh, Tommy! Don't put your gooey hands on the pretty lady's sleeve!"

Jennifer opened her eyes to see a nice chocolate stain on her rayon and silk blend, dry clean only suit coat where Tommy had not been able to resist wiping his fingers on its soft, shiny surface.

"Oh, I am so, so sorry!" exclaimed the friendly woman. "Please let me pay to get it cleaned. And Tommy, shame on you! Here, let me move you over here by your brother, and I will sit next to the pretty lady … I'm sorry, what is your name? My name is Peggy Malone," she continued as she effortlessly picked up little Tommy, sat herself down next to Jennifer, and secured her naughty but cute little son in the seat next to his identical twin brother. All this commotion made Tommy start to bawl while his mother tried to comfort him as best she could. "Now Tommy, why can't you just sit there and be good like your brother."

A flight attendant walked up then and consoled the tubby little toddler with a packet of crackers and some juice in a covered cup with a straw, all the while "oooing" and "ahhing" over the adorable twin boys.

"They are so precious! What are their names?" asked the airline employee.

"Tommy and Timmy," replied their mother proudly.

Poor kids, thought Jennifer unkindly. *Now, no one will ever be able to tell them apart, and even if they do, only one vowel will separate them. They will never have their own identities.*

"Yes, we named them each for their grandfathers. My daddy is Tom, and my husband's is Tim," Peggy Malone explained further.

How very diplomatic of you, thought Jennifer cynically. *That way you can milk the granddads for all the money you can.*

After the flight attendant moved on and the twin "T's" settled back down, Peggy turned her attention back to Jennifer.

"I'm so sorry. With all that disruption, I didn't get your name?"

"It's Jennifer. Jennifer Jacobs," she replied, exhaustedly.

"Do you know if we had had girls, we were going to name them Jennifer and Jessica! What a coincidence!" effused Peggy, smiling from ear to ear, eager to share this choice bit of information with her traveling companion.

Jennifer said nothing but merely smiled another weary half-smile. *Well, you didn't get girls, did you! And I don't give a flying fig what you would have named them! Will this pain in the rump mother never shut up and let me rest?*

"I know you are tired, Jennifer, so I will try not to bother you any more," began Peggy, finally catching on, "but I do want to pay to have your lovely suit cleaned. My boys don't mean to be bad, but being twenty-one months old, they just stay messy a lot. You know how it is with children."

No, I don't know 'how it is with children,' nor do I ever want to know, you ninny. Not every woman in the 1980's wants to spend all her days running around wiping runny noses, messy bottoms, and sticky fingers, and apparently, you aren't doing such a good job even at that! Jennifer continued her uncharitable thoughts.

But she replied tiredly, "Please don't worry about it. The suit needed cleaning anyway. Now, if you'll excuse me, I really have had an awful week capped off by an even worse day today. I am in no more mood for a wedding than I am for a marathon race. I just have to rest some or when I see my sister, I might just snap at her. So, Peggy, if I could just close my eyes and rest for the remainder of this flight, I would be so grateful."

"Oh, sure, honey! I will leave you alone. You just rest now," crooned Peggy, maternally, "and I will do my best to keep my babies quiet. They are really good boys, you know." And to the flight attendant, "Oh, please, could you get Jennifer here a pillow and a blanket, please?"

Having experienced a sleep deficit all week with late evenings and early, pre-dawn mornings, Jennifer was totally exhausted. Thankful for both the pillow and the blanket, she told Peggy so before settling in her window seat snuggly and drifting off to sleep almost immediately to the sounds of the happy mother playing "Itsy Bitsy Spider" with her twin toddlers, their tiny, sweet voices singing along merrily and innocently, their bright eyes shining.

Before long, Jennifer was running, pushing aside the tall, relentless grasses, fighting her way through the darkness, with the cold, pulling, tugging wind ripping at her body. *Oh, No! Someone please help me! Oh, God, please help me! I must find their mother! Stop! Stop! Stop those mowers! There are babies over there! Stop! Please Stop!*

"Jennifer! Jennifer, darlin'! Wake up, honey! Wake up. You're having a bad dream," called Peggy Malone, who was gently patting Jennifer's arm, a look of concern troubling her face.

"Oh! Oh, no! ... Oh ...oh," Jennifer mumbled as she came out of her haze. "Oh ... I am so sorry. I hope I didn't bother you ... or anyone else," she finished, trying to compose herself. Tears had run down her cheeks and she was flushed and slightly sweaty under the wool blanket.

"No, honey. No one else could hear you over the airplane noises," reassured Peggy. "Are you all right, honey? That must have been some awful nightmare. Can I have the flight attendant bring you something to drink?"

"Yes ... yes ... if you don't mind. Could you ask for a glass of wine ... any kind?" Jennifer replied, still slightly shaken and a little dazed. This time she remembered more details of the dream than usual. "I am going to the rest room now to freshen up a bit."

"Sure, honey. Now you just take your time," Peggy instructed kindly, patting her companion's hand comfortingly.

Unsteadily maneuvering her way down the small aisle as she made her way to the lavatory, Jennifer felt slightly weak-kneed. In the tiny bathroom, she straightened up her hair and makeup as best as she could. After a few minutes she felt better but was disturbed at the ferocity of the recurrent nightmare this time. *Why would I dream it here, on this airplane? s*he wondered. When she returned to her seat, the flight attendants were preparing everyone for the imminent landing.

"I'm sorry, Jennifer, but they wouldn't bring you your beverage. They said there wasn't time before the landing," apologized Peggy, her eyes showing true concern for the pretty executive.

"That's okay," Jennifer smiled sincerely, even warmly at the large, friendly woman. "You have been very kind to me, Peggy, and I'm afraid I have been rude. And to a fellow Alabamian, too. It's just not right."

"Aw, that's okay, darlin'," Peggy beamed back at her. "You bein' a powerful executive woman an' all, it's only natural you might get a tad cranky every now and then."

Jennifer smiled broadly at Peggy's unscripted, down-home honesty, and replied, "Thanks for understanding." And she added as she looked over at the now angelic, sleeping little fellows, one's head leaning upon the other's shoulder, "I'll bet you get a 'tad cranky every now and then,' too, looking after those two. They *are* mighty cute."

But she did not stop to think it odd that this was the first time in the flight that she had even bothered to really look at them.

Chapter Twenty-three

" Jennifer! Can you believe it? By tomorrow night at this time, I will be Mrs. Paul Whitfield!"

Susan's eyes glowed, lit by a fire from her heart that shone out of her to any and all who would care to notice. She was the typical radiant bride, or rather, radiant bride-to-be.

It was late Friday night, June 9, 1981, the evening before the wedding that was scheduled for five o'clock Saturday afternoon, and Jennifer and her baby sister were upstairs in Susan's old bedroom lying down on her old double bed, a wrought iron design that had once belonged to their maternal grandmother. The pretty patchwork quilt they were resting on was also handmade by their grandmother. Since Susan still possessed several of her old teddy bears and other stuffed animals and dolls that were displayed along the shelves and bookcases of the flower strewn, wallpapered room, the space appeared as if its occupant was much younger than the twenty-four-year-old about to become a wife. The Jacobs' siblings were both too tired to sit and talk, but wanted to fellowship this one last time as sisters without a brother-in-law/husband to separate them, so they just lay there, staring at the ceiling and sharing old memories, reminiscing about their girlhood, and enjoying this special time together.

The wedding rehearsal had been quite successful with all the wedding party rejoicing with Susan and Paul. Paul's brother, Carl, had made everyone laugh as he had painted the words, "Help Me!" on the bottoms of Paul's shoes, so that when he rehearsed the kneeling to pray part of the ceremony, the congregation read his plea. It was a stale, old joke, Jennifer had thought, but the rest of the crowd had seemed to enjoy it. *Besides, it is Susan, not Paul, who should be begging for help!* she had thought.

Susan and Jennifer's father, Robert Jacobs, and his wife, Helen, were also in attendance and had been pleasant and kind, trying very hard as a couple not to play the proverbial role of "the bastard at the family reunion." Susan had wanted her daddy to give her away even though Jennifer had thought it extremely hypocritical. She had felt that their father had given them both away when he had walked out on them and their mother those many years ago. Being in his presence tonight had been most uncomfortable for her, but for Susan's sake—sweet, happy, fulfilled Susan—she had made every effort to be "nice" to him ... and to Helen, too. That she had failed miserably, snubbing her father at every opportunity, was unknown to her.

"That's right, little Sis," Jennifer joined in, stifling a weary yawn. "By this time tomorrow night, you'll be wedlocked, all right. I just hope Paul knows how lucky he is. That's all."

"Quit saying that, Jen," sighed her sister heavily. "You must have told Paul that a dozen times tonight alone. He is beginning to think that you don't trust him to take good care of me. And anyway, I'm the one who's lucky. Paul is my knight in shining armor!"

Jennifer grimaced sadly at her sister's naiveté and innocence before responding.

"Just promise me, Susie-cuesie, that if you discover, or rather, *when* you discover that your knight's armor is very rusty, and that *you* are the one who has to sand and polish it, you won't be too disappointed."

Susan propped herself up on her elbows at that remark and looked into her hero of a big sister's face, stating firmly, "Jennifer, I resent that statement. You still act as though I am a twelve-year-old little girl with stars in my eyes and—"

"Have you looked in the mirror lately, Sue?" the elder sibling rudely interrupted, smiling smugly.

"What do you mean?" queried Susan.

Jennifer sat up in bed this time, crossed her legs Indian style, and explained, "Susan, you *do* have stars in your eyes! All brides have stars in their eyes, you know. That's the way it should be, and—"

"I know what you are going to say next, Jen," it was Susan's turn to break in. "You are trying to tell me that our happiness won't last. Like Mother and Daddy's, or some such nonsense. But I want you to know that Paul and I have gone through eight weeks of premarital counseling with Pastor Warren, delving into all types of issues, talking very seriously about what to do when 'the honeymoon is over' so to speak. Paul and I are committed to each other and to this marriage, and I sure do wish you—"

"No! That was not what I meant at all, Sue. Really!" Jennifer inserted. "I believe very much that you and Paul are a good match, Sis, and that you will be happy together. I am not *that* cynical ... Not yet, anyway. And I want you to be among the forty percent of women who are contented in their marriage."

"Forty percent? Where did you get that number?" asked Susan, her brows wrinkling a little.

"Oh, I read it ... somewhere ... sometime ago ... It's common knowledge. But anyway," and here Jennifer lay back down on the bed beside her sister and stared at that small crack in the ceiling that had always been there before she finished, "I am glad to hear that you received good counseling. I'm sure that Pastor Warren told you that your odds for staying married are materially damaged by our own parents' divorcing, but—"

"But because *it did* happen to Momma and Daddy, I am going to make darn sure it doesn't happen to me, Jen! Can't you see that? We are not doomed to repeat the mistakes of our parents, and I sure do wish you could see that and not be so cynical, as you said earlier," Susan stated with passion.

Jennifer did not reply, as she seemingly was involved in a concentrated study of that ceiling crack, so Susan probed further.

"Jennifer ... please don't answer this question if you don't want to. I don't mean to pry into your personal life ... But ..." she took a deep breath and plunged directly into the forbidden waters. "What was it that ...? Why did you break your engagement to Michael Evans?"

Still, there was no answer from her big sister, whose eyes became more veiled than ever.

"I am only asking you because I love you so much, Jenny. And I want you to be happy, too, in the way I am with Paul, I mean." Susan spoke very softly from her heart. "And I know that at one time, you were very much in love with Michael and he with you. It was written in your own starry eyes. If he hurt you in any way, I personally want to go ... Oh, I don't know what! Kick his teeth in! Or egg his car! Or something, Jennifer!" she finished with fervor.

A bitter smile creased Jennifer's lips then, and she turned her head to look at her sweet, compassionate sister, her little sister who was ready to fight for her sibling's happiness.

"I don't deserve such a sweet sister as you, Susie," she remarked and rubbed her gently on the head. Then she stared back up at the ceiling, sighed deeply, and answered.

"Well, Sis, despite what you may have heard from wagging tongues, Michael was the one who rejected me. He didn't really want to marry me ... Not really ... No, he didn't really want to ..." She faded away and her eyes became suddenly hard. Then she finished abruptly. "I don't think about Michael at all, Sue. Not at all. And you don't need to waste one more thought about him, either. It's certainly not worth kicking anyone's teeth in, Sue, as much as I appreciate the gesture."

She attempted a smile, but it was more like a grimace, and she stated with her countenance that this discussion was finished. She would have felt foolish to tell her sister the truth—that she absolutely refused to recall the exact reason for her break-up. She was not consciously aware herself that shortly after the trip to Atlanta, she had stubbornly refused to go back there in her memory ever again. Subconsciously, she had become an expert in selective memory and in consciously forgetting what she could not afford to remember. She only recalled that Michael had told her to trust him and then had betrayed her cruelly. And in that cruelty, she had experienced the ultimate rejection. She would allow herself no further memory.

Enough of that! No more! She shut herself down from years of practice. Sitting up again, she refocused her gaze on Susan and finished.

"Enough about me, already! What is past is past. I want to know about you and Paul. This is your hour, Susan. Promise me you won't worry about me. I am happy in my chosen life, and I want you to be happy in yours ... Now!" And she rubbed her hands together in pretense of fiendish glee, a wicked gleam in her eyes, "Tell me all about this 'secret' honeymoon destination. I want all the details! Tell me all about this 'Pleasure Palace' that Paul has planned."

Susan blushed deeply as she, also, had her sister's curse.

She explained, smiling sheepishly, "Paul is just wanting to keep it a secret because he knows his brother Carl too well. Since they are originally from the hills of West Virginia, you know, they have that dreadful tradition of the shivaree, where the men come around on the wedding night and harass and torment the newlyweds, making rude, crude, and lewd remarks and loud noises, sometimes kidnapping the groom. You know about it, don't you?"

"Yes, I am aware of that barbaric tradition, but neither Paul nor his relatives appear to be hillbillies, Sue, so ..." Jennifer began, laughingly.

"Of course they aren't hillbillies, Jen, but Carl would dearly love to embarrass and torture Paul, to make up for all the mean tricks Paul pulled on his poor younger brother when they were growing up, I mean. Paul was not the kind, protective, older sibling that you were to me, Jennifer." And here Susan broke into very joyful laughter. "In fact, some of the stories he told me about his treatment of Carl made me think twice about marrying him!"

"Like what?" Jennifer began to laugh too, as her sister's laughter was always contagious. "Come on, tell me! Give me a good one."

Susan wiped the tears from her eyes and controlled herself long enough to say,

"Well ... one day they were playing cops and robbers. Paul was about ten years old and Carl, I guess, eight. Anyway, Paul was the cop, of course, since he was older, and Carl, the robber. So, Paul the cop caught Carl the robber, gagged him, and tied him up with a rope to a chair down in the basement. About that time his mother called him upstairs to run a short errand or something, and he told Carl he would be right back."

Susan burst into laughter again, holding her side, new tears forming in her eyes.

Jennifer, laughing right along, managed to get out, "Uh-oh! I think I see where this is going."

"That's right," Susan explained through the laughter. "One thing led to another, and Paul completely forgot about Carl! You know, he has four sisters in addition to Carl, and lots of neighborhood kids to play with, also. So, anyway ... At dinnertime that night ... Oh! I can't laugh anymore! At dinnertime, Mr. and Mrs. Whitfield asked all the children if they knew where Carl was and..."

"Oh, no! Not dinnertime! How long was the poor boy bound and gagged?" Jennifer managed through tears.

"He had been down in that ... Oh, no ... My side is killing me ... basement since about twelve-thirty, just after lunch!" Susan replied, holding her side again and having a hard time drawing breath.

"I'll bet he was ready to kill Paul," Jennifer giggled.

"Paul said that he tried to sneak away from the dinner table nonchalantly. He ran down there and promised Carl he would *do anything, give him anything, be his personal slave for life*, if he just would not tell his parents! But, of course..." Susan collapsed back down on the bed that was shaking and trembling in sympathetic joy from the sisters' convulsive laughter.

"Oh, no! Poor Carl! No wonder he wants to get even. What did Paul's parents do?" Jennifer was able to choke out.

"They spanked him, of course, and made him wash the car, scrub the floors, and—oh, some other things. But what is amazing to me is that Carl didn't grow up to become an axe murderer or something! I mean that has to be pretty traumatic for an eight-year-old boy," Susan finished, her eyes watery but filled with love for her mischievous fiancé. "Oh ... I've got to catch my breath."

Both young women eventually settled back down, and Jennifer yawned, looking at the clock.

"Gee, it's nearly one o'clock, Sue. I'd better let you sleep some ... because," and she leered wickedly again at her sister, saying in a sinister, taunting voice, "it's a sure bet that Paul won't let you get *any sleep* tomorrow night!"

Susan's cheeks immediately grew hot and red while she exclaimed enthusiastically, "Oh, Jennifer! I sure do hope so! It has been so difficult waiting to be ... you know ... intimate with Paul. I was afraid I wasn't going to make it!"

Jennifer sat up immediately and looked at her sibling in wide-eyed comprehension saying, "You mean? ... Oh, Susan! ... That is so wonderful! ... Really! I think that is just grand!" and she hugged her baby sister tightly, tears beginning to form in the back of her eyes. "I'm so proud of you. For waiting, I mean. Proud of you both. I really like Paul now!"

Susan was greatly surprised at her sister's reaction and slightly embarrassed. She pulled back a little from her embrace and questioned her, peering into Jennifer's face.

"But Jennifer. Why are you so surprised? We were always taught that it was the smart thing to do, the right thing to do, the thing God commanded us to do ... to wait for our husbands, you know. And you, yourself, told me to be careful ... that night at Cindy's beach house, remember? I never will forget that, Jen. It really made an impression on me."

"Oh, Susan, I'm so glad you heard what I was trying to say. I have always wanted to protect you."

But she could no longer meet her little sister's intense gaze. She dropped her eyes and patted Susan absently on the cheek, sighed, and affirmed,

"I'm so happy for you, Susan. Happy that he respected you enough not to pressure you. I feel very confident now that you and Paul will be happy together ... For always. You are so much smarter than I am, you know. Always have been."

Susan's brows wrinkled some. *Jennifer! Is that part of what went wrong between you and Michael? If so, I am so sorry. And I do want to go kick his teeth in! I want so much for you to be happily married to a wonderful man, too. I love you so much,* she thought.

Pulling Jennifer's chin up and looking into her eyes, she said, "If I am smarter than you, Jen, which I don't think I am, but *if* I am... It is only because you were always there, looking out for me... sheltering me ... protecting me like you said. And I love you so much, Big Sister!"

And as she embraced her older sibling warmly, kissing her soft, dark hair, she felt Jennifer's tears falling gently down the side of her face as she mumbled, "I love you, too, Susie-cuesie. Happy wedding day."

The wedding was glorious. The morning brought rain showers that made the garden reception appear uncertain, but by early afternoon, the clouds were mostly gone and the sun was shining warmly. Susan was calm and glowing all day, which was a good thing because Jennifer and Betty were as nervous as fifth-graders waiting to give an oral book report, fretting about this, worrying about that, making last minute telephone calls to the florist, the photographer, the caterers, and the musicians, making certain that no one had forgotten their duties on this most important day.

Jennifer in particular, who had grown accustomed to being in charge, was bossing everyone around expertly, acting as if she were the father of the bride. When they had arrived at the church shortly after noon to check out the flowers, she had insisted that Susan's bouquet have more white roses and had ordered at her own expense more floral arrangements to be placed by the altar and next to the pews. She had done the same thing for the reception, which was being held on the picturesque grounds of a local, private supper club. She wanted all the white roses in town! Her sister was a virgin, and she wanted everyone to know it. And didn't white symbolize purity? And she wanted more of those twinkling, little white lights in the potted trees scattered all around. Hang the expense! Her baby sister deserved the best wedding money could buy!

She had phoned the band, too, and told them she would pay the extra money for them to play until the last guest had left to go home. And she did not want any tacky, "fleshly" songs played, either. She wanted them to concentrate on pure, lovely, classically timeless love songs. Songs about love that lasts forever. Her baby sister deserved love that lasts forever. If they didn't know any, they had all day to find some, learn them, and sing them tonight. Sing them wonderfully for her little sister's wedding. Her good, pure, sweet, and innocent baby sister's wedding.

That she was attempting to compensate for her own loss of virginity, her own loss of sweet innocence, and her own phantom wedding that she felt in her heart would never take place, did not enter Jennifer's mind. All she knew was that she loved her younger sister enormously and was very, very proud of her.

And when the five o'clock hour finally arrived, and the two hundred fifty guests all turned around to gaze upon the glowing, lovely, virginal bride slowly gliding down the aisle on the arm of her tall, handsome father, her face beaming out love for her groom, who was standing there transfixed at the vision of his one and only true love who was about to become his wife forever, Jennifer felt so very happy. Happier than she had ever felt in her conscious memory. Her little sister—a beautiful, radiant, pure, and loving bride. Her baby sister—who had told her just last night that she, Jennifer Elaine Jacobs, had encouraged her to protect and guard her virginity, a priceless gift that she could now offer freely, joyfully, with no regrets, to that very fortunate man, her husband, Paul Whitfield—was the most beautiful bride she had ever seen.

At least some good has arisen out of my own sorrow, Susan... if I really did influence you to save yourself for your husband, to protect your heart, to know that you are priceless, she thought while standing there by her sister's side, hearing those timeless, magnificent, gloriously bonding, mystical, mysterious, spiritual words—those eternal wedding vows being spoken sincerely from two hearts that had become one.

"To have and to hold. From this day forward. For better or for worse. For richer or poorer. In sickness and in health. To love and to cherish. 'Til death do us part. Forsaking all others, keeping only unto thee for as long as we both shall live. With this ring, I thee wed, and with my body, I thee worship. With all my worldly treasure, I thee endow. For this cause shall a man leave father and mother, and shall cleave to his wife, and they, twain, shall be one flesh. Wherefore they are no more twain, but one flesh. What, therefore, God hath joined together, let not man put asunder."

Oh, Susan! I am so happy for you! So happy. You will make it, Susan. I just know you will! I love you, Susan! I love you, too, Paul! Thank you for keeping my little sister pure. Thank you for guarding not just her body ... but especially ... her heart. Please be good to her always! Please honor and keep these vows you are making. I will hold you accountable. I am witnessing this sacred union, and I will hold you accountable for taking good care of my baby sister. My little Susie.

As these thoughts flooded Jennifer's mind, tears she could not stop flowed freely down her perfectly made-up face. They were only tears of joy, she thought. They were acceptable tears of joy. Joy for her younger sister and her brand new brother-in-law.

But why did they hurt so much?

"Jennifer, you look as lovely as the bride," remarked Sally Parker, a former classmate of Jennifer and a Hillside Church friend as she hugged her at the reception. "And you are still so slender. No fair!"

"Thanks, Sally. You look wonderful, too. How have you been? Mother tells me you are to be married in September," Jennifer returned.

"That's right. But I don't know if my wedding will be as pretty as this one. I can't believe all these beautiful white roses everywhere. And Susan and Paul look so happy together. They make such a great couple, don't they?" Sally continued.

Jennifer nodded, smiling over at Mr. and Mrs. Paul Whitfield who were seated at the table of honor, nibbling at their food but looking longingly at each other, drinking to each other only with their eyes, as the poet what's-his-name had said. The slow, steady burn of their yet to be fulfilled, God ordained sexual passion was clearly visible to anyone with average intelligence who might be observing them.

Sally, who was of above average intelligence, commented astutely, "It appears to me that the new Whitfield's would just as soon get this reception nonsense over with so they can commence with the 'consummation of the union,' as they say, don't you think?"

"I'd say that was a very cogent observation, Sally," Jennifer laughed. "It's so wonderful to see Susan so happy. I do believe that she and Paul will have a long, happy marriage."

"What about you, Jenny? Do you have a special someone in your life?" Sally inquired generously. "If not, I just don't know what's wrong with the men in Indianapolis! You are so beautiful and smart, and you mother tells me you are becoming very rich, too."

"She didn't say that, did she?" Jennifer asked, shocked. "That doesn't sound at all like Mother." She could not imagine her usually tight-lipped, modest mother saying such a thing.

"Well," Sally giggled back, "she didn't say that exactly. What she said was that you were doing *extremely* well in your chosen career and were earning more money than she had ever dreamed possible, climbing very quickly up the corporate ladder there in Indy."

"That still doesn't sound like my mother," Jennifer returned, her brow wrinkling somewhat.

"If I may be honest, Jennifer, and not make you feel uncomfortable or anything..." Sally leaned a little closer to her old friend's ear and explained quietly. "Mrs. Hastings, that nasty gossip, was gloating to your mother earlier this evening that she had heard your old flame, Michael Evans, was marrying Emily Prescott next month, and that she thought you had been foolish to throw away such a fine, good-looking man. Well, your mother just couldn't stand it, and that's when she told her off, so to speak. She said that basically you did not need Michael or any other man to be worthy, successful, or desirable, or something along those lines ... And then she walked off. She did great!"

Sally finished triumphantly and then studied Jennifer's response carefully, for she, too, had never understood how her friend could have discarded that sexy, good looking, silver-throated Michael Evans so many years ago.

Jennifer's face did not change any at Sally's revelation as she had already heard that piece of news. She smiled at Sally's description of her mother's reaction to that hateful, opinionated Fern Hastings, before replying.

"I know about that wedding, Sally, and I have always liked Emily Prescott, as does everyone, you know. She and I were the best of buddies in junior high school, and I think she is the sweetest, kindest, most sincere girl I have ever known, except for my sister ... Oh, and you, too, of course," she added diplomatically.

But the two women merely looked at one another for a moment and then burst into laughter, both at the *faux pas* and the clumsy attempt to repair it.

"You don't have to include me in with Emily Prescott, Jennifer! I am not nearly as nice and kind as she is. Don't pretend to be, either," Sally acknowledged truthfully, still searching Jennifer's face for an answer to her question, but finding nothing in her eyes except a guarded remoteness bordering on hardness.

Jennifer never had "hard" eyes before, Sally reasoned to herself, *or a jaw that was set in a stubborn resolve like hers is now. She was always soft, sweet, and trusting—not suspicious or cynical. Something must have happened between her and Michael that changed all that. What could it have been? He must have broken her heart. But how? And I heard that it was she who broke their engagement, not Michael. How mysterious!*

Their conversation and Sally's ruminations were interrupted at this point. It was time for the speeches and the toast to the bride and groom. As all that was occurring, Jennifer thought about Emily Prescott.

It was so very ironic that Emily should be marrying Michael next month. She and Emily had been bosom buddies during those very awkward, insecure junior high school years. Emily had always been very supportive of Jennifer, had seen to it that she was included in the "in" group at school, and had taken her under her wings to build up her confidence and encourage her in any way she could. Physically, Emily was just the opposite of Jennifer—short and petite, blonde and fair, with pale blue eyes—very small and pretty, almost like a doll. But although she was small physically, she had the largest, kindest, most tender heart of anyone Jennifer had ever known. Also, she was the most sincere Christian that Jennifer had known, living out the teachings of Jesus better than most adults, even back then in junior high and high school.

Perhaps it was her tender, compassionate heart that had led her to "adopt" Jennifer. For the sister of the bride knew that she had been so very needy back then. She had spent most Saturday nights at the Prescott home, with Emily's parents also taking a liking to Jennifer and building her up, loving her, believing in her. Mr. Prescott in particular must have seen in the young girl a tremendous need for a father, because he spoke kindly, encouragingly, and lovingly to her just as he did to his daughter. He could tell that the gangly, coltish, long limbed, skinny adolescent was very insecure, and he would tickle her under her chin and say something about her "dark, gypsy eyes alluring many a young man one day," or something along those lines, Jennifer remembered.

And she remembered, too, what a big difference to her life the Prescott's had made. How much more confident and secure, cherished and worthwhile, they had made her feel. They were the ones that had made her believe that she, too, could one day have a happy family, despite the broken one she had known.

And now their precious Emily was marrying that Michael!

Oh, well, she reasoned, *I have always liked Emily, and I suppose Michael could have changed. We all learn from our mistakes. I have certainly changed. I wish Emily the best, and I'm not going to waste any more time thinking about it. I have my own life now, under my own full control. And with that contract I am going to bring home from Pittsburgh, I should be $10,000 richer, enough to add that bay window seat to my breakfast room and put hardwood floors down in the kitchen and family room of my new house. My investments are doing quite nicely, too, accumulating so that I may be able to purchase that beach house I want so much within the foreseeable future. I am very happy in my own chosen life. Marriage is fine for Susan, but like Mother told that awful Fern Hastings, I don't need any man to make me feel special.*

And just at that moment Susan was tossing her bouquet, aiming it for straight for Jennifer, who lost in thought, let it drop down to the floor right at her feet. The crowd, as one, let out a disappointed, "Ohhhh!" But Sally just kept observing the bride's big sister, more convinced than ever that Michael Evans must have broken her heart. Why else would she not have married him?

Slightly embarrassed at having been caught daydreaming, Jennifer quickly recovered, bent down to pick up the very full floral arrangement with extra white roses, and stated with finesse, smiling and slightly flushed,

"Now you all know why I never made the girls' softball team. Thanks, Susan, for the flowers. I love you! I love you, too, brother-in-law. Take good care of my baby sister, now!"

And she blew her beloved sister a kiss, which was returned and captured on film by the expert photographer to the applause of all the guests.

Yes, thank you, Sweet Sue, for thinking of me. But I don't plan to ever become anyone's bride.

Chapter Twenty-Four

"*Jennifer, darlin'! I've just received some wonderful news about your sister and Paul, and I couldn't wait to call you! You know I don't normally phone you at the office, sweetheart, so please forgive me. I know how busy you stay, but this news couldn't wait!*" began the joyful, excited voice of Betty Jacobs Miller calling the MedTech Center in Indianapolis from Mobile to speak with her newly promoted, Regional Executive Director of Sales daughter.

It was the middle of September 1982, and Jennifer was busily sorting through some stacks of papers on her desk, trying to prepare herself for a director's meeting scheduled in about thirty minutes. As usual, she was up to her neck in work, flying around the office like a whirlwind, overseeing her semi-incompetent staff with a million and one things on her mind. She pressed the telephone between her head and shoulder, continuing to divide the papers as she spoke.

"Don't be silly, Momma. You can always call me at work. You know that. Now, what is this vitally important piece of news," she spoke hurriedly into the mouthpiece. *Gosh, Sarah, you've done it again! How can you be such an idiot to make the same mistakes over and over again?* she thought irritably. *I should have fired you a long time ago.*

"Well ... are you ready for some *really big news*?" dramatized Betty in a manner so atypical of her usual straightforward conversational style.

Jennifer immediately comprehended the change in her mother's mannerism and stopped working, sat down involuntarily, and asked gravely, "You can't mean ... Susan isn't...?"

"Yes! That's right!" Betty raved on, almost shouting into mouthpiece now so that Jennifer had to hold the receiver out a little from her ear for comfort. "Your baby sister is pregnant! I am going to be a grandmother and you, an aunt! Isn't that wonderful, Sweetheart?... Jennifer? Are you still there?"

"Yes, Momma. I'm here. It's just that it's such a shock, that's all. Susan told me that she wanted to wait another year or two so that she would be guaranteed to keep her job if she took a year off for maternity leave," the aunt-to-be responded unemotionally. Her face had turned slightly pale and her breath was coming out more rapidly.

"Maybe that was their plan, you know, but sometimes these things just happen, regardless," Betty answered.

No, they don't "just happen," Momma! How stupid do you think I am? This baby is an accident, an unplanned pregnancy, and why are you pretending otherwise? she thought.

"Aren't you happy, Jennifer? Susan and Paul sure are, even if they were surprised. In fact, don't dare tell her that I told you because I think she wanted to tell you herself. But I just couldn't wait! ... I hope you will be happy for her, honey," Betty added uncertainly, her initial enthusiasm waning somewhat in her conversation with her first born. "She is overjoyed, although beginning to feel a little morning sickness. The baby is due the first part of May."

"How can she be overjoyed while feeling as sick as a dog and tired, too?" Jennifer asked.

"She didn't say anything about being tired, although I suppose that would be expected, Jenny. And she didn't say she was 'as sick as a dog,' either. Honey ... why aren't you happy for your sister? Your reaction is surprising me," Betty asked, concerned. *Surely, you're not jealous, Jennifer. You've always been so proud of Susan and have taken such an interest in her life*, her mother reasoned.

That was a good question. Unfortunately, Jennifer did not know the answer. So she became defensive, as was her usual pattern when under a real or imagined attack.

"I am happy for Susan, Momma! Of course, I am! Why wouldn't I be, for heaven's sake? It's just that I was hoping she and Paul would have more time together without kids to ... you know ... enjoy life without all the worry and exhaustion that children bring. I mean, they haven't even been married two years yet, and—"

"But, children are what *make* a marriage, Jennifer. I know that may sound so hypocritical of me ... coming from my mouth to your ears, Sweetie. Your father and I ... I'm sorry that we didn't..." Betty had interrupted her eldest daughter to explain the joyful blessing that children bring to a marriage, but faltered as she realized the miserable failure her own union had been.

There was a long pause on the other end of the line before Jennifer offered, "Momma, you don't have to apologize to me ... I understand. And I am happy for Susan and Paul. Just surprised ... that's all. Look, might I call you back this evening? I have a very important meeting in about..." and she glanced down at her expensive, status symbol gold watch, "Yikes! About twenty minutes!"

"Sure, dear. I'll talk to you this evening at home. Don't dare tell Susan I told you, okay?" Betty pleaded.

"I won't. 'Bye, Momma," she finished and banged the receiver down on its cradle very firmly.

"Sarah! Get over here on the double and repair this mess you made with these catalog cards again! I can't do my job and yours, too! I've got that meeting in less than twenty minutes, and I need these damned things to be in proper sequence!" Jennifer unloaded on the unfortunate Sarah, who rushed over to her desk muttering under her breath, "Hell hath no fury."

"And Dan, please run down to technical support and ask Joan Matheson if she can join me in this meeting at two. I have been trying to phone her, but her line has remained busy. Tell her I need that presentation video clip on the new CAT scan equipment," his boss requested of him, the telephone under her ear again as she was attempting to make another call regarding the meeting at two while still sorting through brochures.

"Do you mean the RS-2000 or the RSQ-2002?" Dan inquired, not wanting to pass along bad information to Joan.

"How the hell am I supposed to know, Dan?" she exploded into his face. "That's your job, isn't it? All I know is that I heard from R&D that the new CAT scanner is ready for sale! I would assume it is the RSQ model. That *is* the newest model, isn't it?"

"Not necessarily ... but I will take care of it," the exasperated employee responded as he turned to walk to the elevator, also murmuring softly, "Hell hath no fury, but it may one day when JJ passes on."

"Thank you, Dan!" she called out after him in sarcasm, Anger now back in his rightful position in the driver's seat of her personality.

Oh, Mother! she thought, furiously, w*hy did you have to call me at work with your news? Couldn't it have waited until tonight? People have babies every day! I am busy working my tail off here, trying not to look like an incompetent in this meeting at two, and you interrupt me at the worst possible time! Now I am snapping everyone's heads off and using bad words that only the trashy girls used back in Mobile. And I'll just bet you didn't phone Susan at work last month when I got my big promotion, did you? No! My life is not important enough, is it? But just let Susan have an unplanned pregnancy, and the whole world stops spinning!*

And so her afternoon progressed, the two o'clock meeting going very well considering the frantic, last minute preparations that she had made, further alienating herself from her staff. In hindsight, she always felt bad about these outbursts of temper and would apologize to her people later, taking them by two's to lunch, but justifying her bad mood to them somewhat at the same time.

Some of her employees genuinely liked and admired her, while others just thought of her as a mean, self-centered old witch, a thorn in the flesh of their otherwise good jobs with a growing company in a stable industry. The ones who liked her would often try to get to know her better, inviting her to dinner at their homes or to go out after work for dinner and a movie. But more often than not she would refuse kindly, making some excuse. She seemed to hold them all at arm's length, not allowing anyone to really get to know her.

She could be kind and fair, but then again, she could be as hard as nails and twice as unrelenting. And you never knew which Ms. Jacobs was going to show up for work. Lately, the least little frustration would send her over the bend, and her staff walked on eggshells around her, trying to avoid her as much as possible.

That she did not have even one close friend did not bother Jennifer much. She was her own best friend, she knew. She enjoyed her own company, and she stayed so busy that she had no time for friendships anyway. Ferdinand and Isabella were also great comforts to her, and they seemed to enjoy her companionship, always meeting her at the door when she arrived back home from business trips, jumping up on the sofa, curling up in her lap while she read at night or watched television, and of course sleeping by her side or on her pillow, their rich purring humming her to sleep.

So when the clock on the office wall showed six-thirty that Friday evening in September 1982, Jennifer being the only one of her group still hard at work, she drew a deep, cleansing breath and said aloud to no one,

"I'm going to call it a day. I've got to go home and do laundry and prune that old elm tree by the driveway while there is still some daylight left."

Pulling into the garage of her relatively new house that late summer day, a country Victorian revival house with a large, wrap-a-round porch set back in a heavily treed, one-acre lot, gingerbread scroll work embellishing its natural charm, she felt a sense of pride. She was purchasing this house all by herself while most of her neighbors were two-income families. She was woman, hear her roar! She loved using her spare time working on it, too, planting flowers and shrubs, shopping for accessories, pictures, just the right antique to fill a corner of the living room.

She was taking her time furnishing it because she wanted the joy of the project to last as long as possible. Something deep in her soul told her that were she ever to finish this project completely, there would creep into her heart that old, restless longing again. That depression that was always hanging around somewhere in the background of her life, telling her that despite her success at MedTech, she was really wretchedly unhappy.

And still many evenings she found herself waking up in the small hours of the morning crying out in heaving sobs. Why this should be, she did not know nor did she want to explore it. She was successful.

Her dreams were coming true. That was all she wanted to know. And anyone with half a brain was blue every now and then because of all the sadness in the world, she knew, so she was doing " just fine." Surely she was fine.

But her blue periods were not in her thoughts at all now as she was finally home. She punched in the security code as she entered the back door into the kitchen. The telephone was ringing, so she placed her briefcase and purse on the counter, kicked off her expensive Italian pumps, fell down onto the cushiony loveseat, stroking the cats with one hand while grabbing the receiver with the other.

"Hello, Jennifer speaking."

"Well, Jenny, I'm sure you already know my news. I could tell from Momma's reaction when I phoned her this morning that she wasn't going to wait until this evening for me to call you," Susan's happy voice traveled through the line.

"Don't let her know that you know she told me, Susie. She wanted me to make you think that she didn't tell. But anyway, congratulations, Sis. I hear that Paul has gotten you into trouble, that old rascal. And to think that I once liked him, too." The soon-to-be-aunt tried to sound upbeat, still stroking the cats, her face completely blank.

"Oh, I'm in trouble, all right, Jen!" Susan played along, laughing. "But nothing that about seven-and-a-half months won't fix. I'm due May second, or did Momma tell you that, too?"

"Yeah, a little birdie told me something about a package arriving around the first of May," the elder sibling responded, her tone becoming flatter.

"Can you believe it, Jen? Me, a mommy! It just doesn't seem possible, except I am feeling very sick ... in the morning, mostly," Susan continued, her joyful voice dancing across the miles.

"Oh ... I'm sorry, Susie," was all Jennifer said.

There was silence on both ends before Susan resumed, a slightly disappointed expression in her voice.

"You don't sound too happy for me, Sis. I thought you would be looking forward to becoming an aunt and everything."

Why should I be so gosh-darned excited about becoming an aunt? Jennifer wondered. *Really, Sue, you and mother need to wake up and realize it is 1982 and the world is changing for women. Diaper pails and playpens are not what motivate a lot of us to wake up every morning.*

"Nonsense, Susan!" she replied, trying very hard to sound enthusiastic. "I am very happy for you. And for Paul, too. Mother said he was ... 'overjoyed' ... I think, was the word she used."

"Yes, he is. He was shocked at first, as I was, because this wasn't exactly planned, you know, and he asked me how this could have happened." And here, she began laughing very hard. "'How could this have happened?' Can you believe that question, Jen?"

"Yeah. I can believe it ... Go on," Jennifer responded with no emotion once more, staring straight ahead, unseeing, stroking the cats harder and harder as their fur floated heavily in the air.

"Well ... but anyway, once he got used to the idea, he was puffing up like a rooster, strutting around and telling all his co-workers and friends. And I just know he is going to make a wonderful father; don't you think so, too?" she begged her hero-of-a-big-sister for an affirmation.

How the heck am I supposed to know, Susan? He's your husband, not mine, for heaven's sake! the hero-of-a-big-sister thought in exasperation, but stated quickly, dumping the cats off her lap and standing up,

"I'm sure both of you will make very fine parents, Susan. Look, do you mind a lot if I phone you back later this evening? I'm about to run out of daylight here, and there is a branch on an elm tree that I am afraid may fall down on top of my mailbox and wipe it out. They're predicting a storm tonight, and I need to—"

"Don't bother, Jennifer! I'm certain that your mailbox is *much, much* more important than my news anyway! Forgive me for troubling you at all!" replied her baby sister angrily before slamming down the receiver.

"Well, fine!" screamed Jennifer back into the dead telephone line. "Hang up on me, Susan, and just see if I care! The whole world doesn't revolve around yours and Paul's reproductive systems, you know!"

She ran upstairs, furiously tearing off her office work clothes as she went, changed into her yard work ensemble, and grabbed the pruning shears. In the garage, she found the ladder, moved it up under the offending tree branch along the driveway and began to trim it off a little at a time, all the while fuming.

I am happy for you Susan! Didn't I tell you that? Do you want me to do cartwheels or back flips or something just to prove that I care about you?

As she hacked away in anger at the poor tree, the Kowalski family from across the street pulled their green van into their driveway and began to unload groceries. They could never fit their cars in the garage, as it was packed to overflowing with tricycles, bicycles, inflatable swimming pools, and all sorts of kids' yard toys. There were seven of them in all, two parents and five little ones, ranging in ages from eight years down to nine-months. They all waved enthusiastically at Jennifer, and she managed to smile and wave back despite her foul mood.

"Would you like some help with that?" shouted Jeff Kowalski, cupping his hands around his mouth. He was in his mid-thirties and was very kind and neighborly as was his wife, Judy, as befitted their Midwestern upbringing.

"No thanks! I'm almost done!" Jennifer called back, shaking her head and smiling weakly.

"Okay!" he waved, and resumed helping his wife with the groceries and their squealing, tumbling, pinching, high-spirited, and pugnacious offspring. "Stop kicking your sister, Bobby!" he instructed his eldest in frustration, giving him a corrective little smack across his backside, which the boy neither felt nor acknowledged, but vociferously protested.

"But Dad, *she* started it! She *always* starts it!" And the unrepentant, strong-willed son made another attempt to kick the living daylights out of his annoying younger sister, whose main gift in life to this point was thinking of ways to get him into trouble. And she excelled in that gift, crying loudly with exceptional histrionics and holding her stomach as though she had sustained a mortal wound in the mid-section, although his kick had missed its target by a good three inches.

"I don't care who started it! You are the oldest, and you can stop it! And hush that squalling, Kayla! He missed you by a mile," the voice of the irritated but patiently enduring father trailed off as the Kowalski's entered their sprawling, two-story colonial house.

Jeff Kowalski was a pediatrician, and his professional colleagues often teased him about producing one more child of his own whenever their patient load would slack off a bit.

As Jennifer finished pruning off the last of that irksome branch, she ruminated. *Gee! Judy and Jeff must stay so busy with that gang. I have never seen more hyperactive kids in all my life. I sure do hope Susan and Paul don't want a whole passel of children like that. Surely they don' t. But if Paul doesn't even know 'how it happened'... Who knows?*

And here she stopped in her work, wiped some perspiration from her brow, and began to laugh out loud. Laugh until her side hurt. She could see so clearly in her mind's eye her dear Susan telling Paul she was pregnant, and Paul's face going suddenly white at the unexpected news as he stammered, open-mouthed and wide-eyed, "How ... how did this happen?" She could also see Susie staring back at him at first in disbelief and frustration, but then smiling good humouredly as she explained to him very slowly and carefully in her best second grade teacher manner how sexual intercourse works to produce a pregnancy in the mommy's uterus. She could see it so plainly that her laughter nearly made her fall off the ladder. It felt so good to laugh again, and she enjoyed it for as long as she could. She had not really laughed like this since the night before Susan's wedding.

Oh, Susie, I would dearly love to have been a fly on the wall to see that! Oh, it's just too funny!

She knew then that she had to get down off that ladder and phone her kid sister to apologize or something ... to make it right again. She probably should have shown a little more enthusiasm.

I'm just tired from the work week, that's all, and with Momma calling just as I was panicked about that meeting this afternoon ... That must be why I am not happier about this news ... about this good news. And it is good news. Me, Aunt Jenny. That sounds pretty darn good.

I love you, Susan. I am happy for you! Really I am. Your life is not the one I would have chosen, but ... I am happy for you. And I will gladly help you explain to that husband of yours "how it could have happened" if you need me to. I still have my high school biology book, I think. With pictures and everything!

And she chuckled to herself all the more as she walked into her kitchen to telephone her baby sister to make it right again on that beautiful September day in 1982.

Chapter Twenty-Five

*P*honing Susan and apologizing had been easy because of the tremendous affection the two siblings felt for each other, an affection that was only growing stronger and more secure as the years added the wisdom of age to the young women. Friendship, true friendship, was life's most precious commodity, they each knew. And to have a sister who was also a friend was so rare and wonderful a gift that Jennifer was not about to risk estrangement over a silly misunderstanding. The two sisters had a shared history that bound them to each other in a way outsiders could not possibly understand, so Jennifer had been quick to apologize and make amends.

Besides, Susan was her only true friend. She continued to isolate herself from co-workers, and had not kept in touch with any of her high school or college friends with the exception of Katie McComb Smothers. She and the Smothers' had continued to exchange Christmas cards, and dear Katie still remembered her birthday each year, as it was one day before her mother's, with another card and sometimes a small gift. But that was all the contact she had with them. Katie always included a picture of her little girl born in 1980 in the cards. Jennifer would glance at it and then throw it away while placing the card on her living room mantel alongside all the others she received. She loved Katie and Joe still but could not afford to spend any time and energy focused on her past.

Her focus since Coburn University had been on her future, not the past. And she felt that she had made quite a success of her life.

Again, she had outperformed all the men in her region last year and was sought after by other firms trying to lure her away from MedTech. But with each enticing offer she received, came a larger, more attractive counter-offer from Tom Moyer inducing her to stay put. Tom had told her in confidence that she just might be able to take Bob Brandon's job away from him if she stayed there and played her cards just right. And Bob's job was just one step away from Tom's vice-president's position, which could be hers, she thought, as he was certain to retire within the next five years. Yes indeed, her career was unfolding even better than she had hoped.

Realizing the accomplishment of yet another goal, she had saved up enough money to make a large down payment on that beach cottage on the Gulf of Mexico that she had always desired and had a couple of real estate agents searching for just the right property even now. Whenever she would feel blue or empty or that strange sense of melancholia that was never too far away, she would use her imagination to dream of long, carefree days at the seashore, watching sunsets and writing messages in the shifting sands to refocus her thoughts and refire her ambition to "succeed." And it worked like a charm.

The only sad event that had occurred in her future since Coburn had been the death of her sweet cat and friend, Isabella, last January. The animal had begun to lose weight, and Jennifer had taken her to the vet only to be told that she had a pernicious form of cancer of the bowel. "It would be best to put her to sleep," the vet had told her. She had done so with many tears, and a lingering depression had settled over her at that time, not unlike the restless sadness that she seemed to experience every year around the middle of March, a depression that she always attributed to the long, Indiana winters.

Ferdie, too, had missed his sister, dragging around the house, crying constantly, and sniffing the chair in the bedroom where she had usually slept. Jennifer had tried unsuccessfully to introduce two other kittens into Ferdie's life but had been forced to find them other homes, as the surviving male cat had refused them with violence. He wanted Isabella and none other. So it was just the two of them now, Jennifer and Ferdinand. But the pet's death had occurred months ago, and by now both she and Ferdie were doing just fine.

To her mind, the only troubling aspect of her present life was the recurrence of her unchanging nightmare. She had experienced it again that same evening she had telephoned Susan to apologize for her lack of enthusiasm at her good news, and as usual, was surprised at its unexpected appearance. She had not dreamed it in a long time to that point and had hoped it was gone for good.

She always interpreted the dream to be just a general anxiety nightmare, revealing to herself her own inability to control every aspect of life the way she desired. The crying children merely represented, to her interpretation, whatever project she was involved in at the time and her fears that it might not be successful. Nevertheless, it terrified her and she wished she could stop dreaming it. *But how do I control my own subconscious?* she would reason. So she would continue to press on, trying even harder to be successful in her life.

She had just closed on another large contract this past week, in the middle of Spring, 1983, and Tom Moyer had taken her and Bob Brandon out to lunch to celebrate at the most exclusive restaurant in the downtown area. *Not bad for the little girl from Mobile, Alabama* she had thought, while dining on the sumptuous lobster bisque and the other delectable dishes of French cuisine at *La Maison de la Promenade,* being toasted by the vice-president of Sales.

So all in all, this beautiful spring afternoon in late April 1983 as she opened her mailbox at the end of her long, brick driveway, Jennifer was fairly contented with her life. Not happy … just contented. Unbeknownst to her, she had given up on the idea of being happy many years ago. As she was glancing through her mail, she saw Judy Kowalski, who was pregnant again with Number Six and was out strolling her toddler in the lovely, late afternoon sun. The friendly neighbor, displaying that wonderful Hoosier hospitality, walked up to Jennifer and said teasingly,

"Why, hello, Jennifer. Is that another new outfit? You always look like you stepped out of a fashion magazine, and I hate you for it," and she smiled warmly at her neighbor and kissed her on the cheek.

Judy liked and admired Jennifer but felt a little sorry for her at the same time. How could she possibly be happy without a husband and children? She was constantly arranging blind dates for her pretty, single neighbor only to have them firmly but politely refused. But she was determined. *If I can just invite her over for a barbecue one day next weekend, maybe, and invite Grant Perkins, too, I know they would hit it off immediately,* she was planning even now. *They would be perfect together.*

"Hi, Judy. I see you are out with only one little Kowalski this afternoon," Jennifer smiled back at Judy while merely glancing at the toddler. *If you mention one other man who would be "just perfect" for me, I will scream, Judy, so don't even think about it.* She tried to send her a message using mental telepathy.

"That's right. Jeff could tell that I was about to explode because the kids have been terrible all afternoon. So he told me to go outside for a walk with the baby and he would take over with the others. He's so good to me, you know," Judy beamed, so proud of her husband.

Yeah, he's good to you all right, Judy. Six children good! thought Jennifer uncharitably. *You will never have a life of your own, not to mention a waistline, again.*

"Jeff is a good man, I'm sure," the MedTech executive commented out of politeness as she sorted the bills from the junk mail. "I wonder what this one is?" she questioned aloud, turning over a large, expensive-looking envelope that had "Class of 1973 Planning Committee" embossed on the back flap. "It looks like a formal invitation."

As she began to tear into it immediately, Judy offered, "Maybe it's for a wedding. You know, time is fleeting. Most of your friends are probably married by now, Jennifer, and if you would just let me—"

"Oh, look," Jennifer interrupted her matchmaker neighbor purposely. "It's an invitation for my old high school class's ten-year reunion." And she read aloud just to keep Judy from telling her about another perfect man,

" 'The Planning Committee of the Central High School Class of 1973 requests the honor of your presence at our Ten Year Reunion, to be held at the Grande Hotel, 11001 Gulfview Boulevard, Mobile, Alabama, on June 8, 1983.' And there's other information here and an RSVP envelope ... Ooooo! The cost is $75.00 per person, or $145.00 per couple! They must be going to put on quite a show. I think I just might go ... if I can work it out on my calendar, that is. The Grande Hotel is very luxurious, and I could see my sister's new baby, too, while I'm down there," she finished enthusiastically.

She would love to go and show off to all her old friends. *Let them see for themselves how well the little gal from Mobile has done way up there in "Yankee land,"* she thought.

"Oh, has your sister had her baby yet?" inquired Judy, very interested.

Glancing up quickly as for a moment Jennifer had forgotten her neighbor was there, so lost was she in her own daydream of impressing the socks off her old classmates, she stated simply,

"No, not yet. She's due early next week ... really any day now."

"No, it won't be any day now, Jennifer. Not if it's her first baby, like you said. Why, with my first one, I was two and a half weeks late, had to be induced with a drip I.V., and was in labor for over—" Judy was just warming up to her favorite topic of conversation, childbearing and birthing, when Jennifer broke in.

"Sorry to interrupt you, Judy," she lied, "but I do need to go in and phone my sister to see how she is getting along, and I'm about to wet my pants because I was too busy to visit the ladies room at work, so if you don't mind?"

As if on cue, Little Brandon Kowalski began to tune up, demanding to either be strolled as he was expecting or to be let out of the vehicle that was imprisoning him.

So his mother announced upon parting, "I need to go, too. Okay, Brandon, we're going! Just let Mommy tell Jennifer 'goodbye.' Now Jennifer, if you could come over next Saturday afternoon for a barbecue ... you know Jeff grills great barbecue chicken ... I have a friend that would be just perfect for you. You don't want to go to your reunion *alone*, do you?"

But Jennifer was already backing down the driveway towards the safety of her house, making a bold attempt to escape from Judy's latest scheme, calling out as she hastily retreated,

"Sorry, Judy, can't make it next Saturday ... Have plans ... Thanks, anyway! See ya later!" and she closed the door securely behind her, breathing a sigh of relief at another narrow escape.

"Sure, I want to go my reunion alone!" she announced out loud to Ferdie, picking up the big cat and rubbing him under her chin as he purred rapturously. "I don't need any man to make me feel special, or attractive, or desirable, do I, Ferdie! No sir! I am confident on my own. Most of my married friends are about ready to file for divorce about now, anyway," she stated assuredly.

Meanwhile, outside, neighbor Judy was thinking, *Poor Jennifer!* She continued her walk with Brandon, an adorable little redhead who was now happily kicking his small feet against the bottom of the stroller and blowing bubbles with his spittle as he crooned merrily. *She is going to be so miserable at that reunion without a husband <u>or</u> a date!*

Later that evening as Jennifer was returning home from her health club after a long, hard workout under the auspices of that horrible Tonya person, a former Marine Corps drill instructor who loved to work the Friday evening aerobics class and make the young and not-so-young women sweat and groan, she picked up the ringing telephone.

"Hello, Jennifer speaking," she said. *Ouch! It even hurts to pick up the phone. That wretched Tonya.*

"Jennifer Jacobs! I'll bet you can't guess who this is!" said the energetic, feminine voice in a thick, Alabama accent.

"No ... to tell you the truth, I can't quite place ... Wait a minute. Is that you, Sally Parker?" she risked hesitantly as she sat down slowly, easing her already sore body into her favorite chair. *She must be calling about the reunion,* she reasoned.

"It's Sally Parker Freeman now, Jennifer. Last time I talked to you was at your sister's wedding about two years ago, remember? And I got married the following September," responded Sally.

"Yes, that's right. I just couldn't remember your new last name. Your husband wasn't from Mobile, was he?" she replied politely and tried to shift her stiffening body into a more comfortable position. *I'll go take a long soak in a hot tub after this call to loosen up some,* she planned. *That, and a nice, tall glass of wine should help things some. That Tonya is sadistic!*

"No, Ken is from Mississippi, and I hope I will be able to introduce you to him at the good ol' Central High reunion. I received my invitation yesterday. Did you get yours yet?" Sally inquired.

"Yep. Mine came today. Are you and Ken going to be there?" she asked.

"Yes, we are, Jennifer, and I sure do hope you can come. Do you think you can?" Sally inquired hopefully.

"I'm planning to, Sally, after I check my calendar. I don't think there's anything that can't be rescheduled that weekend. I would love to see you again," Jennifer concluded.

"Great! That's wonderful! The reason I am calling is that I was 'recruited,' so to speak, to phone fifty former class members to beg them to please fill out the information update sheet that was included in with the invitations as quickly as possible, like even this weekend if you can, so the committee will have time to print up a booklet to pass out to all the attendees," Sally explained.

"Oh, yes ... I see it right here," replied Jennifer as she leafed through the packet that was on the end table. "Sure, Sally, I'll get right on it either tonight or first thing tomorrow and mail it Monday morning. How's that?"

"Fantastic! And the committee is also asking any and all '73 graduates to send copies of any snapshots or film clips of any high school events, like dances or ball games, awards banquets, and things like that," Sally continued, "that you might have on hand. They want to make some kind of movie or slide presentation, or something along those lines."

"Gee, the committee must be planning quite a spectacle, Sally. I am looking forward to it," she mused. "But all my memorabilia from those days is back at my mother's house, and I doubt if I would have much of interest anyway. I'll see what I can do, however."

"Thanks, Jen. You're such a good sport. You're right about the committee. It's led by Jim Martin, you know, who was always political even way back then, and I think he wants to impress all of us so that when he runs for Congress or President or something, we will all vote for him," and Sally chuckled. "Though I wouldn't vote for him for dogcatcher! I still think he stuffed the ballot box when my brother ran against him for President of the Junior Class back in 1971." And she laughed even more.

"You may be right, Sally," the former classmate replied diplomatically. Jennifer had never liked Jim either. A little too effusive, egotistical, and insincere, she thought. Would make a perfect Congressman, unfortunately.

"Well, I won't take up any more of your evening, Jen, and I've got about forty more phone calls to make, so ... Oh! Remember we were talking about Emily Prescott at Susan's wedding? Well, I just spoke to her before I phoned you, and she and Michael are planning to attend, too. I know you told me that you always liked and admired Emily, so I just thought I would pass along that bit of news," Sally relayed, still fishing for clues as to the mystery of Jennifer and Michael's broken engagement so many years ago.

"That's great, Sally. It will be fun to see Emily again ... and everyone else. Look, thanks so much for calling. I will complete this information sheet without delay and ask mother to get out my old boxes of junk and scrap books to search for anything useable, okay?" Jennifer responded very smoothly, not giving Sally's inquiring mind any additional information.

"Thanks, Jen. Goodbye, and I'll see you in June," and Sally hung up the phone with slight disappointment.

As Jennifer placed the receiver on its cradle, she glanced over the questionnaire that the committee wanted all '73 class members to complete. It inquired after the usual things—current address and phone number, current career, position, and title, spouse's name and children's names and ages, any awards or special presentations, and things along those lines. She flipped the form over and over in her hands while staring out into her lovely family room. Ferdie jumped up in her lap, making her squirm a little.

"Ow, Ferdie! I am sore from Attila the Hun's workout, you know. Be careful," and she stroked him absently, her mind engaged elsewhere.

So, Emily and Michael are going to be there, huh? That doesn't bother me a bit. No sir. Not one bit. I will just plan to dazzle every one of my former classmates, including those two. Then, they will all see that I don't need to have a spouse or children to be successful.

I chose a fulfilling career path instead. And I'll just bet I am much better off than most of them!

She slowly pulled her aching body out of the chair and walked gingerly to the refrigerator, removing a nicely chilled bottle of red wine. She filled a large wine glass, with a bowl big enough to serve soup in, almost to the brim. She then walked carefully upstairs and ran a nice, hot bath for herself in her large whirlpool bathtub. She lit some candles around the huge master bathroom, turned out the lights, and placed a classical music tape in her stereo system. As she eased her sore muscles into the very warm bath water and found a comfortable position in the tub, she sipped at her glass, listened to the soothing music of Mozart, and planned.

That's right. I will dazzle every one of my former friends and classmates. I will purchase the sexiest, prettiest, most expensive dress I can find and make all the woman jealous of me and all the men lust in their hearts for me. I will write down every one of my achievements on that questionnaire and hint broadly at how successful I am ... at what a hugely successful and prosperous business executive I am. Then, everyone there, including Emily and her poor choice of a husband, will know that I am very, very happy.

As she relaxed there in her whirlpool tub and looked at her reflection in the mirrored walls surrounding it, she knew she could carry out this plan to perfection. She knew she was beautiful, much more attractive than the awkward, insecure girl of eighteen she had been back in 1973. Why, tonight alone at the health club, two or three men had tried to obtain her phone number or buy her a drink at the juice bar, gazing longingly at her lovely face and figure! She took pride in her appearance, and it showed not only in her faithful attendance at the gym but also in the expensive tailored clothing and accessories she wore, the fashionable hairstyle and manicured nails she maintained, and the shiny jewelry she lavished on herself.

That's right. When my former classmates and friends see how good I look, they will know that my singleness is my choice ... that I have chosen a career over marriage and children ... that I could win the love of any man I wanted, but that I don't want to. I will show them. I will convince them that the little girl from Mobile has made it, and made it on her own ... without any man!

So she stayed there, pampering her aching body in the warmth of the swirling waters, listening to the comforting, timeless strains of the musical genius from Vienna, and closing her eyes to visualize her success at the Class of '73 Tenth Reunion. She could just see herself now, the center of attention, laughing and making witty conversation with everyone, subtly answering all their questions about her life in a way that let them know how happy and successful she had become, dancing with all the men while their wives looked on in envy, letting Michael know that she had never needed him at all and was much better off without him. She stayed there in her bathtub until all the wine in her glass was gone and the bath water became chilled.

Then she dried herself off, blew out the candles, crawled into her bed, and fell to sleep immediately, thinking still, *I will show all of them, all right. Especially Michael.*

She awoke to find herself lying in a beautiful, flowering glade, tall shade trees along the perimeter and an abundance of soft petaled, fragrant flowers forming a bed all around and beneath her. It was Paradise! Sparkling sunlight was filtering through the towering trees, and birds were making lovely music, singing the melodies of Mozart, while large, brightly colored butterflies were flitting around, sipping nectar out of the flowers. A small waterfall was over in one corner of the garden, spilling its clean, pure water over the white pebbles of the reflecting pool it emptied into, making soothing, comforting sounds.

She was there, in that sweet-smelling, soft flowerbed, making love with Michael. Glorious love, passionate love, pleasurable love! Making love, loving, and being loved. Totally enthralled and enraptured with his love. Totally in tune with the awesome beauty and rhythm of nature and natural desire for her lover, her best friend, her husband-to-be.

Then, very suddenly, the sky darkened, and all the woodland creatures began to run away as fast as they could, terrified, as from a monster. Michael, too, was running. Running very fast away from her, leaving her all alone in the now terrifying forest that was becoming colder, darker, and more frightening with every passing second.

"Michael!" she called out, stricken with a paralyzing fear. "Michael! Please come help me! Please don't leave me here all alone! Michael! Where are you? Please! Please come back and help me!"

But he was gone! He was gone, and she was all alone! All alone to face the monster that was fast approaching! She tried to run, but her feet were like lead. She tried and tried to run, but could not move even one inch, a wicked vine, now wrapping around her feet and ankles, tying her down in place.

"Oh, Michael!" She called out, crying in anguish and terror, *"How could you leave me here ... All alone?!"*

She awoke quickly, tears streaming down her face, her heart beating wildly in her chest. She saw from the clock by her bed that it was two a.m.. She lay back down and breathed deeply, extremely troubled at this dream ... this new nightmare.

Please, please don't add this dream to that other, horrifying one! she begged the cruel demons in her subconscious.

What she did not know was that this was not a new dream. Not at all. In fact, this dream had always preceded the recurring nightmare with which she was so familiar, but it had never awakened her before as it did tonight, so that she could not recall it in the morning. This dream was, in fact, part of the overall nightmare that was continually plaguing her, tormenting her, following her around from house to house, from hotel room to airplane, from her mother's house to the beach house of Susan's friend, Cindy.

But now, tonight, she was so tired from her busy week, the grueling workout, and the relaxing bath, that shortly she fell back to sleep, this time resting for the remainder of the night.

And when she awoke Saturday morning, Ferdie purring in her ear and sunlight streaming in through her window, she had exorcized all the troubling details of the nightmare from her conscious memory, only vaguely recalling that it was a sex dream about her and Michael and had an unpleasant ending. Nothing else.

Must have been because of all that reunion planning I was doing before falling asleep, she explained to herself. *After I see him and Emily there in June, I'll just bet I won't dream it anymore.*

Chapter Twenty-Six

S he did indeed complete the questionnaire, describing her accomplishments in what she hoped was the most glowing of terms while still appearing to be modest and self-effacing, two qualities that are most highly prized among Southern women. It was a tough balancing act, but she thought she had managed it quite expertly. She mailed it the first thing Monday morning and checked her calendar, finding to her surprise that she actually had some free personal time that she might use during the week preceding the date of the reunion.

At first she had thought she would fly down, but upon further reflection she decided to take that whole week off and enjoy a much-needed vacation, driving down leisurely in her new German-made, convertible sports car. Driving down through the beautiful regions of southern Indiana, Kentucky, and Tennessee, on into her lovely home state of Alabama, passing rich farm land, rolling bluegrass country, green hills and rocky outcrops, lush river valleys and pine forests. Driving home, stopping at antique stores and historical landmarks, taking her time, enjoying the late spring sunshine, feeling the soft wind blowing through her hair. Yes. That sounded just right. And she should arrive in Mobile refreshed and relaxed, renewed and restored, ready to take on all contenders at that Class of '73 high school reunion.

And that way, they will see my expensive, foreign car, too, and I won't even have to brag! she reasoned. *And I won't drink any alcohol at all. I will need to stay focused and in control at all times, saying just the right things, making just the right gestures, smiling and flirting with just the right men. Yes, that's right. No alcohol. Not even one glass of wine.*

So with her plans all firmly made and her course all plotted out, she was feeling more confident and secure with each passing day, eagerly awaiting her day in the sun.

But in the meantime, Friday of that same week as she was at the office working, she received two happy phone calls that resulted in her flying home that afternoon, just for the weekend, about one month before the scheduled reunion.

The first call was from a real estate agent who said he had found the perfect beach house for her. It had three bedrooms, a large front porch overlooking the gulf, one and one-half baths, and a newly renovated kitchen. And best of all, it was a divorce sale, being bargain-priced accordingly, and only a forty-five minute drive from Mobile. Could she please fly down to see it this weekend because he was certain it would not stay on the market for long.

She had answered with a resounding "yes!" and had put Sarah immediately on the phone to arrange for her air travel. She had no more hung up the phone from that call when she received more good news. It was her mother telling her that Paul had just phoned to let her know he was driving Susan to the hospital for delivery. Jennifer told her mother she was flying home that afternoon to check out a beach house and would meet her at the hospital tonight, as soon as she could get there from the airport.

How exciting! Two big days for the Jacobs' girls, she had thought. *I may be getting my dream vacation home, and Susan will become a mother! And all in the same weekend.*

She rushed through the rest of her work day, behaving remarkably well toward her staff considering the pressure she was under to get out of there quickly. They were all surprised at her light-heartedness. She was actually humming and smiling while sorting through papers and giving them instructions. Maybe this was a new trend in her personality, they hoped rather than believed.

As she left the office, drove home quickly, threw some clothes carelessly into a suitcase, and then raced for the airport to catch the flight home, her heart was a mixture of joyful excitement and anticipation tempered with a small but gradually increasing amount of strange uneasiness.

I just feel it in my bones that this is the beach house of my dreams! she was thinking while humming. *I can't believe that I will soon be realizing a long-term dream come true. I hope Susan is doing okay, too. She and Paul and the baby will be able to visit me all the time at my new vacation cottage. Won't that be fun!*

So as she was leaving the rental car office at the airport in Mobile that Friday evening, May 4, 1983 and driving toward the Hixson Memorial Hospital, she was elated. *Won't Susan and Paul be so happy for me, and I for them! What a great day. I wonder if the baby is a boy or a girl. Did the agent say the house had wood or tile floors? I hope Sue didn't suffer too much. I wonder what labor and delivery are really like. I can't remember where that agent said to meet him... at his office or at the cottage itself? I wonder if Paul fainted. Will I have to maintain a seawall to counteract beach erosion? Will the baby be bald or have a head full of hair, like Susan did?*

These thoughts were somehow all jumbled up, disjointed, and lacked sequencing by priority in her mind as she pulled into the hospital parking lot about eight o'clock that evening, and she was beginning to feel slightly disoriented and was having trouble concentrating. That same odd sensation that she had often experienced in the past came over her, the feeling of somehow standing outside herself, observing her life as from a slight distance away, wondering what was going to happen to her next, like watching a movie version of her own life while not acting it out herself. *It's just the excitement of this day's news that's making me feel like this,* she rationalized. *It will pass.*

She inquired at the information desk, "Could you please tell me the room number for Susan Jacobs—Susan Whitfield, I mean?"

"Is it the surgical ward or maternity?" asked the receptionist kindly.

"Maternity," Jennifer replied. *For Pete's sake, why does it matter?* she thought, beginning to feel oddly anxious.

"Ah, yes, here is it. Room number 236. Take the elevator there and then turn left on the second floor. She just delivered this afternoon at

3 o'clock. A little girl, 7 pounds, 10 ounces!" responded the smiling receptionist with joyful enthusiasm.

It was the happiest part of her job to tell visitors of new babies, although she thought this young woman looked strangely unhappy and uneasy. She inquired out of curiosity,

"Are you a relative or a friend?"

What business is that of yours? Jennifer thought crossly, but answered flatly as she walked toward the elevators,

"Susan is my sister."

"Congratulations then, Auntie!" called out the woman to Jennifer's retreating back. But she received no reply from the new aunt.

Alone in the elevator, Jennifer's heart began to race and she could feel beads of perspiration forming on her forehead while her underarms began to feel clammy. *What in the world?* she thought, as she listened with growing apprehension to the pounding of her pulse in her ears. *I hope I'm not coming down with the flu or something. If I'm sick, I shouldn't go in to see Sue or the baby. Or the BABY! Wow! Susie has a baby girl! Didn't she always want a girl? Or was it a boy she wanted? Or did she want both? Why am I so dizzy and breathless? My baby sister now has a baby daughter of her own. What am I supposed to do? What is my role in all this? Why am I here anyway? What do I know about motherhood and babies? I don't know what I'm doing here ...*

But as the elevator door opened on the second floor, she took a deep, cleansing breath, tried to compose herself, and walked resolutely toward the left, looking for Room Number 236. Still she could not shake the feeling of panic, of somehow standing outside herself, watching, waiting, to observe, rather than to participate in this miraculous event, this brand new life that her dear sister had just produced. Her breath was coming out rapidly and she felt a little faint, but she pressed on. Standing in front of the partially closed door of Room 236, she peeked in cautiously without being noticed.

In the soft glow of a single lamp on a nightstand, Susan was sitting up in the hospital bed, humming tenderly, ethereally, her gown opened at the front, smiling down in the rapturous glow of maternal love at the tiny creature sucking at her breast, her first born child, a little baby with a mass of dark curls on her tiny head. Paul was seated by her side on the edge of the bed, radiant with paternal pride, looking on as if he were a protecting guardian angel, gently rubbing the dark head of his newborn daughter with his fingers and singing softly to her as she nursed.

It was simply the most beautiful scene Jennifer had ever beheld. Truly, a holy moment, she knew to the core of her being.

Suddenly, the hallway began to darken and the floor to give way under her feet. A nurse at the station a couple of yards away waltzed over quickly, grabbed her around the waist, and walked her slowly over to a chair in a corner of the hall, sitting her down and issuing instructions.

"Just put your head down over your lap … There, that's right. And take a deep breath. Good. One more. Good. Just relax, dear… That's right … Now sit up … Very good. Yes, you're beginning to get some color back into your cheeks. One more deep, long breath. Good."

The nurse, a woman of about fifty years with graying hair and merry blue eyes, smiled down at Jennifer and continued,

"I understand, dear. That scene you just witnessed is very powerful, isn't it? It's the thing that keeps me working the maternity ward, even when my aching feet and back are telling me to pursue some less strenuous career."

Jennifer said nothing but tried to smile back into the nurse's kind face. The nurse just patted her absently on her knee saying,

"You sit right here for a couple more minutes. I'll be right back with a cup of orange juice." And she disappeared momentarily.

But Jennifer thought, *I can't go back in there now. I'm an intruder. I'll go downstairs to the gift shop. I can't believe I left all my gifts for the baby back home in Indianapolis.*

She was feeling better, though still strangely outside herself. She sneaked away before the nurse returned with her juice, took the elevator down to the gift shop, and leisurely perused the small store, purchasing a stuffed animal—a fat gray hippopotamus wearing a pink ballerina tutu, corresponding pink satin ballet slippers, and sporting a pink flower wreath on its head. When you pushed its middle, it played "The Dance of the Sugarplum Fairy" from *The Nutcracker Suite*. She also purchased a bouquet of yellow roses,

Susan's favorite, and a "Congratulations on the birth of your baby girl!" card into which she placed a check for one thousand dollars.

Approximately thirty minutes had passed, and she felt she could now return to Susan's room. This time she marched back to the elevators with determination. *This is absolutely ridiculous,* she thought. *Women have babies everyday. Why am I reacting like this?* But still, she could not shake the strange sensation of unreality and fogginess that was surrounding her. However, she was determined to conquer it, whatever it was, though part of her felt like running away—away from this hospital as fast as she could.

Instead of running away, this time she walked with strength and purpose up to Room Number 236, smiled her apologies to the kind nurse at the station who just winked at her, knocked firmly on the door, and walked in as Paul and Susan both said, "Come on in" in unison.

Her brand new niece was now sleeping in her own little bassinet beside the bed, all wrapped up in a pink blanket with a pink cap on her head and turned on her side, her back toward Jennifer.

"Jennifer! I can't believe you're here!" Susan said with enthusiasm though she appeared to be very tired, and she stretched out her arms and leaned forward in her bed to embrace her big sister. "Oh, and you shouldn't have bought me those expensive roses from the gift shop. It's highway robbery, what they charge down there. But they're so lovely and smell so good! Thanks, Sis!"

"Nothing is too expensive for you, Susie-cuesie," Jennifer replied, still hugging her sister tightly, reluctant to let go. "Nothing. Nothing at all."

Paul took the flowers from his sister-in-law, whose arms were still wrapped around his wife's shoulders and whose eyes were tightly closed. He also took the fat hippo toy while offering his observations.

"Look at this Susan. Doesn't it remind you of that picture of yourself we saw last week in your mom's photo album? You know, the dance recital in the fourth grade?" he teased.

Susan, who had been "pleasingly plump" during her elementary school years before slimming down nicely in junior high school, grimaced at her husband and scolded playfully.

"After twelve hours of excruciating labor to bring *your daughter* into the world, this is the thanks I get?"

She pouted, pretending hurt feelings, while Jennifer, who was now hugging him, hit him playfully on the back with her purse and agreed.

"That's right, Paul! You've got a lot of nerve. Especially since *you're the one* who made her fatter than she's ever been in her entire life, you know." And she kissed him on the cheek and whispered, "Congratulations, Daddy," in his ear.

Susan chuckled and then added gently, gazing down lovingly at her sleeping newborn,

"Oh, but it was worth getting fat again to get *her,* Jennifer! Come over here and just look at her, Jen. Isn't she the prettiest little baby you've ever seen?"

On tiptoe, as if she were afraid her footsteps would awaken her sleeping niece, Jennifer stepped softly over to the bassinet and peered timidly into the tiny, pink face, taking in the delicate shape of her almost translucent ears, the perfect roundness of her tiny nostrils, and looking down on the exquisitely formed little fingers and fingernails, as the sleeping infant produced tiny little grunts while her mouth made sucking noises. She appeared to be a little baby doll, not a real baby. She was indeed the prettiest little baby Jennifer had ever seen, and she could not say anything but just looked up quickly from her niece to her sister and nodded her head, her eyes filling with tears.

Susan seemed to understand her sister's heart. While looking deeply into her eyes, she asked tenderly, "Aren't you going to ask me what we named her?"

Jennifer said nothing but merely shrugged her shoulders a little while shaking her head, still looking at her baby sister, her eyes moistening even more.

"We named her Ashley Jennifer Whitfield. We're going to call her Ashley. Actually, we thought Jennifer Ashley sounded much better, but then realized that her initials would be 'JAW' and didn't want that... Although when she nurses ... Ouchie! 'Jaws' might have been the right name for her after all!" Susan laughed.

The brand new aunt sat down on the bed and just embraced her sister, her baby sister who now had a baby of her own, a baby daughter whom she had named for her, and whispered, "Thank you," in her ear.

Susan whispered back, "You always were my hero, you know."

"Ohhhhhh! Booo Hooo! Ohooooo!" Feeling slightly out of place and embarrassed, Paul mocked the two sisters in pretended satire to lighten up the heavy emotional outpouring of the moment. He plopped down on the bed beside the two of them and threw his arms around both their slender shoulders as he "cried" right along with them.

They started laughing together, and Jennifer finally pulled herself loose, drying her eyes while she inquired,

"So, did Momma leave before I got here? I didn't even phone her from the airport because I wanted to get here before it was too late." She glanced down at her watch, "Oh my, it's already nine o'clock, and I know you must be tired, Susie. Were you really in labor twelve hours? Did it hurt much?"

"No, not too much," Paul volunteered instantly, grinning widely. "I feel fine now."

His wife threw her pillow at him and responded, *"Yes, it hurt,* Jenny! It felt like a Sherman tank forcing its way through my abdomen. But not really all that much until close to the end of labor. And yes, it was twelve hours, but I've been told that's not too bad for a first baby."

"You should have heard her language, Sis-in-law," Paul tormented his wife further. "I was totally shocked! I didn't know Sue knew words like that. And I was in the Navy for four years, you know."

Jennifer was smiling now and looked at Susan questioningly, as her sister laid her weary head back on her pillow and blushed, saying,

"It wasn't that bad, Jen. Paul is just teasing me. I didn't say anything that doesn't appear in the King James Version of the Bible."

"Oh," responded Jennifer, smiling still while pushing some stray hairs out of her sister's eyes and patting her hand. "Then it was just the emphasis placed on the words and the order of their usage that made them sound bad, and not the actual words themselves."

"That's right, Sis," Paul contributed, thoroughly enjoying himself. "It was 'hellfire and damnation,' all right. And I got it all on video tape for Pastor Warren to hear at the next deacon's meeting!"

Just then a nurse came in to check Susan's blood pressure and take her temperature. While that was going on, Jennifer arose preparing to leave as Paul answered her original question.

"Your mother was here all day and left about thirty minutes before you arrived. She said she didn't know if you had a key to the house, so she wanted to be there in case you went home first."

"So who's going to stay here with Sue tonight? I can, you know," Jennifer offered.

"No, Sis. No way. I'm staying." He waved his arms across his body for emphasis. "That chair over there makes out into an extremely *un*comfortable bed I'm told, and I feel that's my penance for putting your little sister through all this. And it's a small price to pay, at that." He grinned some more. Then his face grew serious. He gazed back down at his sleeping newborn and stated firmly but tenderly, "Besides, I don't want to be away from that little lady over there, either. The two women I love most in the whole world are going to be sleeping in this room tonight, and that is where I want to be, too."

Jennifer gazed at her sister's husband very warmly but could not say anything. She smiled appreciatively and patted his shoulder.

"What are the two of you discussing over there?" Susan asked through a yawn. "Include me, please, if it in any way concerns me."

"Paul was just telling me he is going to play nurse tonight. That's all, baby Sis. Look, I'm going to leave now so maybe you can get a little rest … Oh, and before I forget, here is a little something to put in little Ashley's college fund," she said, taking the envelope from her purse and handing it to Paul.

"Hey! No fair, Jen. You can't leave. You just got here. And you should give that envelope to me, not to Daddy Warbucks over there. I did all the work, remember?" Susan replied and yawned again.

Paul whistled as he opened the envelope, his eyes widening, and remarked, "Jen, this is way too much! We can't accept this."

"Let me see." Susan snatched it from her husband's hand. "Wow, Sis. I know you're rich, but this is far too generous."

"Nonsense, you two. How often am I presented with a niece … and a namesake, at that? And I'm told that if you put that check into a good mutual fund and just leave it alone, it should grow into enough money to put her all the way through college. Don't laugh, Paul! I heard an expert just last week say that he thought the market would top eight thousand, maybe even as high as ten thousand, before this century is over. Really! Quit laughing, Paul," Jennifer lectured while Paul doubled over in laughter.

"That'll be the day, Sis," he remarked, grinning at his very generous sister-in-law. "But in answer to your question, we will gladly present you with a niece or nephew each and every year if you will give us a grand each time, right Susan?" He winked at his weary wife.

"If I weren't so tired I would get you for that one, Paulsky," the new mother said and yawned some more.

"Well, changing the subject before Susan kills you, Paul … I don't mean to brag … but," Jennifer began, wanting now to share her good news with the couple, "I am meeting with a real estate agent in Gulf Shores tomorrow who thinks he has found the perfect beach cottage for me! You know, like one I have always wanted to own. Now we can all vacation together at the beach, and the two of you could use it on weekends, too, anytime you want to! Isn't that great?" she asked enthusiastically.

"You mean the *three of us* now, don't you, Jen?" Susan asked, smiling wearily.

"Isn't that what I said?" Jennifer inquired, her brow wrinkling.

"No, you said, 'the two of you,'" Paul corrected, a wicked twinkle in his eyes, "But don't worry, Sis, 'cause I like your idea better, anyway. We'll just dump little Miss Priss there in the bassinet, off at her grandma's house on the weekends, and Susan and I can go on a second honeymoon. How about it, Hot Stuff?" and he leered playfully at his wife, tickling her toes.

"Don't even think about it, Paulsky, darlin'," and she yawned again, finishing with, "Oh … excuse me. That's real good news, Sis.

Really. I hope it's just the beach home you've always wanted." And the exhausted new mother yawned again.

Jennifer was slightly disappointed at the reaction of the Whitfield's to her great news. But then, she also recognized that her sister must be completely worn out. She stated with finality,

"Look, I must be going. You are about done in, Sue, so I'm going to leave now. I will come see you tomorrow afternoon. Maybe I will have some snapshots of the beach house to show you."

But before she could kiss the new mother goodnight, little Ashley Jennifer Whitfield began to cry, a newborn, bleating-lamb-kind-of-cry, and Susan remarked worriedly,

"Oh, dear, she must be hungry again. She didn't take much that last time. I do hope she's getting something, as I can't tell yet. I'm all new at this milking machine job, you know. Aunt Jenny, would you please hand her to me?" she requested of her sister as she was rearranging her gown to nurse her infant.

Immediately, Jennifer bent down to pick up her niece.

But she could not.

The newborn was squirming and turning red in the face, crying more loudly and more insistently with every second, and her brand new aunt froze in place, unable to lift the baby from her crib, afraid she might somehow break her, drop her, do something wrong to harm her. Her heart began to race again and her face went white, as panic and fear swept over her, like in her recurring nightmare. She stared at the crying newborn, wanting desperately to help her, to comfort her, to protect her, but experiencing terror as she had not known in her lifetime—a gripping fear that she would somehow hurt the precious, defenseless infant.

"Jennifer, please give me the baby," Susan asked again, this time more firmly, not glancing at her sister at first, still preparing her lap to receive her child. But when her hero of a big sister did not place the infant into her arms as she expected, Susan gazed intently with growing apprehension into her pale, terror-stricken face, and then quietly redirected her request to her husband.

"Paul, dear, will you please pick up Ashley and give her to me?"

As Jennifer stepped stiffly to one side, he walked quickly over to the bassinet and gently scooped up his little girl, softly clucking over her as he placed her into his wife's arms.

"There, there, darlin.' Supper's on its way. Don't cry now, sweetheart. Everything's okay," he crooned.

Jennifer grabbed her purse quickly and fled the room, calling out a weak "goodbye" to the new Whitfield family. As she left, the breeze from the closing door blew the thousand-dollar check off the table and onto the floor. Paul bent down to pick it up, flipped it back and forth between his thumb and index finger, and looked at his wife thoughtfully.

"What in the world is wrong with your sister?" he asked.

At first, Susan said nothing, concentrating all her efforts on the task of getting nourishment to her tiny daughter. But after baby Ashley was positioned comfortably and was busily nursing, she looked into her husband's eyes with gravity, her eyebrows knitted together in concern, and replied,

"I don't know, Paul. And I'm afraid to guess." *And I hope so much that it's not what I am thinking,* she finished to herself. *Oh, Lord, please don't let it be what I am thinking.*

Chapter Twenty-Seven

*T*he Planning Committee of the Central High School Class of '73 Tenth Class Reunion—composed of the former President of the Student Council, Jim Martin, who was now an aid to a United States Senator with political aspirations of his own, and his hand picked crew of eager volunteers—had simply outdone themselves.

The hotel ballroom literally sparkled and bedazzled the twenty-eight-year-olds as they entered. There were polished silver and brass candelabras on each and every table with huge, floral centerpieces containing an abundance of fragrant blossoms. The linen tablecloths sported expensive bone china and gleaming silver-plated flatware while etched crystal stemware reflected the flickering candlelight. Overhead in the dining area, several large, leaded crystal chandeliers emitted just the right amount of light to illuminate the twenty-foot-high ceiling embossed with decorative moldings and faux marble painted finishes without interfering with the soft, romantic glow of the candles. Underfoot, a burgundy and gold patterned carpet contributed to the regal air of the room. Huge, gilt-edged mirrors lined the walls of the palatial space and seemed to enlarge it infinitely.

Beyond the tables and through an arched alcove, the brightly polished wood flooring of the dance area beckoned the young adults to participate in the live band's golden oldies and contemporary classics. Strains of the song, "My Cherie, Amour," were now being played, and played quite well, too, considering the band was a local one and was found at a reasonable price. Overhead the much lauded and equally maligned mirrored disco ball scattered its innumerable patches of light all around the room in a way that had always made Jennifer think of snowflakes whirling around in a blizzard. She, being born and reared in south Alabama, had not seen snow until she was twenty-one. But as a young adolescent she had always loved the disco ball at school dances because it made her think of snow—a cool, refreshing mental image in the midst of the sweating teenage dancers valiantly gyrating their way across the floors of the hot, non-airconditioned gymnasiums of her youth.

As she entered the ballroom, Jennifer felt confident, beautiful, and slightly haughty. She had spared no expense in her costume, had gone to her old, favorite hair dresser who had never let her down, and also had indulged herself with a professional manicure, something she usually did herself. She was wearing her wavy hair much shorter now, which was more becoming to her face and features than her longer hair had been. Her dress was a rather low-cut, black crepe cocktail length design with black satin spaghetti straps and sequined bodice accents and featured a slit up one side showing off her long legs, which were covered in sheer black stockings. Her shoes were costly Italian black heels, and she carried a matching small clutch purse accented with decorative beads and sequins.

To counteract the classically understated dark outfit, she accessorized with large, reflective diamond earrings, which her shorter hair showed off brilliantly, and a necklace composed of a one-carat diamond pendant, surrounded by smaller, bezel-cut, diamond chips on a shining gold chain. Her mother had lent her a diamond cocktail ring that had first belonged to her grandmother, and she wore bracelets of sparkling gold that made a pleasant jingling sound on her slender wrists. Expensive French perfume emanated pleasantly from her as she walked slowly into the already crowded room. She had taken extra pains with her make-up and it showed. Her eyeliner, eye shadow, and mascara accentuated her large, brownish-black eyes, and the moist, rose-colored lipstick gave her full lips an extremely sensuous appearance. The black dress complimented her tanned olive skin and was very becoming to her slim but shapely figure.

She was indeed much lovelier and more alluring than she had been ten years ago, a mature woman in the prime of her beauty instead of an insecure, uncertain but sweet, adolescent girl. But upon closer observation, those of her high school acquaintances who greeted her enthusiastically with hugs and kisses noticed a very pronounced change in her aura—a hard, steeliness in the core of the once soft dark eyes, a mocking, cynical turn of her mouth as she smiled, and a coarseness to her speech and jokes that were far removed from the innocence of her high school days.

But what surprised them most was that she was still single. The men all admired her appearance tremendously just as the more insecure of the women envied it. She heard over and over again from her old girlfriends their disbelief that some man had not snatched her up and given her children yet. They all told her tales of the beginnings of their own families, including how long they were in labor with their first-borns and how their husbands had fainted in the delivery rooms. Jennifer listened to their tales politely but assured them that she was desirous of neither a husband nor children at this point in her life. She was fulfilled and quite content with her successful business pursuits. *Can't they see this? Why must they all be so conventional and so middle-class?* she thought.

As she embraced and chatted with old classmates, her eyes carefully searched the groups of people in the room looking for Michael and Emily, but so far they were not to be found. Her heart was thumping wildly in her chest. *I can carry this plan out like a professional, can't I?* she questioned herself.

"Hey, Jennifer Jacobs! Can that be you?" A voice that she recognized as Joe Smothers' arose from the group of people around her, and before she could respond he had pushed his way to her side. His firm, strong arms lifted her slightly off the floor, and he twirled her around. "Boy, oh boy, don't you look sexy!" he said enthusiastically as he kissed her lightly on the cheek and embraced her warmly.

"Hey, Katie!" he shouted behind him to his wife, who was busy catching up with some of the others. "Come over here and see Jennifer Jacobs!"

With a squeal of delight, Katie fought her way over to Jennifer, and the two old friends hugged each other affectionately.

"Wow! Jenny! Where did you find that dress? You look absolutely gorgeous!" effused Katie sincerely.

"And so do you, Katie," responded Jennifer gracefully, though she thought that Katie, and Joe too, for that matter, had both put on more than a few pounds since she had seen them last.

"How long has it been, Jennifer? Tell me it wasn't at our wedding that we last met!" Katie continued.

"Yes, I guess it was. Five, no almost six years ago, wasn't it?" Jennifer nodded in reply.

"That's right. We'll celebrate our six-year anniversary next month. Can you believe it?" Katie said excitedly. "And you knew, didn't you, that we now have *two* children. In fact, I'm sure you noticed that I have gained a few pounds. Our youngest baby, a boy, is only six-months-old, and I just haven't been able to get back to my pre-pregnant weight yet. Joe says it's the cookies and brownies, but I told him it's my metabolism," she rambled on, giggling at her own joke. "Anyway, you sure do look slim and trim. I don't know how you do it, Jenny, but you look prettier and slimmer now than in college! When you finally settle down and 'tie the old knot', as they say, and start having babies of your own, you'll see just how hard it is to stay skinny."

Had Katie stopped chattering long enough to see, she might have noticed the subtle change in Jennifer's expression when she started to talk about Jennifer having babies. Her smile became more fixed, and a thin veil covered her eyes. She felt all the more uncomfortable discussing such matters. *Is childbearing all these women can think about?* she wondered.

So she changed the subject quickly, "Tell me, Katie, what are you and Joe doing now? You haven't moved down here to Mobile, have you?"

"Oh, I wish we could! I miss my parents, and we sure could use some free babysitting services. No, we live way up north in Birmingham now. You must have noticed our address change on our last Christmas card—" Katie began but was interrupted,

"Eeeeeee! Jennifer Jacobs! Is that you? It can't be!" squealed a voice from behind her. She turned around to find herself being hugged by another old Hillside friend and fellow yearbook editor, Denise Samples.

"It's so good to see you, Jennifer! Boy, do you look sensational! How are you?" Denise inquired excitedly. "Oh, and hello to you, too, Katie. So good to see you again."

"Hey, Denise," Jennifer returned, and the three girls exchanged light kisses on the cheeks. "You look wonderful, too. I am doing really great, working based out of Indianapolis now although I travel a good bit. How about you?"

"Oh, I'm great, too. I live in Nashville now, you know, and you won't believe it, but I am engaged and going to be married in September! I'm not going to be an old maid after all!" Denise related enthusiastically before stopping herself awkwardly in embarrassment and adding clumsily, "Not that you're an old maid, Jennifer. You are much too beautiful to ever be thought of as an old maid. You probably have to beat the men off with a stick."

Denise had already read the profile on Jennifer in the reunion contact book and knew that she was still unmarried, and she blushed at her thoughtless and insensitive remark.

Before Jennifer could reply, Katie came to her defense with, "Jennifer is not only beautiful, Denise, but she is a *very, very* successful businesswoman, earning more money than you could spend at the mall in a lifetime."

Although she was grateful for Katie's attempt to defend her honor, Jennifer was faintly amused and not offended in the least at Denise's statements, considering their source. Both in high school and college, Denise had been so absolutely boy crazy and desperate for male companionship that it was a wonder she had not scared away any and all potential suitors.

So Jennifer continued on with a slightly superior smile and offered, "That's okay, Denise. Although I do love my single state and am so busy with work that I don't have time for a man in my life, I am happy for you. Who are you engaged to? Anyone I know?"

I hope it's not that dullard you dated for so long ... Larry what's-his-name. What a loser! You'd be much better off as an old maid, she thought unkindly.

"Yeah, you know him," Denise recovered her poise and responded proudly. "I finally talked my old boyfriend, Larry Mathis, into getting wedlocked! Can you believe it? We first started dating in the eighth grade and were on again and off again for so many years, but I guess it was just Fate or God or something that dictated our ultimate union because the knot is going to be tied on September 10th! And I can't wait! Larry couldn't be here tonight, though. Had a business engagement out of town," she bubbled on not stopping to draw breath.

"And guess what?" Denise winked conspiratorially at her old chums. "We see your old beau, Michael Evans, and Emily Prescott... You knew they married a couple of years ago, didn't you? Joe was one of the groomsmen, wasn't he, Katie? Anyway, Larry and I see them just about every week now because we go to the same church. And did you also know that Emily is eight months pregnant? Can you believe it? Old guitar-strumming, heart-breaking Mikey from Coburn University, the one you tossed aside like an empty Coke can, is going to be a daddy now! They're coming to this little shindig tonight, too. They ought to be here by now."

This time Denise did stop to draw breath, and, as usual with her, she wished she had thought more before she spoke. Somewhere in her babblings on and on, she noticed that Jennifer's countenance had noticeably altered. The color seemed to drain from her dark complexion, though her smile remained fixed, and her eyes no longer were focused on Denise, as she had turned her head slightly to the left and was staring at the wall a few feet away.

Katie noticed it too and thought, *Oh, gee! Why did Denise have to open her big mouth about Michael and Emily?* And her eyes told Denise to drop this topic and change the subject.

But Denise had already sensed it. *Gosh, I have blown this conversation big time with Jennifer. First I called her an old maid and then I opened up a can of worms. I guess I thought Jenny would have gotten over Michael by now. College romance and all that. And from what I heard, she broke up with him. In fact, I'm really surprised that she doesn't have her own husband here with her tonight, as beautiful as she is. Does she even have a date?* While

Denise was quietly kicking herself for her own faux pas and trying to think of something to say to make it right, Katie came to her aid.

"Denise, I think I hear Janet Pugh calling you over there." And she motioned to the rear left corner of the ballroom. "She has been searching for you all night. Said something about getting revenge on you for that awful snapshot of her in a facial mud mask and pink sponge hair curlers that you placed in the 'Student Life' section of the year book."

"Uh-oh," responded Denise gravely with mock concern. "I thought we had worked that out years ago. I guess I had better go talk to her, though, before I wind up with a dead horse's head or worse in my bed. I'll talk to ya'll more before the evening's over, okay?" And with another quick hug, she was gone.

While Katie and Denise had been talking, Jennifer's mind was racing. *Why did I think I could ever carry this reunion off? I have to get out of here! I must get out of here! I don't really want to be here. What do I have to prove to all these people anyway? And why do I feel so suddenly panicky and faint?*

"Jenny, are you okay? Are you all right?" It was the voices of both Joe and Katie directing their concern at their old friend's sudden paleness. But their voices sounded muffled and distant to Jennifer.

"Come on, Jen," Joe directed quickly. "Let's get you out of this room and into some fresh air. It's getting more and more crowded in here."

Katie, gravely concerned, followed them both out the doors. As Joe gently led Jennifer toward the door, he grabbed a glass of wine off a silver tray being carried in their direction by one of the many waiters wandering around and offered it to her. She gladly accepted it as she sat down on a round banquette that surrounded a fountain and flower garden located in the exterior courtyard of the hotel.

The air in the courtyard was refreshing, and the glass of cold wine brought both a sense of warmth and a measure of peace back into Jennifer's mind as she sat there with Katie by her side for about three or four minutes. Joe had judiciously left the two women alone, returning to the ballroom.

As the two former roommates sat there, Katie tried to think of something to say to fill the awkward silence between her and her old friend but was afraid that any remark she might make would be the wrong one. Denise had really upset Jennifer just moments before, mentioning Michael and Emily and all, and Katie was determined not to make matters worse. So she just sat there, smiling a concerned, half-smile and patting Jennifer on the arm every few seconds as she finished her glass of wine and they both listened to the soothing sounds of water spilling into the fountain.

The early evening sky was just beginning to fade into dusk, and there was a gentle breeze stirring the soft, fragrant air. In the peaceful surroundings, Jennifer's thought processes slowed down to a manageable pace and her uneasiness abated. She smiled wordlessly back at Katie and took a deep, cleansing breath as she collected herself.

If I leave now, what will Katie think? She will think I am still in love with Michael, that's what, and tell Joe, too! And then Joe might tell Michael. She knew that wasn't true. She knew down to her toes that she no longer possessed any feelings that in any way resembled love for Michael. *Then why did I feel so strange when Denise told me he and Emily were here?* she questioned herself, puzzled. *I knew they were going to be here. I wanted them both to be here. That was the biggest part of my plan ... to show him how well I am doing. I didn't know Emily was pregnant ... but so what? Several of the women here are pregnant. That can't be it. What is it then?* But there was one thing she did know. *I have to go back into that ballroom now and be the life of the party, just like I planned. I am okay now. I can do this. I am woman; hear me roar.*

She took another deep breath, put down her wine glass, smiled, and said,

"Dear Kate, I am sorry I ...I just don't know what came over me. I think my pantyhose are too tight or my heels too high or something. I just all of a sudden felt odd ... like my brain wasn't getting enough oxygen or something. Thank you and Joe for taking care of me. Let's go back in and get something to eat. That will help my blood sugar, too, which may be low. I haven't eaten anything yet today because I've been so excited to see everybody again."

Relieved, Katie examined her old friend carefully and responded, "Your coloring certainly looks much better now." Then, she impulsively placed both arms around her former roommate, gave her a tight bear hug and said, "Are you sure you feel like going back in there? I will gladly sit out here with you. Lord knows, I don't need to eat anything, and I would love to catch up on your life. I have missed you, Jennifer."

Touched by Katie's kindness but annoyed at her own weakness, Jennifer remarked,

"I have missed you, too, Katie. I didn't know how much until now." Then she jumped up from the bench and exclaimed, "But to answer your question ... Sure, I want to go back into the ballroom! Let's go back in there and eat and party and kick up a ruckus on the dance floor! Class of '73, look out, 'cause here come one bad mama and one bad sister!" She laughed an artificial laugh, and pulled her former roommate up from the bench to join her.

The two women re-entered the ballroom, which was still buzzing with pleasant conversation and music, just as the alumni were beginning to sit down to dinner. Joe, who was waiting for them, had saved two places next to him and ushered them in, pulling out their chairs like the gentleman he was. He had not been privy to the conversation they had had before, so he did not know the reason for Jennifer's weak spell. He had just assumed it was a "female thing." As he helped them into their seats, he glanced across the room and a few yards away he saw his old pal, Michael Evans, and his expectant wife, Emily.

"Hey! Michael Evans!" he called out above the rumbling of the assembly. Waving his arms wildly above his head, he caught the couple's attention. "Come on over here and eat with us! There is plenty of room."

As Mr. and Mrs. Michael Evans made their way to the table, Jennifer knew that the thought had never entered Joe's head that she and Michael were anything to each other now except old high school and college buddies, a couple who had broken up but still remained friends, so she was not in the least aggravated with him. How she wished that she had not felt weak when talking to Katie and Denise! She could not afford to meet Katie's gaze for the rest of the evening, she knew, if her plans were to succeed. Katie was not stupid. Katie had incredible intuition. And Katie knew something was wrong.

Jennifer knew that something was wrong, too, but could not begin to think of what it could be. She knew she had not loved Michael for many long years now. That could not be it. And she reminded herself that she had always liked Emily. She had no problem with Emily. Emily was very sweet and sincere. So her problem must be with Michael.

Yes, her problem was with Michael, she now realized with all the energy in her body and soul. She had a big, unresolved problem with Michael! How could she have been so foolish as to think she could pretend differently? Why would she have wanted to come to this reunion so badly and show off in front of him otherwise? And what about that horrific sex dream concerning him she had experienced a few weeks ago? Yes, she had a big time problem with Michael. But what was it? And what a completely miserable time it was to realize this fact. Why now? What awful luck that this knowledge was so evident to her now while he was rapidly approaching her dinner table with his pregnant wife.

There was no escaping, but that tall glass of wine on the table in front of her appeared to be a lifeline to her drowning self-confidence. That was it! With glasses and glasses of wine she could somehow make it through this evening's trial, and she would try to figure it all out later—somewhere in private. She immediately forgot her original plan to abstain from all alcoholic sustenance and was swiftly swallowing the remains of the already half-empty glass when Michael and Emily arrived at the table.

"Look who's here, Michael and Emily," Joe announced to the newcomers. "Doesn't Jenny look beautiful?"

Poor, thick, Joe had no idea what had transpired between Jennifer and Michael when they had broken up so many years ago now. He had simply taken Michael's explanation at the time—that Jennifer had convinced him that they were not suited to one another and had split up amicably—at face value, even though Michael had been broken-hearted afterwards. And tonight he thought they might enjoy catching up on each other's lives as old friends. Katie, however, could have kicked Joe for his insensitivity, and it would not have been the first time, either.

Michael, who had first noticed Jennifer as he was only a few feet away from the table, leaned over before he sat down, held out both his hands toward her, and smiled a kind smile, forcing himself to look into her eyes.

He had been devastated when she had broken their engagement. It had taken him three years to recover fully from his suffering, mostly because of the secret, buried guilt he harbored coupled with the fact that he had truly, passionately loved her. He had for many years now deeply repented of his treatment of her and had often toyed with the idea of trying to contact her or write her a letter conveying his regrets. But in the end, he had always backed down, not knowing if his actions would be well received or even proper. He had tried to speak with her at Joe and Katie's wedding back in 1977, only to find her actively avoiding him, fleeing whenever she saw him approaching, refusing even to look in his direction throughout that horrible weekend celebration.

And because her rejection of him had been so devastating, he had thought he might never be able to love again. Until he began to court Emily. Emily's sweetness and tender love had helped him heal, along with the passage of time. And although his heart had been healed for some time now and he had no lingering romantic feelings for his first true love, his first true lover, he still had been silently dreading this uncomfortable meeting. And yet, there it was. There she was. More beautiful than ever ... but different, too. Very different.

"Hello, Jenny," he said softly as she reflexively and automatically held out her hand to him.

His appearance had not changed much in the past eight years, except that his hair, too, was shorter and he somehow appeared more mature about the eyes and slightly heavier. He was as handsome as ever. He gently took her hand in both of his and absently patted it briefly as he searched her face. But she would not meet his gaze, her eyes focusing somewhere in the vicinity of his chin.

"You look so lovely tonight. Of course, you remember my wife, Emily?" he finished and placed his arm around his wife's shoulder.

At his words, "my wife," Jennifer felt a totally unexpected knife cut through her heart, and dreaded tears formed at the back of her eyes, though she did not know why. She knew that Emily was his wife, so why the tears? She involuntarily inhaled quickly, not allowing the tears to mature, and smiled in Emily's general direction.

Emily reached across the table to touch Jennifer's very cold hands, offering warmly,

"Hi, Jennifer. It is so good to see you again. You certainly do look beautiful, as usual."

Using all the will power she could muster, Jennifer stood up to reach across the table to Emily and squeezed her hand, smiling into her sweet countenance, which appeared to be truly concerned for her. *I have always liked Emily,* she thought. *Emily is kind and good. A sincere Christian.*

"Hello, Emily," she began, her voice surprisingly steady as she was once more feeling as though she was standing outside herself. "You are very kind, as usual. I hope you are well ... and your dear parents, too. Please tell them 'hello' for me, and that I remember them so fondly."

The second glass of wine was working its way through Jennifer's system now, giving her false confidence. *There. That wasn't so bad. I can do this! I can do this!* she told herself over and over again as she sat back down, her racing heart beginning to settle down somewhat.

As the others seated at the table continued the greetings, Jim Martin, class president, called over the public address system for everyone's attention.

"Attention, please, Class of '73! Now that we have all had time to meet and greet and imbibe some of those potent potables that are being passed around ... Much better stuff than we used to get out of the trunk of Bill Curley's '62 Chevy on Prom Night ... No offense, Bill."

And on cue, Bill Curley, now balding and with a decided beer belly, stood up and bowed while the group chuckled appreciatively as Jim continued.

"We will begin our sumptuous repast that was planned so carefully by our reunion committee. Incidentally, will all the members of that group stand up now and receive their just recognition?"

As the committee received polite applause, Jennifer accepted another large glass of wine from a waiter in a white dinner jacket and proceeded to drink it down quickly. She was beginning to feel more relaxed and like her old self again. *I don't need any man to make me feel special,* she thought. *I don't have to be anyone's wife or mother to make it in this world.*

For the rest of her life, Jennifer could never recall the conversation that occurred during the meal, or what delicious food was served on that elegant table in that romantic ballroom in that exclusive hotel in Mobile, Alabama on June 8, 1983. Three large glasses of wine drunk quickly out of desperation by a slender young woman with an empty stomach may have accounted for part of the memory lapse. She only remembered that as the meal wore on, her own raucous laughter seemed to be attracting a good deal of attention not just from her table, but from the neighboring ones, too. She thought she was being quite witty, regaling the group of former classmates and one former lover with stories of her sales exploits and dirty jokes that she had been told over the years, which for some reason or other all returned clearly to her memory now.

She ate most of what was on her plate, thankfully, as she had one-and-one-half more glasses of wine, and managed to keep from making direct eye contact with Katie, Emily, or that dreadful Michael, who appeared to be giving her a disappointed expression. Or was her mind making this up? And Emily, too, whose mid-section Jennifer absolutely refused to look upon, seemed out of the corner of her eye to be looking at her with a sympathetic, compassionate, but sorrowful face.

A plague on them both! she thought. *Am I to be pitied? No, it's probably just my overactive imagination.*

As the last dessert plate was finally removed, Jim Martin came back on the loud speaker. " Ladies and Germs," he began with a conceited, self-aggrandized and yet confident expression.

There were groans from the crowd and someone yelled, " For Pete's sake, Jim, can't you come up with something more original than that?"

"I repeat, beautiful Ladies and you bunch of lousy Germs," Jim Martin, undeterred, continued on.

And the drummer performed one of those little drum roll, cymbal clash numbers reserved for stand-up comics when they deliver a bad joke. The crowd chuckled. But for some reason to Jennifer the drum roll/cymbal clash was extremely funny, and she emitted a very long, very loud belly laugh, crying tears and holding her side, so funny was that joke. Her riotous laughter penetrated to the far corners of the huge ballroom, and the Class of '73 all turned their heads in her direction and wondered who in the heck that was and wished they had some of what she was drinking.

"At least *someone* in this ballroom has a sense of humor," observed Jim.

"Either that," called out a loud male voice, "or else *someone* has been out by Bill Curley's car trunk!"

As if following a stage direction again, Bill Curley stood up once more and took a very long, very pronounced bow to the applause, laughter, and hisses of the crowd amidst one more drum roll and cymbal clash.

"You all really are in rare form tonight, and I predict some heavy hangovers tomorrow. But if I might continue on ..." said Jim as the noise died back down again. "We will now view our Feature Presentation, an award winning film which was put together by Phil Johnson, formerly of the Central High Audio/Visual Squad, and his lovely wife, Laura."

" 'Lovely' wife, Laura," whispered Jennifer too loudly with a cruel giggle and a sneer. "Her face looks remarkably like a bulldog's to me."

While some who heard her obviously agreed with her assessment of the canine aspects of Mrs. Phillip Johnson's physiognomy and laughed along, those of her friends gave her a disapproving look, and Katie placed her finger over her lips and whispered, "Sh-h-h, Jenny. Not now."

From the podium, Jim Martin continued, "This film was assembled from various and sundry home videos taken by the many proud parents of the remarkable Class of '73 and local television sports highlight shows, and I am certain is of Academy Award winning caliber."

Jim was having the night of his life, enjoying his moment in the limelight like only a prospective, ambitious young politician can.

"After the picture show ... and by the way, during the presentation, Steve Elliot will be selling popcorn at the back for only ten dollars a box."

And the room chuckled as all remembered that Steve Elliot—who had possessed extreme entrepreneurial skills even in the tenth grade and had always thought of ways to make money off them back at Central—now owned his own successful popcorn and potato chip company.

"Anyway, after the show, we will be presenting the Class Awards. You know, like who came the farthest to get here, who has the most children ... Legitimate ones, that is ..." More groans and a little laughter emanated from the group. "And stuff like that. Then, some remarks from any former teachers who are brave enough to face this group again, and after that ... Party and dance until dawn ... or at least until two in the morning when we have to leave this lovely facility. So, with no further ado ... Class of '73, this is your life!"

With those last remarks, there was a dramatic drum roll, and the band started playing "Those Were the Days." Jennifer was the only one in the ballroom who began to sing the lyrics out loudly in between giggles and inebriate gestures that emphasized the rhythm of the song, while those attendees seated with their backs to the podium began to stand up and turn their chairs around to face the front. As they performed this task, many amused dinner guests craned their necks to see who that drunken woman was and to laugh either at her or with her. Was it really that sweet and bashful Jennifer Jacobs making such a fool of herself, and wasn't she always a tea-toting Baptist? Oh well, just goes to show you that people change. She is certainly entertaining us all tonight, if nothing else.

Michael stood up, too, and turned both his and his wife's chairs around as the lights in the room dimmed and a movie screen was lowered in the front of the ballroom. But the look he directed first at Jennifer and then at Katie was not one of amusement but of sorrow mixed with serious concern.

Katie leaned over to Jennifer and whispered, "Why don't you visit the Ladies Room with me?" She needed to talk to her friend in private if possible, and discover what was wrong.

Jennifer was surprised to find the room swaying a little as she made her way out with Katie. As they entered the luxurious powder room and the women automatically surveyed their reflections in the brightly lit, Hollywood style mirrors, Katie began.

"Okay, give now, Jenny. Something must be bothering you. You are not acting like the Jennifer Jacobs we all knew and loved. What is the matter? I want to help."

As if she did not hear her former confidante, Jennifer reapplied her lipstick and picked at her hair with a comb, saying,

"What a mess I am! Why didn't you tell me I had a little white string across my dress front?" She was applying translucent facial powder now and looking at her eye makeup, which had smudged a little with her tears of jocularity.

"There is nothing at all wrong with your appearance, Jennifer," Katie pressed on, grave distress on her face. "You are one of the most beautiful women here, as you well know. What I want to know is ... Why are you acting like you are? Why are you drinking so much?"

Again, Jennifer feigned deafness and headed into the toilet area. Remaining in the outer room in frustration, Katie sighed, peered at her reflection, played with her hair and makeup a little, and wondered if she should try one more time with her old Coburn companion. Being the kind, loyal friend that she was, she did not want her dear, former roommate to be etched into the minds of the other attendees in a less than superior manner. And she knew instinctively that Jennifer was not happy. No, more than that—Jennifer was miserable. Inside. Why else would she be drinking so much? The Jennifer she had known never had to resort to inebriation in order to enjoy people. What in this world could be wrong? Was it Michael and Emily? What was it?

When Jennifer emerged from the other room, she offered lightly,

"Well, ready to go attack the rest of this evening with me and show the Class of '73 what we have made of ourselves, Katie, old pal?" A studied, contrived smile creased her full lips but refused to travel to her cold, increasingly dangerous eyes. "And don't worry, old Coburn buddy-of-mine! I can handle my liquor! Yessirree, Bob, if there's one think … thing … I've learned in my 'old maid' days, as daffy Denise would say, it's how to handle my liquor! And I'm ready and rarin' to dance, Katie old pal! Come and dance with me! Okay?" And she did a little tap dance and then spun around, grabbing at the doorframe to steady herself.

But it was not okay. Katie made one last attempt, this time placing her hand firmly but gently on Jennifer's arm, her face directly in front of her friend's to make eye contact, pouring out her concern and her love.

"All right. One last time. Jennifer, *please* tell me what is wrong. I care about you! I am your friend, remember? I want to help if I can."

But Jennifer pulled herself free from the loving grasp and exclaimed in an exasperated tone, eyes flashing,

"Good God, Katie! Must something be 'wrong' for me to cut loose on occasion and have a little wine and laugh a little at others' expense! Why must something be 'wrong?' Why are you such a little prude, that you would deny your old buddy a little fun in this God forsaken world? Nothing is 'wrong' with me! What is 'wrong' with you?"

With those angry, harsh, and unkind words, Jennifer pushed the door open with a tremendous blow and walked on ahead of her old friend. Katie, who stayed behind in the powder room for a few more minutes collecting herself, forgave Jennifer quickly and began to worry even more.

Something was terribly wrong with the one she loved. Something that changed not only her relationships with people, but also with God. The Jennifer she knew would never have misused His name.

Chapter Twenty-Eight

"*I see a bad moon rising. I see trouble on the way*,"* the hired band played and sang John Fogerty's song on into the evening, playing well but so loudly that it was almost impossible for the reunited Class of '73 members to communicate with each other without standing close and literally shouting into each other's ears.

"You didn't really do that!" yelled Sissy Campbell into Jennifer Jacobs' ear, chuckling at her more than slightly intoxicated former classmate's retelling of a recent victory over a scheming co-worker's plan to stab her in the back during a meeting.

"Yeah, I really did!" Jennifer shouted back. "He won't mess with me again! None of those sorry, wretched guys will ever mess with Jennifer, 'JJ' Jacobs again! The lousy, sorry scoundrels!"

She laughed the mocking, uncontrolled laughter of a woman who had consumed three more glasses of wine and was working, though half-heartedly, on a fourth since her conversation in the Ladies Room with that uptight, stick-in-the-mud friend, Katie, over an hour ago. As she laughed, she swayed slightly on her expensive high heels and held on to the occasional arm of whoever happened to be standing next to her for support.

She was having the time of her life with the aid of the wine, she thought. Why had she only saved it for bedtime before tonight? And why only one or two glasses? How stupid of her! What a waste of good wine! Why, it opened up a whole new world of enjoyment, pleasure, and witty conversation.

She had hardly spoken to her old flame and his pregnant wife, although she was constantly aware of their whereabouts in the room. And she had danced—and provocatively, too—with most of the good-looking men, both former classmates and the spouses of the many Class of '73 wives, who did indeed look on with envy and disapproval.

"Well now, partiers and all night revelers," came the voice of the bandleader, a good-looking man about the same age of his audience who had had his eyes on Jennifer all night, as she was flirting shamelessly with him. "We in the band are going to take a fifteen minute break, and then we'll be right back with more of your favorite golden oldies and contemporary classics."

To the crowd whose ears had been assaulted with music at the decibel level of a jumbo jet on take off for over an hour, the silence was a welcome relief. Their own voices, which had grown hoarse from all their shouting, could now be heard, and lip reading and sign language were no longer necessary for communication.

Unfortunately, someone forgot to tell Jennifer that loud speech was not needed any more, for her voice could still be heard around the room. The bandleader walked over to her and wrapped his arms around her waist, which she greatly appreciated at that moment as the room was beginning to spin once more. He hugged her and whispered something in her ear, which made her laugh riotously and reply salaciously, wickedly.

"Oh, I know you can talk the talk, but what I need to know is, can you walk the walk?"

He then whispered something else, which made her smirk and giggle, patted her lightly and playfully on her rear end, and walked away.

All this was observed by Mr. and Mrs. Michael Evans and Mr. and Mrs. Joseph Smothers, who were thinking the same thing but not vocalizing it. One of them needed to see that Jennifer was going to make it home safely. They did not want to abandon their old friend but did not know how to deal with her tonight. She was as prickly

---

"*Bad Moon Rising" by John Fogerty, ©1969 Jondora Music (BMI). Copyright renewed. Credit: Courtesy of Concord Music Group, Inc. All rights Reserved. Used by Permission.

as a cactus whenever any one of them came around her. Anyone but Emily, that is. She would just walk away from Emily as fast as her legs would carry her whenever Emily approached. No prickles there; just plain avoidance.

As the rumbling sounds of the crowd echoed all around her, Jennifer noticed that those two couples were looking at her with concern, disapproval, and pity. And something clicked inside her now chemically altered brain. Something angry and sinister. Who were they to pity and disapprove of her? Who died and made them judges of the quick and the dead? How dare they sit in judgment over her! She would just go over there and set the record straight. Maybe then they would leave, and she could enjoy the rest of the evening.

As she wobbled her unsteady way over to the four, she forced a mischievous, silly grin, placed her finger over her pursed lips, and whispered loudly,

"Sh-h-h, don't tell anyone, but I think I have a date with that lesh... lesht ... lech-er-ous bandleader after the show."

Though her eyes were hard, she giggled some more and then continued, giving her former friends and one former lover some inside information regarding her plan.

"At least, *he thinks* we have a date. What I plan to do is this ... I'll tell him to meet me here after the show and that I'll do all sorts of things ... And then, when the performance is over, I'll just not show up!"

She laughed louder and wobbled around some more, instinctively grabbing the nearest arm for support, which happened to be Michael's. When she realized whose arm it was, however, she quickly and reflexively pulled away, like a hand is withdrawn from a hot stovetop.

She continued on as the others did not reply, "So if the four of you are worried about your old buddy an' pal ... Don't worry! I have it all unner ... unn-der control." Her speech was becoming more slurred as she went on.

"I used-t to do this, and still on occasion haff to, on business trips. Sh-h-h, don't tell anyone." She put her finger over her lips again. "Those marvelous old husbands who travel with me on business sometimes have *monkey business* on their minds. Sh-h-h, don't tell! So I love to tell them, 'okay' ... And then just not show up!"

She laughed a raucous, evil sounding laugh and continued.

"Can't you just pish ... pisher ... pic-k-ture it? Those lust-filled husbands sitting up in their rooms, all hot and bothered, waiting for that sexy boo ... boo-nette ... bru-nette to show up ... And I never do!"

The uncomfortable group of four had trouble holding her gaze, looked away from her face to the floor, and still said nothing. So she went on.

"I don't answer the phone or the knocks on the door and just lie in my bed and laugh and laugh into my pillow! What can they do about it? Complain to the 'Big Cheese' that I refused to be an adultiterous... aduliteromous ..." she slurred, "Oh, what do you call her when a woman sleeps with a married man?"

"Adulteress?" Katie volunteered softly, feeling helpless.

"Yes! That's it! Good job, ol' Katie, ol' Coburn pal o' mine! You always did have a good voca-boo-l'ry. An adulder-teress!" she finished, smiling slyly, swaying, and very proud of herself.

The foursome witnessing the demise of their longtime friend were embarrassed and silent, as they could not think of what to do or say. For Michael in particular, watching his former fiancée in such a drunken condition was heartbreaking. He could not help but remember the sweet, innocent, trusting young woman she once was not so very long ago, and her brokenness was affecting him in ways he did not know how to explain—except that he knew that he was, in large part, responsible. And that, though he was responsible, he could not now restore her.

Joe was just bewildered. He could not imagine what could have changed Jennifer so. She had always abhorred liquor of any sort.

"What's wrong, guys?" Jennifer challenged, losing patience and beginning to get a pick-a-fight look in her eyes. "Why are you all looking at me with such pitiful faces? I do not need nor do I desire your pity! That's right! I neither need nor desire your pity! I was top salesperson in the whole damn country las'h year! Did you know that? I earned six ... Count 'em," And she held up six fingers in front of their faces, "Six figures las'h year! To be precise, I made

$181,456.24 las'h year alone. That's right! $181,456.24 ! Don't you dare forget the 24 cents!"

The successful female sales executive was becoming angrier and more obnoxious as she continued.

"I told my accountenant ... accounterent ... you know, the guy who does my taxes ... Anyway I told him, 'Don't you even *think* about dropping the 24 cents from my tax return, damn you! I earned *every penny* of that 24 cents and I want ... No! ... *Demand* to have it on my 1040! It won't affect my taxes any, but buddy, I want the *whole world* to know that I, little Jenny Jacobs, formerly of the Hillside Baptist Church, in Mobile in the Great State of Alabama, Coburn University graduate, Class of 1977... I, sweet and lovely Jennifer Jacobs, earned $181,456.24 in the year of our Lord 19 and 82!'"

Her long time acquaintances were still silent, feeling more helpless than ever as Jennifer now had the attention of most of the couples on the dance floor, many of whom were snickering softly while Bill Curley encouraged her with, "Give 'em hell, Jennifer!"

She became even louder.

"Yep! I was top salesperson! I beat every *man* in the country! Beat 'em, I said! Yes, I beat the gray, pinstriped suit pants right off their shiny little backsides. The guy that came in second to me only made eighty-six measly thousand bucks," she laughed cruelly. " Can you believe that? Only eighty-six thousand paltry little dollars. Boy, what a lily-livered loser! What a sorry louse!

"And I own my own little beach house, too, right on the shoreline of the boo-tiful Gu'f of Mexico!" she slurred on smugly, her facial features becoming more contorted and her dark, hard eyes more angry as she published abroad her great accomplishments to those judgmental, fuddy-duddy, old friends of hers.

"Did you know that? Huh? Did the four of you looking at me so pitifully know that? Yessir! And I bought it *all by myself*, too, without one little measly penny from anyone else. No sir! Not one red cent came from *Mr.* Anybody Else! I bought it from the proceeds of *my* great successes, you see, 'cause, in the words of my boss, Mr. Thomas Moyer, Vice-Presh-ident of the MedTech Enterprises, Inc., and I quote ... 'Jennifer, you are one *helluva* salesman! Yessir! *One helluva of salesman!'"*

And again she laughed loudly at her own conceited recital and wobbled dangerously on her heels, spilling some of her wine onto the glossy surface of the dance floor.

Michael could stand it no longer.

"Lower your voice, Jennifer! For heaven's sake, take some pride in yourself, and don't make such a scene," he stated softly but firmly as his blue eyes narrowed, instinctively grabbing her arm to steady her.

He quickly regretted his words and actions, however, for his remarks threw gasoline on the already smoldering embers of her anger and rage.

"Take your nasty little hands off me, *Mr.* Michael Evans!" she exploded into his face, her dark eyes now filled with fury as she pulled herself away. "Who gave you permission to touch me? Who are you to tell me how to behave? You have no right to tell me *anything*!"

As she spoke those last words, the band began to tune up for the second half.

Michael automatically responded, "You're right about that, Jenny. I was only concerned for you as an old friend and as a sist—"

He broke off suddenly and with shame, his eyes falling away from her face. He was going to say "as a sister in the Lord," but before the words came out of his mouth, he realized the hypocrisy of them. Had any young man dared to treat either of his sisters the way he had treated Jennifer, he would have strangled them. He could, even now, feel his fingers around the throat of any man who had behaved toward one of his sisters they way he had toward Jennifer.

At his faltering explanation, however, Jennifer's angry tone immediately changed, and she doubled over convulsively with mad cackling.

"As a 'sister,' you were going to say!" she observed derisively. "You are concerned for me as a *'sister'*? That is just too funny, Mikey, old friend! Yeah, that's just too, too funny!'" And she held her side as she bent down in mocking laughter once more.

Then suddenly, even through the cloud of liquor shrouding her thinking, she thought of Emily and glanced at her. She had no intention of hurting Emily. Emily was kind and good. Too good for the likes of Michael.

But Emily was only looking sadly at Jennifer and even more sadly at her husband.

To try to save the situation, Joe Smothers had an idea, a very rare occurrence for him. Obviously there was something that needed working out between Michael and Jennifer, but the center of the dance floor of the Tenth Class Reunion amidst the stinging stares of the callous crowd was not the proper place for it.

He offered, "Katie and Emily, would you please come with me to the refreshment stand. I think we could all use something cold to drink. Jenny and Michael, there is a storage space I discovered while searching for the Men's Room—about ten feet from the doorway there across the hallway—where you can talk about the old days in private if you'd like to."

After Michael quickly signaled his wife with a look and she signaled him back, the two women gratefully took Joe's arms as he led them across the room, leaving the two former lovers standing there by themselves. The crowd around them magically dispersed, too, as embarrassed wives took their husbands hands and led them to the dance floor. This mass exodus had been so swift that neither of them had had much time to respond before their friends and his wife were gone.

Michael then asked bravely, "Jennifer, do you want to talk?"

She was taken totally by surprise and said nothing but just stared at him. Oddly, much of her anger had dissipated in the verbal tirade and tongue-lashing she thought she had delivered so well just moments before, and she was slightly taken aback now, not knowing how to respond.

So he addressed her once more, hesitantly but with determination. "Now that Joe has given us the opportunity ... There *are* some things I have wanted to tell you ... for many years, now ... if you would like to hear," he offered once more.

He knew in his heart that this might be the only chance he would ever have to try to convey to her his remorse and regret, asking her forgiveness for his past treatment of her. They had parted with so much unfinished business between them. So much that needed to be said. Perhaps there was some resolution, some closure to their heartbreak that honest talking could bring about. He wanted to try it anyway, if only to soothe his own guilty conscience.

Jennifer, still in a sort of shock and confused by the wine and the abrupt invitation to "talk" merely shrugged her shoulders and nodded her head. *Why not hear what the sorry so-and-so has to say?* she thought. *It should be entertaining, if nothing else.*

He led the way to the storage facility Joe had discovered. As he opened the door, the two found a room about fifteen feet by twenty feet that had a few tables and chairs stacked against the walls. One table was set up in the center of the room and was holding a small pile of folded tablecloths and napkins with two chairs drawn up to it.

The band was playing "Light my Fire," as they entered and Michael closed the door. An awkward silence filled the space between them, which made the lyrics of the song even more pronounced.

"You know that it would be untrue. You know that I would be a liar, if I was to say to you, 'Girl, we couldn't get much higher.' Come on, baby, light my fire. Come on, baby, light my fire. Try to set the night on fire."

"Would you like to sit down?" Michael asked as he pulled a chair out from the table.

Although he wanted to express to her his regrets at the dastardly way he had treated her and ask her forgiveness, he was at a loss as to how to begin. And though he was completely in love with his wife, Emily, he still cared for Jennifer deeply, truly as his sister in the Lord, even though it had sounded so hypocritical coming from his lips. And in addition to confessing his own guilt, he wanted so badly to see her restored to the Jennifer he had known. Restored, healed, happy, and content with a husband and a family of her own. Her brokenness was obvious to anyone who knew her in the past, and was so painful for him to witness.

She refused his offer of a chair, however. She was confused, not just from the alcohol, but also from his actions and words. What did he want to tell her? They both remained standing about five feet apart, just staring at each other, she with a puzzled expression and he with an awkward embarrassment.

"Come on, baby, light my fire! Come on, baby, light my fire! Gotta set the night on FIRE!" The lead singer was becoming more passionate.

Suddenly, in the uncomfortable silence, Jennifer burst into laughter again as the strange irony and absurdity of their situation played inside her alcohol influenced brain.

She exclaimed cynically, "Man, oh man, Mikey! You and I sure did 'light each other's fire,' didn't we, old chum! We sure did set some nights on fire, didn't we, old Hillside Baptist brother-of-mine!"

She laughed derisively again and then stopped herself suddenly, "Hey! That's sick, isn't it? You and I, 'brother and sister' in the Lord, setting some real bonfires together! That's inces-shoo-us, isn't it?" she slurred as she looked him directly in the face, a mocking, cruel smile creasing the corners of her full lips, her eyes as hard as stone.

He dropped her gaze and stated stiffly, clumsily,

"Jennifer, that's what I wanted to talk to you about ... I wanted to tell you ... that I'm sorry for the rotten way I treated you. For seducing you and talking you into ... honeymooning before the wedding and everything. It was very wrong of me. I misused you and I wanted to ask you ... to please forgive me," he began falteringly and with great frustration at his speech.

These were not the eloquent words and phrases that he had needed and wanted to communicate his regrets to her. They sounded so stiff and so inadequate to his ears. *How do you ask forgiveness for taking away what can never be replaced?* he wondered to himself. *How do you ever make it up to someone you once loved so passionately and yet wounded so deeply?*

But she responded immediately.

"Forgive you? You wanted to ask me to forgive you?" she began. Her shoulders shook as she laughed. "I'll tell you something, Mikey, old man." And again she placed her finger over her pursed lips, wobbled a little closer to him, and whispered loudly, "Shh-h, don't tell anyone. But do you know what? I *liked* being with you. Yeah, I did! And, old buddy, 'It takes two to tango', as the saying goes, doesn't it."

She stepped back and waited a few seconds for his response. As he did not reply but just looked at her slightly confused and embarrassed, she burst forth in self-revelation.

"Hey! I've always wanted to tell you to go to hell for the way you treated me, and now that I have the chance, whadda ya know? I find that I, myself, am taking the blame! Well, what about that? *'In vino veritas.'* That's Latin, you know, for 'In wine there is truth,' or 'There's truth in wine,' or somethin' like that. I know Latin, you know. I made straight 'A's' in Latin for three years. Did you know that? Yep, I, little Jenny Jacobs, made the Latin Club Honor Roll for three straight, in-suff'ra-bull years at good ol' Central High School. And I'll just bet you didn't know that! No sir! You don't know everything about me, you know. Although you 'knew' me in the Biblical sense, you don't know everything 'bout me, Mr. Michael Evans."

And she glanced back at him with a sarcastic expression and laughed cruelly.

He said nothing but looked at her in dismay. Why did he think he could talk to her seriously when she was in this condition?

"Yeah, that's just too funny, Mikey, old pal," she went on, backing away a little more. "Now that I have the chance to tell you off … I blow it! Ain't life funny. Ain't life just too damn funny!"

She looked down at her hands and seemed surprised to find a half empty wine glass in one of them. She quickly drained it and placed it on the table. As he still said nothing, she continued, eyeing him now with contempt.

"Do ya wanna know somethin' else, Michael Evans? You probably won't give a rat's fat fanny, but I'm gonna tell ya anyway. Do ya know that I have *never, ever* been with another man? That's right! Never!" She laughed a sarcastic, malicious laugh and continued, "Oh, a lot of men have tried, let me tell you. And not just those lusty husbands on business. No, sir! Some real attractive single guys, too. Some even as handsome as you, Mr. Michael Evans, and—"

"Look, Jennifer, I'm sorry, but this is going—" he attempted to speak. *Why did I think this could ever be resolved? This is only making matters worse,* he thought in frustration.

But she rudely interrupted him again.

"No! Shut up and hear me out! You owe me at least that much, Michael!" her eyes blazed at him as she confronted him head on. "I want you to know that you are the only man I have ever let ... touch me in that way."

And again she insulted them both with vicious laughter. "I was *not* going to be tricked *twice*, by Granny's garters! No way, Jose! No sir! I learned my lesson well, you see ... And I was going to tell you off and now ... Poof!" And she snapped her fingers, or at least tried in vain to snap them. "The chance is gone! But I will tell you one thing, Michael Evans. I said I liked being with you, and I did ... But ya wanna know why? Do ya wanna know? ... Huh?"

Again she put her finger to her lips and said, "Shh-h, don't tell anybody." She cupped her hands around her mouth and leaned over to whisper in his ear. "I liked it ... because I loved you!" She then backed away and finished. "Yeah, that's right! I loved you! I loved being with you, feeling part of you. I loved your strong mastks-cu-linity. I loved the way you made me feel ... special and beautiful and fem-me-mimn ... I loved the way you sang me love songs ... Remember? You used to sing 'The Nearness of You' to me?"

"Jen—" he begged, his eyes imploring her, but she would not let him speak.

"No! Let me finish!" her eyes flashed at him. "I loved your eyes, and your hair, and your sense of humor, and your smile, and the way you smelled when we were close ... And, you know what? I 'specially loved the way you wrote and sang songs about God and Jesus an' all."

As she talked on, reminiscing, she began pacing the room, clasping and unclasping her hands as she recalled long suppressed memories.

"Yeah, I really loved that about you, Mikey ... It made me feel safe, like I could trust you, you know. You being such a spiritual man an' all. I loved you 'desperately and completely,' Michael Evans. Did you know that? I read that in a book somewhere. Some poor sap-of-a-girl loved some poor jerk-of-a-guy 'desperately and completely,' spirit, soul, and body, an' all that. I loved you like that ... and I thought you ... I thought you loved me, too."

She was becoming serious for a moment, but then burst out into a contemptuous cackle again as she turned around to face him.

"Can you believe that, Michael Evans? I actually thought that you loved me, too! You certainly did ack ... acktt ... like it! And you told me you did. Even had it 'nscribed on a bracelet. What a joke!"

"Please, Jenny—" he tried again but was interrupted.

"That's right, I loved you 'desperately and completely" ... Spirit, soul, and body, Michael Evans, and I thought you felt that way, too."

She stopped pacing for a moment and ran her fingers up and down the stack of folded tablecloths as she continued talking without a break.

"Imagine my shock and surprise when I found out it was just my *body* that you loved. What a shock!" she derided herself and him, and continued before he could say anything. "I shoulda' listened to Old Mother Hubbard ... What's her name? ... Oh, yeah ... Mrs. Muriel Hubbard, at good ol' Hillside Church. While all the other women were telling all us girls to stay pure because God wanted us to, Old Mother Hubbard said—"

She then gave a very credible imitation of Muriel Hubbard.

"'Now remember, girls! Why should a man buy the milk cow when he can get the milk for free!'"

She laughed wildly again, turning her hard eyes toward him, mocking them both.

"She was a practicable ... prackical ... woman, that Mrs. Hubbard. I shoulda' listened to her."

This time Michael did not let her interrupt him. As ashamed as he was over his past behavior, he could at least justify himself on this one account. He said quickly, searching her face,

"Jenny, don't you remember that it was *you* who broke off our engagement? It was *you* ... and *not me.*"

"Our '*engagement*'? Our '*engagement,*' did you say?" She laughed in contempt and began circling the room again as she sneered at him. "What a ruse and a sham! What a travesty and a mockery, Mikey-boo! You never intended to marry me, Michael! Not really, did you, old buddy? Why you pretended you did, I'll never know ... unless it was just to get me in the sack." And here she laughed once more sarcastically before adding, "No, you never intended to marry me, and it was *you* who rejected *me*, Michael Evans ... Coldly! ... Cruelly! ... Completely! ... *You* rejected *me!* And after you told me you loved me! How can you be such a low-life liar?"

He was more distressed at these statements than at anything else she had said this evening, and he feared for her sanity. Looking at her with grave concern in his eyes, he questioned her gently, slowly.

"Jennifer ... Don't you remember?... You came to my apartment that day, that Saturday before the football game, gave me back your ring, and told me that you didn't love me anymore ... and that you never wanted to see me again? I had shaving cream on my face, and I begged you for more time. Don't you remember that?"

She wrinkled her brow a little and said,

"No. How can you say ...?" and then she broke off, a very puzzled, troubled expression on her face. She had refused to recall the pain of their separation and its cause for so long that ... Did it happen the way he said?

Suddenly new insight fell heavily upon Michael as he observed her troubled countenance, so suddenly and with so much force that he had to sit down and quickly exhale. *How could I have been so blind, so stupidly blind, so thick and so foolish*? he thought. *Of course Jennifer felt rejected—coldly, cruelly, completely—rejected, when I insisted that she terminate the pregnancy! She did not want to do it. I pressured her, and pressured her hard. How could I not know that she received that as the ultimate rejection of her?*

He thought about Emily. How would Emily have reacted when she rushed into his office that day seven months ago and told him she was carrying their child, if he had said, "Wait just a minute, sweetheart. Let me grab my car keys and we'll run right down to the woman's clinic and take care of it." *Wouldn't she have felt coldly, cruelly, and completely rejected, too?*

Walking with Emily through her pregnancy had given him insight to that mysterious, marvelous connection between a woman and her unborn child—that indeed, Emily was connected to their unborn baby and he or she to her, both physically and emotionally. That though she was one woman in her present state, she was sheltering and nourishing a totally separate person, a person she would gladly sacrifice her life for if necessary. She had already told him as much. She had said that if something were to go wrong in the delivery room and it was either her life or the baby's, she wanted the baby to live. *How could I have thought that I could reject the pregnancy and not reject Jennifer, too? How foolish, oh God, how foolish of me! No wonder she despised me ... wanted to be as far away from me as she could!*

His mind and soul had been opened up to this insight in the length of about a second or two, at the speed of thought. He looked up at Jennifer standing there, still looking troubled and confused and knew that she had repressed the truth all these years because it was so wrenchingly painful. Should he now beg her forgiveness for taking her to Atlanta that day?

No! Not yet! She's not ready quite yet, came a strong impression, an inner voice that originated in his spirit and traveled to his ears. *Just listen. Just be still and listen.*

In the brief second or two that had transpired, Jennifer, with the aid of the truth potion in the wine, had recalled that what he had said was true. She *had* been the one to return his ring. But even so, it was only a symbol of what he had already done to her—of what he had symbolically done to her. Of that unspeakable thing he had made her do. And she began to feel very uneasy, almost panicky, very troubled in her soul. *Change the subject!* her subconscious screamed.

So she responded nervously as she continued pacing back and forth, alternately wringing and waving her hands in emphasis, her golden bracelets jingling on her slender wrist.

"Oh, I don't remember 'xactly how we split up, but what difference does that make now? It's all water under the bridge, as they say. It's all a moot point, don't you see. I love that phrase ... A 'moot' point... Doesn't matter a hill of beans, Mikey. And don't feel bad about it now, Michael! Don't apologize. I don't love you anymore. No, sir! Not any more. You are very safe from Ms. Jennifer Elaine Jacobs and her 'desperate and complete' love. I don't love you anymore ... And I haven't loved you for a long time now ... A very long time now." She stared off into space, before continuing. "So you don't have to apologize to me. I am fine! I am woman, hear me roar, 'member?"

And once more she turned her granite-cold, dark eyes in his direction.

"Jennifer," he stood once more and began, relieved that she finally allowed him room to speak, although it was very difficult to look into those dead eyes of hers. "I know you may not believe me, but I always did care for you ... loved you, and admired you very much. You are a very intelligent, talented, loving, and beautiful woman. I know you have what it takes to be successful in whatever you want to do and to be whatever you want to be. That's why it hurts me ... hurts all of us ... Katie, Joe, Emily, your former classmates and friends ... to see you—"

She interrupted him angrily, banging her fist on the table in emphasis.

"To see me *what? What,* Michael, *what?* I *am* successful, damn it! I *have* made it! What do you all want from me?"

Her words came out rapidly now, in a torrent of emotion, leaving him no place to get a word in. The sarcastic, drunken laughter was gone, and in its place were eight long years of bottled up bitterness, pain, and rage.

"You said that you thought I could be whatever I wanted to be! What a crock! What a sorry, sad crock of bullshit, Michael! You said that you 'cared for me' and that you 'loved' me! What a liar you are, Michael! What a damnable liar you are! Oh, I was good enough to be your lover, I suppose! I was good enough to be used in bed, all right! But I wasn't good enough to have your children, was I now, Michael Evans! Was I! Oh, no, not good enough to be the mother of—"

She broke off for one brief moment.

She had not meant to go this far! This was a door that she had kept locked up tightly for almost eight years now. She had never intended to open this door, to enter a room with such fearsome and dreadful occupants.

But somehow, something inside her soul knew that *this* was the issue that she and Michael needed to resolve if she was ever to be free. *This* was the thing that finally had to be aired between them! She was scared to death at the thought of it, but this door had to be opened, forced open if necessary, for the sake of her ultimate freedom. This was the painful truth that had to be exposed.

Suddenly, she collapsed onto the table and cried out loudly, her head in her hands,

"Oh, Michael! How could you have taken me to that awful, horrible place? How could you have left me in there *all alone*? Did you not have a heart? Did you think that I wanted to be in that awful place ... *all alone!*"

"Jennifer!" He leapt over to her side and tried to place his arm around her shoulders.

But she brushed him off with violence and turned stormy, hate-filled eyes toward him.

"Don't you touch me, you selfish, cold-hearted, lying bastard! You unfeeling, cowardly son of a bitch!" she screamed at him in pain. "You said that you loved me, but you left me in that cold, awful place when I was so frightened and so ... so all alone ... so terribly all alone... and so very, very scared!" She began to weep uncontrollably, her slender shoulders shaking, her hands covering her face. "And you knew I didn't want to be there! *I didn't want to be there!*"

He winced in pain at the forcefulness of her words, as if she had slapped him across his face with all of her strength. Yet he knew he deserved them. He knew he deserved much worse. And he wanted to somehow ease the tremendous, wrenching suffering of her soul now, but he knew he could not touch her. He knew his words would do little to comfort her, but he had to try. He stood by her side as she sat on the table and searched her face as he spoke, trying frantically to make eye contact so that she might know of his terrible remorse and guilt.

"Jennifer! You must believe me!" he began with a quiet desperation and urgency in his voice. "I have kicked myself over and over again for what I did to you that day! I have gone back there *so many times* in my mind and tried to change what happened! If I could do it over again, I would *never* take you there! You must try to believe me! You must try to forgive me!"

"Forgive *you*, again!" she raged on at him. "Forgive *you?* What good will that do now? How will that change things?" She had large tears flowing down her lovely face.

Michael knew instinctively that the best thing he could do now was to listen ... to let her vent her heartbreak and anger.

And it was the most difficult thing he had ever had to do.

He sat down in a chair next to her and listened, his eyes never leaving her face as she recounted her long repressed nightmare to him there in that luxury hotel storeroom that June night of 1983, while the band played on, oblivious to the drama unfolding in the room across the hallway.

"You left me there all by myself ... I was so very frightened ... I wanted to leave that place ... But where could I go?... What could I do?"

Her words were spoken with raw emotion and sobs punctuating the phrases, and still the tears flowed freely.

"I couldn't tell Mother. I tried to tell Daddy. Did I ever tell you that? It was when we stopped for gas at that station just outside of Atlanta. What a joke! I tried to call up my father who doesn't know me and doesn't care and tell him. He could tell something was wrong, but do you know what he asked me? He asked if I needed any money! Can you believe that? There I was, pregnant and unmarried, scared and all alone, and my father knew something was wrong but asked if I needed money! How sad! How very pitiful!"

At her words, "all alone," a great stab of guilt cut through Michael's spirit. He had been there, but he had not been the responsible, compassionate man he should have been. That she had felt "all alone" made him very, very sad. He did not know whether the unborn child that his wife was carrying was a daughter or a son. They wanted to be surprised. He thought about his daughter's being in Jennifer's place and feeling "all alone," and he shuddered inwardly.

"As I sat in that clinic ... that cold, cold clinic ... You remember how hot it was outside that day? It was over one hundred, wasn't it? But they had the air-conditioning turned down very low ... It was *so cold* in there. I just sat there by myself ... shivering ... and filled out the paperwork. I kept thinking, maybe Michael has changed his mind. Maybe he will come running in here, grab me by the arm, and say, 'Let's get out of here, Toots. Come on. Let's go home and get married. I will take care of you and the baby.'... But you didn't come! ... *You didn't come!*"

And her shoulders shook more violently as her tears fell unimpeded.

Michael's hands were making fists as he listened, and he was hitting himself in the legs as she talked. Tears that he would not permit to fall were forming at the back of his eyes. He wanted to hold her so badly, to try to comfort her, but was terrified of her reaction. She might stop the recounting of the tale that was a first step towards her healing. And it would be unwise on his part, too, given her loveliness and the passion he had once felt for her. So all he could do was to listen ... and to beg her forgiveness.

"I'm so sorry, Jennifer. Please forgive me. Please ..." he stated softly.

But she barely heard him, so lost was she in her agonizing recollection.

She continued on, "Then ... when it was my turn ... my hands were so cold and my legs were trembling as I walked back there, down that long, dreadful hallway. When I had taken off my clothes and had on the gown, I knew there was no turning back now."

She stopped talking briefly and began to cry even harder.

"But, you know," she sobbed, "even then, I kept hoping that you would kick down that door and come take me home! *I wanted you to come take me home!*" she cried more loudly, not even trying to wipe the tears from her face as they ran down unhindered onto her chest.

Had she really seen Michael, she would have noticed that his face was as white as a sheet, his eyes had a stricken look, and that he was vicariously reliving her every word, despising the memory of the young man he had been then.

But she was too caught up in her own misery to notice. She just looked through him, back into the past, to that ghastly day in Atlanta in August of 1975.

"As I crawled up on that ... table and placed my feet in those ... stirrups," she cried, "I wanted to hop down and run as fast as I could away from there! Run until I dropped down! But where could I run? There was no place to go! No place!"

She wiped her eyes with a napkin that her hand found on the table, staining it with her black mascara, and continued as best she could while he listened in agony.

"I had never even had a pelvic examination before. Did you know that, Michael? No one had ever touched me ... there, before … except you, in love. I felt so ... so violated ... and so … so humiliated and exposed ... and so very frightened! And I wanted them to stop! I told them, *'Stop! Please stop!'* But they said it was too late! And the doctor yelled at me to 'just hold still, for Christ's sake!' That's what he told me, Michael ... to 'just hold still *for Christ's sake.'* But I knew just then that 'for Christ's sake,' I shouldn't have been there *at all!* No, not at all! I knew it then, Michael! I had not known it before, but I knew it right then! ... But it was too late! It was *too late,* Michael, don't you see, when I suddenly knew it!"

She looked into his own distressed, haunted eyes for a brief second as she relived the awful torment of that moment, knowing he would comprehend with her the grotesque absurdity of the doctor's statement, her lovely shoulders shaking more as she wept bitterly.

But there was nothing he could say or do now to make it right, he knew. He could only sit and listen. He could only repeat his own remorse and regret, begging her forgiveness.

"Oh, Jenny!" he whispered. "I'm so sorry! ... So sorry! ... Forgive me! ... Please!"

She continued through tears, "And the kind nurse told me, 'Now, honey, when the machine gets started and you feel the pain, just hold on tight to my hand and squeeze. I won't mind.' And I said, 'What do you mean?' She said, 'Oh, don't you know? You did not have enough money for the anesthesia. It is going to hurt some.'... I should have taken that money that Daddy offered, then, don't you see? If I had known, I would have taken it! But then again … I deserved the pain! *I deserved it*, don't you see!"

She buried her head back into her hands and sobbed violently, while choking out between fast catches of breath,

"*You lied* to me, Michael! You *betrayed* me! You told me to trust you! You said this was going to make everything all right again! But I knew as I lay on that cold, hard table and felt so ... so terrified and... so abused ... and so wicked and ashamed … that this was making everything all *wrong*, Michael! And it would be all wrong *forever!* All wrong *forever*, Michael! *All wrong ... forever!*" She shook with terrible remorse

Tears were now flowing down Michael's cheeks, too. He could not stop them. He did not want to stop them. He sat and just watched her, listening to her recount her pain. He knew that this was what he should do, though he wanted to run out of that room, too, like Jennifer had wanted to run out of the clinic. But this time, he would not fail her! This time he would just sit and listen and wish this were all a bad dream from which he could awaken. How could he have been so deceived and so blind?

He whispered once more, this time almost inaudibly, "I'm so very sorry, Jennifer. ... So very sorry ... I didn't know ... I didn't know ... I had no idea ... Please, please try to forgive me."

Again, she was almost deaf to his words. She gazed over his head, unseeing, as she recalled that most dreadful day. That miserable, hot day in Atlanta, in that frigid, cold clinic, where she had lost the biggest part of herself.

"The pain was unbearable ... It couldn't hurt worse than that to have a baby ... They were having a hard time ... removing ... whatever was inside me. It seemed to take a long, long time ... Whatever was there didn't want to ... come out that way ... They kept pulling and tugging on me. And I wanted them to stop! I wanted it so much! I wanted them to stop!"

Her whole body was shaking and quivering with her sobs, her hands completely covering her face so that he could not see her eyes. And he looked away, unable to watch such suffering, feeling so powerless to make it right ... to make Jennifer right again ... to erase her awful torment ... to comfort her in her grief.

Finally, she drew a deep breath, removed her hands from her face, looked in his direction and finished.

"And when it was over, and they were cleaning up some ... I overheard one of them telling the other, 'Be certain to check well for everything. It was twins, you know.'"

She jumped down from the table now and cried loudly, her broken heart completely open, spilling out all its buried pain and suffering, her words falling one upon another very quickly as she looked him in the face, her large eyes no longer cold but naked with anguish, grief, and deep, deep regret.

"It was *twins,* Michael! I never told you that before! I never told you anything *at all* about that before! I told myself I was going to *forget* what happened! That I would *never, ever* allow myself to even *think* about it again! Never, ever! And I never did! I never told *anyone, not anyone*! You never told anyone, did you Michael? Please tell me you never told anyone!" Her plea was one of desperation.

At this revelation from his former lover, his former fiancée, Michael felt as though he had been kicked in the stomach.

No! Not twins! he thought. *Not two innocent lives!*

But he could not fully assimilate this knowledge now. He had to try to comfort Jennifer. But he would not tell her a lie to do so. It took all his courage, but he told her the truth. They had been living a lie for too long now. It was time for truth. He wiped his eyes and stood up in front of her, trying to take her hands. But she withdrew them.

He said gravely, kindly, "Jennifer, I didn't tell anyone for a long, long time. Not anyone. I remembered our pact." He looked her squarely in the eyes with all the tenderness of his heart and continued, "But when Emily told me that she was expecting our baby ... It just all of a sudden hit me what you and I had done ... what *I* had done *to you.* Oh, I had thought about it some before, but like you, had tried to forget it ever happened ... But I couldn't forget when Emily told me. She could tell something was badly wrong with me ... so I told her."

"Oh, Michael, no! Tell me Emily doesn't know! How could you break your sacred oath!" she cried, her face full of new agony. "How could you tell Emily—sweet, innocent Emily—of all people? No wonder she has been looking at me with those sad, cow eyes of hers all night! How could you betray me so, Michael?"

She was becoming angry again.

"Jennifer, I had to tell Emily! She will never tell anyone! She is my wife; can't you see that? I can't keep such a secret from her!" He begged her to understand as he instinctively grabbed at her hands once more, his eyes pleading with her.

Again, she pulled her hands away in frustration and bitter disappointment and cried out,

"No, no! I can't understand! How can I understand what it means to be someone's *wife?* I am damaged goods, Michael! Can't you see that? I am defective merchandise! No decent man would ever want to marry me now! Not if he knew!"

She stood before him, baring her soul as she had never done when they were body intimate but still soul strangers in many ways. She continued her passionate outpouring and her self-disclosure as though she had no control over it. *In vino veritas.* After eight long years, she was no longer able to hide the Truth of her brokenness from her former lover ... or from herself.

"When they cleaned me out at that horrible place, they must have removed my woman's heart, too! I stopped loving then ... Love hurts too much, Michael! Love hurts so very much! I stopped loving then... Stopped loving you, stopped loving God, stopped loving myself ... Stopped loving."

She began to cry bitterly again and continued through still more tears, "There is no hope for me, Michael! No hope at all. I have lost my woman's heart and don't know how to find it again!"

He immediately reached out again and took her hands gently but firmly. This time she did not repulse him. He pleaded passionately, begging her to hear his words, his own heart breaking for her deep wounds—wounds that he had unwittingly inflicted on the one he had dearly loved.

"Jennifer! Look at me! That is *not* true! There *is* hope for you! It was all *my* fault, not yours! I take full responsibility for the abortion! *There is hope for you!* There is always hope in the mercy and forgiveness of God! Jesus has not left you, Jenny!"

She pulled away from him one last time and exclaimed through still more tears,

"Oh, Michael! That is so easy for you to say! You are married to the sweetest girl in the whole class who is going to present you with a child in just a few weeks ... One of many, I am certain. And Katie and Joe are going home tonight to each other and to a new baby and a cute, freckled, little three-year-old daughter ... I have seen her picture in their Christmas cards ... But what about me?"

She extended her arms out slightly and cried between broken sobs, " My arms are empty! ... My arms are empty! ... And I can't even hold my sister's baby! I can't even pick up ... my precious little niece from her crib ... to comfort her when she is crying! My arms are empty! And there is no hope for me!"

With that horrific statement, she ran past him to the door, opened it, and fled down the hallway, still crying.

"Jenny!" he called out after her.

But he knew it was of no use.

Years later, Michael would still recall the irony of the song the band was playing as his inconsolable former lover fled the scene: "How Can You Mend a Broken Heart?"

Joe, Katie, and Emily were in the hallway, standing not too far from the storage room. As Jennifer ran out, Katie instinctively pursued her. Joe and Emily walked quickly up to Michael. They could tell something dreadful had happened. His face had the appearance of one who had just witnessed a grizzly accident or a murder.

"Joe, go find Jennifer and please drive her home! She is in no condition to get behind the wheel. She will kill herself or someone else. Lasso her if you have to, but whatever you do, please don't let her drive!" Michael begged Joe, grabbing his arm, his eyes completely open and naked with fear and grave concern as he communicated his sense of urgency to his old college buddy.

Joe said nothing, but acknowledged his friend's request with a knowing look and a tight squeeze on his forearm as he searched his face. He quickly pursued Katie and Jennifer.

After Joe left, Michael walked wearily back into the storage room, violently kicked the large, heavy table, dislodging it a few inches as it shook and shivered, and then collapsed into a chair. With his head hanging, he beat his fists repeatedly on that same poor table at his own impotence to repair the situation. His mind was racing with the new knowledge he had gained in those few, terrible minutes there in that room. Knowledge of Jennifer's excruciating agony and suffering all those years. Suffering that he, in ignorance, had brought upon her. And he now knew more of his own great loss.

Emily walked quietly in, closing the door behind her. She wisely said nothing but just stood beside her husband and cradled his head against her chest.

Just then, the baby in her womb began to kick and to move around.

"Oooo," she murmured softly, as she gently caressed her swollen abdomen. "It must be the relative quiet in here after so much noise out there."

As Michael felt his unborn baby moving, he could no longer contain himself. In the presence of his wife's unconditional love, he let the tears flow, sobbing like a child, his shoulders shaking much the same as Jennifer's had done just moments before, his head in his hands.

"Oh, Father God! ... Oh, dear God! ... Lord Jesus!" he cried between broken sobs. "I'm so sorry! ... So sorry! ... Can you forgive me? Can you ever forgive me? Can you heal Jennifer? ... I'm so sorry, and it's all my fault!"

Emily remained silent, stroking her husband's hair gently and praying silently for him, tears running freely down her own cheeks. She could easily imagine how dreadfully painful and tormenting the past thirty minutes had been for him and for Jennifer.

After a few minutes, he was able to look up into her compassionate, understanding eyes. He explained as he brushed away his tears,

"Jennifer went through hell and ... is still so broken ... so very broken." He swallowed hard and managed to choke out the words, "And ... It was ... twins ... God forgive me, it was twins!" before the shaking began again.

Chapter Twenty-Nine

*G*lancing in his rearview mirror occasionally for the signs of state troopers, Joe Smothers was speeding down the interstate highway about eighty miles per hour in a hurry to get his sobbing, broken-hearted former classmate home where he hoped she could find some comfort for whatever the heck it was that was affecting her so badly. He was completely bewildered as to what Michael and Jennifer could have said to one another that would have distressed them both so much.

Were they still in love? No. No way. Joe had been a groomsman at Michael's and Emily's wedding and had seen them together several times in the past year. If ever there was a couple completely and totally enraptured with one another, it was Michael and Emily. Their commitment to one another was strong and permanent, he knew. And they were extremely happy about the approaching arrival of their baby in one month. They had the nursery all prepared and everything. And Jennifer, too, had given no indication that she was still in love with Michael, Joe reasoned. He recalled her behavior at the party. She had seemed extremely angry with him—but certainly not in love. No, it couldn't be that. Then what in the world was the problem?

In the back seat of the speeding blue minivan, Katie had Jennifer's head cradled on her shoulder, her arms around her disconsolate friend, softly stroking her hair.

"Shh, shh, now, Jenny. It's going to be all right. Everything's going to be all right now. It's all right," she was repeating, trying to comfort her dear friend as she did her little girl when she was upset.

Katie was relieved that they were away from the hotel and the rest of the Class of '73. It had hurt her deeply to hear the cruel and insensitive statements her former classmates were making regarding Jennifer's ribald behavior at the party. Katie cared too much about her former roommate to leave her there. Even though Jennifer had insulted her earlier and had rudely avoided her for most of the evening, Katie knew that the woman who exhibited such coarse behavior at the reunion was not the real Jennifer. All evening she had been pondering the mystery of the cause of such a change in her character and why she was so angry. No, it was more than anger. It was fury. But why? What could have made Jennifer so full of rage and fury, so willing to trample on the feelings of those she used to love, so desperate to avoid confronting that mysterious "something" that she had to dull her senses with alcohol?

Now, an idea, an appalling, terrible idea, began to form in the back of Katie's mind suggesting to her the reason. And Michael's expression when he emerged from the store room coupled with Jennifer's heart-rending tears reinforced Katie's suspicion as to the cause of such pain and suffering. For Katie was not stupid, as Jennifer had known from the beginning of the evening. Even though her husband was mystified, Katie now knew. She finally knew the reason for such heartbreak. *Jennifer had experienced an abortion back at Coburn! She and Michael had aborted their baby!* There could be no other explanation for the evening's events.

Poor, poor, Jennifer! Oh, my poor, poor friend! And poor Michael, too. How guilty he must feel now! What regret they both must feel! she thought sadly. *Oh, Jenny, how I would love to tell you that I know now, and that I do not judge you, dear friend! That I know, but for the grace of God, it could have been Joe and me suffering the way you and Michael are now.*

But just as instinct had told Katie what the problem was, it also warned her that now was not the time to verbalize her thoughts to Jennifer. The time was not right now, as the wound was too fresh and raw. *Oh, Jenny, I do hope that someday you feel that you can tell me—that you know that I will love you anyway, and that I understand the desperation and helplessness that you must have felt back then.*

Katie knew there was no way that she could sit in judgment of Jennifer, dear, sweet Jennifer who had been so desperately in love. She had known all along that she and Michael had been sexually intimate back at Coburn, though Jenny had never confided it to her. There had been too many unexplained late night absences, too many weekend disappearances for it to have been otherwise. And the way they would look at one another, the intimate, sensual, seductive glances they would exchange, had been poor concealment, indeed, of their sexual activity and had left Katie with no doubt whatsoever as to the nature of their relationship.

Suddenly, Michael and Jennifer's strange behavior the day they returned from that "baseball game" in Atlanta was explained to her. His pleading phone call to her that evening at the dorm asking her to please "look after" Jennifer. He had sounded so very troubled and anxious, she remembered.

How could I have been so blind as not to know it then? And the week before, when she was ill with a "stomach flu." That was morning sickness! And Jennifer's breaking their engagement just weeks after that Atlanta trip and moving to Montgomery on her own, getting as far away from Michael as she could. Katie knew Jennifer had never been the same girl after that. It all made sense to her now.

Katie also knew that she and Joe, themselves, had crossed the line into very dangerous territory many times and could easily have been in Michael and Jennifer's shoes back at college. And she still regretted that she had not waited until her own wedding night to consummate the marriage, but had finally given in to her desires and had slept with Joe only a couple of months before their wedding. She had felt quite the hypocrite in her snow-white wedding gown, she remembered. And she had been so afraid that her father might have found out and throttled Joe.

Just two months, she thought. *You'd think we could have restrained ourselves for only two little more months.* Katie knew the awesome, explosive power of sexual passion and sat in judgment of no one on this issue. And she knew the tremendous pressure the couple must have felt to conceal the pregnancy—how it would have been so miserable for them to reveal it to their friends, families, and the church. Katie also knew that at that time, the moral and spiritual aspects of abortion had not been discussed in their church nor in their communities at large, so that her dear friends were probably very ignorant of its consequences on many fronts. No. She sat in judgment of neither Jennifer nor Michael. How she wished she could tell Jennifer this! Instead, she just sat there, soothing and praying for her precious Jenny. *Oh, dear Lord, please, please comfort and heal Jenny,* she beseeched God silently for her friend. *And remember Michael in Your mercy, too.*

Jennifer herself had sobered up very quickly. The first expression of her deeply repressed, severe psychological and emotional trauma sobered her up in record time. *In vino veritas.* The Truth—pushed down, ignored, denied, and silenced in so many different ways for so many long, hard years—had finally surfaced, but the cruel manner in which it had surfaced left Jennifer feeling more desolate than ever. Michael had been right in insisting that Joe drive her home. She never would have made it otherwise.

Even as Katie was trying hard to comfort her, Jennifer could not stop herself from weeping, though she desperately wanted to stop. The truth to her words, "my arms are empty," filled her with an aching emptiness that seemed to stretch all the way down to her toes. Seeing so many of her former classmates with proud, loving husbands had made Jennifer feel cheated in a way that she could not explain. She knew that she had been lying to herself all those years—lying to herself and convincing herself of the "truth" of those lies. Lying to herself that she did not need any man in her life. That a husband was an evil thing. That families were all doomed to failure. That true love did not exist, or if it did, it did not last for long. These lies, which had somehow given her false comfort and strength for so many years, now mocked her cruelly. *My arms are empty ... There is no hope for me ... I have lost my woman's heart ... No decent man would want me now.* These thoughts replayed themselves in her mind as the tears flowed down her face and onto Katie's dress in the backseat of that speeding blue minivan in Mobile, Alabama, that June night of 1983.

But she knew she must somehow stop the tears before she arrived at her mother's house. The thought of having to deal with her mother after such an emotionally chaotic evening gave her the strength she needed to stem the flow, even as Katie kept her arms tightly about her shoulders.

As she tapped into her iron will once more and found the ability to compose herself somewhat, she thought, *Dear Kate, how can I ever thank you enough? I have treated you so badly tonight, and yet you still care for me.* She wanted to verbalize this to Katie, but knew it would only bring on more crying. With the last of her will power, she began to stop the tears. *If I can just make it to my bedroom, I will be okay.*

As Joe pulled into the driveway of Jennifer's mother's house, she was much more collected. How she hoped her mother had already gone to bed! She knew she could not survive the close scrutiny of her mother's many questions about the reunion tonight. Not tonight. Tomorrow, maybe, but not tonight. *Please, oh, please be asleep, Momma,* she prayed. She pulled out her compact and dabbed powder under her swollen, red eyes.

Then she thought suddenly of her automobile left at the hotel. *My car! How can I explain away my missing car? I'll have to think of something.*

"Jenny," Katie began tentatively as the car came to a stop, her eyes filled with sympathy. "Would you like me to walk inside with you? Or do you want to go for a walk somewhere and just talk?"

"Oh, no ... No, thank you, Katie. I appreciate it so much. But no, thank you. How can I ever thank you for being so ... so kind and so patient with me tonight? I have been such a mess. And I have been so mean to you. Please forgive me." And she hugged Katie tightly, blinking back more tears. "And thank you too, Joe ... for driving me home ... and everything."

Joe felt embarrassed in this awkward situation but said, "Sure, Jen. Anytime ... You know that. Here, let me at least walk you to the door."

"Oh, no, that's not necessary, Joe," she replied quickly. "But I do have a big favor to ask of you ... if you don't mind, that is, after helping me so much already."

"Sure. What can I do?" he asked, eager to be of service.

"Would you mind too much driving my car back to me tomorrow? I know that's a lot to ask and if—"

Before she could finish, he answered enthusiastically, "Oh boy! Sure I will! I would love to drive that Mercedes convertible. Are you kidding?"

Joe would have gladly exchanged both Katie's minivan and his '79 sedan—and his house, too, for that matter—for Jennifer's expensive sports car. Jennifer gave him the keys and thanked him.

With that said, and final hugs and kisses exchanged, Joe and Katie got back into their van.

"I'll call you tomorrow, Jen. Maybe we can have a late lunch. Please take care of yourself. We love you," Katie called out the window as they drove away and then added, "And let me know if you'd just like to talk."

Betty Jacobs Miller was not asleep when Jennifer came through the front door, of course, as she had never been able to sleep until her daughters were home safely. Just because her first-born was now twenty-eight-years-old, that fact had not changed. How she wished Jennifer was married to a good man like Susie was, so that she would not worry about her so much.

"Hello, dear. I didn't hear your car pull into the garage. How was the party? Tell me all about it. You look so tired and pale. Are you okay?"

Betty could not help but observe the pinched, fatigued look of her daughter's face. She looked so different now than when she had left. Her makeup was all smudged and her eyes were inflamed and extremely puffy, like she had been crying and crying a lot, too. Immediately her mother's heart was engaged. What could have made Jennifer cry at the reunion?

"Oh, Momma, I *am* tired ... Very tired ... from all the dancing and partying, and my feet are killing me from these blasted heels." She kicked her shoes off and continued. "Joe and Katie Smothers drove me home. My car wouldn't start ... the battery or something ... so Joe volunteered to take care of it for me tomorrow and drive it here."

Jennifer did not like lying to her mother, but to tell the truth at this moment would have been impossible. Besides, her mother had never known "the truth" about her anyway.

"And I have a headache from all that loud music that the blasted band was playing," she went on. "I don't feel too good and would like to just go upstairs, take a hot bath and a couple of aspirin, and go to bed. Could I tell you all about it tomorrow, please?"

She tried to keep her back towards her mother by walking to the refrigerator and pouring herself a glass of water.

Not so easily thrown off the scent, her mother persisted. She walked over to her daughter and placed her arm around her slender waist saying,

"Jennifer, what's wrong? Didn't you have a good time? Why have you been crying? Did someone say unkind things to you?" Betty Jacobs Miller was not stupid either.

"Oh, Mother!" she exclaimed, exasperated, and escaped her mother's embrace. "Everyone was very nice, okay? No one was mean to me! Please, just please, let me go to bed like I asked you to and I promise, I will tell you all about it in the morning."

"All right, dear, if that's what you want," Betty replied, only slightly offended.

As a woman who had never spoken all of her mind to anyone, not even either of her two husbands, she understood the individual's right to privacy of heart and soul. She only wished that her daughter trusted her more. That neither of her girls had ever truly confided in her she knew very well, and had attributed it to the divorce. But her mother's heart was troubled by the fact that she was in many ways a stranger to her own flesh and blood. But what could be done about that now, she thought sadly.

"Thanks, Momma," was her daughter's reply. "I'll see you in the morning. I hope I didn't keep you up too late waiting for me. I don't think I'll go to church with you tomorrow, if you don't mind. I need to rest. I have a busy week next week ... Meetings and all." And she gave her mother a careless peck on the cheek while avoiding direct eye contact.

"Goodnight, sweetheart. I hope you sleep well. I won't wake you then. Get some rest and we can talk at lunchtime."

As Jennifer walked upstairs to her bedroom, Betty sighed. Something upsetting had happened at the reunion. Something that had disturbed her daughter very much. Was it Michael Evans and his wife? Did Jennifer still love Michael?

Betty still did not understand what had made Jennifer break up with Michael. She knew that her daughter once had loved him very much. Lately, however, she had begun to wonder what it was that Jennifer had tried to tell her that Sunday she had fled Michael, driving down to Mobile by herself—that Sunday he had pursued her and had embraced her so ardently, telling her of his undying love here in her kitchen. Could she have been pregnant, she wondered? Surely not, but still ... What could it have been to make her so upset that she had to flee her fiancé? At the time, she had been relieved that they seemed to have made up that day. It had been just one less thing for her to worry about at the time that her own marriage to Bill Miller was ending.

That Jennifer had never had another boyfriend and did not seem at all interested in marrying and having children bothered Betty, though. But what could she do? Jennifer could be stubborn and strong-willed when she wanted to be and would not allow anyone to pry open the door of her heart. She had said that she never wanted to marry, that marriage was old-fashioned and only made women doormats for men.

Lord knows, her and Jennifer's father's divorce, coupled with her later breakup with Bill Miller, had given her daughter no reason to believe anything else. And yet she knew her eldest was not happy with her life even though she was an extremely successful businesswoman. She felt a brokenness in her beautiful daughter, with important, vital, pieces of her missing and damaged, not very much unlike her own brokenness. How she longed for a better life for her Jennifer than the one she had given her!

O God, she prayed. *Please help my little girl, Jennifer! Please fix whatever it is that is wrong with her.* As she sat in her chair and picked up her Sunday school lesson for tomorrow, she could hear the bath water running upstairs and the semi-stifled sobs of her daughter as she wept into a towel. *Please, dear Lord, wash away all the pain and heartbreak that her father and I have brought upon our little girl.* And as she prayed, a tear escaped her eyes and gently fell onto the pages of her opened Bible.

Chapter Thirty

"*L*adies and gentlemen, please bring your seat backs to their full, upright position and make certain that your seatbelts are fastened. Also, please lock your tray tables and make sure all your bags are safely stored in the overhead compartments or under the seats, as we are making our final approach into Indianapolis. The current temperature is 82 degrees under partly cloudy skies," said the flight attendant exactly one month after the Central High Class of '73 had celebrated their reunion.

Jennifer had never been more grateful to get back to Indianapolis than she was on that Friday afternoon in July. She was returning from a five-day business trip that had taken her to Chicago, Milwaukee, Cincinnati, Detroit, and Buffalo. The two weeks before that, she had been busy training new employees, and the week before that she had been on business in Louisville, Asheville, and Atlanta. And, of course, the week before that she had begun her drive back to Indianapolis from Mobile the Monday following the reunion disaster.

The car trip had taken her two days—two long, hard, lonely days with nothing to distract her from the memory of what had been said at the reunion. That her plans had gone terribly awry in Mobile was the understatement of her life. Just another huge disappointment in her tragic life. She had managed to get through Sunday with her mother by being her usual vague self in her presence, and had politely turned down Katie and Joe's invitation to lunch or dinner, saying that she had to pack as she was leaving early Monday morning. Katie had looked straight into her soul, Jennifer feared, and seemed to know her heartache.

Had Michael or Emily told? She did not think so. *Perhaps Katie just figured it out*, she had thought. *Katie has unbelievable intuition. But then again, maybe not. After all, Katie still seemed to love me. She wouldn't love me anymore if she knew. Being the mother of two little ones, she would find what I had done to be unforgivable.* At this point, however, Jennifer neither knew nor cared very much. The dreadful memory of that day in August of 1975 in Atlanta was out of the closet now, and she knew she could never lock it up again. It was a wild animal that once let out of its cage, could never be recaptured and tamed.

Jennifer's reaction to facing the truth of that most traumatic experience had been that she seemed slightly dazed and more aloof than ever to her co-workers and associates. In private, she was either crying or at the point of tears constantly, as if all the tears she had repressed during the past eight years were now given permission to flow freely.

Now that her rage and bitterness toward Michael had been released during their confrontation, the buried anger and desire to compensate her loss that had fueled her tireless pursuit of success in the business world were gone, much like a huge, bulging reservoir that finally breaks through an earthen dam and then spends its energy, leaving in its place a large, flat lake. But instead of leaving a peaceful lake in its wake, Jennifer's constant companions now were regret and pain. She was having trouble concentrating on her work, something she had never experienced before because her work had been her salvation. A creeping depression seemed to be invading her waking moments and robbing her of much needed sleep. She did not believe that she would ever have a peaceful night's sleep again. And the old nightmare was still occurring.

But more disturbing than that, she was beginning to experience flashbacks to the abortion, which were terrifying, making her believe that perhaps she was losing her mind.

The first one of these occurred during a meeting at her office. The custodian had just left the conference room, vacuuming the carpet of some spilled crumbs from a cake the staff had purchased for Tom

Moyer's fifty-sixth birthday. As Jennifer sat down for the meeting, suddenly she was back lying on the table in the women's clinic in Atlanta in 1975. She was there at the most traumatic point in the procedure, frightened out of her wits, in pain and emotional agony, and feeling totally helpless and powerless, as in her nightmares. Her heart had begun to pound rapidly and she had felt the room whirling around her, as an overwhelming sense of panic and terror invaded her mind. She had excused herself quietly and had run to the ladies room, shut herself up in a stall, and cried until she felt some relief from the awful memory. It must have been the sound of the vacuum, she later realized, which triggered this memory—the same sound that the vacuum had made in the clinic during the suction abortion. But what if this flashback should occur again? How could she cope with that?

She had gone to her doctor and obtained tranquilizers from him under the pretense that she was just overworked and overwrought at the office, a lie that her physician seemed to buy, as she appeared to him to be a very successful businesswoman. But even with the aid of the pills, she had experienced another flashback, this time while standing in line at the grocery store behind a very pregnant woman, who also had a toddler in her shopping cart who was crying inconsolably. "Mommy! Mommy! Me hurt! Me hurt!" he had cried out repeatedly, showing his mother his mashed finger. That time, she just left her grocery cart there and ran out to her car, in panic and fear.

She had begun taking two sleeping pills and two or more glasses of wine to try to sleep. And still, she would wake up at three o'clock some mornings, a dark void gnawing away at her soul. How could emptiness hurt so much, she would wonder? The empty, yearning of her spirit was calling out, she knew. But to whom was it calling?

Michael had said that God still loved her, that Jesus had never left her. But try as hard as she could, she did not feel His comforting presence, that comforting presence that had encouraged her so often as a young person at Hillside Church. She would open her Bible only to find empty words and meaningless phrases. How could the Lord have gone with her into that clinic anyway, she would think? Perhaps He had abandoned her. Perhaps she had committed the unpardonable sin. It certainly felt like it, as an overwhelming sadness and despondency seemed to be invading the inner recesses of her personality.

Still, Jennifer had never been one to give up easily. If she could just get some time off from work, she felt she could regain her momentum. But her schedule was so very busy. There was no time to deal with her soul.

As she wearily opened the door to her house and dragged her suitcases behind her, a huge pile of mail that her neighbor had brought in greeted her on the kitchen table. In the pile was a fat, large, yellow envelope addressed to her in Michael's handwriting.

An ache arose in her heart as she saw her name written in his handwriting. The last time she had seen this was in Coburn, Alabama, in the summer of 1975. He had often left her love notes hidden in her school notebooks. The pain arose not from the fact that she still loved him, she knew, but rather from the idea that the sight of his handwriting evoked in her mind the memory of her *feeling* loved. Her depression worsened at the thought. She had thought that Michael had loved her and had staked her very personhood, her most intimate self, her mind, soul, and body on that premise. And he had failed her. She knew after their painful conversation in Mobile that on some level he had loved her, but not with the kind of deep, abiding, immutable, unfathomable love that she had so desperately needed all her life. A love she needed still—now more than ever. A love she could not find.

Now, why in the world would Michael be writing to me? And what is this thick item in the envelope? she wondered, feeling the bulge of a small, rectangular package inside the manila envelope.

"Meow," called Ferdinand as he brushed up against her legs, welcoming her home.

"Oh, Ferdie, did you miss me? I'm so glad that you missed me."

Jennifer picked up the feline and stroked him over and over again as his rich purring sounds filled her kitchen. He reveled in the attention and rubbed his head under her chin.

"Oh, Ferdie, *you* love me, don't you, sweet kitty? Sweet, sweet, kitty cat. At least *you* love me," she continued, her ubiquitous tears falling onto his soft gray and white fur.

Placing him down, she said to herself out loud, "Okay, enough of this sadness. Enough, already. I can't change the past. Enough sadness, already."

She opened the kitchen junk drawer and searched for the letter opener. As she pushed around the various papers, rubber bands, twist ties, and tape dispensers searching for it, she pulled out the invitation to the class reunion. The memory of her gut-wrenching confrontation with Michael leapt to the forefront of her mind. She had unintentionally opened up to him and, more importantly, to herself, the very disturbing past she had concealed for so long. But she could not see that anything of value had come from it. From her own perspective, she was much worse now than before. Wasn't opening up and delving in to suffering from your past supposed to purge and cleanse you?

At last, she discovered the letter opener. What in the world could be inside? She spilled its contents onto the counter. There were two letters in two separate, sealed envelopes addressed to her. One was from Michael and the other from someone with a feminine handwriting. It must be from Emily. And there was an audiocassette tape in a plastic cover. In Michael's writing was the title, "If You Were Mine ..." taped on a piece of paper on the outside of the cover.

"What in the world is this?" Jennifer asked aloud to Ferdinand.

"Meow," Ferdinand replied.

Carrying the contents of the envelope into the family room, she collapsed onto the sofa. She opened Michael's letter first. It was dated exactly one week ago. She read aloud to Ferdie, who curled up next to her and purred as she carelessly stroked him while reading.

"Dear Jennifer,

I don't even know how to begin this letter to you, so please be patient and try to discern what my heart is attempting to say. I am afraid my words will fail me here.

I want you to know that I meant every word I said to you that night at the reunion, that awful night at the reunion, more awful for you than for me, I know. If you knew how much I have regretted what I did to you (and by that I mean using your body when I had no right to, as we were not married yet, and especially taking you to that clinic in Atlanta) Anyway, if you knew how much I have hated myself for what I did to you, did to hurt you, perhaps you could find it in your heart to forgive me. I know I don't deserve to be forgiven, but then again, that is what mercy is for, isn't it? To forgive someone when they don't deserve it.

The thing you said that disturbs me the most, disturbs me the most because I know it is true, is that you trusted me back then because I was "spiritual," presenting myself to you and to the world as a "man of God." <u>Jennifer! I am so sorry! So very sorry</u>! I was the biggest hypocrite of all time! I had fallen away from my walk with the Lord, as you well know, because of my own selfishness, because I wanted to have you when I had no right to, because I didn't want to hear the Lord telling me, "No!" I turned deaf ears to Him, and in doing so I not only betrayed my faith in Him, but I also hurt you terribly, Jenny. And destroyed innocent lives.

I have repented before God many times now, as Peter did when he denied the Lord those three times, remember? The scripture says that Peter then went out and <u>wept bitterly</u>. I have bowed down before Him so many times and wept bitter tears, despising my sin, wishing I could in some way go back and change my behavior. Especially undo the damage that my own sin brought upon your sweet, vulnerable spirit, Jennifer. I regret that the most. I pray that you can receive the grace of God to forgive me, although I don't deserve it, for your own sake, Jennifer. You know what bitterness and unforgiveness can do to you. Please, for your own sake—not for mine, but for yours, forgive me.

You called me some harsh names, and believe me, I deserved most all of them! I have called myself much worse over the years because of my treatment of you. You called me a selfish coward. I thought that those two words described me the best—selfish—cowardly. Oh, I tried to convince myself at the time that the trip to the women's clinic was best for you, for our families, for the church, (we couldn't risk embarrassing the church!) and for me. But in the clear light of day with all my defenses stripped away, I know now that it was mainly ME, THE GREAT MICHAEL EVANS, SUPER GOOD GUY, that I was thinking of the most. I was not thinking of anyone else as much, Jenny. Not even you. I despise myself for it now!

And "cowardly." As much as that word hurts my pride, I have to admit to God and to you that I was a wretched coward! I was trying to run away from my responsibilities, run away from the consequences of my sinful treatment of you, Jennifer. Run away like the coward that I was. Can you forgive me?

But one thing you said to me in anger, I hope you did not mean. You called me cold-hearted and unfeeling or something like that, implying that I never loved you (you must know in your heart that I did love you) and that I never thought about the loss of our child—No, the loss of our <u>children</u>! Twins! Oh, Jennifer, I am so sorry about that! Please try to forgive me! I can't imagine how difficult it must have been for you to keep that a secret all these years.

I take full blame for the abortion, Jennifer. *I* was the one who pressured you. *I* was the one who told you it would make everything all right again. And I was the one who was so horribly deceived, so abominably wrong! But *you* are the one who has suffered the most for my sin. I had no idea of the great extent of your suffering, Jennifer, until the reunion. I have hardly been able to sleep since then, recalling your words that described your awful agony, Jenny. <u>I had no idea back in 1975 what I was asking you to do,</u> although I should have known. I should have done research. I should have known, Jennifer, and I beg you to please try to forgive me! I did not mean to hurt you. You must believe that!

I <u>have</u> thought about that despicable day in Atlanta very much, especially since my baby is expected to greet this world any day now. (I hope my mentioning this does not hurt you more, but I want you to know why I am concerned both for you and for the children we lost together.) I did not realize at the time I took you to Atlanta that we were destroying our children. I was ignorant, and I guess I wanted to believe that they were not babies yet. It was only later, when I reviewed one of my father's medical books and saw unborn babies in the womb at eight weeks gestation, that I realized what I had done. In truth, however, I now know that life begins at conception, so it doesn't really matter what I tried to convince myself of back then to "escape" our problem. I was wrong.

I have recently been mourning their loss, Jennifer. Our loss, Jenny. Actually, the world's loss, I believe. Every child is God's gift to the world. I know that now. How I wish I had known that then! And I know that our children would have been very special, Jenny. (It breaks my heart to know it now, Jennifer! I was so blind and foolish. So foolish!)

I wrote and recorded (with the help of some friends) a song about my longing to get our babies back. I am sending you a copy, hoping that you will hear in the song better than in the words I have written on this page, my regret and longing, and my broken heart.

And Jenny, you said that you had lost your woman's heart. I don't believe that for one minute! Not one minute! Please let that tender heart emerge from you again, Jennifer. I am praying that the Lord will send you someone special to cherish that sweet, loving, gentle woman's heart much better than I did.

Please know that I care.

With regret and yet, somehow, unexplainable hope,

Michael

P. S. I asked Emily to read this letter, as I don't want to have secrets from her. She is also writing to you. Emily cares for you very much too, Jennifer. She remembers you and her in junior high and high school together so fondly, and we both pray for you daily."

Jennifer did not know what to make of his letter. She had continued her quiet weeping as she read the letter aloud to herself and to Ferdinand, who continued his purring throughout, a purring that in some unexplainable way comforted her at that moment. She believed that Michael was sincere in his distress concerning his past behavior toward her. She had believed that since Mobile. But what did he mean about "mourning the loss of our children?"

"Our 'children'?" she asked aloud. "What 'children?'" *We never had 'children' together, Michael,* she thought. *The visit to the women's clinic took care of that. How can you mourn the loss of someone you never knew?*

She had vented to Michael in that hotel storeroom, her anger and rage over feeling abandoned, used, and cast off by the one she had loved 'desperately and completely,' the one she had trusted, the one she had believed loved her, too. She had expressed her fury at him for his ultimate rejection of her as *the potential* mother of his children, even though he had been her passionate lover, the one who had impregnated her. She had let him know that she felt somehow unworthy to become a wife and mother now.

But she had never thought consciously about her actually carrying "children" in her womb. *It wasn't really babies yet, was it? It was just "tissue," wasn't it? Products of conception, right? Potential babies but not really "children"? Right? And what did he mean when he wrote about life beginning at conception? Was that correct? What was the basis of that knowledge?*

Suddenly, she stood up from the sofa, dumping Ferdinand off her lap as he gave a disconcerted "meow." She walked swiftly to her room, tore off her costly business suit, and dressed herself in her workout clothes with a tremendous urgency. She had to go outside, get out of this house, out into the sunshine, out into some fresh air! She had to walk and walk and walk to clear her troubled mind! Exercise had always refreshed and revitalized her before. Exercise was supposed to cure depression and confusion. She had to get outside!

She grabbed her portable radio/cassette player and headset as she always did when she jogged or walked. As she began to open the door, her hand trembled slightly on the doorknob.

What can Michael's song possibly say that will comfort me? Why does he want me to listen to it? He said that it reveals his heart better than his letter does. Can I afford to know his broken heart? What good will that do now?

Impulsively, she picked up his cassette and re-read the title, "If You Were Mine..." *To whom does the "you" refer? And why the small row of periods after the title? That's called an ellipsis, isn't it? That usually indicates an incomplete thought or an unfinished, interrupted sentence, doesn't it? Or does it mean something is left out? Is missing?* she pondered.

Somewhere deep in her heart she knew that her suffering would not be eased until she knew the answers to those questions. With trepidation accompanied by a somewhat mysterious resolve, she placed the cassette in the tape player, closed and locked the door, and headed outside for the walk she hoped would bring peace to her anxious thoughts.

Chapter Thirty-One

*T*he sun was shining warmly in the late afternoon of that July day in Indianapolis. It was about five-thirty with a good three hours of daylight left as Jennifer began the brisk walk around her neighborhood. There was a small park around the corner from her house that featured shade trees, playground equipment, rusted-out stationary barbecue grills, and picnic tables. It was usually filled with playgroups of mothers and children on lovely summer days such as this. These informal groups were composed of pre-school and elementary age children and their stay-at-home moms, who would meet to fellowship and encourage one another in the many thankless tasks that they performed in the daily grind of child-rearing. The mothers would always laugh and say that the playgroups were formed for them, not for the children, as it gave them both an outlet to converse with other sympathetic adult women and an excuse to leave some important but disagreeable chore unfinished. Nevertheless, both mothers and children appreciated the time spent together in the park with their peers.

For some reason unknown to her, Jennifer had always avoided the park even though she liked the beauty of the natural setting. But today, she felt she wanted to walk that way to see the birds and the squirrels and the lovely old hardwood trees. She thought the happy setting might help to bring her some peace. The sunlight and the clear skies were already helping her spirits rise somewhat.

As she rounded the corner and entered the park area, she saw small children running and playing, and mothers chasing toddlers, bouncing babies, and cleaning up messes. One young woman was nursing her newborn. She pushed down the "play" button on her cassette player.

Strains of a very lovely, touching melody, much like a lullaby, played by piano, acoustic guitar, bass, cello, and Irish flute introduced the recording. Then Michael's wonderfully soft, clear tenor voice began to sing the lyrics. His voice was so tender, so filled with a quiet passion, and evoked such a sad longing that Jennifer immediately began to shed tears, even before she understood the meaning of the words.

"When my heart is troubled

And I am weighed down,

Then I like to think of how this lonesome world would be

If I could see your face

Or hold you in my arms,

If you were mine ... If you were mine ..."*

At this point in the song, a woman's sweet soprano voice joined in, humming and harmonizing. All at once, Jennifer knew to whom the "you" was referring in the title and haunting refrain of Michael's song—the "you" were their twin babies! And it was their twin babies who were crying for their mother in her nightmares. And simultaneously, she knew beyond a doubt that the row of periods after the title represented the way in which their tiny, still-forming bodies and lives had been so violently and suddenly removed and destroyed.

Jennifer's heart felt as if it were being ripped open, and she began sobbing, much as she had done back in that hotel storage room in Mobile. She began to run, looking for somewhere to hide in the park

---

*IF YOU WERE MINE by Fernando Ortega, © 1998 MargeeDays Music (Admin. by Dayspring Music, LLC), Dayspring Music, LLC. All Rights Reserved. Used By Permission.

so she could grieve alone and unobserved. She found a spot behind a large oak tree in a corner of the grounds and continued crying. Large, heavy tears that seemed to be coming from the deepest recesses of her soul poured from her eyes and ran down her face unheeded. The lyrics continued, Michael's voice crying out.

"If you had a bad dream,

I would jump inside it,

And I would fight for you with all the strength that I could find!

I would lead you home

By your tiny hand,

If you were mine … If you were mine …"

As these words sounded in Jennifer's ears, she fell down to a sitting position on the ground behind that great tree, pulled her legs to her chest, put her head in her hands, and shook intensely with heart-wrenching grief, her tears flowing like a waterfall.

She knew now what she had so vehemently refused to acknowledge in the aftermath and shock of that tragic, traumatic August day in Atlanta so many years ago. She knew in the very core of her mind, soul, and spirit, in her heart of hearts, in that tender, mother's heart that God gives every young woman, that she had lost her precious twin children that day. Children she could never retrieve. Children she would never be able to hold in her arms, soothe and comfort, guide and direct. Children that would never play in the park, be pushed in a swing, sing silly songs, and laugh into the summer sunshine like the children all around her were doing. Children that would never walk into her kitchen at bedtime, teddy bear under one arm, children's book in hand and say, "Mommy, read me a story."

There was an instrumental interval in Michael's song now, with the Irish flute sending its sorrowful but sweet tones straight into Jennifer's grieving heart. She knew now what Michael had meant about mourning the loss of *their* children. *"Our" children,* thought Jennifer. *What would "our" children have been like? Mine and*

Michael's. What would they have looked like? What would have been their gender? Two boys? Two girls? A girl and a boy? Would they have been dark like me or fair like Michael, or one of each? Would they have had his lovely voice, his voice that even now was calling out to them, longing for them? What would they have been like?

All these thoughts were arising almost instantaneously from Jennifer's soul, falling one upon another as she sat under that oak tree unobserved, grieving vicariously with the father of her children their loss—their tragic loss by their own parents' desperate, ignorant decision.

I must get out of here! I have to go home and scream and yell and cry until there is no more sorrow left in my heart! How long will that be? How long will it take to remove this awful, horrible sorrow and regret from my heart! O my babies, my precious little ones! What did I do to you? What did I do? Can you ever forgive me?

She jumped up and began running home as fast as she could as Michael sang softly, like a lullaby, the third and final stanza.

"I would sing of love

On the blackest night.

I would sing of God and how His goodness fills our lives.

I would sing to you

'Til the morning light,

If you were mine … If you were mine …

I would sing to you

'Til the morning light,

If you were mine … If you were mine …"

As she ran toward the safety and refuge of her house, she passed Judy Kowalski sitting on her front porch, gently rocking and singing her newborn baby to sleep.

Chapter Thirty-Two

Not even Ferdie's purring and constant rubbing against Jennifer's arms and legs as she half-sat and half-lay on the soft carpet of her family room could provide even the smallest amount of comfort to her now. She had burst hysterically into the room, thrown herself down on the carpet placing her face into the expensive fabric of the sofa cushions, and cried aloud the bitter tears of mourning and sorrowful remorse known only to those who have experienced a great loss, a very great loss of their own making. Mourning a loss that could never be retrieved. Grieving for dreadful mistakes of the past while knowing that nothing could ever be done to make it right again. The tearing, ripping anguish of her broken spirit seized her violently and forcefully, while cries of deeply wounded emotions made her whole body rock and quiver uncontrollably.

She pounded on the sofa pillows with clenched fists, as her torment would not abate. *Oh, Michael! How could you have done this to me? Why did you want me to listen to your sad, sad song? Why did you want me to tear myself apart like this, mourning the loss of our babies that we can never get back? What were you thinking, Michael? What were you thinking? You have betrayed me again!*

Had Michael known what her reaction was going to be, he never would have sent her the tape of his song. He had presumed that she was feeling the same loss as he. His situation, having a pregnant wife who had come into his office that evening eight months ago beaming with the news that she was carrying his child, his living with her through morning sickness and ultrasounds, and his listening to his baby's heartbeat at the two month obstetrical visit had forced him to recognize the humanity of the unborn. He had assumed that Jennifer knew this intuitively. He never again wanted to hurt her and would not have dreamed that she would have responded in this way. He had only wanted her to know of his own heartbreak, hoping that it would in some way comfort her, helping her to know she was not grieving alone.

How long she sat there weeping, she never knew. It seemed to her like days and days. The room began to darken, but Jennifer did not bother to turn on any lights. She just sat there crying, but receiving no comfort from her tears. And it seemed to her that if she cried from now until the end of the world, she would never get relief from the terrible, wrenching, aching sorrow that left her so very shattered and disconsolate.

What she had always subconsciously feared had fallen upon her. She had instinctively known in her deepest soul that she, by herself, could not deal with the destructive consequences of what had happened to her that abominable day in Atlanta. She had known that she was not equipped to handle the terrible emotional, psychological, and spiritual damage that was done to her that day *all by herself.*

And she had been *all by herself* throughout the tragic ordeal of the pregnancy and its termination. Sure, Michael had been there physically, had driven her to the clinic and had paid the fee for the procedure, but in refusing to go with her inside, he had abandoned her emotionally. He had actually abandoned her from the moment he requested that she terminate her pregnancy, she knew. From that moment on, Jennifer had known she was on her own. A young, frightened, woman—barely twenty-years-old—facing a crisis pregnancy all alone.

Jennifer had been all alone, and she knew she could not deal with this pain and trauma alone. Deep in her subconscious mind, she had known that she would fly into a million pieces and not be able to piece herself together again if she acknowledged what she had experienced in that clinic—the pain, betrayal, heartbreak, and violation she had experienced there. The terrible loss of her innocence, the loss of her tender woman's heart, the loss of her ability to love and trust men, and most of all, the loss of her precious little children, were much too severe for her to assimilate or even recognize by herself. How could she have possibly dealt with these things all by herself?

She had known this subconsciously, that hot August day in Atlanta as she sat in the recovery room in that clinic, and had coped the only way she could—by shutting down her woman's heart, by slowly but surely putting to death the maternal instinct that could so mercilessly and completely accuse her now, by using all her conscious will power and mental strength to forget that excruciating, torturous event. By extreme denial.

And in order to maintain that extreme denial, she had been forced to break up with Michael. She had lost her ability to trust him there in that clinic, even though he had acted in ignorance, and with that loss of trust, came the inevitable loss of her love for him. She had known subconsciously that the only way she could forget that awful trauma was to move away from him, to try not to ever think of him again. Because each time she saw him, she was reminded of what he had done to her, of his betrayal of her, even though it was unintentional.

And to make matters worse, he would continually try to force her to revisit that painful day, as he knew what had happened to her there had changed her personality and he wanted her to be restored. But ironically, his insistence that she address the issue was what had eventually forced her to break their engagement, to leave him once and for all. To forget him. To forget all the painful past. To start anew, somewhere far from him and all that reminded her of him—of him and of that horrible day.

This hardening of her heart had taken a few years, and its work might have been completed except for her sister's pregnancy and subsequent baby ... and the Class of '73 Reunion. Seeing so many of her classmates with child, hearing them discuss their children ... and especially seeing Emily eight months pregnant with Michael's child, had forced Jennifer to dredge up from the hidden places in her psyche The Truth.

The Truth that had been safely and securely locked up in her memory behind a thick steel door with armed guards on both sides and rolls of barbed wire stacked up in front. The Truth that had a large sign in front of that steel door that read, "DANGER! DO NOT ENTER! EVER!"

But The Truth was supposed to set her free, wasn't it? But now, Jennifer did not feel free in the least. She felt as though she were locked in another prison, a prison of inconsolable grief, self-reproach, anger, and remorse. A prison of guilt and shame from which she could never escape.

The breaking of her once hard heart, there in her beautifully decorated family room in her lovely house on that pretty July day in 1983, was complete. The hardness was totally gone. But the spiritual, psychological, and emotional distress that it brought was also complete. Jennifer could not see it then, but that terrible breaking of her stony heart, as painful as it was, was somehow necessary if she was ever to be whole again. A whole woman. A tender, compassionate woman. A woman of true, not false, strength again.

How could I have done this terrible thing? How could I not have protected my own little babies? How can God forgive me? How can I forgive myself? Oh God, please, please help me! Oh God, Michael said You had not abandoned me! Where are You? Why can't I feel the comfort of Your mercy?

I'm so sorry, dear Lord! I am so sorry, but how can I ever make it right? How can I get my babies back inside my womb and give them life? I would if I could! Oh, You know I would if I could! But I can't! Oh, Lord! ...Oh, God! ... Jesus, help me! ... Please, please forgive me! Help me, please!

As Jennifer prayed these words from the deepest, shattered places of her young, wounded soul, she felt a firm but gentle voice arise from the center of her being. Not an audible voice, not words spoken to her physical ears, but a strong, persistent impression that spoke directly to her spirit and seemed to say,

"You did not open the second letter, Jenny. Open the second letter, Jennifer!"

Sensing the complete authority and yet compassionate comfort of those words spoken to her spirit made Jennifer stop her anguished lament almost immediately, and she felt chill bumps arise on her arms. She knew this had to be the Lord speaking to her, as those words did not come from her own broken mind and heart. She had not been thinking along those lines at all. In her sorrow, she had completely forgotten about Emily's letter. She had been in extreme distress, and those words were spoken with tenderness and peace. They had arisen from the center of her being and not from her own troubled thoughts. She remembered the scripture in which Jesus had said, "My sheep hear my voice," and she knew.

She stemmed the flow of her tears with quick catches of her breath, as she calmed herself as best she could after spending three long hours of that evening crying hysterically. She slowly arose from the floor, walked over to the end table where she had dropped Emily's letter earlier, flipped the switch to turn on the lamp, and picked up the letter.

It read, "For Jenny" on the outside of the sealed envelope. Still trying to compose herself and return her fast, short catches of breath into a more natural breathing pattern, Jennifer picked up a tissue from the holder, dried her eyes which were blurred from all the weeping, and sat down in her softly upholstered club chair to read the letter.

The envelope was bulging and as Jennifer opened it, she discovered that the letter was five pages long, written on the front and back using feminine stationery that had flowers and vines along the borders. It was in Emily's fine, small, lady-like handwriting, petite, neat, and pretty just like Emily herself. It must have taken her at least an hour or two to compose such a volume, Jennifer thought. She began to read,

"Dear, Sweet, Jenny-Penny, (You remember, don't you?)"

Jennifer almost half-smiled. She had nearly forgotten the silly, early teenage nonsense of junior high school girls. She had been Jenny-Penny, Emily had been Emmy-Simmy, and the third "musketeer" of their group had been Molly-Dolly. They had been the closest of friends throughout seventh and eighth grades. How did Emily remember such things after all these years? She continued reading.

"Oh Jennifer, you remember how close we once were back at Harris Junior High, don't you? When I think of the sweetness and innocence of those days, of how frightened and insecure we all were back then—wow! It seems so long ago. And yet I know that the wishes and dreams we had then are not so far removed from what we still long for today, are they?

We both wanted a cute boyfriend to take us to the school dances (all two of them!) and to carry our books home from school, and to write us notes in class. Remember those horrible, cheap, heavy roped chrome I.D. bracelets? We wanted to wear a cute boy's I.D. bracelet, didn't we, Jenny? We wanted to feel special, and that we belonged to someone. We wanted to hold hands, but we didn't want to be kissed, did we? We were frightened of being kissed, remember? We would practice in the mirror and talk about how it might feel and fret and worry about it. Yes, how sweet and innocent we were then!"

Jennifer stopped reading for a moment to dry her eyes and blow her nose. Yes, she remembered all this. But where was Emily going with this letter, she wondered? She continued.

"I don't know why I am remembering this, Jenny, except to say that I want you to know that in my mind and my heart you will always be that same sweet, innocent, vulnerable Jenny Jacobs, no matter what! I want you to know that I do not look down on you or judge you in any way for what happened to you, for what occurred between you and Michael, Jennifer.

I know this is awkward and strange, but I want you to know that I will never, ever tell anyone your secret, Jenny! Never! I can so easily put myself in your shoes. It could have been any one of us girls who were capable of the same tragedy that happened to you, Jenny. Please know that I understand that much!

When Michael first told me about what had happened, I felt very betrayed and angry with him. I am sure you can understand that. But he was so broken and devastated and repentant that I had to forgive him. He didn't know what he was doing, Jennifer. I mean, especially about the clinic visit. I know he had no idea of what he was putting you through. He had no idea of the long-term consequences of his actions."

Again, Jennifer stopped reading and thought, *Oh, Emily, you always were the sweetest girl in class. But how can you know what I went through? Michael did not treat you badly. Michael married you and wanted you to be the mother of his children. How can you possibly understand?* She read on.

"Jenny, I know that you were just plain old looking for love, for true love, for real, lasting, permanent love, for a strong, masculine love, like all of us girls were. I remember when you used to spend the night with me in school. We would have so much fun doing our hair and makeup and nails and day dreaming and singing all the pop songs on the radio together. We both had braces on our teeth and were at that awkward, gangly age. We felt unattractive and clumsy.

That was when we both needed a daddy's love so badly! I honestly don't know how I would have made it through those rough adolescent years without my daddy's telling me I was beautiful and loveable! I knew that you so hungered for a father's love, too, Jenny. I remember how you would just love to be around my daddy. He would always tickle you under the chin and say that those 'dark, gypsy eyes of yours were certain to allure many a young man and capture many a heart.' Remember? We used to laugh together at the way Daddy phrased things!"

This time Jennifer did actually smile a little at the remembrance. How kind Mr. Prescott, and Mrs. Prescott, too, had been to her! She continued reading.

"I also remember one night after the lights were out and mother had told us 'for the last time' (about the fiftieth time, that is!) to be quiet and go to sleep, that I heard you softly crying. You thought that I was asleep, but when I heard you I asked you what was wrong. Remember? And you said that you wished that you were my sister and that my parents were your parents, too. You said that you knew that was wrong of you, but, oh, how you wished you had a happy home like mine! Remember, Jenny?"

Oh, Emily, of course I remember. How could I forget such a poignant statement! How I envied you your happy home, your stay-at-home, attentive mother, and your adorable, kind father. Jennifer stopped reading to dry her eyes once more. At this point she was having trouble reading through her watery eyes. But when her vision cleared, she continued.

"I recall how sad I felt for you, Jenny. I knew things were not happy for you at home, that you hardly ever saw your father, and I so wanted you to have that security that I had. I remember praying to the Lord very often, asking Him to send you a happy home and a good father to help you through this world. All girls need a good father, I knew. It helps so much.

As we entered high school and sort of drifted apart, you with your drama and journalism and me with my cheerleading and art, I still cared very much for you, Jennifer. I still prayed for God to send you a good father. When your mother married Bill Miller, I thought that maybe my prayer was answered. But sadly, that was not to be either.

When Michael told me about everything, I wept for you Jenny. I was angry with God for not answering my prayers for a good father for you! I felt that if you had known that strong loving father, he would have been able to protect your heart and make you feel special so that it would have been easier for you to resist the temptations that we all experienced as young women at college. Please don't think that I am in any way criticizing you here, Jenny. I only want you to know that I think I understand what was motivating you at the time you and Michael became physically involved. Again, I know this is awkward and embarrassing, but I feel such an urgency to get all this aired and out into the open."

At this point, Jennifer had a complete understanding of Emily's mind and heart. She was not in the least offended, but marveled at Emily's merciful, forgiving nature. She read on.

"Anyway, one night last week as I was again praying for you, Jenny, (Michael and I pray for you daily. We are both so concerned for you, especially after the reunion. I don't mean for this to make you feel uncomfortable in any way, but I want you to know that both of us care about you and want you to be healed of all this sorrow.) Anyway, as I was saying, as I prayed, I became angry with the Lord and said to Him, 'Why didn't You ever answer my prayers for Jennifer to have a good father?'

And, Jenny, please don't think I am crazy or that my hormones have made me insane, but immediately there came a response to my soul and mind which I am certain was from the Lord saying,

'I AM that good Father to Jennifer! I have never left her, not for one moment! I have seen every tear that she has cried. I have felt every pain in her soul. I know the deepest longings of her heart. I AM her eternal Father, and I will care for my daughter!'

Oh, Jennifer, I still get chills and cry when I recall that awe-filled moment, that holy moment! I am as certain of that being the Lord's voice as I am certain of anything! It was spoken to my heart so fiercely and so powerfully, Jenny! I know that it was God's voice, because He loves you fiercely and powerfully, Jennifer. Loves us all that way. Please believe it!"

As Jennifer read this incredible account, there was an indescribable witness to her own spirit that this was indeed the tender, comforting, yet powerful, forceful voice of the Lord that she had known as a young girl at Hillside Baptist and at home saying her prayers at bedtime. She had once known the sweet comfort of God's presence. She had once felt His loving arms around her during worship at church or in her quiet time at home with her Bible open, or way up there in her trees. She had heard in her spirit His voice telling her that He would be the Father that she never had, her Heavenly Father. But it had been so long, so very long, since she had known the sweet sound of His voice speaking words of love and joy to her soul. She had stopped believing on the same day she had stopped feeling, stopped loving—on that dreadful day in Atlanta. Her eyes became blurry again but she squinted and read,

> "Jenny, I just want to encourage you in your faith—to remind you of our extremely merciful, forgiving, and understanding God—to remind you of His loving heart for His children, a heart that keeps on loving His precious children even when we walk away and stop believing. Forgive me if I sound as though I am preaching to or lecturing you, Jenny. I don't mean to do that, but I so badly want you to know that nothing, absolutely nothing, that you or I or Michael or any of His children can do, is able to make the Lord stop loving us!"

Here, Jennifer stopped reading and wept yet again. But this time, she was beginning to feel the hope that having a loving Heavenly Father brings to the human heart. This time her tears had the promise of being the kind that cleanse and heal. She was still very broken in spirit, but she could almost see in her mind's eye a faint light of hope out there in the not too distant future beckoning her onward. She was suddenly reminded of a stanza in an old hymn she used to sing, "*O Joy, that seekest me through pain; I cannot close my heart to thee. I trace the rainbow through the rain, and feel the promise is not vain, that morn' shall tearless be*". After a few moments, she was able to finish Emily's letter.

"This brings me in a very round-about way to my main purpose in writing to you, Jenny. I met a very wonderful young woman in our Sunday school class two weeks ago. As we were talking, I asked her where she worked, and she told me she was a volunteer counselor who works with women who have experienced the pain of abortion. She said that she herself had been traumatized by two abortions when she was in high school, and that she had experienced great healing in a group such as the one she now leads.

She said that the groups are now nationwide and that the only women who can attend are women who themselves have known the heartache and suffering of losing their child or children in this way. The groups meet one night a week for nine to twelve weeks. There is absolutely no hypocritical condemnation or Pharisaical judgment of any kind placed on the women who attend these groups meetings. Everyone is kind and supportive. She said she has seen so many wonderful, precious women find freedom and restoration in her groups.

I obtained a phone number from her for the national headquarters, and was able to discover that there is a group such as this in Indianapolis. It is called "Streams of Hope" there in Indy, and I am enclosing the telephone number, contact person, and address.

Oh, Jenny, I hope you don't mind that I did this! I just believe that you might be able to find the sympathy and understanding that can heal your wounds there. I know that sometimes the enemy of our souls likes to make us think that no one else in the whole world has ever experienced our sorrow or could possibly understand our suffering. He likes to isolate us and make us feel so lonely and hopeless. Knowing that other women have lived through similar emotional turmoil and have found help has to be encouraging, don't you think?

Anyway, I hope I haven't taken up too much of your time with this lengthy letter. I hope, like Michael, that you can read past the words I have so poorly written here and find not only my love and concern for you, but also the strong, loving hands of your Heavenly Father that are reaching out to you, even in the midst of your pain.

I will always love you, precious Jenny-Penny!

Emily

P.S. If you ever want to talk to me about this or about anything at all, please call me! You are also welcome in our home anytime."

Dear, sweet Emily. What a kind friend you still are. I find your loving heart in every word, thought Jennifer as she finished the letter.

After several minutes of just sitting there in the chair by the soft glow of the lamplight, drinking in the words of Emily's letter and pondering—as much as her weary mind could ponder after such an emotionally draining evening—how it was she came to read that letter in the first place, Jennifer stood up and walked to her telephone. She dialed the number Emily had written her.

Chapter Thirty-Three

*T*here were butterflies in Jennifer's stomach as she stepped out of her car in the parking lot of the strip mall where The Safe Haven Crisis Pregnancy Center had its offices. It was a fairly new, pleasant building with trees scattered around the parking lot and flowers growing in the many concrete planters that were placed along the sidewalks by the entrance to the Center. The summer sun was still shining even though it was early evening. This was the Wednesday following Jennifer's phone call on Friday to the number Emily had written her.

The young woman who had answered her call that Friday night was a warm, friendly-sounding person named Laura Post. She had been the volunteer who had taken the crisis "hotline" home with her that evening and had been in her kitchen preparing dinner for her two-year-old son and her husband when Jennifer had phoned. Immediately the volunteer counselor could sense that the caller was in tremendous need and had dropped her dinner preparations, retreated into her bedroom, and closed the door to have a private conversation.

From the quaking voice on the phone, Laura could discern a tremendous sadness and need for understanding. She had assured the caller that her conversation would be held in the strictest confidence. She had only asked for Jennifer's first name and had prayed silently that her concern for this yet unknown fellow sufferer would be transmitted through the telephone lines.

Laura's prayer had been answered as Jennifer had immediately sensed a camaraderie with this kind, sympathetic woman. She briefly told her that she needed information about the next Streams of Hope group meeting. It just so happened that Laura herself was leading that next group which would have its first meeting on Wednesday evening. How she hoped that Jennifer would be a part of the new group, Laura had said. She had given her directions to the Center where the group met, telling her she should park in the back and enter by the back door. She had said that this was just a precaution to protect the privacy of the five or six women who usually composed the groups. Laura had finished by telling Jennifer that she would love to meet her and hoped to see her Wednesday night at seven o'clock.

Jennifer had felt so confident and relieved at the time of that telephone conversation last Friday. It had made sense to her that only other women who had experienced similar trauma and pain could possibly understand what she was going through. But now, five days later, as she was walking up the two steps leading to the back door of the Center, her legs were weak and her heart was pounding.

What am I doing here? What is going to happen inside this place? I hope I haven't made another mistake. I'm not certain that I want to open myself up to a group of total strangers. This may not help me at all, she fretted, opening the door.

But her fears were quickly placed to rest as she stepped inside. There to greet her immediately, smiling a warm, welcoming smile, was none other than Laura Post. Jennifer knew this because the attractive, red haired, freckled woman about her own age standing there wore a hand labeled nametag that read, "Hi, My Name is Laura." And Jennifer was immediately drawn to her. Laura had the kindest, most understanding green eyes and met her gaze full on. The volunteer group leader was ready and excited to take on the challenge of this new group of women in general, and this beautiful, dark brunette in particular.

"Hello! My name is Laura Post. I'm so glad you came this evening." Laura took Jennifer's hand and squeezed it gently.

"Hi. I'm Jennifer. Jennifer Jacobs," she replied, feeling less nervous and attempting a weak smile.

Laura had a very disarming demeanor and openness about her appearance that immediately made Jennifer feel more secure. She seemed "normal."

"Jennifer ... Jennifer Jacobs. Oh, that's right. I received your phone call last Friday night." Laura recalled, genuinely interested.

She nodded, "Yes, that's correct."

"Well, great Jennifer. I was so hoping to get to know you better. You have such a wonderful Southern accent that I dearly love. My favorite grandmother was from South Carolina, and when I hear that drawl, it puts me in the middle of her kitchen eating homemade chocolate chip cookies. Speaking of which, come on inside and help yourself. We have sandwiches, chips, cookies, cake, coffee, tea, soft drinks ... you name it, supplied by the sweet women of the Center auxiliary. Obviously, they don't care at all about our figures," Laura laughed and ushered Jennifer into a very lovely conference room. "You're not from South Carolina, too, are you? Oh, excuse me one moment, I hear some more ladies coming up the steps. Please make yourself at home, Jennifer," and with that, the group leader walked back to the door to welcome the newcomers.

This gave Jennifer time to look around the room. She grabbed a diet soft drink off the table and gazed at the facility. There was a dark wooden conference table in the center of the room that would seat about twelve people in the comfortably padded and upholstered chairs. The colors in the room were blue and yellow, with a rich, patterned area rug under the table. There were pretty pictures on the walls, mostly landscapes and floral designs. Bookshelves lined the walls and contained books, attractive vases, candlesticks, greenery, and other bric-a-brac. It was a very inviting, feminine room, and there was soft instrumental music coming through the speakers in the ceiling. Jennifer thought she recognized a few of the melodies.

What is the name of that song? she mused. *Oh, yes. These are old, sweet hymns from my childhood.* She recognized "Sweet Hour of Prayer," while the timeless, lovely old melodies evoked in her a sense of peace. In fact, mysteriously the whole room seemed to whisper, "Peace, peace," to her heart. She became more relaxed and comfortable.

Four other young women had entered the room in the meanwhile. They appeared to range in age from not quite twenty to thirty something and looked like any other women Jennifer might see around town in the shopping centers or at the grocery store. *Gee, these ladies appear normal also,* Jennifer thought to herself. *I don't know what I was expecting them to look like, but they appear normal like ...*

Suddenly, she realized that subconsciously she had always marked herself as "not normal." And she had always suspected that others might be able to see through her and suspect her dreadful secret. That was the main reason she had refused to allow anyone to grow close, had refused to have a real, true friend. That, coupled with the fact that she was punishing herself in isolation. This insight surprised her greatly because she had consciously been very proud of her appearance and accomplishments all those years. She had desired to have friends *outwardly.*

But *inside*, she was wearing her own version of Hester Prynne's scarlet letter, a very visible crimson "A." Only this time the "A" had stood for "abortion," not "adultery." She had marked herself with this secret letter "A" and had been terrified that someone would discover it if she had let them really know her. And she had felt that she did not deserve to be loved, anyway, after what she had done. No, she did not deserve a true friend, she had believed down deep inside.

She was amazed at this sudden insight and was still pondering and processing these thoughts when Laura spoke to her and the other four ladies.

"Well, everyone, I hope you don't mind wearing one of these very lovely self-adhesive name tag things, guaranteed to ruin even the loveliest outfit, with just your first name on them. I know many of you are much like me ... terrible at remembering names and things... and the name tags will help us for a couple of weeks, if you don't mind. Meantime, I will make introductions as you are writing them to test my own poor memory." She laughed lightly and warmly.

Boy, Laura sure would make a great salesperson in my company, Jennifer said to herself. *She certainly knows how to work a room and make everyone feel welcome and special.*

"Let's see," Laura began, smiling, "to my right here is Sarah..."

And Jennifer smiled at a rather plump, sad-faced woman of about thirty-two, she would guess.

"And next to Sarah is Janie ..." Laura continued.

Janie was tall and blonde and very, very skinny, almost appearing anorexic, and it was hard to guess her age.

"And then across from me is Kathy ..." the introductions went on.

Kathy appeared to be about Jennifer's age and was an immaculately groomed, attractive African-American woman, sporting an expensive outfit and manicured fingernails, and had thick, wavy hair and guarded, veiled eyes.

"Then, there is Debbie," Laura smiled at Debbie who had the deepest dimples Jennifer had ever seen and very curly hair. She appeared to be very young, the youngest in the group, and reminded her of Shirley Temple. *How could anyone have done that to you, Debbie?* she wondered.

"And finally, to my left here is Jennifer," Laura finished. "Jennifer, I hope you don't mind, but since you called so late, I did not have the opportunity of meeting with you privately as we usually do before the first group meeting, to let you know about our program here. So I will briefly tell you, and this can be good review for all of us."

She smiled very warmly, looking directly into Jennifer's eyes and explained, "What we do here is conduct an eleven week session, meeting one night per week here at the Center. And there are only three rules, which is good for me because I am not a very good 'rules' person myself," and she laughed at herself before going on.

"The first and foremost is that we maintain strict confidentiality. We don't tell anyone at all whom we meet here, and if we see each other out of the Center somewhere, we don't mention to any other person standing around how we know each other. Of course, later on, after our work here has been completed, some of you may not mind sharing your experiences here with others ... or you may. It is entirely up to you. Some of our 'graduates,' so to speak, become involved in helping other post-abortive women, and some prefer not to. But in any case, none of us here will ever tell anyone else outside this room of our sessions together without the consent of the other party, okay?"

Jennifer replied, "Okay. I understand." And the others all nodded.

"Now Rule Number Two is that we want you all to be committed to attend all the meetings for the next several Wednesdays and to complete your assignments. These assignments should not take more than three or so hours a week. You can take longer if you want to, but this is an estimate of how long most women take on each task. It's important because each week we will explore a new aspect of our hearts and of what the Lord wants to do to restore us fully. Full restoration. That is our goal. Okay?"

Laura smiled again from her tender heart as all the women replied, "Okay."

Full restoration. Jennifer thought. *Is that possible, Lord? Can this aching in my soul ever be fully healed?* She had begun to pray again and to believe that the Lord was there for her, though she was not yet able to experience His presence fully, the way she had in the past. *How I hope it is possible!* she thought. *Laura certainly doesn't appear to be broken. She appears to be at such peace with herself.*

"And the final rule is that we will all offer each other non-judgmental feedback. No raised eyebrows. No 'How could you do that's?' Nothing at all like that. We are all here to listen, to understand, to love each other, to help each other, and encourage each other. We must be totally honest, of course, and take responsibility for our actions, but we all need that sense of safety and security that refusing to judge each other brings. Okay?" She smiled at the group as they gave her the final, "Okay."

"Okay! Great! Let's all sit down and get comfortable around the table here. Then I want to begin our group tonight with a word or two to the Heavenly Father, if you don't mind."

And she prayed, not closing her eyes and bowing her head as Jennifer had always done, but looking up at the ceiling and smiling at God, her face radiant.

"Oh, Dear Father, thank you so much for this lovely group of women you have sent here. Thank you for working in each and every one of their hearts and souls, and for preparing this session in advance for each one of them. Thank you for Sarah and Janie and Kathy and Debbie and Jennifer. Thank you, most of all, that you will in some way reveal yourself to each one of these ladies over these next few weeks; that you will comfort, heal, forgive, and guide them to walk in paths of newness of life ... life to its fullest ... and will help them walk away from the clouds of death and darkness that have been hovering over their heads. Thank you, merciful Father ... In the name of your dear Son. Amen."

Once again, tears formed in Jennifer's eyes. *Clouds of death and darkness. That's right. That is what I have felt like for these past eight years. Like my heart has been under clouds of death and darkness.*

"Now for our first session this evening, all we will do is to share our individual stories," Laura continued. "Our stories of how we found ourselves in the abortion clinic or clinics. You may take as long as you need to, or be short if you feel you can't go further at this point. Whatever you can do. I will start and share with you my own sad story. It is important, however, that we all share. You know as well as I do that our pain thrives so well in secret ... in keeping our own dark secrets from any living soul. Shame, guilt, and despair love secrecy, silence, and concealment. The first step toward freedom is to bring it all out into the light ... out into the light of love, such as we find in here, in this room tonight."

Laura continued looking at each woman present with a totally honest, open expression, and with the most understanding eyes Jennifer had seen in a while. She felt safe with her.

Laura went on, "You see boxes of tissues on the table so that each of you can reach them as you need them. Let's not hand each other the tissues, as sometimes this communicates to the person crying that they need to stop the flow of tears. That's not necessarily so, you know. I know with myself, my tears are very often what the Lord uses to bring my healing. There is a scripture verse that tells us God keeps all our tears in a bottle ... or writes them on a scroll or something. I love that one. I just want you to know that crying is perfectly acceptable here. Okay?"

And she smiled so sweetly one last time as the women all said, "Okay" in unison.

"Well, my story begins with ..." and Laura Post, red-haired, freckled Laura Post who looked like the All-American girl next door, raised on a farm in southern Indiana, shared her story. It was a story not so very much unlike Jennifer's. She had gone steady with a boyfriend whom she loved very much, whom she trusted, whom she thought would marry her if she ever "got in trouble," but who, in ignorance like Michael, drove her to an abortion clinic instead. And her pain and suffering while in the clinic and afterwards were not so very different from Jennifer's, except that she had been able to talk about it almost immediately with her boyfriend. He, however, had not wanted to listen and had told her to "just forget it." But she, instead, "just forgot" her boyfriend, breaking up with him within two weeks.

She, too, had experienced nightmares afterwards and flashbacks to the clinic episode. And she had begun self-destructive behaviors that she had not participated in before, such as using drugs, letting her grades fall by the wayside, and alienating herself from her family and friends. Depression had also set in. But her mother, with whom she had always enjoyed a close relationship, had finally been able to get her to open up and to reveal to her the dire secret she had been hiding.

They had cried together, her mother and she, there in her bedroom sitting on her bed, holding each other very tight. That was the only time that Laura, herself, had cried in re-telling her story ... when she recalled her mother's tears and the words she repeated over and over while holding her red-haired daughter, rocking her in her arms, "Oh, my baby! ... My poor, poor baby! ... My baby! ... Why didn't you tell me? ... My poor baby!"

All the women seated around the table had cried right along with Laura Post, had related to her own story in a deeply personal way. The tissues were being put to good use.

And as cute Debbie, "Shirley Temple" Debbie, was next to share her story, the tears flowed even more freely. Everyone there would have protected adorable little Debbie from her agony if they could have. She was only fifteen when she had visited the clinic. But unlike Laura, Debbie's mother had known about her pregnancy and had actually driven her to the clinic and had paid for the procedure... again, in ignorance, thinking it was the best thing she could do for her little girl. Later on after she was educated about the emotional trauma that abortion can bring, her mother had sincerely repented of her action and had begged her daughter to please forgive her. Debbie, now eighteen, was having trouble doing that, she said, and hoped that what she learned in this group would enable her to finally forgive her mom. She wanted to forgive her, she said, but she was still angry and was hurting so much inside.

And as Janie related her story, more tears of sympathy fell. Janie had actually experienced this heartbreak three times, one boyfriend at a time. How could she ever find forgiveness, she asked out loud? Laura assured her that she would find forgiveness here and encouraged her to stay with the sessions, not giving in to despair. "Hope and freedom are just around the corner, Janie," Laura said with tenderness and confidence as she wiped her own tears away. And the others agreed, trying to relay to Janie their concern for her, their belief in her, even though she had been a total stranger to them before this night.

Sarah, the oldest in the group, told perhaps the most heart-breaking story, at least to Jennifer. Sarah had been married at the time she had terminated her pregnancy. She never told her husband about either the pregnancy or the abortion, she said, because she felt he would be angry with her and not understand. She had believed the rhetoric that what was growing in her womb was not a baby, and had simply driven herself to the nearest clinic without his knowledge when she discovered she was pregnant in the first year of her marriage. "We were barely able to pay our bills, and I had to keep my factory job, which I wouldn't be able to do if I was pregnant. Pregnant women weren't allowed on the assembly line where I worked because of health risks to the baby," she explained through tears.

But after her clinic visit, Sarah had withdrawn from both her husband and all her friends and had fallen into a deep, dark depression that had required a brief hospital stay. And while the medication that she had been given had helped her to function, she knew that it was not addressing the real cause of her sadness. She had finally received the insight to connect the depression with the abortion from watching a Christian television program by "accident" one evening, where the story of the young woman on the TV screen had been much like her own experience. "But my husband still doesn't know. I am so scared he won't love me anymore if I tell him," she cried, as the others wept with her. "I can't ever tell him."

When Kathy related her experience, she was completely unemotional and flat at first. She said that she had been routinely sexually abused as a little girl by a relative and had learned not to feel anything at all in order to cope. She had begun to have sex with various boyfriends at an early age and had become pregnant at fourteen. Her grandmother had taken her to the clinic, and it was there that Kathy said she felt she had been raped once more. It made her so angry that she ran away from home and lived out on the streets for a while. A kind, Christian home for runaways had taken her in, and it was there that she found a new beginning to her life. But she still struggled daily with depression. Lately, she said, she felt the Lord speaking to her heart to revisit the abortion experience. She told the group that she believed that the Lord wanted to do some deep healing in her heart—that he had wanted to do this for a long time—but that he was waiting for her. Here in her story she shed one tear. She said he spoke one question to her heart last week: "Are you ready to heal?" She said she was.

Finally, it was Jennifer's turn. She told her story simply, relating to the group all the details she could recall, details she had not revealed to Michael there in that storage room in Mobile as she had not been able to remember them then. But for some reason, here, in the company of the understanding sisterhood of post-abortive women, she was able to recall dreaded details long forgotten. Of sitting in the recovery room after the procedure was over with a group of four other young women who were weeping ... No, not weeping really. Their heart-wrenching, soul-rending cries could hardly be called 'weeping.' They were wailing. Wailing out their agony, realizing what had happened to them there, realizing their incredible loss and knowing they could never go back to the way they were before they entered the clinic doors.

She poured out her heart, telling her fellow sufferers of her fear and shame, of her regret and pain, of her isolation, despair, and loneliness, of her anger and outrage, of her betrayal, powerlessness, and sense of violation ... and mostly of her grief. Her overwhelming grief that crushed her spirit when she overheard the workers in the clinic talk about her twins.

"My twins!" she lamented aloud to the group. She cried violently and was surprised at her own tumultuous eruption but was unable to hold it back. "My precious twin babies! I had always wanted twins! Oh, my little twin babies! I can never get you back! I can never get you back! How I wish I could get you back! How I wish you could come home to Momma! My babies … Oh, my babies!"

Her shoulders shook just as they had when she had finally acknowledged her story to Michael there in Mobile, but her hands did not cover her face this time. No, this time in the presence of the kind, loving, sympathetic sisterhood of understanding mourners who were weeping right along with her as she poured out her grief and heartbreak, she was able to hold her head up and to look them in the eyes, knowing they comprehended her suffering, as her tears fell in never ending rivulets down her cheeks.

And as she grieved her great loss in the presence of this group of mourners, Jennifer realized now, for the very first time, that it was indeed possible for her deep, deep wound to be healed. She could already sense the beginnings of the release of the poisons and trapped toxins which had built up in her soul around that yawning, festering, gaping wound that had lived way down in her spirit for so long. The wound that had existed there in darkness and in secret, thriving and growing more venomous and rancid with every passing year, poisoning her soul with anger and bitterness, making her hard-hearted and hateful and self-destructive, isolating her in total loneliness from intimacy and true friendship with others. And most importantly, keeping her estranged from sweet fellowship with her Creator.

Yes, she could tell already, as she shared her heartbreak with these dear women—these soul-sisters who were on the same pilgrimage as she, from the land of slavery to their painful, regrettable past toward the promised land of healing and restoration—that her agonizing, aching wound was being opened up to drain out all the putrefying infection so that the healing balm she so desperately desired could soon be applied.

And wholeness awaited her, she knew. Wholeness and healing. A gift from a very merciful, forgiving God.

Chapter Thirty-Four

"*H*ello, young lady," said the sweet, old gentleman who was on the welcoming committee of the Harvest Place Fellowship Church as he handed Jennifer a bulletin and gave her a friendly handshake. "So glad to see you're out on such a rainy Sunday," he finished, smiling.

It was indeed a very rainy Sunday in early August, but Jennifer had arisen early that morning to begin working on her new assignment for Wednesday's Streams of Hope meeting before attending church. How she had missed the Lord! She had begun to attend services regularly again, and had not realized how much she had missed her faith during the past eight years until now. As she sat down in the sanctuary awaiting the beginning of the service, she pondered the assignment for her next group meeting, week number five.

Specific healing for anger, unforgiveness, and depression or any other symptoms of post-abortion trauma was the topic. She and the other group members were asked to identify the areas in their lives that needed healing, and then to begin to apply what they had already learned about the character of God—His great mercy, forgiveness, and boundless love—to their own lives and to the lives of those who had hurt or betrayed them.

Jennifer was having a difficult time with this one.

Her favorite scriptures about the forgiveness and mercy of God flooded afresh into her thoughts as she listened to the beautiful music being played on the piano.

"If we confess our sins, He is faithful and just to forgive us our sins, and to cleanse us from all unrighteousness ... The Lord is compassionate and gracious, slow to anger, abounding in love. He does not treat us as our sins deserve, or repay us according to our iniquities. For as high as the heavens are above the earth, so great is His love for those who fear Him. As far as the east is from the west, so far has He removed our transgressions from us."

How she loved these and other words from the sacred book! But she also knew that in order to receive God's forgiveness, she too, must forgive. *"Blessed are the merciful, for they shall obtain mercy."* And she recalled from Matthew Chapter 18 the parable of the unmerciful servant, who had been forgiven a huge, impossible debt, only to turn around and demand payment in full from a man who only owed him a few dollars, and who had begged for mercy but had been shown none. The wicked, unmerciful servant had been handed over to the jailers to be tortured, because he had refused to forgive his fellow man a very small amount after his master had forgiven him a gigantic sum that could never be repaid. So offering forgiveness to others was not an option if she wanted God's forgiveness for herself.

She knew she had already forgiven Michael. He had not intended to harm her. She knew that quite well. He had acted in ignorance, fear, and confusion, just as she had, and not maliciously. He had begged her to forgive him both at the reunion in June and in his letter in July, and she could not withhold her forgiveness from him. Amazingly, she had found it surprisingly easy to release him freely.

She had also admitted to herself in an assignment two weeks ago, that she and she alone was primarily responsible for the termination of her pregnancy. Sure, Michael had pressured her. But he had not forced her. She knew in her heart of hearts that she could have refused his request. She could have refused the clinic visit, and Michael would not have insisted that she go. He would have married her, she knew now. And even if he had not, she could have found help to carry her babies to term from some other source. Her mother would not have abandoned her. Not at all.

She knew that she too, had received counsel from that diabolically wicked duo, Fear and Ignorance, in that most important decision of her life, that decision that would shape how she saw herself for so many agonizing years, that decision that had extracted from her a fee she had never meant to pay, the lives of her irreplaceable children. In Fear and Ignorance, she had been led to believe that she could somehow terminate her pregnancy and never acknowledge her loss, much less mourn for her babies. And in isolation, grief, and loneliness she had been abandoned by that mocking duo to deal with her suffering and agony in secret for eight long years.

In addition, Fear and Ignorance had been pleased to find a limited partner in her Pride. It had been her Pride, which would not allow her to force Michael into an early, secret wedding, that had motivated her into agreeing to the abortion—her Pride, coupled with her love for him and her desire to please him. But ironically, her love for him was destroyed almost immediately as she lay on her back on that table in the clinic, her feet up in those stirrups, experiencing the painful violation, humiliation, betrayal, heartbreak, and anguish of her many losses that day.

She realized now that she had placed Michael up on a pedestal, worshipping him instead of her Creator, trusting him instead of trusting God, and trying to find in him that unconditional, boundless, fathomless love that only God could bring to her soul. She could not hide this fact from herself anymore. She had to be honest if she was ever to be free and whole.

God's voice calling out to her spirit those eight years ago had been trying to warn her not to make the wrong choice, she now knew. That was why she felt so uneasy and frightened at the prospect of the clinic visit. That was why she told Michael that a very large part of her "welcomed the trap" she was in, because she knew that was where she should have stayed. God's voice speaking to her heart was trying to warn her way back then, but she did not obey Him. She obeyed Michael instead. Her false god, Michael. Michael, who was "so horribly deceived, so abominably wrong," as his own words had stated later.

And she had not even thought to open up her Bible to search for God's perspective on her situation, she admitted to herself. How she wished she had maintained her close walk with Him, searching for his heart in his words! How she wished she had sought wise counsel from Knowledge, Courage, Strength, and Wisdom before rushing off to the women's clinic!

"Before I formed you in the womb, I knew you; before you were born I set you apart," God had spoken to the prophet Jeremiah in chapter one of that Old Testament book.

"For You created my inmost being; You knit me together in my mother's womb ... My frame was not hidden from You when I was made in the secret place ... Your eyes saw my unformed body. All the days ordained for me were written in your book before one of them came to be," King David spoke of God in Psalm 139.

God is the Creator of life. God is the One who knits each child together in his mother's womb. God is the One who loves us and longs for us, even before one day of our lives has come to be. The Eternal, Timeless, All-powerful, All-knowing, Creator God who knows the end from the beginning. She knew this of a certainty now. Why did she not know it then?

But ... God is merciful and forgiving, she knew. He forgives any and all who repent and confess, turning to Him in faith, she knew. Jesus paid the price for *all her sins* with His own life, she knew, and *all her sins* included even abortion. And she also knew that she had invited Him into her heart many years ago, loving Him, believing in Him, trusting that it was *her* sins that He had borne that awful day He was crucified, that dreadful day He wore *her* crown—that ugly crown of thorns.

And she must release herself, too, accepting God's forgiveness. She must release herself from the punishment her sins deserved, or else refuse to believe in God's mercy, placing herself higher than He is. She could not place herself above God, so she gratefully received His forgiveness both for the abortion and for the premarital sexual relationship with Michael that was the cause of the crisis pregnancy in the first place. For some strange reason, however, it was much more difficult for her to release herself than it had been to forgive Michael.

But somehow, in spite of all this, there was a very insistent pricking of her conscience telling her she still needed to forgive someone else. All was not forgiven yet. Not quite yet.

She knew that it was not the clinic workers. They had been professional, and one or two had been kind to her, like the nurse who told her to squeeze her hand. Even the doctor who had told her to just hold still had done so to prevent her injury. She had walked into that clinic of her own free will, she knew, making her "choice" herself. She did not blame them or hold anger against them.

Who then, could it be? To whom do I still harbor bitterness and resentment? she wondered as she sat there. *Please show me who it is, Lord, and help me forgive,* she prayed silently there in her chair as the service started.

After the congregational singing and just before the sermon, a young woman with a lovely soprano voice sang a very poignant, moving solo that Jennifer had never heard before. As the lovely lyrics reached her ears and traveled mysteriously, purposefully directly to her soul, she felt God's peace in a way she had not experienced since she was a child.

"I've seen pain and sorrow, while walking in the light.

And I have seen good men losing the fight.

I have seen babies die. I've been there when the widow cries.

And I have learned that joy returns in the morning light.

While holding to the Master's hand.

Holding to the Master's hand.

I can go throughout the day, and what comes my way

won't fill me with fear.

While holding to the Master's hand.

He helps me to understand,

Though I am so weak and frail,

And sometimes fail to see His hand,

He's holding on to me!"*

She closed her eyes as the tears begin to stream down her face once again. *Oh, Lord, I let go of your hand when I placed myself in Michael's, and I followed him instead of you. Please forgive me!*

And yet, even as I walked away from you, not intentionally, but walked away just the same, you were still holding on to me! Oh, thank you, Lord, for still holding on to me!

Suddenly, she saw as plain as day even though her eyes were tightly closed, a vision. She was lying on the table in the women's clinic in Atlanta, in terror and humiliation, realizing that what was happening to her was wrong and wanting it to stop, wanting to get up and run but feeling powerless to do anything ... at the point in the procedure that was the most painful physically, emotionally, spiritually. But instead of the kind nurse holding her hand, she turned her head and looked up to see *Jesus*!

He was holding her hand very tightly and was looking down on her in love, forgiveness, and compassion, tears falling down His cheeks, loving her, crying for her, understanding her pain! Yes, *He* was there, loving her and weeping not only for her and her precious babies, but also for Michael, suffering torment out in that parking lot, and for the clinic workers all around her.

He was loving them all, while mourning and weeping for their pain, heartache, ignorance, and sinful hardness of heart. He was mourning the loss of Jennifer's twins with her and grieving for her terrible, awful heartbreak and despair. Yes, *He* was there, loving her, forgiving her, and loving her still, more and more! Michael, her false god, had refused to go with her, to hold her hand on that table. But Jesus had not left her! She was not alone in that clinic, like she thought she had been. *He* had gone in there with her, because He had promised her never to leave her or forsake her. *He* had seen her broken, repentant heart and had forgiven her. She was His, and He would go with her anywhere! *He* had not let go of her hand! He had not let go of His Jennifer!

"He's holding on to me! He's holding on to me!
When I am so weak and frail, And when I fail to see His hand,
He still holds on to me."

The soloist finished the song as the vision faded from Jennifer's eyes. She sat there in a holy silence, crying silently streams of healing tears as her heart drank in and returned, in gratitude, the overwhelming, unconditional, boundless love of her Savior, who had not let go of her hand.

"Excuse me, please, but am I anywhere close to Maple Grove Lane?" Jennifer asked the youngster who was out riding his bicycle with a football tucked under one arm on that very warm August day.

"Yep. It's just around the corner there. Really, around two corners. The road kind of twists and turns. Here, lady, just follow me on my bicycle. That'll be a whole lot easier," responded the stocky, sandy-haired boy in braces who appeared to be about ten or eleven-years-old.

"Thanks so much," she smiled back at him and rolled up the window of her rental car so the air-conditioning would not escape out into the hot day.

It was the last week of August, and Jennifer had flown to St. Louis on business yesterday, but today had taken personal leave for the purpose of visiting her father. He lived about an hour's drive outside of St. Louis in a small, southern Illinois town, and she had not been to visit him in so long that she had forgotten the exact location of his house. The neighborhood had changed, too, with new shopping centers and widened traffic lanes to accommodate them, so she felt slightly disoriented while searching for 4020 Maple Grove Lane, making her grateful for the guidance of the cute little boy on his bicycle.

The reason for her visit was simple: she needed to forgive her father.

Robert Jacobs, CPA, was the person she had resented and refused to forgive for so many years. This had been revealed to her in a Streams of Hope meeting just two weeks ago as she had shared her dilemma with the group, the dilemma of feeling there was someone she still had not forgiven, but not knowing who it was.

Laura Post had been the one to whom the insight was given. She remembered from the first group session Jennifer's retelling of her phone call to her father that August day in 1975, when she was just outside Atlanta. Laura had rightly guessed that she deeply resented her father's not being present enough in her life to discern her great need for him at that crucial moment.

This revelation had landed on Jennifer very heavily. She knew for certain the truth of Laura's words as they were still coming from her lips, and a lump had formed in her throat at the memory of their pay phone conversation on that dreadful day.

So Jennifer had driven home from her support group meeting and called her father that very night, asking if she could come visit him on August 27th and spend the night there at his house with Helen and him as she was going to be in St. Louis on business.

Forgiveness was not optional for her at this point in her recovery, she knew. Really, forgiveness was never optional for a true Christian. So she had phoned him right away with stubborn resolve, not allowing herself the luxury of thinking it over for even one twenty-four hour period, perhaps rationalizing another way out. Jesus said to forgive, so forgive she must. And how could she withhold forgiveness from her father when the Lord had forgiven her so much ... so very much?

Bob Jacobs was overjoyed at the prospect of her brief visit, though very surprised. He had not spoken to his first-born daughter more than three or four times in the past twelve months, because her resistance to his numerous attempts to talk to her on the phone or to visit her over the previous eight years had simply worn him down.

He knew she was angry with him for some reason. He was not stupid. Susie loved him, he knew, and was always so happy to hear from him or to see him. But Jennifer, who, like her mother, had always been more serious in personality than his happy-go-lucky Susie-cue, had avoided him and shunned him at almost every turn since her graduation from college. No, maybe it was before then that she had seemed to turn on him. When was it exactly? Right at the time of her broken engagement to that miserable young man, Michael Evans, wasn't it? Or was it? He didn't know for certain.

And his own guilt arising from the divorce kept him from making any serious attempt to discover the reason for her anger of late. He had sighed as he hung up the phone after telling her he was looking forward to her visit. He had done the best job at long-distance fathering he could do, to his mind, and there was no use in beating himself up at this point in the game. What good would that possibly do? And if she wanted to stay angry with him, what could he do about it now?

But he was optimistic today because her voice had sounded almost happy to speak with him last night when she had phoned him after her business meeting to tell him what time to expect her. And the prospect of spending an entire day with her, and by means of her own initiative, too, gave him hope of having some sort of affectionate relationship with his highly successful, intelligent offspring. So he had gladly taken a personal day off from the office to spend with his daughter, and was out in the front yard checking the mailbox as she pulled into the driveway, waving a "thank you" to a boy on his bicycle who waved a "you're welcome" back to her.

As she was exiting the automobile, Jennifer took a deep breath. She did not know exactly what she was going to say to her father on this visit. She had prayed and asked God for wisdom and for the proper words to use when she saw him, not knowing exactly what could be said or done to heal their relationship in less than twenty-four hours. But she knew she needed to try. She had to try, at least. She did not want any root of bitterness to poison her life ever again.

"Hello, Jennifer! I can't believe you're here, Sweetheart," her father welcomed, opening her car door for her and smiling. "You get more beautiful and grown up every time I see you."

To his surprise, she actually reached up to hug him, all six-foot three inches of him, and gave him a brief kiss on the cheek. He was very grateful because she had neither embraced nor kissed him for over eight years, and had avoided him as much as possible at Susan's wedding and his few subsequent visits. But now, she not only hugged and kissed him, but also smiled a little timidly into his eyes. And her eyes looked a good deal softer than they had appeared in years. He was very pleased.

"Hello, Daddy," she replied simply. "I can't believe I forgot how to find your house."

"Well, it's been years, Jenny, you know," he began somewhat awkwardly. "Here ... let me carry your suitcase inside. Let's get out of this heat and humidity, and I'll make you a lemonade like I used to do when you were a little girl ... or don't you drink lemonade anymore?" he queried, grabbing her bags and leading her into his modest ranch style house.

"I'd love one of your famous, hand-squeezed, pink lemonades, Daddy," she returned, her eyes beginning to mist slightly, though she could not guess why, other than it really felt good to be here with her father and not be mad at him. She continued as she sat down at the kitchen table looking out at the backyard while he concocted her beverage.

"The trees in your backyard have really grown a lot. I remember them being just tiny little sprigs when Susie and I played back there in the summer as little girls. And where is Helen? Is she at work?"

"That's right. She thought you and I might like some time together alone, and she was needed at the office today because one other lady is on vacation all week. She will be home about five-thirty," he replied taking the ice from the freezer and opening the cabinet to get the sugar. "You're right about those shade trees, Jenny. It's a pity that it took almost twenty years before we got any shade from them," he agreed.

As he worked on the refreshments, Jennifer stood up from the table and began to wander around the kitchen/family room area of her father's twenty-five-year-old house. There were several pictures of Susan and her as little girls adorning the table tops and the fireplace mantel—most of them being those awful school portraits that the harried and hurried photographers snap in a "ready or not" fashion, and which do little justice to the objects of the camera lens, producing a result that only a parent would love and proudly display. However, she did enjoy the one of Susan as a snaggle-toothed kindergartener, grinning as wide as the sky despite her temporary toothless condition, her eyes sparkling merrily.

Jennifer, herself, smiled involuntarily back into the adorable face of her little sister as a five-year-old as she lifted the photograph from the table. *Five-years-old. Susie at five. Smiling so big ... Just three years before the divorce,* she contemplated. *Oh, Susie, how I wish I could have spared you your tears when Daddy left!* And a little lump began to form at the back of her throat.

She replaced the photograph and studied some others as she slowly walked around the room. She was especially drawn to a Polaroid snapshot that Helen must have made of her father and her at her graduation ceremony from Coburn, and which was stuck to the harvest gold refrigerator door by a magnet in the shape of a carrot. Try as hard as she could, she could not recall that picture ever being taken, and only vaguely remembered her father's presence at her college commencement. But there he was, his arm proudly around her shoulders as she stood there in her off-white cap and gown, her face somber, unsmiling, her eyes cold and hard, standing very rigid and stiff, her whole countenance stating that she would rather be somewhere else—anywhere else—than in her father's embrace.

How very telling, Lord. I am sorry, she prayed silently, sadly, sincerely.

In contrast, there was another instant snapshot right beside it of Susan and her daddy taken at her wedding reception. Susan was radiant. She literally glowed and had her head pressed close against Bob Jacob's chest and her arm around his waist as they both smiled broadly into the camera, so happy and joyful.

This is really a very good picture, almost of professional caliber, Jennifer thought. *It should be enlarged, framed, and displayed in a place of prominence. Forgiveness must come so easily to you, Susan. I should have learned from your example, Little Sis. You always did remind me of Jesus.* The lump in her throat grew larger.

"There ... I think I'm done now. One lemonade for you and one for me," Bob Jacobs brought her back to the present, smiling again, and they both sat down at the knotty pine kitchen table. "And one and one make two. Two lemonades, for me and my gal. How's that for fancy accounting from the CPA," he winked at her, emboldened at her newfound kindness towards him.

"I'd say that is very fine accounting, Daddy. I'm sure you'll be up for promotion if you keep that up," she smiled back, almost flirting with her father as her eyes misted mysteriously again. "Did I ever tell you I made a ninety-two in that very tough, fourth-year accounting course I took back in Montgomery, the course that nearly half the class failed?" She tasted her drink adding, "Oh, this is a very good lemonade. Thank you."

"No, darlin', you didn't tell me that. That was a real fine accomplishment for you because I know math was never your favorite subject," he replied, sipping his own drink. "Don't you think this needs a little more sugar, Jenny?"

"No, mine's great," she stated to his back as he got up to get more sugar from the pantry. "How did you know that math was not my favorite subject?" she wondered, her brows knitting in contemplation.

He looked at her in surprise as he sat back down and answered, "Sweetheart, I knew you were majoring in English and journalism at first ... and that you always liked words, diagramming sentences and things. In fact, I was surprised when you decided to switch to business in your junior year. I thought you might not like that as much as your language arts. But I sure guess I was wrong. You have done so well at MedTech. I am very proud of you, Jennifer."

"Really, Daddy? Are you really proud of me?" she asked sincerely, peering steadfastly into his eyes. It had never entered her mind that her father might be proud of her success at MedTech.

"Darlin', don't you know that I have always been proud of you... and of your sister, too?" he asked, surprised, looking at her face, but then averting his eyes to the side before adding awkwardly, "Jennifer, I know that ... I mean ... I realize that my ... divorcing your mother those many years ago was ... a terrible thing to do to you and your sister. But, I hope that you know that I have always loved you... and your sister, too."

He stopped. There was so much more he wanted to say, but he did not know how.

They were both silent for a moment, hearing only the ticking of the clock on the wall and a dog barking outdoors in the distance. When her father returned his gaze to look into her face once more, Jennifer began honestly, looking back deeply into his eyes, replying softly,

"No, Daddy. I didn't know that ... I didn't know that at all."

This was a hard thing to tell him. But she had not driven all this way to remain a stranger to her father. She felt she must tell him the truth ... as kindly as possible.

Observing his troubled, questioning expression at her remarkably frank statement, she elaborated as gently, as lovingly as she could, attempting to explain to him what she meant.

"Oh, I suppose I knew in my *head* that you loved me, Daddy... I mean, if someone had asked me point blank, 'Does your father love you?' I probably would have answered, 'Yes.' But, Daddy ... here..." and she placed her hand on her chest, her voice, now almost a whisper, beginning to tremble slightly. "*Here* ... in my *heart*, Daddy... I didn't know it. I didn't know it at all."

Her large, dark eyes were as transparent as glass as she gazed once more with simple, childlike trust into her daddy's face. And before she could stop herself, words that expressed her sorrow and heartache, her still broken, little girl heart, began to spill out of her involuntarily, one after another, like a waterfall overflowing a dam. And tears began to flow again as she could not stop herself, crying out all the pain and emotional turmoil that had grown and multiplied in her soul for the past eighteen years—a shocking response to his simple declaration of love, which took them both totally by surprise.

"I didn't know it at all, Daddy! When you left home when I was ten, I felt so abandoned and so ... so frightened ... and so worthless, Daddy! I was so frightened! I needed you, Daddy! I needed you so desperately ... *But you weren't there*! You weren't there, Daddy! You left me, Daddy! You left me and Susie and Momma *all alone! You left me, Daddy!*"

She quaked with her sobbing, her lovely face contorted in overwhelming grief and pain, her tear-filled eyes tortured and haunted, as her poor accountant father, stunned, just sat and looked on, listening to her heartbreak and not knowing what to do.

He had no idea that his little girl had experienced this brokenness, as she had always been such an excellent student and model child. And as a young adult woman, she had appeared to be so self-reliant, strong, and independent. How could she have felt this way all these years? Her words cut his heart in two.

"It was so hard for us ... for Susan and me and for Momma, too, though she tried very hard. She would tell me that you loved us, and that you had left *her*, and *not us,* but I couldn't understand it, Daddy! I couldn't understand it *at all!* I thought that if you really loved me, you wouldn't have left! You wouldn't have left me, Daddy, if you really cared ... if you knew how much I needed you!

"I don't mean to tell you this to make you feel bad, Daddy, but... but ... Oh, Daddy! ... I needed you so much! I needed you to hold me in your arms and tuck me in bed at night, saying our prayers the way we used to do! I needed you to tell me I would always be your own, special little girl, Daddy, and that you would always be there to take care of me ... To love me! I needed you so very, very much! *And you weren't there!*

"Oh, Daddy! Oh! ... Daddy! How could you have left me ... when I needed you so very much? How could you have left your little girl? Oh, Daddy! ... Daddy!"

As she sobbed uncontrollably, her slender shoulders shaking, her hands continually wiping away old tears as new ones were constantly coursing down her pretty cheeks, her father, not knowing what else to do, began to weep, too.

He did not attempt to defend himself. He did not try to explain away her feelings, insisting that he *did most certainly* love her all those years; how could she have thought otherwise? He did not tell her of all the monetary sacrifices he had made for her and Susie, proving his love. He did not remind her that he had always told her she could phone him, anytime, day or night, if she needed him. Instead, he did the right thing.

He understood.

As he looked at his daughter crying her heart out there at his table, he saw, not the savvy, beautiful, twenty-eight-year-old, successful businesswoman she now was, but rather the abandoned, fearful, shattered, ten-year-old little girl she had been. The little girl who had known nothing of the tortuous complexities of marital estrangement, infidelity, and divorce, but the little girl who simply had needed him. Had needed him desperately. And he had walked out on her. He had walked away from his two delightful, sweet daughters, leaving them so vulnerable and unprotected.

And so, he understood ... Although it broke his heart, he understood.

He moved his chair over next to hers and took his trembling daughter in his arms, and they wept together. He kept repeating softly, over and over again, as he caressed her soft, dark hair and moistened it with his tears,

"I'm so sorry! Oh, Jennifer, I'm so sorry! Please forgive me. I'm so sorry. I do love you! I've always loved you."

That she was totally surprised and amazed at her own tumultuous emotional eruption was an understatement. Jennifer thought that she had banished that broken, fragmented, abandoned and fearful little girl from her personality many, many years ago. She had believed that she had accepted her fate as the child of divorce long ago and had coped with it very well, leaving behind all the pain and heartbreak, choosing to walk into the future with no heavy chains binding her to the past. She had never intended to break down in this fashion in her father's company. Rather, she had visualized a rational, quiet discourse with him, calmly and logically telling him about herself and inviting him into her life once more.

But as that little girl that lay buried deep in her psyche unexpectedly resurrected herself and burst upon the scene, dressed still in her grave clothes of fear, feelings of worthlessness, rejection, abandonment, anger, and grief, Jennifer experienced a catharsis and a cleansing that she had not thought possible as she wept there with her father, locked in his embrace.

"I forgive you, Daddy! I do. I forgive you," she responded through tears, her voice muffled though passionate as her head was buried in his chest. "And I love you, Daddy. I never stopped loving you! Not really. I was very angry and hurt with you, but I never stopped loving you! You're my Daddy."

They stayed there, crying together, arms wrapped around one another for several minutes more before she backed away slightly, drying her eyes, and stating,

"But Daddy, there is one thing I have to tell you. I have to tell you because I need to know." She made direct eye contact before continuing, "Do you remember that day I phoned you at your office? That day I told you Michael and I were on our way to Atlanta ... to a baseball game? Do you remember?"

He released his tight grip on her shoulders and sat back in his chair, wiped his eyes, and replied, "Yes. I remember it well. You sounded upset, and I was very worried."

"*Oh, Daddy! I wanted you to come get me!* I needed you to come get me! You would have come to get me, wouldn't you? You would have, if you had known?"

And she shook once more, almost frantic with her sobs, still the broken child who had needed her father's protective arms so desperately that day so long ago and yet so fresh in her memory now.

"Come to get you from where, Jennifer? Now calm down some, Sweetheart, and explain what you mean. Calm down now, Jennifer. That's right. Explain to me, please, what you mean."

He took tissues from off the kitchen counter top and offered them to his daughter, embracing her shoulders firmly and taking masculine authority over her approaching hysteria. It worked, as she steadied herself, looked him fully in the eyes once more, and cried,

"Michael was taking me to an ... *an abortion clinic*, Daddy! *And I didn't want to go!* I wanted you to come get me ... but I didn't know how to tell you! But you would have come, if you had known? You would have come for me, wouldn't you, Daddy? You would have taken care of me? Wouldn't you?" she sobbed again, shaking violently as she relived the anguish and desperate fear of that day in Atlanta, where she had felt so abandoned and all alone.

Bob Jacobs' face went white. Then he hugged his beautiful, dark-haired daughter to his chest very, very tightly, as if he could somehow go back to that day in 1975 and rescue her if he held her tight enough now, eight years later. The muscles of his arms were very firm and tense, and he kissed her dark hair as she cried in his arms, as she shook in his embrace.

"*Yes!* I would have come for you, Jennifer! I would have left whatever I was doing and hijacked the next airplane if I had to, to come for you, Sweetheart!" he spoke passionately, his deep voice quivering. "Why didn't you tell me? Why didn't you let me know? I would have been there as soon as I could, and I would have strangled..." but he could not finish, so intense were his emotions at that moment.

"That's what I hoped you would say, Daddy," Jennifer choked out after she had spent so many of her tears. "That's all I needed to know... I just needed to know you would have come for me."

After a few moments, her sobbing stopped and his arms relaxed a little, enough to allow her to sit back and take a deep breath. Then she clarified,

"Please don't hate Michael, Daddy. He didn't know what he was doing. Neither of us did, and he feels so bad about it now. He has begged me to forgive him and ... and … I could have ... I should have refused, anyway. He would have married me, I know. Please don't hate him. And … Daddy?"

She paused here and looked into his eyes once more, her wounded soul completely open, her voice trembling.

"Daddy? ... Will you please forgive me?"

"Oh, darlin'! Forgive *you?* How can you think *I* need to forgive *you?* I love you so much, Jennifer! I feel somehow responsible for the ... whole thing," and he embraced her tightly again. "If I had been the father you needed ... then …"

But he could not finish.

He kissed her dark hair again and just held her close to his heart… where she had always been... but did not know it.

Before she left the next day to go back home to Indianapolis, she hugged her father tightly one more time. Hugged Helen, too, the first time ever, and then embraced her father again before sitting down in her rental car. They had fully reconciled the previous day. She had told him that even though she was twenty-eight-years-old, she still needed her Daddy. Would always need him. She had invited him back into her life, had asked him if he would phone her once a week, like Mr. McComb used to do for his Katie, and still does, she knew.

They had already set a date two weeks from next Friday, when he and Helen would drive over to her house in Indiana for the weekend. He had never seen her new house. And they tentatively scheduled a weekend at her new beach cottage for the middle of October to get together with Susan, Paul, and baby Ashley. It would be Susan's birthday.

She smiled and waved at the pair as she backed out of the driveway praying, *Thank you, Lord, for giving me back my Daddy. And I am beginning to believe that "full restoration" is possible after all.*

Chapter Thirty-Five

"Hey, Jennifer, care to join me at the Corner Café in about thirty minutes for lunch? Oh, sorry. Didn't see you on the phone," apologized Joan Matheson standing in front of Ms. Jacob's piled up desk in the MedTech Center the third week of September.

Jennifer smiled up from her chair, motioning to Joan to please wait just a moment for her reply as she finished her telephone conversation.

"Great, Sister Mary Margaret! I have wanted you to come see me in Indianapolis for so long now. And yes, I will make reservations at the most expensive restaurant in town ... Yes, it will have strawberry cheesecake." She then laughed into the phone and smiled at Joan once more before finishing, "Yes, I know. I do owe you, big time. Yes ... Okay ... God bless you, too. Next Tuesday, then. Bye, now."

She hung up the phone and addressed her co-worker with enthusiasm, "Joan, that lunch sounds fantastic! After talking to that dear Sister Double M about the food we are going to be eating together next week, my appetite is raring to go *now*. How about it? Can you get away now?" Jennifer inquired.

"Yep. Let me just run upstairs and grab my purse," Joan replied.

"Not necessary. This will be my treat," Jennifer stated with authority while grabbing her own pocketbook, throwing her sweater around her shoulders, and calling out loudly into the next room,

"Hey, Mike, Dan, we're going to lunch at The Corner Café. Ya'll care to join us?"

Unfortunately, neither man could go but thanked her for "the invite" anyway. And as Joan and Jennifer made their way toward the elevators, both the males wondered for the umpteenth time these past few weeks just what had happened to change their boss so much... for the better!

Now, she was actually what could be termed "friendly" or "neighborly," not standoffish and aloof, as she had been before. And she was not nearly so quick to lose her temper these days. And even if she did become angry, she was more composed, carefully choosing her words which were missing the four-letter variety that, even though found in the King James Bible, had been misapplied in her speech patterns before. And now her smiles actually made it all the way up to her eyes, which would sparkle and glow a little. Dan noticed this right away. He had always thought that JJ's eyes were as hard as steel, even when she used to smile. Dan was an "eye man" himself, and believed he could tell all about a woman's character just from carefully observing her eyes. No doubt about it, Ms. Jacobs' eyes were much softer and kinder than they had been before.

The "Hell hath no fury" phrase was being slowly replaced by "What hath God wrought?" in a tongue-in-cheek manner among her staff. For they all believed that it could only be some miraculous power that could have made such a transformation in their superior's personality. And for that, they were truly thankful.

As the two ladies walked into the cozy restaurant across the street and sat down in a booth by the front window, they were chatting about work at first. But then, as women are wont to do, although Jennifer had not allowed it in her past, they moved the conversation naturally towards family and relationships.

"I do hope my youngest is feeling better," Joan fretted as she glanced absently at her menu. "She complained of a very sore throat this morning. But I never know if she is really sick, because she will definitely try to deceive me if she can to get a day off from school. She is not the scholar that her brother is."

"Really? Perhaps she feels threatened by his success," Jennifer offered as she closed her own menu. She always ordered the same thing here anyway, and wondered why she even bothered to peruse the menu in the first place.

"Yeah, her father and I have thought about that, and we try not to compare the two of them, but ... Kids pick up on the smallest things, you know. I do hope she is okay. I gave my beeper number to the school secretary to use if she really did start to feel bad," Joan remarked with worried eyes.

As if on cue, her pager sounded its annoying alarm right at that moment. The two women locked eyes briefly and grinned. Then Joan looked down at the number on the read-out screen and said, sighing,

"Yes. It's the school, all right. Speak of the devil, and there he is. Let me go use that pay phone over there. Don't order for me, Jennifer, because it appears as though I will be leaving post haste. Hazards of motherhood, you know," and she scooted out from her seat with a weak smile and walked to the pay phone.

Normally Joan's parting, offhand remark about "the hazards of motherhood" would have offended Jennifer, or at least, would have made her eyes drop down their well-worn veil. But not now.

She was beginning to feel as though she could one day become a mother herself. She was experiencing for the first time since that trip to Atlanta back in 1975, the beginnings of the awakening of her long-dormant woman's heart, a yearning for a husband and a family of her own.

Her career had been wonderful in many ways, but she was beginning to desire someone to come home to at the end of her day, someone other than Ferdie, dear though he was. Someone to give her heart fully to, to love and to serve. Someone who would return that love and service into her own bosom. Her love song, which had been silent within her breast for so many years, was just starting to tune up again, to rehearse itself, to do the basic, vocal exercises necessary to prepare for the full concert that was forthcoming and inevitable. Her own, unique love song. Like none other ever sung—as are all love songs. All unique. All so vitally needed and necessary in this tone deaf, bleak world. All providing beauty and meaning.

Joan walked back to the table with a resigned expression, looking at Jennifer with determination.

"Well, just as I thought. I've got to go pick up Heather from school. No lunch here with you today ... Hey! And you were treating! No fair!"

"That's right, Joan. You were a very cheap date today. But not to worry. Let's try it again tomorrow," she laughed at her co-worker who was fast becoming her friend. "I hope Heather feels better very soon."

And she waved at Joan through the window as she crossed the street heading back to the office.

The waitress then came over, took one look at Jennifer and observed, "Don't tell me. Caesar salad with grilled chicken and a cup of minestrone soup. Iced tea with extra lemon and two packets of pink sweetener."

"I had hoped I was more mysterious than that, but you've got me pegged," replied the regional sales director from MedTech with a grin.

Just then, walking behind the waitress and stopping to look at Jennifer before taking her seat, Laura Post beamed,

"Jennifer! Fancy meeting you here!" and she bent down to embrace her friend and fellow sister-sufferer.

There was man with Laura who looked remarkably like her, only taller, with hair almost as red and face just slightly less freckled. He could have been Huck Finn, so down-home-farm-boy did he look, only more mature and dressed nicely in a suit.

"What are you doing here, Laura? Have a seat and eat with me! My lunch partner just left to go pick up her sick daughter from school, and I do so hate to eat alone," responded Jennifer heartily as she hugged Laura's neck.

The young man there with her smiled very warmly into her eyes as she embraced the group leader. *What a pleasant, friendly smile,* thought Jennifer. *Makes me think of a nice, steaming cup of tea on a very cold day.*

"Oh, may we? This is my brother, David Stephens," Laura said while straightening up and grabbing her brother's arm to pull him forward toward the table. "David, this is my new friend, Jennifer Jacobs."

"Hello, Jennifer Jacobs," the brother responded while smiling still and reaching out to shake her hand.

"Hello, David Stephens," Jennifer returned, not missing a beat, smiling back into his kind eyes, offering him her graceful hand.

Laura, you and your brother have the kindest, warmest, most open, sincere eyes of any two people I have ever met, she thought as the two of them slid into the booth opposite her.

"So what are you doing in the downtown area, Laura?" Jennifer asked as the waitress passed out menus to the newcomers.

"I came down to take my big brother to lunch for his thirtieth birthday. He had a doctor's appointment down here, and I just love this little café. They have the best apple pie a la mode in town," Laura explained.

"Happy Birthday then, David. Many happy returns of the day," Jennifer stated as she could not help but grin at Huck Finn over there. *You may be thirty, but you will always look like you are seventeen-years-old,* she thought.

"Thanks," he began. "Actually, my birthday was *last Tuesday*, but Laura here, who *has never been on time for anything at all in her entire life,* just now remembered it," he teased his kid sister while winking at Jennifer.

"At least I remember your birthday! As I recall, you have never sent me a card or given me a present or taken me to lunch at all on my birthday," his sister returned, undaunted.

"But I do always phone you, Sis. And I don't even reverse the charges," he finished. "And it's always on the *day of*, not one or two *weeks after*, your actual birthday."

The waitress then returned and took their orders, bringing Jennifer her iced tea.

When she left, Jennifer remarked, "I hope you are not ill, David. There is so much flu going around."

"No, not ill. I'm in perfect health, I hope. It was just my annual physical. A required thing that I hate so much, as there is one sadistic technician there, known as Dracula, who just loves to stab you about four or five times before finding just the right blood vessel to drain out about a quart—" David began, looking at Jennifer and illustrating his story with his hands, making his finger poke up and down his arm as he searched for that perfect spot to jab the needle in, until Laura interrupted him in disgust.

"Da-a-a-vid! Must you be so graphic? We are in a restaurant, you know. People are trying to eat." And she hit him softly but repeatedly on his arm with her purse.

He looked at his sister in mock concern and grinned, "Sorry, Sis. Didn't realize you had such a delicate constitution, growing up on the farm and all, hosing out the hog sty, shoveling up the cow—"

"David! Watch your tongue! There are ladies present!" Sister remonstrated.

"I was going to say 'cow *manure*,' Sis. You're the one with the dirty mind!" Brother teased.

"Jennifer, he is going to sit here and torment me until you say something to stop him. Please!" Laura begged her friend playfully, as she tried to pinch her pesky brother's arm.

But Jennifer was thoroughly enjoying the brotherly/sisterly exchange between the pair. She had always wanted an older brother and envied Laura hers at this moment. But she came to the aid of her group leader inquiring of David,

"So your company requires an annual physical exam? To keep health insurance rates down?" she asked, focusing on the very kind green eyes of Laura's big brother.

She also noticed that the hairs on the backs of his strong, masculine, callused hands were a blondish red, and that he did not wear a wedding ring. And was that a cute little dimple in the center of his chin, like Cary Grant's?

"Actually, I am a pilot for a major airline, and we have to stay healthy. Or as one of my favorite authors, P.G. Wodehouse says, we must stay 'in mid-season form,' so the passengers don't have to worry about us fainting or having a heart attack on take-off," he explained to the beautiful, dark-haired woman across from him, a faint smile on his lips.

He also noticed that she was not wearing a wedding ring, and he looked at her eyes thinking, *Those are the darkest, largest, most mysterious eyes I have ever seen. A man could get lost in them ... and not want to find his way out again. And what a beautiful, glowing complexion.*

"Oh, I love P.G. Wodehouse! Bertie and Jeeves are so much fun! And I dearly love that vague old gentleman ... Oh, what's his name ... You know, the absent-minded one, the one with the pig, The Empress of Blandings. Lord or Earl something-or-other," she replied enthusiastically, snapping her fingers softly as she tried to nudge her memory.

"Yes, I know who you mean, but I can't recall his name either. It's been a while since I read about him," the pilot responded, warming up more to this very lovely friend of his sister. "Not meaning to change the subject, but where do you know my kid sister from, Jennifer Jacobs? And where are you from originally? I just love your Southern accent. Makes me want to call you 'Miss Jennifer, Ma'am,'" and he searched her face.

But immediately knew he had said something to make her uncomfortable.

"Jennifer and I met while we were with a group of some other women at a—" Laura began from practice to protect her fellow sister-sufferers, not herself here, as her brother and all of her family knew of her own abortion. She had shared this information with the Streams of Hope group just last week.

But Jennifer interrupted her with a firm, honest reply.

"I met your very dear, sweet sister at The Streams of Hope group that she leads ... And we are just about finished with our sessions, and I am going to miss her terribly," she stated from her heart, her eyes looking straight into his and then moving to Laura's at the end of her statement.

This was the first time she had ever let any friend or outsider know of her sorrowful past, of her dreadful mistake, of the crimson "A" that she used to wear. But somehow she felt she could trust this brother of her sweet, sympathetic group leader, and she suddenly felt freer than she had felt in a long time. In a very long time.

After a brief pause, David replied softly, kindly, "Oh, I see."

He met her gaze with compassion and understanding. Then he placed his arm around Laura's shoulder, hugging her warmly, looked at her face and stated,

"I do love to torment my sister, here, but I am very proud of her for many things. The thing she does that makes me the proudest is leading that Streams of Hope group. I know she must be dynamite at it!" he finished appreciatively.

"Yes, she is that. She is dynamite at it all right. With the red hair to go along with it," Jennifer smiled her sincere thanks to her mentor. "And when our sessions are over, I hope we can still get together, Laura, and stay friends."

"Of course, Jennifer!" Laura responded with emotion. "You betcha! I have truly enjoyed getting to know you and very much think of you as my friend already."

Their food was being set down on the table, so their conversation was momentarily put on hold. When it resumed, David offered,

"I know it must have been difficult for you to tell me that, Miss Jennifer Jacobs. I want you to know that on some level, I think I understand. We all have things in our past ... mistakes and regrets ... that can haunt and plague us. I know I have more than my share."

Here he faltered a little as Jennifer had looked down at her plate when he had begun talking. *Perhaps I should not have said anything about this now,* he doubted himself.

But she raised her eyes to meet his as he finished his thoughts with, "I just want you to know that I think you are very brave to confront your past and to deal with it. I hope you don't mind my saying this."

"No, I don't mind. Not at all. Thank you for encouraging me," she stated simply, her mouth smiling slightly but her eyes with a tinge of sadness.

Laura, who had been silently observing the conversation and the attraction between her brother and her new friend, was thinking, *Not yet, David. Don't pursue Jenny yet. She still has a little way to go before she is whole enough to see you, I think. Wait just a few more weeks. She has been hurt badly and needs a little more time.*

"You never did tell me where you are from," he continued addressing the beautiful MedTech director between mouthfuls. "Let me guess ...Texas?"

"No, but the people from Texas come to my state to learn how to talk properly," Jennifer played along, her eyes beginning to shine some.

"Oh ... okay, then ... Well ... Mississippi?" he smiled back, lifting his eyebrows questioningly.

"No, but you are getting warmer," she drank from her iced tea glass and winked at Laura, who was also smiling.

"I've got it! Louisiana! You have some Creole blood in you, for sure!" he stated emphatically, assured of his correct response this time.

"I don't know if I have Creole blood in me or not, but I will go ahead and tell you before you have to get out your geography book," she said, laughing. "I am actually from L.A.!" She finished with aplomb, her eyes twinkling mischievously.

The brother/sister pair looked at her incredulously, wrinkling their brows before she finished with enthusiasm.

"L.A.! You know ... Lower Alabama. Mobile, actually." she grinned.

"Of course! I should have known! The Heart of Dixie," David added, chuckling at her humor. "I was stationed at Maxwell Air Force Base in Montgomery when I was being trained in the Air Force. I know it well. How about that?"

Before she could reply, David's pager began to beep and he looked at it saying, "Uh-oh. Looks like I'm needed to fly. I'm on call today, and someone must be sick or have an emergency or something."

"That's too bad, Davey," whined Laura playfully. "For your birthday celebration and everything. And you haven't even had your dessert yet, either. But that's okay, because Jennifer and I will eat it for you." And she winked at her friend.

"No you won't, baby Sis, because I am going to take a slice of that pie with me. I can eat it in the car. And you owe me a homemade birthday cake, too, remember?" He kissed his sister on the cheek as he scooted out of the booth saying, "Thanks for the belated lunch. Tell Rick and my nephew 'hello' for me. Sorry I have to leave early."

He then looked at Jennifer with a very kind smile and even kinder eyes.

"And Miss Jennifer, Ma'am, it was a real pleasure meeting you." And he reached out to shake her hand in parting as he finished. "I do hope I may enjoy the benefit of your company again sometime soon, ya'll."

Yes, I would like that very much, he thought, enjoying the reddening of her pretty cheeks as she returned his smile and squeezed his hand gently.

She dropped her eyes shyly and responded, "It was wonderful meeting you, too." *I think I would dearly love to get to know you better, Huck Finn,* she thought.

As he left, Laura searched Jennifer's face carefully.

"I know he is going to ask me for your telephone number, Jenny. But I'm not sure if you're ready. Tell me."

Jennifer toyed with the food on her plate before she looked up with her reply.

"I honestly don't know, Laura. Maybe. I mean ... I have avoided men like the plague for so many years now ... I was afraid, you know. Afraid of their finding out and not wanting me ... And afraid of being hurt again," she expressed her thoughts sincerely.

Laura patted her hand in sympathy, responding, "Yes. I know, Jenny. I know exactly what you mean." Then she gazed off into the distance and finished, "I felt like that, too, until I completed our little course here. And then, a year later, when I met Rick, my husband... He was so kind and sweet to me. I told him on our third date of my... sorrow ... thinking he would never want to see me again, but you know what?"

"What?" Jennifer asked, looking at her red-haired, freckle faced friend.

"Rick said he understood. Said he still wanted to see me, if I didn't mind. Said that everybody makes mistakes, and he was sorry for my pain. Said he would beat up my old boyfriend, if I asked him to," and her eyes twinkled.

"No! He didn't say that, Laura!" her friend stated in disbelief, smiling. "And what did you say?"

"I said that that was the sweetest thing any man had ever said to me, or something like that, and started blubbering and crying like a silly baby!" Laura reminisced as her eyes misted slightly through her smile. "And then I told Rick that assault and battery were not necessary, that I had forgiven my old boyfriend, and that, anyway,

I didn't want him to serve time behind bars on my account. Or something like that. And the rest, as they say, is history."

Jennifer's eyes teared up, too, as she rejoiced in her friend's freedom and joy. She observed from her heart,

"I'm so happy for you, Laura. God is very good, isn't He."

"Yes ... He is. He is that ...Very, very good. And very merciful," and she squeezed Jennifer's hand, searching her eyes. They were silent for a moment before she asked,

"So, what do you want me to tell David when he asks me for your phone number?"

"What makes you so all-fired sure he is going to ask you for my phone number?" Jennifer inquired, grinning.

"I know my brother ... and I'm not blind or stupid, Jen. There was some pretty serious chemistry going on here at this table. And chemistry was my weakest subject in school, too," she began in fun, and then grew more serious as she elaborated. "David's wife died of acute, pernicious leukemia less than two years after their marriage. That was three years ago. They tried everything. Even a bone marrow transplant. But she was so weak by that point and ..."

"Oh, I'm so sorry," Jennifer responded softly. "There is so much sadness in this world."

"Yes ... There is that ... But anyway, he has only begun to date again in the past year or so. I think he wants to re-marry now and raise a family," Laura continued. "He is a very wonderful man, though I do say so myself, Jenny, but I will gladly tell him to wait a while. No problem."

Jennifer thought for a moment and replied, peering deeply into her counselor's eyes, "Maybe that would be best for now. Just a little while longer, I think. Not much. There is still an area ... Laura, I think the Lord planned this meeting with you today ... because I am struggling with this week's assignment."

"Oh, really? Tell me about it." Laura said kindly, patiently, lovingly.

This was a tough assignment, she knew. This was the time to reconcile with the lost child or children, to ask God to reveal to your heart who your child was, and to begin to think of something tangible to do to memorialize the child or children. Many women wrote letters, either to the child or to God. Some made quilts or quilt squares. Some planted gardens or trees. Some painted pictures. There is even a National Memorial to the Unborn in Chattanooga, Tennessee, where women can purchase a plaque to add to the thousands that are already there to honor the memory of their lost children.

And although this was a difficult assignment, it was a necessary one, as this was so often the time where the true, deep, inner healing took place—where the post-abortive woman could finally find release and peace, as she officially mourned her lost child or children and surrendered them into the hands of their loving Creator.

Laura never ceased to be amazed, to stand in awe, of how God honored the hearts of these precious, grieving women, revealing miraculously to them the sex of their child and some type of knowledge of what the child was like, of his personality and talents. She recalled how she had known beyond a shadow of a doubt that her lost baby was a boy with freckles like her but with blonde hair like his father. And he was mischievous and boisterous, always active and into "trouble."

And she had grieved for him terribly.

But God had healed her grief, had let her know her son was safe in His hands, and had comforted her in a way she had never thought possible. God had been so very real to her.

So she encouraged Jennifer gently, warmly, compassionately.

"You can tell me, Jennifer. I understand," she said tenderly.

She began timidly, not quite knowing the words to say, tears in her eyes, "I guess ... I think ... I am afraid, Laura. I mean ... I always wanted twins, you know ... And I love them so much now ... I know that sounds nonsensical. But I love them so much now, already ... Not even knowing who exactly they were ... are ... I mean. And, if I let the Lord tell me who they are exactly, it may be so hard ... wanting them so badly and all ... that I won't ever be able to heal. To get over my grief. Do you know what I mean?" she asked, her voice trembling, as she wiped away her tears.

"Yes, Jenny. I do. I know exactly what you mean," and Laura was crying now, too. She squeezed Jennifer's hand again and continued softly, "I felt just that way ... Just the way you feel, too. But the Lord is so kind and gentle. Remember the verses in Isaiah?... *'He tends his flock like a shepherd: He gathers the lambs in His arms, and carries them close to His heart; He gently leads those that have young.'"*

And here, Laura's voice broke, too, as she dried her own tears with her napkin before swallowing and continuing.

"And that is how He will reveal your precious twins to you, Jenny... Gently. Very gently ... And He will carry you through the grieving, too ... *Close to His heart* ... Close to His heart, Jennifer, where we all are, anyway ... And when the grieving is over, you will walk away from the pain ... *for good*!   Although you will always miss them. You will always miss them, Jen, and have a type of aching longing for them. But the terrible pain will be gone! I have seen it so many times. So very many times ... God is good! He is very, very good.

"And Jenny, I know this sounds hard, but ... unless we give a face to our loss, we can never truly mourn them. You can't truly mourn what you refuse to acknowledge. And unless we truly mourn our lost babies, we can't be healed *way down deep* ... in our hearts, you know. *Down deep* where it hurts so much! Like Jesus said, *'Blessed are those who mourn, for they will be comforted.'* We have to fully mourn so we can be fully comforted. Does that make any sense?"

Jennifer nodded as both women were crying silent tears while holding hands and looking into each other's eyes, sitting across the table from each other in The Corner Café. And it must have appeared odd to any passerby.

But to Jennifer Jacobs, Regional Executive Director of Sales for the MedTech Companies, Laura's sweet words encouraged her greatly, witnessing to her own spirit the truth of what she had felt the Lord speaking softly to her heart.

Of course, He would lead her gently ... very gently ... carrying her close to His heart. He had never let go of her hand. He would lead her gently through her grieving process, and she would walk out into the sunshine again. Out into the sunshine of His unconditional, healing love.

Chapter Thirty-Six

*I*t was another one of those nearly perfect days, a gorgeous spring day, April 16, 1984, a Sunday, and Jennifer was visiting a church she had never before attended in Nashville, Tennessee. Outside the church building, the dogwood trees and azaleas were in full bloom, and there was not a single cloud in the sky. The birds were all rejoicing from their nests in the treetops, fluttering over their new families or busily pecking at the ground and along the sidewalks, searching for food for their young ones, enjoying some of the leftover rice from the wedding that had occurred there the previous evening. The warm sunlight was flooding in through the stained glass windows into the sanctuary, spilling glorious, colorful rays onto the members of the congregation as they were singing the closing hymn, one of Jennifer's favorites from her childhood.

"O, for the wonderful love He has promised, Promised for you and for me. Though we have sinned, He has mercy and pardon, Pardon for you and for me. Come home! Come home! Ye, who are weary, come home! Earnestly, tenderly, Jesus is calling. Calling, 'O Sinner, Come home!'"

She had driven down from Indianapolis yesterday for the purpose of completing the last step she felt was required for her total restoration. Although she had finished the required meetings with The Streams of Hope group back in October and had indeed felt free for the first time in over eight years, walking away from the agonizing pain of her troubled past, she had somehow known that she must speak to Michael and Emily again.

Because she had not spoken with them nor communicated with them in any way since the reunion, they had not known how she had reacted to their letters or even if she had received them. She had thought about writing to them or phoning them, but in her heart, she felt she needed to see them in person, to let them see, rather than just believe or hope that she was restored, that she was no longer the broken, bitter, lost and wounded soul she had been at the Class of '73 Reunion. They had loved her enough to pray for her and to write her letters and share songs from their hearts, and she wanted them to know that their prayers had been answered. She wanted to tell them both, "thank you." And she felt she had to see Michael one last time—one last time for the sake of closure. One last time, sober and in her right mind—at peace, and in forgiveness.

She had phoned them that morning and asked if she could speak with them both after church. They had sounded very surprised to hear her voice over the phone and had said they really looked forward to seeing her. They wanted to sit with her in the congregation, but both were committed to sing in the choir. But they would look for her and meet her in the foyer of the sanctuary just as soon as the service was over. And would she go out to lunch with them afterwards?

And they had both smiled down very warmly at her from their seats in the choir loft. She had returned their smiles, feeling strangely more at peace than she ever thought she would. She had no lingering romantic feelings for Michael, but still she cared for him as her brother in the Lord. And she had always loved Emily, dear, sweet, Christ-like Emily. She just wanted them both to know that she was healed; wanted to close this sad chapter of her life so she could begin again. Except ... she would always miss her babies.

So she walked back to the foyer of the church as the congregation was all spilling out into the beautiful spring sunshine and the organist played the postlude. Friendly faces smiled at the pretty visitor and wished her a good day. And then a feminine voice punctuated the air.

"Jennifer! Oh, sweet Jenny-Penny! I can't believe you are here!" Emily ran up to her and embraced her old friend tightly, tears in her eyes. "And you are all better! I could see it, even from up there in the choir loft! I'm so glad you are all better, Jenny!"

Jennifer hugged Emily warmly and whispered, "Yes, Emmy. I am all better. Thank you for your sweet, gracious letter."

And as the two of them separated somewhat, she added, "Wow, Emily. You sure have shrunk! You are back to your tiny, petite self, I see. Last time I saw you, you were out to here!" and they both laughed as Jennifer illustrated the swollen abdomen that her delicate friend had sported at the reunion.

Just then Michael appeared, still wearing his choir robe. He walked very quickly over to the pair, placed his arms around them both and hugged them. Looking at Jennifer's face with a mixture of concern and joy, he stated very warmly,

"I can hardly believe you are here, Jennifer. It is *so good* to see you again! I know this may be awkward, but ... It really is good to see you again. How are you?"

She looked him squarely in the eyes and answered, "I am fine, Michael. I really am. That's why I wanted to come down here and see you both." She looked at Emily, too, before continuing. "I wanted both of you to know that I am fine now. Better than fine. I have been... oh, 'healed,' I guess is the word. Like you wrote, Emily, in your letter. 'Healed from all this sorrow.' I know I was such a mess the last time you both saw me ... And I appreciated your letters so much... and your song, too, Michael." She looked back at him and smiled sadly before dropping her gaze. "And your prayers, too, which the Lord has so mercifully answered," she finished.

"That is so good, Jennifer! Such good news to me—to both of us, Jenny," Michael said very thankfully, and hugged her once more in a loving brotherly fashion before removing his arm.

"So you found a group ... like the one I mentioned in my letter, Jenny ... to help you?" Emily questioned, her eyes full of love for her old friend, her slender arm still around her waist.

She nodded her head, "Yes, just the one you mentioned, Emmy. In fact, I phoned the number you sent on the same evening I first read your letter. It was that group that the Lord used to ... restore me ... to heal me ... to cleanse me. Thank you so much. You are such a dear friend," she smiled sincerely into Emily's kind, sympathetic eyes.

"I'm so glad, Jenny," she replied very softly. "God is so very faithful, isn't He."

Jennifer nodded, her eyes misting as he three of them just stood there for a minute, no one saying anything, until Emily clapped her hands together and opened her eyes widely, exclaiming,

"Oh, golly! We forgot the baby! I'd better go get him before the nursery workers call me everything but a lady." Then she blushed a little and looked into Jennifer's eyes saying, "Oh, I'm sorry, Jenny, if that statement appeared insensitive. You don't mind, do you, if I go get little Joey and bring him here. Just tell me if you do because—"

"No, don't be silly, Emily! I am fine, really. And I would love to see your baby! I love babies again. And I can even babysit my little niece now, for a whole weekend while my sister and her husband take a couple of days off. I did it with Mother just last month, in fact," she smiled at them both.

"Okay, then, I'll be right back."

And she left, squeezing Jennifer's hand and looking into her eyes deeply before she went.

As the two former lovers were left alone, a slight embarrassed silence fell between them. Then they both spoke each other's names simultaneously, chuckled nervously, until Michael said,

"Go ahead, Jennifer. What were you going to say?" And he looked into her face kindly.

"I just want to let you know ... that ... I realize you didn't know what you were doing ... That neither of us knew at the time ... That I realize that you did not intentionally hurt me, Michael, with the clinic visit and everything. I knew, even back then, that it was not intentional on your part, but ... I had to forget, don't you see? I had to forget that clinic visit to survive. And every time I saw you, I remembered ... And I want to let you know that I have forgiven you."

She chose her words very carefully and stated them seriously from her heart as she looked into his eyes—eyes she once knew so well but now seemed slightly foreign to her. Eyes that now belonged to Emily.

"Thank you for that, Jenny," he responded warmly, looking intently at her also. "I know I don't deserve your forgiveness. It is like you said, though. I was so ignorant at the time ... And so selfish, so immature and foolish ... I'm glad you know I never, ever meant to hurt you, Jennifer. I just wish ..."

And he dropped his eyes and his speech.

"I know ... I wish, too," she replied flatly, looking down at the floor a moment before continuing. "But I also feel I need to ask you to forgive me, too, Michael ... No, don't say anything yet, please," she added quickly, placing her hand up for emphasis as he tried to interrupt her. "I need you to forgive me, too, because I knew in my heart that ... I knew it, Michael, and I could have refused to go, you know ... And I need to know you forgive me, too," she finished looking back fully into his face.

"Jennifer, I will say, 'I forgive you,' if you need me to, but I will always feel that it was all my fault ... All *my* fault, and not yours ... But, I think I see what you are saying, and ... I forgive you, Jen," he finished, looking back into her eyes just as Emily came around the corner.

She held in her arms the biggest, cutest, blue-eyed, blonde-haired, nine-month-old baby boy in the world. He was dressed to the nines in a pale blue sailor suit and had on the cutest little white sneakers Jennifer had ever seen.

"Oh, Emily! Michael! He is the cutest thing! As cute as my little niece! Please, can I hold him?" Jennifer beamed through unexplained tears at the adorable baby, who was smiling broadly at everyone, four little teeth showing through his gums in a big grin, drool running down his chin.

He went readily into her arms, still smiling and she observed,

"Gee! He must weigh a ton! How much did he weigh at birth?" and she bounced him happily in her arms, her eyes misting even more as she kissed his soft cheeks and smelled his fresh, baby smell.

"Eight pounds, fifteen-and-a-half ounces," stated Michael proudly. "And he's never looked back!"

Emily just stood there, glowing, and laughing into the face of her little boy, playing a little game of peek-a-boo as the baby laughed out loud.

434

"Then it's just as they say," Jennifer remarked, as tears were now running freely down her cheeks, though she was smiling widely. "The little women always have the big babies, and the big women always have the little ones."

"Oh, Jennifer, you are crying!" Emily noticed, concerned, and she reached out her arms to take her son, but Jennifer explained as she held on to the infant.

"They are just tears of joy, Emmy. Please, let me hold him a while longer! It feels so good! It's part of my healing; I know that now. I was never able to hold a baby before, you know. Never wanted to be around them at all," and still she beamed at husband and wife in spite of her tears, and kissed the baby's sweet head over and over again as she continued rocking him, bouncing him gently in her arms.

"Sure! Hold him as long as you wish, Jenny," Emily replied with compassion, gently wiping away the tears from her old friend's cheeks with the soft corner of the baby blanket and whispering, "I love you, Jennifer." But she had tears in her own eyes now, as did Michael, who could not even speak at that moment.

"I know. I love you too, Emily," she responded softly. Then, she cleared her throat a little and asked, "So, did I hear you say that his name is Joey?"

"Yes, Joseph Michael Evans. We named him for my daddy and for Michael," Emily replied proudly and sweetly.

"That's right. Dear Mr. Prescott! Your daddy is so great, Emmy. And Michael promised Joe Smothers that he would name his first-born for him, too. Remember?" she reminisced, looking over at him and grinning.

"That's right. I had forgotten about that," he smiled back and then looked at his wife, explaining, "Joe and Katie helped me move furniture one very hot day back at Coburn, and I told Joe I would name my first-born after him in payment."

"And Joe said he would rather have a steak dinner and couple of brews as I remember, didn't he?" Jennifer laughed into the faces of the couple before adding, "But he wouldn't say that now, if he could see this precious little fellow."

And she continued hugging the baby against her chest, smiling and crying simultaneously.

No one said anything for a minute or two except baby Joey, who was gurgling and cooing merrily, entertaining this unusual group of three.

"You know, as one of my assignments in our group sessions, I asked the Lord to reveal to me who our babies were ... and ..." Jennifer stared out into the room as if recalling her dream, her voice very soft, as if speaking from a distance, "I had a dream, that very night after I prayed. There was a very beautiful meadow that was also a garden. It was so lovely there, so perfect ... with all kinds of flowers—roses and gladioli and daisies and lilacs, and some other flowers I have never seen before. It smelled so sweet, like newness and freshness, like there was no corruption or decay around anywhere. I don't know quite how to describe it ... And, anyway, there in this meadow and garden, suddenly two little children appeared—"

"Don't tell me, Jenny," Michael interrupted quietly. He, too, was gazing out the front door as if recalling a vision. "They were a boy and a girl, the boy being dark like you, dark hair and eyes and olive-skinned, and the little girl was blonde and fair with blue eyes, like me."

She stopped bouncing Joey and just stared at him.

"How? ... How did you ...?"

He looked at her and replied, "When I was recording my song, 'If You Were Mine,' I closed my eyes the way I always do when I record, to shut out the visual so I can concentrate on the sounds of the music ... and ... There they were!" He almost whispered, lost in reverie. His eyes grew watery at this point and his voice broke some as he continued, peering out beyond the room again.

"They were out on a type of gravel road, it appeared, in a garden, too, but the gravel was soft and not crunchy. I remember that because I was afraid they might fall down and scrape their knees. They had on short pants, you see. They were riding little tricycles and couldn't be older than two or three, I guess. Anyway, they were racing each other down that soft, gravel path, pumping their little tricycles as fast as their chubby, little legs would go ... Laughing out loud ... Laughing so hard ... Having such a great time ... They were so beautiful!"

He could not go on.

They were all silent for a moment. Then Jennifer spoke softly, still rocking Joey in her arms, as he was now resting his head on her shoulder and sucking his thumb.

"I saw them in my meadow, holding hands and running like the wind ... Running and laughing ... Looking at each other and then looking straight ahead ... The little girl had on a long, white dress, down below her knees, and wore a big, blue bow in her long, blonde hair. The little boy wore white bib overalls with a pale blue shirt to match his sister's bow ...They were so happy! ... And I wanted to be there with them! ... Wanted it so badly! Wanted to hold them in my arms *just once!* Wanted to tell them how much I love them! ... And to ask them to please forgive me!"

Her impassioned voice broke and she stopped, allowing Emily to dry more tears from her face with the blanket, even as she dried her own. Michael let his tears fall unashamedly, as he listened and mourned with her, his desires being, once more at that moment, the same as hers.

No one said anything. It was very quiet. And peaceful. There in the church vestibule.

After the silence, Jennifer continued, very softly and tenderly.

"I named them Julie and Jamie. Continuing the 'J' thing, you know," and she smiled poignantly.

"Julie and Jamie," Michael repeated quietly, wiping his tears away. "I like that just fine."

"And I planted a garden in their memory in my back yard," she went on, "with two, baby oak trees that will one day be strong and tall. Mother drove up from Mobile and stayed with me all week and helped me. My neighbor told me I planted them too close together... that as they grow, one day their branches and root systems will become intertwined ... But I said that was okay ... I sort of liked it that way."

She paused a moment to compose herself before continuing.

"We placed rhododendrons and rose bushes and evergreen shrubbery around them, and a birdbath. I plan to add annuals every spring, and maybe even a fountain—you know, an angel fountain or something—and a park bench. I had workmen place a white picket fence all around it with a bronze plaque on the gate that says,

"'For Julie and Jamie, You lived within my body for a very short while, but you will live on in my heart for always. I would sing to you 'til the morning light ... if you were mine. Love, Momma'"

In the still, sweet silence that followed, interrupted only by soft sniffling, the three of them were bonded in a way that outsiders who knew their story would have found impossible to believe.

"I will send you a picture, if you like," she finished, looking at Mr. and Mrs. Evans.

"Yes, please do," Michael replied while Emily just nodded her head and dried her tears.

"And God is keeping them for us ... in Heaven, you know," she said tenderly.

"Yes ... I know," he agreed and swallowed hard. "I know," more softly.

Baby Joey was now asleep on Jennifer's shoulders, his breathing soft, his face angelic.

"And you know something else?" announced Jennifer with conviction first born of pain, and then, from its release, new tears running down her pretty face. "I think ... No, I *know* ... I can actually become a wife and mother, too! ... Someday!"

"Of course, you can!" cried both Michael and Emily simultaneously as they encircled Jennifer with warm embraces, placing their arms firmly around her shoulders, the tears now flowing again down all three faces.

"Wow," remarked Jennifer, gently laughing through tears along with husband and wife at their spontaneous, identical outbursts. "You two really *are* married, aren't you! You must have been made for each other."

They made a very strange, impossible picture standing there in the church foyer. A new father and his wife, surrounding his former lover who was holding his sleeping baby boy in her arms. His former lover who had also carried his children inside her womb for a short time. Too short a time. All crying tears of regret, pain, joy, and hope somehow all mixed up together.

Especially hope. Hope for a future for the deeply wounded ones left behind in the war fought for innocence and for life.

Yes, the picture they made in a church in Nashville, Tennessee, on that warm, spring day in April of 1984 under the blossoms of the dogwood trees was an impossible one, all right.

Impossible for anyone ... but God.

"For I know the plans I have for you, declares the Lord,
Plans to prosper you and not to harm you,
Plans to give you hope
And a future."
Jeremiah 29:11

For information about help that is available for those experiencing pain and regret following abortion, including support groups similar to the fictitious one mentioned in this novel, please refer to the following resources:

-Care Net's Post Abortion Counseling and Education (PACE) programs are similar to the fictitious "Streams of Hope" group in this novel:

www.optionline.org
(800) 395-HELP (4357)

-Ramah International offers help, resources, and information to those suffering from past abortion(s).

www.ramahinternational.org
(941) 473-2188

-Project Rachel is an outreach of the Catholic Church open to all those dealing with abortion loss:

www.hopeafterabortion.com
(800) 5WE-CARE -- (800) 593-2273

Additional Song Lyric Acknowledgements